Studies in European Culture and History

edited by

Eric D. Weitz and Jack Zipes
University of Minnesota

Since the fall of the Berlin Wall and the collapse of communism, the very meaning of Europe has opened up and is in the process of being redefined. European states and societies are wrestling with the expansion of NATO and the European Union and with new streams of immigration, while a renewed and reinvigorated cultural engagement has emerged between East and West. But the fast-paced transformations of the last fifteen years also have deeper historical roots. The reconfiguring of contemporary Europe is entwined with the cataclysmic events of the twentieth century, two world wars and the Holocaust, and with the processes of modernity that, since the eighteenth century, have shaped Europe and its engagement with the rest of the world.

Studies in European Culture and History is dedicated to publishing books that explore major issues in Europe's past and present from a wide variety of disciplinary perspectives. The works in the series are interdisciplinary; they focus on culture and society and deal with significant developments in Western and Eastern Europe from the eighteenth century to the present within a social historical context. With its broad span of topics, geography, and chronology, the series aims to publish the most interesting and innovative work on modern Europe.

Published by Palgrave Macmillan:

Fascism and Neofascism: Critical Writings on the Radical Right in Europe
by Eric Weitz

Fictive Theories: Towards a Deconstructive and Utopian Political Imagination
by Susan McManus

German-Jewish Literature in the Wake of the Holocaust: Grete Weil, Ruth Klüger, and the Politics of Address
by Pascale Bos

Turkish Turn in Contemporary German Literature: Toward a New Critical Grammar of Migration
by Leslie Adelson

Terror and the Sublime in Art and Critical Theory: From Auschwitz to Hiroshima to September 11
by Gene Ray

Transformations of the New Germany
edited by Ruth Starkman

Caught by Politics: Hitler Exiles and American Visual Culture
edited by Sabine Eckmann and Lutz Koepnick

FREEDOM AND CONFINEMENT IN MODERNITY

KAFKA'S CAGES

EDITED BY

A. KIARINA KORDELA
AND
DIMITRIS VARDOULAKIS

First published in 2011 by
PALGRAVE MACMILLAN®
in the United States—a division of St. Martin's Press LLC,
175 Fifth Avenue, New York, NY 10010.

Where this book is distributed in the UK, Europe and the rest of the world,
this is by Palgrave Macmillan, a division of Macmillan Publishers Limited,
registered in England, company number 785998, of Houndmills,
Basingstoke, Hampshire RG21 6XS.

Palgrave Macmillan is the global academic imprint of the above companies
and has companies and representatives throughout the world.

Palgrave® and Macmillan® are registered trademarks in the United States,
the United Kingdom, Europe and other countries.

ISBN: 978–0–230–11342–8

Library of Congress Cataloging-in-Publication Data

Freedom and confinement in modernity : Kafka's cages / edited by
A. Kiarina Kordela and Dimitris Vardoulakis.
    p. cm.—(Studies in European culture and history)
    ISBN 978–0–230–11342–8
    1. Kafka, Franz, 1883–1924—Criticism and interpretation. 2. Liberty in
literature. 3. Self (Philosophy) in literature. 4. Imprisonment in literature.
I. Kordela, Aglaia Kiarina, 1963– II. Vardoulakis, Dimitris.

PT2621.A26Z719926 2011
833'.912—dc22   2010042508

A catalogue record of the book is available from the British Library.

Design by Newgen Imaging Systems (P) Ltd., Chennai, India.

First edition: May 2011

10 9 8 7 6 5 4 3 2 1

Printed in the United States of America.

CONTENTS

ABBREVIATIONS OF KAFKA'S WORKS

Each edition is indicated by the year of publication next to the initial.

A

Amerika. Translated by Willa and Edwin Muir. New York: Schocken, 1962.

Der Verschollene. In *Kritische Ausgabe*. Edited by Jürgen Born, Gerhard Neumann, Malcolm Pasley and Jost Schillemeit. Frankfurt a.M.: Fischer, 2002.

C

The Castle. Translated by Willa and Edwin Muir. New York: Schocken Books, 1982a.

Das Schloß. Edited by Malcolm Pasley. *Kritische Ausgabe*. Frankfurt a.M.: Fischer, 1982b.

The Castle. Translated by J. Underwood. London: Penguin, 1997.

The Castle. Translated by Mark Harman. New York: Schocken, 1998.

HA

"A Hunger Artist." In *The Complete Stories*. Edited by Nahum Glatzer. New York: Schocken, 1971.

"A Starvation Artist." In *Nachgelassene Schriften und Fragmente 2*. Edited by Jost Schillemeit. *Kritische Ausgabe*. Frankfurt a.M.: Fischer, 1992.

"A Hunger Artist." Translated by Willa and Edwin Muir. In *The Complete Stories*. New York: Schocken, 1995.

"Ein Hungerkünstler." In *Kritische Ausgabe*. Edited by Jürgen Born, Gerhard Neumann, Malcolm Pasley and Jost Schillemeit. Frankfurt a.M.: Fischer, 2002.

MM

"The Metamorphosis." In *The Complete Stories*. Edited by Nahum Glatzer. New York: Schocken, 1971.

The Metamorphosis: A Norton critical edition. Translated and edited by Stanley Corngold. New York: Norton, 1996.

"Die Verwandlung." In *Erzählungen Franz Kafka: Gesammelte Werke (Taschenausgabe in acht Bänden)*. Edited by Max Brod. Frankfurt a.M. Main: Fischer, 1998.
Metamorphosis with the Judgement. Translated by M. Hofmann. London: Penguin, 2006.

OP

"On Parables." In *Gesammelte Schriften*, Vol 5. Edited by Max Brod. New York: Schocken Books, 1946.
"On Parables." In *The Basic Kafka*. New York: Washington Square Press: Pocket Books, 1979.
"Von den Gleichnissen." In *Sämtliche Erzählungen*. Edited by Paul Raabe. Frankfurt a.M.: Fischer, 1985.

RA

"A Report to an Academy." In *The Complete Stories*. Edited by Nahum Glatzer. New York: Schocken, 1971.
"Ein Bericht für eine Akademie." In *Gesammelte Werke in zwölf Bänden*. Band 1. Edited by Hans-Gerd Koch. Frankfurt a.M: Fischer, 1994.
"A Report to an Academy." Translated by Willa and Edwin Muir. In *The Complete Stories*. New York: Schocken, 1995.
"Ein Bericht für eine Akademie." In *Erzählungen Franz Kafka: Gesammelte Werke (Taschenausgabe in acht Bänden)*. Edited by Max Brod. Frankfurt a.M. Main: Fischer, 1998.
"Ein Bericht für eine Akademie." In *Kritische Ausgabe*. Edited by Jürgen Born, Gerhard Neumann, Malcolm Pasley and Jost Schillemeit. Frankfurt a.M.: Fischer, 2002.
"A Report to an Academy." In *Kafka's Selected Stories*. Norton Critical Edition. Edited and Translated by Stanley Corngold. New York: Norton, 2007.

T

The Trial. Translated by Willa and Edwin Muir. Harmondsworth: Penguin, 1953.
Der Prozeß. In *Gesammelte Werke*. Edited by Max Brod. Frankfurt a.M.: Fischer, 1965.
Der Proceß. Edited by Malcolm Pasley. *Kritische Ausgabe*. Frankfurt a.M.: Fischer, 1990.
The Trial. Translated by Willa and Edwin Muir. New York: Schocken, 1992.
Der Prozeß. Munich: Deutscher Taschenbuch Verlag, 1998.
The Trial. Translated by Breon Mitchell. New York: Schocken, 1999.
Der Prozeß. Norstedt: Verlag für Akademische Texte [Isbnlib], 2008. Accessed 15 July 2010 http://www.isbnlib.com/preview/3640226976/ Der-Process

CONTRIBUTORS

Karyn Ball is associate professor of English and Film Studies specializing in literary and cultural theory at the University of Alberta. Her articles have appeared in *Cultural Critique, Women in German Yearbook, Research in Political Economy, Differences,* and *English Studies in Canada.* Recent publications include "Primal Revenge and Other Anthropomorphic Projections for Literary History," *New Literary History* 39 (2008), "Melancholy in the Humanities: Lamenting the 'Ruins' of Academic Time Between Bill Readings and Augustine," *Alif* 29 (2009), an edited collection entitled *Traumatizing Theory: The Cultural Politics of Affect in and beyond Psychoanalysis* (Other Press, 2007), and *Disciplining the Holocaust* (State University of New York Press, 2008).

Christophe Bident teaches at the Université de Picardie Jules Verne, and his research focuses on literature and philosophy of the twentieth century, as well as contemporary theater, and particularly issues of mise-en-scène. He is the author of numerous articles and three books—*Maurice Blanchot, partenaire invisible* (Champ Vallon, 1998); *Bernard-Marie Koltès, Généalogies* (Farrago, 2000); *Reconnaissances—Antelme, Blanchot, Deleuze* (Calmann-Lévy, 2003)—as well as the editor of Blanchot's two volumes of critical essays: *Chroniques littéraires du* Journal des débats (Gallimard, 2007); *La Condition critique* (Gallimard, 2010; forthcoming). Together with Hugo Santiago, he co-scripted the film *Maurice Blanchot* (INA, 1998).

Howard Caygill is professor of philosophy at Kingston University, London, where he teaches philosophy, aesthetics, and cultural history. His publication include: *Art of Judgment* (1989); *A Kant Dictionary* (1995); *Walter Benjamin: The Colour of Experience* (1998); and *Levinas and the Political* (2002).

Stanley Corngold is professor emeritus of German and Comparative Literature at Princeton and formerly adjunct professor of law at Columbia. His more recent books are *Lambent Traces: Franz Kafka* (Princeton University Press 2004); a Norton Critical Edition of *Kafka's Selected*

Stories (2006), which includes new translations of thirty Kafka stories; and *Franz Kafka: The Office Writings* (Princeton, 2008), which he co-edited. Northwestern is publishing his and Benno Wagner's new study of Kafka's professional and intimate writings, titled *Franz Kafka: The Ghosts in the Machine*; and Norton is publishing his translation and Critical Edition of *The Sufferings of Young Werther.*

Peter Fenves is the Joan and Serapta Professor of Literature at Northwestern University. He is the author of *A Peculiar Fate: Kant and the Problem of World-History* (1991); *"Chatter": Language and History in Kierkegaard* (1993); *Arresting Language—From Leibniz to Benjamin* (2001), *Late Kant: Towards Another Law of the Earth* (2003), and *The Messianic Reduction: Walter Benjamin and the Shape of Time* (2010). He is editor of *Raising the Tone of Philosophy: Late Essays by Kant, Transformative Critique by Derrida* (1993), co-editor of *"The Spirit of Poesy" Essays on German and Jewish Literature and Thought in Honor of Géza von Molnár* (2000), and translator of Werner Hamacher's *Premises: Literature and Philosophy from Kant to Celan* (1996).

Chris Fleming is senior lecturer in philosophy and anthropology in the School of Humanities and Languages at the University of Western Sydney, Australia. He has written a book on the work of René Girard (Polity, 2004) and for journals such as *Body & Society, Anthropological Quarterly,* and *Philosophy and Social Criticism.*

A. Kiarina Kordela teaches at the Department of German Studies, Macalester College, Saint Paul, Minnesota. She is the author of *$urplus: Spinoza, Lacan* (SUNY, 2007) and several articles on subjects ranging from German literature to philosophy, psychoanalysis, critical theory, sexual difference, film, and biopolitics, published in collections and journals such as *Spinoza Now* (University of Minnesota Press), *European Film Theory* (Routledge), *The Dreams of Interpretation* (University of Minnesota), *Literary Paternity—Literary Friendship* (University of North Carolina), *Modern Language Studies, Angelaki, Cultural Critique, Parallax, Rethinking Marxism, Radical Musicology, Political Theory,* and in translation, *Monokl* and *Hihuo kukan.*

John Mowitt is professor in the department of Cultural Studies and Comparative Literature at the University of Minnesota. He is the author of numerous texts on the topics of culture, theory and politics, most recently his book, *Re-Takes: Postcoloniality and Foreign Film Languages* (2005) and the co-edited volume, *The Dreams of Interpretation: a Century Down the Royal Road* (2007), both from the University of Minnesota Press. In 2010, he collaborated with the composer Jarrod Fowler to transpose his book, *Percussion: Drumming, Beating, Striking* (Duke University Press, 2002), from a printed to a sonic text. His current project, *Radio: Essays in Bad Reception* is forthcoming from the University of California Press later this year. He is also a senior coeditor of the journal, *Cultural Critique*, a leading Anglophone academic publication in the field of cultural studies and critical theory.

John O'Carroll is currently a lecturer in Literature and Communication at Charles Sturt University in Bathurst, Australia. He has worked at a range of Australian Universities as well as at the University of the South Pacific in Fiji. He has published (with Bob Hodge) *Borderwork*, a book on Australian multicultural theory, and (with Chris Fleming) a number of essays in the fields of literature and philosophy.

Ross Shields graduated from Macalester College and was a DAAD fellow at the Humboldt University in Berlin, Germany. He is currently pursuing graduate studies in the Department of Comparative Literature at SUNY Buffalo, New York.

Henry Sussman's forthcoming book, *Around the Book: Systems and Literacy* (New York: Fordham University Press, 2010), is a progress report on this venerable tradition and medium in the context of contemporary systems theory. In important respects, the present contribution to *Kafka's Cages* is a direct outgrowth of this long-standing interest on the author's part. Another backdrop to the essay is Sussman's *The Task of the Critic* (New York: Fordham University Press, 2005). Sussman is also the author, coauthor, and editor of several books on critical and literary theory, psychoanalysis, philosophy, and literature. He currently serves as a visiting professor in the Department of Germanic Languages and Literatures at Yale University, as well as professor emeritus, Department of Comparative Literature, University at Buffalo.

Dimitris Vardoulakis teaches at the University of Western Sydney and is the author of *The Doppelgänger: Literature's Philosophy* (Fordham University Press, 2010), the editor of *Spinoza Now* (University of Minnesota Press, 2011), and the co-editor of *After Blanchot* (University of Delaware Press, 2005).

Kafka's Cages: An Introduction

A. Kiarina Kordela and Dimitris Vardoulakis

Kafka's literary universe is organized around constellations of imprisonment. All his novels present states of confinement. In *Amerika*, Karl Rossmann arrives in New York like a prisoner and then he is soon trapped in different circumstances. In *The Castle*, the elusive castle on the top of the mountain and its officials exercise such an attraction to the landsurveyor that he is unable to leave the village. And in *The Trial*, Josef K. is found guilty without being told what crime he is accused of. This sense of imprisonment is also crucial in the novella *The Metamorphosis*, in which Gregor Samsa is confined to his room. It is also prevalent in the short stories; for instance, in Georg Bendemann's senseless condemnation to death by his father in "The Judgement," in the chilling description of the torture machine "In the Penal Colony," and in the cages of "A Report to an Academy" and "A Hunger Artist," to mention just a few.

Traditionally, Kafka's hermetically confined world has been conceptualized as a reflection of Kafka's own life. Kafka was trapped by his family circumstances and his domineering father in particular. He was "in prison" while working at the office, unable to devote himself to writing, and felt encaged even in his engagements with women. Broadening this perspective, the predominance of arbitrary confinement in Kafka's writings is conceptualized as a wider metaphysical or religious quest to show the fallen world of modernity, in which man is trapped in his complete separation from spirituality. This interpretation can be further nuanced by introducing the idea of existential anguish: Kafka's depictions of imprisonment are a reflection of the nothingness of human life. All of the above interpretations share as their common premise the supposition of a distinct, and ultimately oppositional, alternative to imprisonment. A sense of redemption, salvation, or freedom is the ideal or aim that the tortured Kafka heroes strive for but cannot attain.

The present collection proposes a different way of grasping the figure of the cage in Kafka's writings. According to this approach, imprisonment signifies neither a tortured state nor the striving toward something unattainable. Rather, it is the very critique of a culture that first posits a clear-cut opposition between confinement and freedom, and then sets up freedom as an ideal, which, conceived in such absolute terms, is by definition unattainable. In its laborious and exhilarating pages, Kafka's work probes the arsenal of the configurations through which such a culture reduces freedom to the bait whose promise and impossibility torment people.

* * *

To understand Kafka's critical intervention requires situating him within a certain literary and philosophical tradition. On the one hand, foundational texts of the literary canon are narratives structured around a confining frame. Homer's *Iliad* recounts how the Greek army is stranded outside Troy for ten long years. The stories of *The Arabian Nights* are framed by the narrative of Scheherazade telling Shahryar a tale every night, hoping that in this way he will not kill her like his other wives. More modern classics, as well, are narratives of confinement, such as Boccaccio's *Decameron*, the collection of stories narrated while a group of people are confined in a villa in order to avoid the plague. On the other hand, it is often overlooked that the issue of freedom does not arise as a question for philosophy and political theory until the seventeenth or eighteenth century, with the emergence of the bourgeois individual. The Greek classics of political philosophy or ethics, for instance, do not emphasize freedom at all. Plato's *Republic* is an inquiry into justice and the best possible government, while the linchpin of Aristotle's *Nicomachean Ethics* is the issue of friendship. Even if one considers the medieval legal notion of *legibus solutus* or its subsequent reformation as the sovereign's prerogative—that is, the standing of the king or the sovereign above the law—then it is clear that this exceptional right is not grounded on a presumed freedom on the part of the king or the sovereign.

The reason for this lack of reference to freedom prior to the seventeenth or eighteenth century is that striving toward freedom is an idea that presupposes the formation of the individual as an autonomous agency, in order for it to make sense in the first place. It is the construction of individuality that allows for a discourse on freedom to develop both in literature—as in the eighteenth-century novel—and in political philosophy. From this perspective, Kafka's topoi of imprisonment—his *cages*—take on a radically new meaning. Rather than being images of the failure of the individual to attain the ideal of freedom on the metaphysical or social level, they are instead images of the failure of freedom to define the individual. In short, Kafka's cages can be understood as a reaction to the promise of freedom— the means by which the individual is both defined and ensnared.

This way of understanding imprisonment in Kafka is radically different because Kafka's cages are no longer seen as a fault or source of anguish. Instead, the cages in Kafka's works become the means for Kafka to engage in the political and philosophical debates of his—and our—time. The vitality of the condition of encagement has ensured that Kafka's works continue to have a cultural resonance long after his death, in a century that saw the emergence of concentration camps, and in a new century that started with the establishment of new camps to incarcerate without charge "enemy combatants," "illegal aliens," and suspects of "terrorism."

* * *

The chapters collected in this volume respond to this way of understanding Kafka's cages, and each addresses them on several literary, philosophic, aesthetic, and sociopolitical levels, as well as through rich and thoughtfully conceived interdisciplinary methodologies. The chapters have been clustered according to the emphasis they place on certain aspects— interpretative, theoretical, or performative—of the cages in Kafka's work and the ways in which they reflect modernity.

The following summaries are only meant to indicate the salient features of the various cages of modernity addressed by each author.

Stanley Corngold's chapter "Special Views on Kafka's Cages" shows how Kafka constructs, through an incessant metamorphosis of the cage— ranging from culture to the skull—a "writerly ontology," in which the cage embodies the paradoxical coincidence of a confining cell full of negative openings and a protective fortress full of negative walls. Drawing on Friedrich Nietzsche, Bertolt Brecht, Walter Benjamin, and others, as well as Claude Lefort's, rather than Max Weber's, reading of Marx, Corngold advances the thesis that in Kafka even the bureaucratic office becomes a trope-like space enabling erotic play among its parts, for, as a cage, it is itself animate and charismatically charged.

Engaging with Eric Marson, René Girard, Benjamin, and Stuart Lasine, Chris Fleming and John O'Carroll argue in "Delusions of Agency: Kafka, Imprisonment, and Modern Victimhood" that Kafka's *The Trial* portrays the encagement of specifically *modern* victimhood. It does so, first, because of its double absence of agency: the victim lacks moral agency, just as the bureaucratic law functions like a mob in that no person can be singled out as responsible for K's death. Second, the legitimacy of modern victimization lies, as Max Weber pointed out, not in a "reasonable" basis, but in "scapegoating." This is an anthropological, rather than morally based, procedure that aims at generating social unanimity against the designated scapegoat, whereby the scapegoat bears no moral agency. It is for these two reasons that Josef K.'s primary error lies in his delusion that he is an *agent at all.*

In his dialogue with Derrida's readings of Kafka's *Before the Law*, in "Kafka and Derrida *Before the Laws*," Howard Caygill expands exponentially the text's framing layers, whereby the play of mise en abyme that Derrida finds exemplary in this uncontainable story is shown to be itself mise en abyme, due to its (re)publications prior to both *A Country Doctor* and *The Trial.* In Caygill's deferred analytical itinerary, Kafka's story intertwines literary, political, cultural, and historical contexts, thereby transforming itself from a narrative about the tension between the universality of the law and the singularity of any entrance to it, as it is canonically read, to a story about failed emigration/immigration, which becomes even more plural as, depending on its position between other of Kafka's stories, it is narrated from either perspective—the immigrant's or the guard's.

In John Mowitt's "Kafka's Cage," Kafka and John Cage form an allegorical parallelism between music and literature, showing their shared epistemological difficulties: how to write critical musicology in the wake of Arnold Schoenberg's "new music" (Jean-François Lyotard's question) and how to read after the novelty of (Kafka's) "new" literature. In both cases, ever-proliferating compartmentalizations disciplining sound and thought vie over what determines the intelligible and its proper interpretation. Mowitt reads Cage's and Kafka's works (especially "Das Schweigen der Sirenen") through the work of Walter Benjamin, Theodor Adorno, Max Horkheimer, Sigmund Freud, Jacques Lacan, and Louis Althusser, to debunk the purported opposites of silence and to propose that only through a reconceptualization of "influence" and "inscription" beyond the cage of linear causal reductionism can critical musicology and literary criticism articulate the cunning means by which to theorize the "new" music and literature.

Dimitris Vardoulakis's "'The Fall is the proof of our freedom': Mediated Freedom in Kafka" reads the cages in "A Report to an Academy" and "The Fasting Artist" against the background of Levinas's critique of the humanist ideal of freedom as the clear-cut opposite of confinement. Vardoulakis shows that in both short stories, laughter collapses this ostensible opposition, leading to disembodiment and the loss of singularity, thereby undermining the further canonical oppositions between, on the one hand, the empirical, finitude, and singularity, and, on the other hand, the abstract, infinity, and the universal. Rather, Vardoulakis argues, singularity is the way that the empirical and the limitless are held in a productive and yet irresolvable suspension that allows Kafka's cages to intertwine judgment, singularity, and mediated freedom.

By rereading (*re-legare*) Kafka's 1918 fragment "Die besitzlose Arbeiterschaft," Peter Fenves offers in "'Workforce without Possessions': Kafka, 'Social Justice,' and the Word *Religion*" a radical redefinition of "religion." Fenves argues that Kafka's fragment is not a defense of either the October Revolution or any Zionist or socialist and communist programs in Kafka's time—which, at best, aimed at an equal distribution of goods among their peoples—but a universalist manifesto against the cage of any possession whatsoever, by dint of the fact that for religion possession is simply impossible. The *res religiosae* postulates that a thing that belongs to someone must become no one's, and since prior to be acquired by someone, everything belonged to no one, "no one" is the sole just proprietor of everything "religious." Kafka's "Workforce" is a bond [*re-ligare*] among those who in the eyes of the law are no one, so that what belongs to them is made "religious." Only former-proprietors-become-workers-without-possessions can make the world religious.

In "Kafkaesque: (Secular) Kabbalah and Allegory," A. Kiarina Kordela invokes Kant, Benjamin, and Lacan, as well as obliquely Spinoza and Marx, to unravel the logical structures of kabbalist thought and allegory as philosophical and literary modes specific to secular epistemological exigencies. Albeit Kantian in its mission, the Kafkaesque, as a specific allegorical mode, revises transcendental criticism by constructing empirical reality as the unknowable index of its own transcendental Truth and Law, thereby challenging the postmodern epistemological confinement in cultural relativism. In her dialogue with other thinkers, such as Weber, Blanchot, Foucault, Deleuze, Jameson, and Žižek, Kordela morphs the Kafkaesque into a blueprint of concepts that range from parable, desire, and redemption to set theory, the gaze, and perversion.

In Ross Shields's "The Ethics and Beauty of *The Trial*: Kafka's Circumscription of Failure," the paradoxes and failures so characteristic of Kafka's writings take on the significance of expressing allegorically the specific modes of failure of the sexed subject and the apparatus of imprisonment that delineate his or her limits. Drawing on Deleuze and Guattari's work on Kafka and on Lacan's topology in his seminar on ethics, Shields identifies a paradigm shift in *The Trial* from the transcendent totality and objective rationality of the male position of enunciation to the immanent incompleteness and impossible desire of the female position of enunciation. This shift entails a reconceptualization of desire, beauty, ethics, and their interrelations.

In Karyn Ball's "Kafka's Fatal Performatives: Between 'Bad Conscience' and Betrayed Vulnerability," a stichomythia between Kafka and Nietzsche reveals the latter's "fatalism" as a double mechanism of fatal performativity, in which proclaimed guilt is internalized as one's own desire, while the moral values purported to ground laws are themselves the effects of the laws they ground. The (post-)modern quasi universalization of the cage, in which one can be arrested without charge or trial, is not reducible to either Nietzsche's "bad conscience" or Freud's human instinctual aggression (Nietzsche's primal vitality). In this context, as Ball's reading of Kafka, and particularly *The Metamorphosis*, shows, art is confined to refracting a death-driven modernity, but only by itself executing the fatal performative it stages; thus, it itself dies as a figural world, while its demand for solidarity outlives it to reproach us (readers), now.

In "How Is the Trapeze Possible?" Christophe Bident's reading of Kafka's 1921–1922 story "First Sorrow" shows that, unlike any actual trapeze artist, the *essence* of the trapeze artist consists in desiring nothing other than trapezes, so that the trapeze artist's desire coincides with his prison. Bident links Kafka's story to the 2005 show *I Look Up, I Look Down,* in which trapeze artists Chloé Moglia and Mélissa Von Vépy pierce through the aerial cage of the trapeze-artist-being by means of the (philosophical) voice. Through this encounter of the spectacle and the voices of Bachelard, Deleuze, or Jankélévitch, a narrative emerges that questions all possible borders, from that between desire and risk, physical performance and meaning, physics and metaphysics, to poetics and politics.

Henry Sussman's "With Impunity" traces the narrative chiasma of rhetoric and (political) act in Giorgio Agamben's *Homo Sacer,* through which impunity emerges as the performative tact and fundamental attitude of biopolitical power. In Sussman's reading of *The Castle,* its official is endowed with the same impunity that marks both Agamben's biopolitical power and Weber's charismatic leader. In the biopolitical coincidence of body and law, of which Kafka offers unparalleled fictitious descriptions, bureaucratic mechanisms, not unlike those of the camps, become a digital (i.e., purely relational/syntactical) readout to what was once an ecology of analog (i.e., meaningful) relations. By invoking Jacques Derrida, Sussman appeals to the university's and psychoanalysis' "unconditional" freedom of expression as the sole sites of a potentially revolutionary impunity against the extant rule of totalitarian impunity.

Part I
Interpreting Kafka's Cages

CHAPTER ONE
SPECIAL VIEWS ON KAFKA'S CAGES

Stanley Corngold

Main Entry:
cage
Pronunciation:
\\'kāj
Function:
noun
Etymology:
Middle English, from Anglo-French, from Latin cavea *cavity, cage, from* cavus
hollow—more at CAVE
Date:
13th century
1: a box or enclosure having some openwork for confining or carrying animals
(as birds)
2 a: a barred cell for confining prisoners b: a fenced area for prisoners of war.
—Merriam-Webster Online Dictionary[1]

1. Wreathes and Cages

Germany, as the sublime commonplace has it, is "das Volk der Dichter
und Denker" (the people of poets and thinkers). The Austrian writer and
publicist Karl Kraus twisted the stereotype ferociously as "das Volk der
Richter und Henker" (the people of judges and hangmen).[2] You find this
thrust in Kraus's *Sprüche und Widersprüche* (Dicta and contradictions),
which the English translator elaborates as "The Germans. 'Nation of bards
and sages'? Cremation and bars and cages!"[3]

Kraus, writing in Vienna as a subject of the Austro-Hungarian Empire,
would have had few qualms in referring his critique to his own nation(s).
I will presume to speak for him: "Subjects of Vienna. 'Empire of bards and

sages'? Cremation and bars and cages!" This trope brings us by an eccentric path to the cremation and bars and cages felt by a greater subject of the Empire—Franz Kafka of Prague. His writing is haunted by these figures, but they are again twisted—in the manner of helixes. You do not see real bodies on fire in Kafka (it is an odd and important revelation). You see "experience" on fire, and this is a beneficent flame. It is part of a complex braid of images of neo-Gnostic inspiration. You see abundant bars and cages, though they are not only or essentially nationally inflicted.

The cage is prominent, even aggressive and mobile, in one of Kafka's Zürau aphorisms of 1919 (packaged in prayer cloth by Max Brod as "Reflections on Sin, Suffering, Hope, and the True Way"). Referring, very likely, to a deep sense of himself, Kafka wrote, "A cage went in search of a bird."[4] I believe Kafka has condensed into this movement all the ways that his strongest abilities only served to capture and stifle life—or what he tirelessly called "life." To understand this claim, we need to have Kafka qualify the agent (the cage) and the object (life). Here is one such elaboration, a lament that Kafka wrote to Max Brod, on July 5, 1922, after a tormenting night,

When I let everything run back and forth again and again between my aching temples during last night's sleepless night, I became aware again of what I had almost forgotten in the relative calm of the past few days—what a weak or even nonexistent ground I live on, over a darkness out of which the dark power emerges when it wills and, without bothering about my stammers, destroys my life. Writing maintains me, but isn't it more correct to say that it maintains this sort of life? Of course, I don't mean by this that my life is better when I don't write. Rather, it is much worse then and wholly intolerable and must end in insanity. But that [is true], of course, only under the condition that I, as is actually the case, even when I don't write, am a writer; and a writer who doesn't write is, admittedly, a monster asking for insanity.

But how do things stand with this being a writer (*Schriftstellersein*)? Writing is a sweet, wonderful reward, but for what? During the night it was clear to me with the vividness of childish show-and-tell: it is the reward for service to the devil. This descent to the dark powers, this unfettering of spirits bound by nature, dubious embraces, and whatever else may go on below, of which one no longer knows anything above ground when one writes stories in the sunlight. Perhaps there is another kind of writing, I know only this one; in the night, when anxiety does not let me sleep, I know only this. And what is devilish in it seems to me quite clear. It is vanity and the craving for enjoyment, which is forever whirring around one's own form or even another's—the movement then multiplies itself, it becomes a solar system of vanities—and enjoys it. What the naive person sometimes wishes: "I would like to die and watch the others cry over me," is what such a writer constantly realizes: he dies (or he does not live) and continually weeps about himself. From this comes a terrible fear of death, which does not have to manifest itself as the fear of death but can also emerge as the fear of change.... The reasons for his fear of death can be divided into two main groups. First, he is terribly afraid of dying because he has not yet lived. By this I do not mean that wife and child and field and cattle are necessary to live. What is necessary for life is only the renunciation of self-delight: to move into the house instead of admiring it and decking it with wreaths. Countering this, one could say that such is fate and not put into any man's hands. But then why does one feel remorse, why doesn't the remorse stop? To make oneself more beautiful, more attractive? That too. But why, over and beyond this, in such nights, is the keyword always: I could live and I do not....

What right have I to be shocked, I who was not at home, when the house suddenly collapses; for I know what preceded the collapse, didn't I emigrate, abandoning the house to all the powers of evil?[5]

This is writing of such beauty and intensity as to punish students eager to repeat Benjamin's jealous aperçu that Kafka's friendship with Max Brod was "probably...not the least of the riddles in Kafka's life."[6] Granted the constraints of home on his choice of friends, in supposing Brod a fit recipient of such confessions—of so "complete an opening out of body and soul"—Kafka will have embraced Brod, if intermittently, as his friend.

On the strength of this letter, the English elaboration of Kraus's aperçu might have read, "...bars and *wreathes* and cages." The image of wreathes, with their suggestion of garlands, tropes, ornaments commemorating a death, are, for one moment, the bars of Kafka's cage. Part of the conclusion to the letter reads:

What I have played at will really happen. I have not ransomed myself by writing. All my life I have been dead, and now I will really die. My life was sweeter than that of others, my death will be that much more terrible. The writer in me will, of course, die at once, for such a figure has no basis, has no substance, isn't even made of dust; it is only slightly possible in the maddest earthly life, it is only a construction of the craving for enjoyment. This is the writer. But I myself cannot live on, since I have not lived, I have remained clay, I have not turned the spark into a fire but used it only for the *illumination* of my corpse.[7]

This illumination (*Illuminierung*) of his corpse is at once a burnished clarification, with final insight, of the death-in-life of being a writer. It is also, more literally, a furnishing it with figural decorations, as a manuscript is illuminated. The light of an unlived life glances through the bars of his cage, producing letter-like figurations, embellishments, the sort of figures that, *In the Penal Colony*, delay any possible understanding of the ethical commandment one has betrayed—which is to say, the truer design of one's life.

These illuminations, figurations, embellishments might well be a synecdoche of what is called "culture"—the play of aesthetic experience (*Erlebnis*) and the memory of shaped practices (*Erfahrung*) that Kafka excoriated as schemes to muddy the knowledge of ethical failure. The attack on epistemic and aesthetic (viz., non-tragic) culture is exemplary in Kafka's interlocutor Nietzsche. Consider among many examples Nietzsche's unpublished notes on "European Nihilism": "Morality is disintegrating: but if the weak are going to their ruin, their fate appears as a self-condemnation, the instinctive selection of a destructive necessity. What is called 'culture' is merely merciless self-analysis, poisoning of all sorts, intoxication, romanticism...."[8] This rattling (from within) of the bars of culture is audible in texts of Kafka throughout. There is his reading of the Biblical story:

> Since the Fall we have been essentially equal in our capacity to know Good and Evil; nevertheless, it is precisely here we look for our special merits. But only on the far side of this knowledge do the real differences begin. The contrary appearance is caused by the following fact: nobody can be content with the knowledge alone, but must strive to act in accordance with it. But he is not endowed with the strength for this, hence he must destroy himself, even at risk of in that way not acquiring the necessary strength for this, but there is nothing else he can do except this last attempt.... Now this is an attempt he is afraid to make; he prefers to undo the knowledge of Good and Evil (the term "the Fall" has its origin in this fear) but what has once happened cannot be undone, it can only be made turbid [*trübe*]. It is for this purpose *motivations* arise. The whole world is full of them: indeed the whole visible world is perhaps nothing more than a motivation of man's wish to rest for a moment—an attempt to falsify the fact of knowledge, to try to turn knowledge into the goal.[9]

The key word "motivations" is smartly paraphrased by Joyce Crick as the negative in Kafka's "radical project"—viz. "to transcend, in the asceticism of his writing, what he called the 'Motivationen' of discourse, ideology, interest, the constraints of historical location, the claims of the social order, the needs of the body, into a realm of purity and truth."[10] (She might have added the aesthetic factor—what Kafka, in the letter to Brod earlier cited, called the drive "to make oneself more beautiful, more attractive.") Motivations feed on local knowledge, and Kafka's were well provided for, since he read voraciously and in seven languages. Furthermore, as a skilled practitioner within the geographically, not trade-based, Imperial Austrian system of workmen's accident insurance, he was obliged to master the protocols of production of everything manufactured under the aegis of high industrial modernism in the whole of the Czech Lands of Bohemia ("the

Manchester of Central Europe") in factories, quarries, farms, spas. The important fact about so much knowledge is that it irrupts into Kafka's aesthetic drive, a fact that matters when his stories are read as the records of "thought experiments" with the major currents of the epistemic culture of his time.[11] In this way, the two categories of epistemic and aesthetic experience mingle, as in this late letter to his fiancée Felice Bauer:

> I strive to know the entire human and animal community, to recognize their fundamental preferences, desires, and moral ideals, to reduce them to simple rules, and as quickly as possible to adopt these rules so as to be pleasing to everyone...to become so pleasing that in the end I might openly act out my inherent baseness before the eyes of the world without forfeiting its love—the only sinner not to be roasted.[12]

Such texts speak of ethical failure, the failure to do the right thing ("to move into the house") and of the great distraction: the accumulation of "alibis" as pieces of knowledge and the cultivation of a "pleasing" "literature." With the "adoption" of the rules of the discipline of anthropology, Kafka is surely referring to his own artistic practice—to packing his writing with so much cultural knowledge as stuff to be transformed. (In what other medium could he plausibly say that he had adopted the rules reflecting the "fundamental preferences, desires, and moral ideals...of the entire *human and animal community*..."? [emphasis added, SC]). This accumulation of "alibis" in empirical life—or literature—undoes the mandate of "acting in accordance with the knowledge of Good and Evil" that leads to "life." And what, furthermore, is it to "undo" a knowledge that cannot be undone if not to *disbelieve* it? Kafka wrote: "It is not a bleak wall, it is the very sweetest life that has been compressed into a wall, raisins upon raisins."—"I don't believe it."—"Taste it."—"I cannot raise my hand for unbelief."—"I shall put the grape into your mouth."—"I cannot taste it for unbelief."—"Then sink into the ground!"—"Did I not say that faced with the barrenness of this wall one must sink into the ground?"[13]

A certain dialectic indwells this refusal, which—N.B.—ends with a sadly brilliant alibi. We have been hearing about the sinful refusal to eat of the Tree of Life ("We are sinful not merely because we have eaten of the tree of knowledge, but also because we have not eaten of the tree of life").[14] Whereupon the speciously positive arm of the dialectic is raised up as another wall—of sweetly compressed explications grounded on "I"'s concluding alibi. This surplus of sweetness has a musical counterpart in the great lament:

> Have never understood how it is possible for almost everyone who writes to objectify his sufferings in the very midst of undergoing them; thus I,

for example, in the midst of my unhappiness, in all likelihood with my head still smarting form unhappiness, sit down and write to someone: I am unhappy. Yes, I can even go beyond that and with as many flourishes as I have the talent for, all of which seem to have nothing to do with my unhappiness, ring simple, or contrapuntal, or a whole orchestration of changes on my theme. And it is not a lie, and it does not still my pain; it is simply, a merciful surplus of strength at a moment when suffering has raked me to the bottom of my being and plainly exhausted all my strength. But then what kind of surplus is it?[15]

In the letter to Brod of September 1922 quoted earlier, *it* is "a sweet, wonderful reward, but for what? [...] *It* is the reward for service to the devil." The condition of the reward is a musical death-in-life, life in a certain hell—the steel-hard cage of culture—read: devil's work, as in the Gnostic myth that Kafka employed: "No people sing with such pure voices as those that live in deepest hell; what we take for the song of angels is their song."[16]

2. The Happy Fortress

Everything is fantasy: family, office, friends, the street, everything is fantasy, whether farther or nearer, woman the nearest, truth however is only that you press your head against the wall of a window- and door-less cell.[17]

Kafka is so drawn to the image of himself encaged that Kafka's biographer Reiner Stach speaks of "the cage" as itself a cage: he means that Kafka imprisoned himself handily in the view, in this metaphor with claws:

A life in a cell, in a cage, a life that threatens to choke on itself. The private myth gives one purchase, it offers a theory of one's own history, one's own being that literally *makes sense*. But the costs are high, spontaneous action is scarcely possible any more, insignificant irritations waken the threat of "collapse" [Kafka's word: *Zusammenbruch*], less and less does Kafka feel able to bear new experience, however promising.[18]

There is good evidence throughout the diaries for this picture of Kafka, most succinctly in the formula "Meine Gefängniszelle, meine Festung (My prison cell, my fortress)"[19]—stress on "fortress."[20] Here we have the most compressed account of the two torques of Kafka's cage: the cage torments the prisoner, as a place of airless oppression, a suffocation of the "spark," and it gives him "purchase" (Stach). Two successive notebook entries in 1921/1922 read (1) "The war with the cell wall" and then (2) "Undecided."[21]

The metaphysical foundation for these two moments is found in an aphorism from the same pages of Kafka's notebooks: "There is no having, only a being, only a state of being that craves the last breath, craves suffocation."[22] "Being" (*Sein*), as Kafka notes, means in German both "existence" (*Da-sein*) and "belonging to him" (*Ihm-gehören*).[23] This second provision cancels out the putative freedom of human being. Being is "incomplete," not in the sense that it craves some inner-spatial fullness perhaps available to it, on the model of Gregor Samsa's longing for "unknown nourishment" (MM 1996, 36); it craves its own closing down. Its thrust is toward an ending, which does not entail fulfilment—a sense of fulfilment is contingent—but which in every sense of an ending implies its death, since it is its nature to be incomplete, à la Heidegger, for whom "the Being of Dasein [...] is an issue for Dasein in its very Being."[24]

It would be apt to ask about the place of *writing* in this ontology. "Writing maintains me," we have just heard Kafka saying, "but isn't it more correct to say that it maintains this sort of life?"—this sort of death-in-life? But if writing is to be something more than tapping quickstep in place, then it might well be thought of as an *enactment* of this final conatus of human being. It aims to perform the completion of its being (that is at the same time its death) by what Benjamin calls "the death of an intention"—here, the writerly intention—in craving a last word, an ecstasy beyond which there need be no more writing.

The fusion of the terms "word" and "breath" has an ancient foundation, as in Psalm 33:6 of the King James Bible: "By the word of the Lord were the heavens made; and all the host of them by the breath of his mouth."

Such writing has little to do with introspective acts focused on a Diltheyan abundance of an "inner world"—even a "tremendous/monstrous/colossal" world[25]—of what Kafka earlier called "lived experience."[26] "How would it be," he writes, "if one were to choke to death on oneself? If the pressure of introspection were to diminish, or close off entirely, the opening through which one flows forth into the world"?[27] Here, one must draw a distinction between the suffocation (*Ersticken*) that human being craves on drawing its last breath and, on the other hand, that "choking *on oneself*" (*an sich selbst* ersticken, emphasis added, SC) that comes from relentless introspection. The risk of not writing would be, quite literally, choking on oneself—and not maintaining a life at issue with itself and full of craving—if even for that other finale in suffocation (there is no more air to breathe, one craves it no longer).

The goal, then, is "not shaking off the self but consuming the self,"[28] where "consuming the self" needs to be understood as a transformation of the standing stock (*Bestand*) of the subject-ego into pure craving...for a last word/the last breath. These sentences were written toward the end of Kafka's life, but even early in his diaries Kafka recorded his desire "to write all my anxiety entirely out of me, write it into the depths of the paper just as it comes out of the depths of me, or write it in such a way that I can draw what I have written into me completely."[29] The thrust of this desire is to transform anxiety into the words of art or an inhalation of what has been written—like breath—the breath of the straitened freedom to crave the last word, the last breath once more.

All this has more than one moving correlative in *The Castle,* the work in which Kafka most fully elaborates this writerly ontology. We can lay stress on two moments—on breath, on home.

The first breath is K.'s breath of pain inside his celebrated embrace of Frieda, the pawn in his pursuit of "entry" into the Castle.

> There [on the floor with Frieda, in a puddle of beer] hours passed, hours of breathing together, of hearts beating together, hours in which K. again and again had the feeling that he was going astray or so deep in a foreign place [or: in a foreign woman, *in der Fremde*] as no man ever before him, a foreign place in which even the air had no ingredient of the air of home, in which one must suffocate of foreignness and in whose absurd allurements one could still do nothing more than go farther, go farther astray.[30]

It is clear: the goal is suffocation, to draw in the last breath, but that last breath may not be a breath of the air of oneself, the afflatus of dog-chase-tail introspection; nor the foreign air (of a woman's body); but of an air that (one postulates, by negation) breathable because unmixed, without its element of filth (*Schmutz*) and putatively natural, suited to a human being that craves a last but not a toxic breath. Where is this purer air? Kafka sought its empirical correlative in the air of the mountains he visited. Its essential kind and place can very well be the air of the final word, a word on the heights, implicit in such statements as: "I can still get fleeting satisfaction from works like 'A Country Doctor....' But happiness only in case I can raise the world into purity, truth, immutability";[31] a place high above the "Niederungen des Schreibens," the lowlands of writing, where the composition of *Der Verschollene* allegedly took place; a leap out of murderers' row, viz.

> The strange, mysterious, perhaps dangerous, perhaps saving comfort of writing: the leap out of murderers' row of deed followed by observation, deed followed by observation, in that a higher type of observation is created, a higher, not a keener type, and the higher it is and the less attainable from the "row," the more independent it becomes, the more obedient to its own laws of motion, the more incalculable, the more joyful, the more ascendant its course.[32]

This "higher type of observation" would presumably be that clear gaze (how Kafka celebrated "die Klarheit des Blickes"![33]) accompanying the last breath, a little, too, like Poseidon's "quick little tour" of the oceans just at the instant the world was coming to an end.[34]

This craving for a finale as a sort of home—in effect a charnel house—is vivid in a passage in *The Castle* recently excerpted and discussed at length by Michael Wood. He studies the passage

> where Frieda, the woman the protagonist K has taken up with, suggests they leave the village where they are living and escape the whole world that depends on the castle K is so anxious to enter. They could go to Spain or the South of France, she says. This is already pretty startling, given the bleak fairy-tale atmosphere of the novel . . . but K's response is even stranger, representing "a contradiction he didn't bother to explain." He can't leave, he says, because he wants to stay. Why else would he have come? "What could have attracted me to this desolate land other than the desire to stay? (Was hätte mich denn in dieses öde Land locken können, als das Verlangen hier zu bleiben? [C 1982b, 215].) What does this sentence mean?

Wood writes:

> It doesn't explain, but it shows. K is not attracted by the desolation, he is driven by a desire for home that overrides all objections. The desolation insures that the desire will remain a desire; that home, even if K should by some freakish accident manage to settle there, will not be any place like home.[35]

In this passage, we recognize the figure of thought we have been exploring above in the exalted language of Kafka's notebooks. But here, in *The Castle*, the figure of suffocation is cast in a local and demotic diction. The German word translated "desolate"—as in "desolate land"—is *öde*; the ordinary sense of *öde* is "dead" (as a party might be dead), "yawn-producing"—hence, airless. So, in K.'s brief speech, we again have the conjunction of a self-reproducing, inexhaustible craving for . . . suffocation, oxygenless, desert air—except, here, it appears in a mode of sad abjection, so demoralized have K.'s longings become. For what sort of air is this, the air of this desolate land? It has presumably stayed in his nostrils as the scent of the beer-splattered floor of the odious barroom on which K. and Frieda married. This nonsensuous figure of airlessness, it is well known, has a general applicability to marriage, as, for example, in the 1914-painting by Walter Richard Sickert titled "Ennui," the portrait of "a marriage suffocating with boredom."[36] All the passages from Kafka cited above prove the seamless continuity of thought and feeling in his life and art.

So, we see Kafka encaged in a Sisyphean circle without fulfilment, longing to die, longing for a perfectly deadly last breath but who, in the figure of K., will settle for an endless inhalation of bad desert air. It is the air of a continuous dying short of death; his words recall the moment before the death of another K. At the close of *The Trial*, Joseph K. is led into a little quarry, "verlassen und öde" (abandoned and desolate) (T 1990, 310). At this moment there is no great difference between the school classroom where K. is employed as a janitor and the stony desert into which K. is led. And there he will die, but "like a dog"; his last breath, his last word, pronounces this judgment. It is a foul breath, afflatus of a barren life that has always, in practice, declared *it* to be a desolate (*öde*) stone wall; but *it* is in truth "the very sweetest life," a wall of sweet raisins pressed together, as we recall, but the Ks cannot (p. 13 supra).

"In me, by myself, without human relationship, there are no visible lies," wrote Kafka on August 30, 1913; "the limited circle is pure."[37] Such a circle is not a cage, not a vicious circle. Kafka merely needs to shear himself of all human connection. But three months before, on May 3, 1913, he spoke, gnomically, of "the terrible uncertainty of my inner existence."[38] The images do not jibe. It is one thing to play off one's purity against the disturbing imagination of others' feelings. But in the absence of that shame, Kafka reverts to his primary insecurity—the broken, not limited, circle of his inner existence—for which the cage is an apt enough figure, for it is a broken circle, an enclosure with gaps, with its openings (its "ways out") too narrow to slip through and narrow enough to hold him. "Kafka's cage" will make us think of the rib cage enclosing friable lungs gasping for clean air. Gerhard Kurz writes about the neo-Gnostic legacy of figures of tension in Kafka—

> anxiety, the experience of death, guilt, and suffering. whose recurrent metaphorical paradigms are . . . homelessness, the loss of orientation, impotence, "thrownness," exposure, vulnerability, anxiety, madness, alienation, *sickness, imprisonment* (emphasis added, SC). All are metaphors of Gnostic origin.[39]

And yet we have also seen this Gnostic prison as Kafka's fortress, a stay against dissolution, against a final death-in-life, mere undeadness: "Meine Gefängniszelle, meine Festung (My prison cell, my fortress)."[40] The paradox of a cell full of negative openings that is at once a fortress full of negative walls again catches the tension.

The conjunction of such torques is not original in Kafka; on the heights of tradition (but in a figure certainly much dimmed-down in Kafka) perches the dubiously "happy prison." Recall the canonical example of *The Charterhouse of Parma*, Stendhal's account of Fabrizio del Dongo's sequestration in the fortress of Parma.[41] Let us cite, for good economy, a valuable source: Martha Grace Duncan's "'Cradled on the Sea': Positive Images of Prison and Theories of Punishment." She writes:

> In Stendhal's novel, *The Charterhouse of Parma*, the prison is constructed so far above the ground that Fabrizio refers to his "airy solitude." On the first night of his incarceration, Fabrizio spends hours at the window, "admiring this horizon which spoke to his soul." In prison, he finds the happiness that had eluded him in freedom: "By a paradox to which he gave no thought, a secret joy was reigning in the depths of his heart." Endeavouring to account for this paradox, Fabrizio reflects: "[H]ere one is a thousand leagues above the pettinesses and wickednesses which occupy us down there."[42]

This is, admittedly, too sublime for Kafka, but it makes the point, Stach's point, with which I began this section: there is masochistic pleasure in Kafka's imagining his incarceration. I would stress that the pleasure comes off the prospect of nourishing his writing with his pain, for by 1920, when he wrote the phrase "My prison cell, my fortress," he could recall having happily imagined the figure of Rotpeter, the literally encaged hero of his published story "A Report to an Academy" (1916) and thereafter the brother of the girl who knocks on the gate, in "The Knock at the Courtyard Gate" (1917), and who is then put on trial in the "tavern parlor." The outcome of his ordeal might be anticipated, for the parlor now "looks like a prison cell":

> Large flagstones, a dark gray, bare wall, an iron ring cemented somewhere into it, at the center something that was half plank bed, half operating table.
> Could I still sense any air [!] other than that of a prison? That is the great question—or rather, it would be the question if I had any prospect of being released."[43]

And Kafka would take pleasure from his expert knowledge of being encaged on writing "A Starvation Artist" (1922)—and all along there are the many unnamed martyrs in his notebooks:

> It was not a prison cell, because the fourth wall was completely open. The idea that this wall was or could be walled up as well was terrifying because then, considering the extent of the space, which was one meter deep and only a little taller than I, I would be in an upright stone coffin. Well, for the time being it was not walled up; I could stick out my hands freely; and when I held on to an iron ring that was stuck above me in the ceiling, I could also carefully bend my head out—carefully, of course, because I did not know how high above the surface my cell was located. It appeared to be

very high; at any rate, in the depths I saw nothing except grey mist, to the right and to the left and in the distance, as well, except towards the heights it seemed to grow a bit lighter. It was a prospect such as one might have from a tower on an overcast day.

I was tired and sat down in front, on the edge; I let my feet dangle below. It made me angry that I was completely naked; otherwise I could have knotted my clothing and towels together, attached them to the clamp above, and let myself down outside a good distance below my cell, where I might be able to scout out a thing or two. On the other hand, it was good that I could not do this, because in my agitation, I would probably have done it, but it could have turned out very badly. Better to have nothing and do nothing.

In the back of the cell, which was otherwise completely empty and had bare walls, there were two holes in the floor. The hole in the one corner seemed designed for defecation; in front of the hole in the other corner there lay a piece of bread and a little wooden bucket with water, screwed down. I concluded that my food would be stuck in through there. (HA 1992, 350–51)

One detail that may strike us is the missing fourth wall, which preoc-cupied Kafka earlier—the *different* fourth wall of Rotpeter's cage in "A Report to an Academy":

After those shots I awoke—and here my own memory gradually takes over—in a cage in steerage of the Hagenbeck freighter. It was not a four-sided cage with bars; instead, only three barred sides were attached to a crate, which thus formed the fourth wall. The whole was too low to stand and too narrow to sit down in. Hence, I squatted with bent, continually trembling knees; and since at first I may not have wanted to see anyone and was eager only to remain in the dark, I faced the crate while the bars of the cage cut into the flesh of my backside. This way of keeping wild animals during the first few days of their captivity is considered effective; and today, with my experience, I cannot deny that from a human point of view this is, in fact, the case. (RA 2007, 78)

Here, the fourth wall (of the cage) is only nominally missing, for it has been replaced by a worse impediment to Rotpeter's freedom. In turning toward the crate wall, the ape consecrates his own unfreedom. This point is quite explicit: "I was eager only to remain in the dark" (78).

Now the "fourth wall" will have another resonance for Kafka, who had a highly developed *theatrical* awareness. "The fourth wall" in the conversa-tion about theater in Kafka's time—especially in the locution "the *miss-ing* fourth wall"—refers to the "naturalistic constraint" on theater, which disappears "when the audience has been assumed to be something other than figures in the dark who stare through a missing fourth wall at peo-ple who ostensibly remain unaware that they are observed."[44] Innovative modernist theater, on the other hand (read: Pirandello, Yeats, Brecht) strove "to liberate contemporary theater from its continuing naturalistic constraints—physical (the 'missing fourth wall') as well as ideological (the 'slice of life')."[45] The ape who faces a missing fourth wall, in this conversation, enacts, in high parodic style, the constraints on the freedom of the theatrical work of art. If the mention of theater seems tactless in a scene of suffering, consider the fact that the ape is on his way to becoming a self-fashioned theatrical work of art. His account of his own education to the "average cultural level of a European" (RA 2007, 83) is possible only because "my position on all the great vaudeville stages of the civilized world [is] secure to the point of being impregnable" (77).[46] But vaudeville stardom, it hardly needs pointing out, is not equivalent to innovating modernist theater. If it is true that Rotpeter finds "a way out" by turning back and away from the missing fourth wall, it is only to peer through his cage at the spectacle of sailors spitting on the deck (a "slice of life") and learning to imitate them: he perfectly incarnates the Naturalist ethic, he is, as Aristotle defined the ape, the *mimic* par excellence.[47]

For one moment, Rotpeter has refused the mode of human being that consists in being-seen—and chosen "darkness." For one moment, he has refused the cage that defines "the I as the eye of the other"—the cage that is indistinguishable from everyday human life. But now, in turning around, finally, in his search for a way out, to face the bars of the first wall of his cage, he presents himself to the view of the others. He adopts the "realism" of inauthenticity, the "presentation of the self in everyday life."

3. The "Iron Cage"

This expression is not Kafka's, and it is not even Max Weber's. Weber wrote "stahlhartes Gehäuse" or "carapace as hard as steel." He was referring to the iron cage of high industrial capitalism, the chain links of its administration—rule-bound, control-seeking, indifferent to the destiny of individuals. The expression famously appears in *Die protestantische Ethik und der Geist des Kapitalismus* via Weber's inversion of the views of the Puritan theologian, Richard Baxter. Weber writes: "The care for external goods should only lie on the shoulders of the 'saint like a light cloak, which can be thrown aside at any moment' [thus Baxter]. But fate decreed that the cloak should become an iron cage (*stahlhartes Gehäuse*)."[48] Benjamin, in a letter to Scholem, makes explicit the connection between Weber and Kafka: Kafka's perspective is that of a "modern citizen who realizes that his fate is being determined by an impenetrable bureaucratic apparatus whose operation is controlled by procedures that remain shadowy even to those carrying out its orders and *a fortiorito* those being manipulated by it."[49]

Thinking, now, of Gregor Samsa, in Kafka's *Metamorphosis*, the scholar of organization theory Malcolm Warner asks whether "the carapace, both the author and the character develop in their figurative and literal respective ways, is a *defense mechanism* against their common exploitation in terms of appropriated 'time.'"[50] Warner then cites Sheldon Wolin: "Everywhere there is organization, everywhere bureaucratization; like the world of feudalism, the modern world is broken up into areas dominated by castles, but not the castles of les chansons de geste, but the castles of Kafka."[51] Of course the word *Schloß* in the title to Kafka's novel also means "the lock," and in various places in the novel Kafka plays with this second meaning.

In the matter of bureaucracy, Kafka may be said to know on his living body those factors profiled in Part III, Chapter Six, of Max Weber's *Wirtschaft und Gesellschaft*. "The management of the modern office," writes Weber,

> is based upon written documents ("the files"), which are preserved in their original or draught form. There is, therefore, a staff of subaltern officials and scribes of all sorts. The body of officials actively engaged in a "public" office, along with the respective apparatus of material implements and the files, make up a "bureau." In private enterprise, "the bureau" is often called the "office"....[52]

The modern "office" may well be considered another profile (*Abschattierung*) of Kafka's cage.[53] But contrary to the doxa that radically separates office from literature, the bureaucracy serves Kafka as a fitting model for the organization of his writing powers. The structure and the image of the former "encage" the latter. This link confirms the point that the office, for Weber and most decisively for Kafka, is ubiquitous and uncanny, "the admired adversary, spreading inexorably into every department of life."[54] In the world of both writers, as Cornelius Castoriadis notes, "bureaucratization (i.e. the management of activity by hierarchized apparatuses) becomes the very logic of society, its response to everything."[55] This mode of management also informs Kafka's "ministry of writing."

The omnipresence of files arises from a continuous amassing of data—rules, procedures, matters of fact—in the service of instrumental logic. If, somewhat counter-intuitively, we now assign "instrumentality" to the activities of Kafka's portable office—to "the tremendous/monstrous/colossal world I have in my head"[56]—we are not distorting the character of his art as he knew it. Kafka did after all write:

> There is nothing to me that...one could call superfluous, superfluous in the sense of overflowing. If there is a higher power that wishes to use me,

or does use me, then I am at its mercy, if no more than as a well-prepared instrument. If not, I am nothing, and will suddenly be abandoned in a dreadful void.[57]

At the same time the cold, instrumental character of bureaucratic ratio-nality is a mask—a trope that Kafka the artist was among the first to exploit erotically, as one whose body bore its brunt.[58] He toyed with its elaborations in his fiction, like so much mind- and body-sustaining play while imprisoned in a cell, whose wall he likened to the inside of his skull: "The bony structure of his own forehead blocks his way; he batters him-self bloody against his own forehead."[59] Unlike Weber's, Kafka's fictional portrait of bureaucracy has room for play and the erotic seduction of part by part—inside the cage.

The personal—or charismatic—face of bureaucracy worn by the office*holder* reappears as a mask of "writerly being." The early picture of the writing destiny cited just above, in which Kafka figures as its "well-prepared instrument," consorts with the impersonal face of bureaucracy. But his bureaucratic machine is once again animate and charismatically charged. In a letter to Milena Jesenská, Kafka describes the "office" as "a living human being, who looks at me...with its innocent eyes...a being with whom I have been united in a manner unknown to me" all the while it remains "alien."[60] The office Kafka is speaking of here is the Workmen's Accident Insurance Institute for the Czech Lands in Prague! And what agency, one might ask, is Kafka speaking of when he writes of "the false hands that reach out toward you in the midst of writing" (T 1965, 316)? These are not the demons of the bureau but archons employed by the "office" of literature; Kafka is referring to the nightly combat that writing forced on him.

The sociologist Claude Lefort has elaborated Marx's insight that bureau-cracy is capable of translating "all social relations into a diction of formal relations between offices and ranks."[61] Lefort reminds us of the absurdity that a correct "translation" would have to include, since "behind the mask of rules and impersonal relations lies the proliferation of unproductive functions, the play of personal contacts, and the madness of authority."[62] This is the ludic dimension that Kafka knows and varies inside his two office cages. As Hartmut Binder notes of Kafka even when encaged in the Workmen's Institute, "he could play with considerable success on the apparatus of [legal] 'instances.'"[63] How much more freely in the fictions!

There is scarcely a moment in *The Trial* and *The Castle* that does not resonate with the terms of Kafka's own writerly bureaucracy. The worlds of both *The Trial* and *The Castle* are marked by an omnipresent traffic in script that goes its way at an immeasurable distance from superior authority.

Precisely this distance, at once playing field (*Spielraum*) and field of care, prompts mad play in both the writer and his hero. "Mad *play*" in *The Trial?* Think of K.'s seduction of Fräulein Bürstner, which employs the theatrical performance of his arrest. "Mad"—meaning "anguished" play? Consider Louis Begley's biographical essay on Kafka—*The Tremendous World I Have in My Head*—which detects all the signs of a simultaneous "nervous breakdown" in both K. (of *The Castle*) and his author.[64] But the latter claim must include the unavoidable if ineffable difference in depth between Kafka and his hero, which allows the collapsing writer free play enough to portray the collapsing hero. "You have to dive down as it were, and sink more rapidly than that which sinks in advance of you."[65] The afflatus of writerly being, always its virtual last, floats, for a time, the iron cage of bureaucracy.

Notes

1. Are there distinctions to be made between "cage" and "cell"? Vis-à-vis prison cells, cages may have a greater degree of transience about them: creatures are caged, as a rule, en route to their permanent destination, which may be more (or less) drastically enclosing than the cage they arrive in: they may be on their way to being put behind the bars—of a cell. But even here, the difference is one only of degree, of short temporal delay. Consider: "A first sign of dawning recognition is the wish to die. This life seems unbearable; another existence seems unattainable. One is no longer ashamed of the desire to die; one wishes to be brought from one's old cell, which one detests, into a new one, which one will shortly come to hate. The remainder of one's faith colludes in the hope that during the transfer the Lord will coincidentally come down the corridor, look at the prisoner and say: 'Don't bother to lock this one up. He is coming to me.'" (Franz Kafka, *Nachgelassene Schriften und Fragmente 2*, ed. Jost Schillemeit, *Kritische Ausgabe* [Frankfurt a.M.: Fischer, 1992], 43.) Some of this knowledge may have informed the author of the dictionary entry above. He or she makes the second meaning of "cage" above equivalent to "cell." Enfin, I shall use the terms interchangeably throughout this essay. Both signify enclosure, incarceration, solitude, helplessness. And both signify a certain openness to the outside, permeability, exposure, because both cages and cells are normally employed to exhibit their prey. In this sense, to cite an aperçu of Virginia Woolf, "The eyes of others our prisons; their thoughts our cages." (*An Unwritten Novel*, 1921.)
2. Karl Kraus, *Die Letzten Tage der Menschheit* (Munich: Kösel, 1974), 200.
3. Jonathan McVity, *Dicta and Contradicta* (Urbana and Chicago: University of Illinois Press, 2001), 114.
4. Kafka, *Schriften und Fragmente 2*, 117.
5. Franz Kafka, *Kafka's Selected Stories*, Norton Critical Edition, ed. and trans. Stanley Corngold (New York: Norton, 2007), 210–12; *Briefe, 1902–1924*, ed. Max Brod (Frankfurt a.M.: Fischer, 1958), 383–86.

6. Walter Benjamin, "Review of Brod's Franz Kafka," in *Selected Writings*, trans. Edmund Jephcott, Howard Eiland, and Others, ed. Howard Eiland and Michael W. Jennings (Cambridge, MA: Harvard University Press, 2002), 3: 319.

7. Kafka, *Selected Stories*, 211; Kafka, *Briefe, 1902–1924*, 386 (emphasis added, SC).

8. Nietzsche, *Sämtliche Werke. Kritische Studienausgabe in 15 Einzelbänden*, ed. Giorgio Colli and Mazzino Montinari (Berlin: de Gruyter, 1967–77 and 1988), 12: 215.

9. Franz Kafka, *The Great Wall of China*, trans. Willa and Edwin Muir (New York: Schocken, 1960), 299; Kafka, *Schriften und Fragmente 2*, 132 (emphasis added, SC).

10. Joyce Crick, a review of James Whitlark, *Behind the Great Wall: A Post-Jungian Approach to Kafkaesque Literature, The Modern Language Review*, vol. 89, no. 3 (July 1994), 803.

11. E.g., Benno Wagner, "Zarathustra auf dem Laurenziberg: Quételet, Nietzsche und Mach mit Kafka," *Literarische Experimentalkulturen: Poetologien des Experiments im 19. Jahrhundert*, ed. Marcus Krause and Nicolas Pethes (Würzburg: Königshausen und Neumann, 2005), 225–40.

12. Franz Kafka, *Letters to Felice*, trans. James Stern and Elizabeth Duckworth (New York: Schocken, 1973), 545; *Briefe an Felice*, ed. Erich Heller and Jürgen Born (Frankfurt a.M.: Fischer, 1967), 755–6.

13. Franz Kafka, *Dearest Father*, trans. Ernest Kaiser and Eithne Wilkins (New York: Schocken, 1954), 297; Kafka, *Schriften und Fragmente*, 334.

14. Ibid., 131.

15. Franz Kafka, *The Diaries of Franz Kafka, 1914–1923*, trans. Martin Greenberg (with the assistance of Hannah Arendt) (New York: Schocken, 1949), 183–4; Franz Kafka, *Tagebücher*, ed. Hans-Gerd Kock, Michael Müller, and Malcolm Pasley, *Kritische Ausgabe* (Frankfurt a.M.: Fischer, 1990), 834.

16. Franz Kafka, *Briefe an Milena*, ed. Jürgen Born and Michael Müller (Frankfurt a.M.: Fischer, 1983), 228.

17. Kafka, *Tagebücher*, 869.

18. Reiner Stach, *Kafka. Die Jahre der Erkenntnis* (Frankfurt a.M.: Fischer, 2008), 483.

19. Kafka, *Tagebücher*, 859.

20. György Kurtág, Hungary's great composer, wrote a song cycle titled *Kafka fragmente op. 24*. Among the textual fragments he set to music is this very line, "Meine Gefängniszelle, meine Festung" (My prison cell, my fortress). The phrase is the third fragment in part III of the cycle, but in Kurtág's manuscript it also appears on top, above everything, as its motto. It is, on Kurtág's account, a phrase eminently "komponierbar" ("composable") and, by dint of its top position, supremely expressive of Kafka.

21. Kafka, *Schriften und Fragmente*, 383.

22. Kafka, *Dearest Father*, 37. "Es gibt kein Haben, nur ein Sein, nur ein nach letztem Atem, nach Ersticken verlangendes Sein." (Kafka, *Schriften und Fragmente*, 120.)

23. Ibid., 123.

24. Martin Heidegger, *Being and Time*, trans. John Macquarrie and Edward Robinson (New York: Harper and Row, 1962), 160. "[Das] Sein des Daseins, um das es ihm in seinem Sein selbst geht...." (*Sein und Zeit* [Tübingen: Niemeyer, 1963], 123.)

25. Kafka, *Tagebücher*, 562.

26. Ibid., 87.

27. Kafka, *Diaries, 1914–1923*, 223; Kafka, *Tagebücher*, 910.

28. Kafka, *Dearest Father*, 87; *Schriften und Fragmente 2*, 77.

29. Franz Kafka, *The Diaries of Franz Kafka, 1910–1913*, trans. Joseph Kresh (New York: Schocken, 1948), 173; Kafka, *Tagebücher*, 286.

30. Kafka, *Selected Stories*, 209. "Dort vergiengen Stunden, Stunden gemeinsamen Atems, gemeinsamen Herzschlags, Stunden, in denen K. immerfort das Gefühl hatte, er verirre sich oder er sei soweit in der Fremde, wie vor ihm noch kein Mensch, eine Fremde, in der selbst die Luft keinen Bestandteil der Heimatluft habe, in der man vor Fremdheit ersticken müsse und in deren unsinnigen Verlockungen man doch nichts tun könne als weiter gehn, weiter sich verirren" (C 1982b, 69).

31. Kafka, *Selected Stories*, 205; Kafka, *Tagebücher*, 838.

32. Kafka, *Selected Stories*, 210.

33. Kafka, *Tagebücher*, 904.

34. Kafka, *Selected Stories*, 131.

35. Michael G. Wood, review of Louis Begley, *The Tremendous World I have Inside My Head. Franz Kafka: A Biographical Essay* (New York: Atlas, 2008), in *The New York Sun* (July 9, 2008). http://www.nysun.com/arts/king-of-infinite-space-louis-begleys-kafka-book/81462/

36. As noted by an unidentified Tate Gallery commentator, viz. http://www.tate.org.uk/servlet/ViewWork?cgroupid=999999961&workid=13385

37. Kafka, *Diaries, 1910–1913*, 300.

38. Ibid., 286.

39. Gerhard Kurz, *Traum-Schrecken. Kafkas literarische Existenzanalyse* (Stuttgart: Metzler, 1980), 150.

40. Kafka, *Tagebücher*, 859.

41. See Victor Brombert, "The Happy Prison: A Recurring Romantic Metaphor," in David Thorburn and Geoffrey Hartman, *Romanticism: Vistas, Instances, Continuities* (Ithaca, NY: Cornell University Press, 1973), 62–79. Cf. "The happy prison of self-promotion," in Stanley Corngold and Irene Giersing, *Borrowed Lives* (Albany, NY: SUNY Press, 1991), 13. Though Kafka does not appear to have read Stendhal, in the mind of more than one reader (W. G. Sebald, in *Schwindel, Gefühle*, for example), these authors are a single literary organism. See, as well, my "Tropes in Stendhal and Kafka," *Literary Imagination: The Review of the Association of Literary Scholars and Critics*, vol. 4, no. 3 (Fall 2002): 275–290.

42. Martha Grace Duncan's "'Cradled on the Sea': Positive Images of Prison and Theories of Punishment," *California Law Review*, vol. 76, no. 6 (Dec. 1988): 1201–1247. Professor Duncan writes interestingly, "Closer to my own work... is Brombert's analysis of the happy-prison motif in nineteenth-century works by major French writers, such as Stendhal, Hugo, and Baudelaire. Brombert explores a number of themes, focusing on the relationship between

physical confinement and artistic freedom. In the concluding pages, however, he suggests that the Holocaust and the Soviet penal camps have changed the way we imagine prison, relegating the nineteenth-century motif to the 'status of a reactionary anachronism.'" (Brombert, *The Romantic Prison: The French Tradition* [Princeton, NJ: Princeton University Press, 1978], 182–83.) He observes that the Romantics' "dream of a happy prison has become hard to entertain in a world of penal colonies and extermination camps, in a world which makes us fear that somehow even our suffering can no longer be our refuge" (209). By contrast, the present study demonstrates that the psychological sources of the attraction to prison are deeper than Brombert perceived, and that, in consequence, the theme of the happy prison has withstood the realities of the twentieth century's particularly nightmarish forms of incarceration." (Duncan, "Cradled on the Sea," 1204.)

43. Kafka, *Selected Stories*, 125.

44. C. W. E. Bigsby, *Modern American Drama, 1945–2000* (Cambridge; New York: Cambridge University Press, 2000), 244.

45. James McFarlane, "Neo-Modernist Drama: Yeats and Pirandello," in *Modernism: A Guide to European Literature 1890–1930*, ed. Malcolm Bradbury and James McFarlane (London: Penguin, 1991), 561.

46. I discuss the theatrical character of the ape's evolution in Stanley Corngold, "Kafka's 'A Report for an Academy' with Adorno," in *Aesthetics and the Work of Art*, ed. Peter de Bolla and Stefan Hoesel-Uhlig (London: Palgrave Macmillan, 2008).

47. Aristotle's *Poetics*, chapter 26, is the "locus classicus" of the term "ape" to characterize the actor whose performance is vulgar and exaggerated. Cf. Hartmut Böhme, "Der Affe und die Magie in der 'Historia von D. Johann Fausten,'" in *Thomas Mann. Doktor Faustus 1947–1997*, ed. Werne Röcke (Bern: Peter Lang, 2001), 116.

48. Max Weber, in *Max Weber (1): Critical Assessments*, ed. Peter Hamilton (London: Routledge, 1991), 294.

49. Walter Benjamin, letter to Gershom Scholem, 1938, in *Correspondence* (Paris: Aubier, 1980), 2: 248. For reminding me of this passage, I am grateful to Malcolm Warner's suggestive essay "Kafka, Weber and Organization Theory," *Human Relations* (2007), vol. 60 (7): 1019–1038, esp. 1027. See also Corngold (with Michael Jennings), "Walter Benjamin/Gershom Scholem Briefwechsel, 1933–1940," *Interpretation: A Journal of Political Philosophy* vol. 12 (2/3) (May and September 1984): 357–366.

50. Warner, 1030.

51. Sheldon Wolin, *Politics and Vision* (London: G. Allen and Unwin, 1961), 354, cited in Warner, 1019.

52. Max Weber, *Wirtschaft und Gesellschaft. Grundriss der verstehenden Soziologie*, 5. rev. edition (Tübingen: Mohr, 1985), 552.

53. The following pages on bureaucracy are freely adapted from my "Kafka and the Ministry of Writing," *Franz Kafka: the Office Writings*, eds. Stanley Corngold, Jack Greenberg, and Benno Wagner (Princeton, NJ: Princeton University Press, 2009), 6–10.

54. R. J. Kilcullen, On *Bureaucracy*, http://www.humanities.mq.edu.au/Ockham/y64l09.html

55. Cornelius Castoriadis, *Political and Social Writings*, vol. 2, trans. and ed. David Ames Curtis (Minneapolis: University of Minnesota Press, 1988), 272. Cited in John Guillory, *Cultural Capital: The Problem of Literary Canon Formation* (Chicago, IL: University of Chicago Press, 1993), 248. This and my next few pages have greatly profited from Guillory's discussion, along with his mention of authorities.

56. Kafka, *Tagebücher*, 562; *Diaries, 1910–1913*, 288.

57. Kafka, *Letters to Felice*, 21.

58. In writing that Kafka's "body" bore the brunt of a "trope," we would be faithful to Kafka's own rhetorical practice: "If the infection in your lungs is only a symbol," he wrote, "a symbol of the infection whose inflammation is called F. [his fiancée Felice Bauer], and whose depth is its deep justification; if this is so then the medical advice (light, air, sun, rest) is also a symbol. Lay hold of this symbol (Fasse dieses Sinnbild an)." (*Diaries, 1914–1923*, 182; Kafka, *Tagebücher*, 831.)

59. Ibid.

60. Kafka, *Briefe an Milena*, 169.

61. Guillory, 250.

62. Claude Lefort, *The Political Forms of Modern Society: Bureaucracy, Democracy, Totalitarianism*, ed. John B. Thompson (Cambridge, MA: MIT Press, 1986), 109. Cited in Guillory, 250.

63. Hartmut Binder, *Kafka in neuer Sicht. Mimik, Gestik und Personengefüge als Darstellungsformen des Autobiographischen* (Stuttgart: J.B. Metzler, 1976), 409.

64. Louis Begley, *The Tremendous World I Have in My Head: Franz Kafka: A Biographical Essay* (New York: Atlas, 2008), 204.

65. Kafka, *Diaries, 1914–1923*, 114.

CHAPTER TWO

DELUSIONS OF AGENCY: KAFKA, IMPRISONMENT, AND MODERN VICTIMHOOD

Chris Fleming and John O'Carroll

In this chapter, we explore the levels of imprisonment in Franz Kafka's The Trial. *These levels include legal arrest, social containment and humiliation, and linguistic entrapment. Our chapter then traces the modernist narrative dream-structure of the novel in order to tease out thematic issues of guilt and innocence. The novel presents its drama in clearly defined domains: the bank, the law, the family, and so on. The tragic action and trajectory of the novel offer an analysis of some key features of modern victimhood. In this respect, the novel as a whole analyzes the modern scapegoat, and does so in terms of victimage within institutional and bureaucratic contexts.*

1. Contexts of Imprisonment

Though I think myself right, his mouth may condemn me;
though I count myself innocent, it may declare me a hypocrite.
But am I innocent after all? Not even I know that...[1]

Everywhere there is organization, everywhere bureaucratization; like the world of feudalism, the modern world is broken up into areas dominated by castles, but not the castles of *les chansons de geste*, but the castles of Kafka.[2]

In this chapter, we explore how the central character of *The Trial*, Josef K., is claimed, trapped, and finally killed by a system whose nature and ambit he never comes to understand, and whose highest representative, the judge, never appears, and whose ultimate court of appeal, the high court, he cannot access. In keeping with the idioms of much modernist writing, and for reasons linked to the nature of modernity itself, the reader has to work to grasp the rules of the presented world, and indeed to make sense of the charges leveled against Josef K. We are readily tempted to the view that the decision readers make concerning the protagonist's guilt or innocence says as much about the framework of reading as it does about the text itself. Yet it will be our contention that the novel is far from equivocal in this respect, that it *does* present cues that astute scholarship has only just begun to grasp, and that these cues *do* allow us as readers to see orders of guilt and innocence, and to form judgments on that basis.

In order to launch our inquiry, the next two sections of this chapter are devoted to the modernist contexts that frame the work, and their relationship to the kinds of imprisonment that Josef K. undergoes. In terms of the framing of the work, we know in advance that in his novels and short stories, Kafka frequently plays out some of the signal shocks of modernity by forcing his readers to grasp the world through the constricted, humiliated viewpoints of his protagonists. That is, Kafka's protagonists are often disoriented, mistaken about realities, and uncertain about what even the near-term future holds. The shocks are often physical, as when at the beginning of *Metamorphosis*, Gregor "awoke one morning from troubled dreams" to find himself actually "changed into a monstrous cockroach in his bed," (MM 2006, 1) or again, as when at the beginning of *The Castle*, an official demands a permit from K. after he has been snoozing at the end of a day's travel (C 1997, 3–6). If the protagonists are disoriented, so are we as readers, as we follow the spiral of these figures away from the world they surely thought they knew and understood down into another whose rules they—and we—only dimly understand.

Once we see the kinds of imprisonment that Kafka's protagonist undergoes, we are then in a position to inquire into the way the "trial" itself works, what is at stake, and ultimately to form a new view of guilt and innocence. After all, this is book about the "process" of a trial, and we as readers struggle to find how guilt and innocence might be established or assessed, and whether indeed we should see his as a story with a tragic trajectory, or whether he is perhaps guilty of some charges unknown to us. *The Trial* is fragmentary and morally complex. It is a tale whose dream-logic defies our attempts to make sense of its welter of heterogeneous materials: these include matter-of-fact statements, K.'s internal bewilderment and question-asking, and the text's own pieces of concrete observation. In treating questions of guilt and innocence as we proceed further into our analysis, we find that these issues of judgment operate in conjunction with the layerings of confinement and imprisonment that permeate the work from beginning to end. In this respect, later in this chapter, we draw on important work by René Girard on the nature of scapegoating and of victimage. In Josef K.'s unsuccessful attempts to claim victim status, we find, paradoxically, a situation in which he is actually the victim of a mechanism of scapegoating—just not the one he himself imagines it to be.

2. Modern Subjectivity

Few who read Kafka miss the traumatic dimensions of the text—even if they hold that the protagonists of his stories and novellas are ultimately guilty. Part of the trauma is indeed experienced by generations of readers as, in page after bewildering page, they encounter the frustrations of modern pettiness, of bureaucracy, of narrow-minded cruelty conducted by apparently well-meaning individuals. The shock of self-recognition has, in part, conditioned responses to the work, partially distorting critical scholarship and perspective and yet, in our view, ultimately supplying a guide to what an adequate ethical response to the text might be. In many respects, of course, Kafka was no more than a product of his time and place: an early modernist, writing in the years of a dying empire. The context is essential for it supplies an understanding of two key dimensions of the books—on one hand, the sense of impending gloom and horror, and on the other a peculiar loss of agency and indeed of personhood in the world. Yet being a product of this time and place, as we shall now see, lent his work possibilities that only those who lived then and there seemed able to realize.

Let us begin with the shock of modernity, its pervading oppressiveness, and horror. For many writers of this era, there was a brief hope that a cleansing war would shake off the torpor of late Romantic Europe. For most, though, a wiser sense of portent, danger, and even claustrophobia was uppermost. Nowhere were all these currents more visible than in the dying Austro-Hungarian empire. Even by the time of Kafka's own death at an early age, this massive empire had dissolved into nothingness. "Artists" of all kinds noticed, and their work still lets us *see what they saw*. The Austro-Hungarian world was a multiethnic imperial space, which generated astonishing critique in a starkly modern idiom, as evidenced by the cynically anarchic humor in Italo Svevo's *Confessions of Zeno*, from the Austro-Hungarian port city of Trieste (in present day Italy), and by Robert Musil (from Vienna), as well as Kafka himself from Prague.[3]

We cannot trace all these links here: Robert Musil's work will serve to illustrate our two principal contentions. First is the shocking onset of modernity itself. Such onset is clearly manifest in the Musil's novels, as in other modernist writers. Musil wrote two major works, *Young Törless* and the *Man Without Qualities*. The first of these two works, written when the empire was still intact, is a horrific tale of induction of a new boy into a military school. The story is as shocking today as it was when it was written. Musil's depiction of brutality in dark private places lends it an intensity, making it even more sinister than Kafka's own works. In one sense, of course, it is a "realistic" story in that we can envisage and understand it in concrete terms. Yet it is so shocking that we are inclined to allegory; that is, to read the terrible story of the impressionable Törless as having wider import. If it is allegorical, and there are those who see it as prophetic of the undercurrent that led ultimately to Nazism, it is at another level just a book about what happens when boys are confined together in brutal conditions at school—a kind of institutionally situated *Lord of the Flies*. The "modernism" is not so much a formal innovation as it is a point of view, and a destabilization of established mores. The horror of the novel is perhaps the apotheosis of the *Bildungsroman* form it fulfils— except that the development is all in the wrong direction, and the idea that children left to themselves will not necessarily find goodness let alone "grow" through their mistakes.

Where the claustrophobic horror of Musil's first novel lets us see how the modern world closes in on its protagonists, his mature work interrogates the very idea that *we have agency as individuals at all*. The tone, of course, has changed. In his later magnum opus, *The Man Without Qualities*, the logic of the shift of Musil's narrative voice is itself terrifying: this novel is at once cool, ironic, and as a rule, even comically detached. This multivolume work—like Kafka's incomplete at the time of the author's death— describes the barbarity of civilized life in a way that makes its allegories less traumatic to read than *Young Törless*, and indeed, Kafka's *The Trial*—but only on condition that we don't reflect on what they mean as a whole. If, in other words, we can see that the Weberian world of rationality, bureaucracy, and state power produces all these works out of the ruins of the earlier imperial memories of faded Austro-Hungary, and it does so in distinct ways in each case. What gathers them together is the fact that the central characters' respective agencies are stripped away. Törless is brutalized, to be sure. In the *Man without Qualities*, however, Ulrich is a protagonist whose defining characteristic *is that he has no characteristics*. The word *Eigenschaften* (qualities) also means something akin to "characteristics" or "traits"—and Musil has an unsettling habit of showing how his main characters struggle to claim or retain "personality" of any kind. For Musil, as for Kafka, there is a deep uncertainty as to selfhood, a sense that modern worldview sociologists like Durkheim describe in terms of disorientation, loss of center, loss of certainty.

Perhaps then a further point: in each of these works is a problem of what might best be called *ethical orders*. In *Young Törless*, we as readers identify with the dilemmas faced by the protagonist. He is young; what would—or could—we ourselves do in the same frightening circumstances? We condemn, straightforwardly, the school system that would allow such a situation to develop. In *The Man Without Qualities*, ethics itself is held up for question as high society ladies (Bonadea, Diotima, and her friends) come to view the spectacle of the trial of Moosbrugger, the murderer-rapist.[4] Yet we see already in all these works, and indeed of other writers from this region at that time, a common concern with ethics, with falsehood, with a certain inner brutality of the human that contrasts strikingly with the shimmer of civil veneer.

We do not need to look far to see similar patterns in Kafka's works (and indeed the ethical issues are so fraught that we need to treat them later in our chapter). At every turn, the central characters are ineffectual, the theaters in which they seek to perform are the wrong ones, and the things they think they need to do are misguided. In "Metamorphosis," indeed, paralyzed by indecision, Gregor is *himself* physiologically metamorphosed. In the case before us, the *Trial*, Josef K., caught in an impersonal judicial process, loses control over his own life—and is ultimately executed, "like a dog." In *The Castle*, *The Trial*, and *Metamorphosis*, we have only the perspective of the central protagonist, and it is to the issue of perspective and the modernist novel that we now must turn our attentions.

3. Modernism: Narrative and Character

Let us see how modernism manifests itself in terms of perspective in Kafka's work. In the modernist novel, we find a destabilization of narrative perspective, as well as of touchstone characters. As a result, much modern writing, whether programmatically modernist or not, undermines the certitudes of the Romantic first person or third person narrator. Such is also the case in Kafka's writing.

When the novel commences, Josef K. rings the bell for his breakfast and is disoriented by the immediate appearance of a warder in his room. Our point of view is his—even though the novel is in the third person. The narrative situation is strange, to put it mildly. The third person typically distances the reader, leading to the expectation of narrative in the omniscient Romantic or even later modern vein. Yet we come to realize very swiftly that our vision is as blinkered as that of the protagonist, and the "objective" vision we get is just that—the *objects that he sees*. There is much to say about the disjunction between the third person and the restriction of our focalization.[5] At the opening of Franz Stanzel's *Theory of Narrative,* we are presented with a "typological circle," which compresses an entire theory of narratology into a single diagram.[6] In his "wheel" of narrative, Stanzel gives examples and situates Kafka's work just across the border from first person narrative, alongside other works like Joyce's *Portrait of the Artist as a Young Man* and Woolf's *Mrs Dalloway*. The perspective is internal, like a Romantic first person novel, but the character is told in the third person. The effect is unsettling, disturbing the workings of the novel, as we become less and less sure of what we initially took to be certitudes.

In a novel like this one, from the beginning we tend, as readers, to align our viewpoint with the character whose focalization defines the field of what we learn. We experience the world through Josef K.'s experience, and we tend in the first instance to trust his viewpoint. Yet we are constantly reminded that his experience is not ours—he is he, and we are we—and this is a third person narrative, after all. When at the beginning, Josef K. is told all this is happening because it is the law, he (as we might ourselves) says: "I don't know about this law," to which he is told, "All the worse for you" (T 1953, 13). This passes beyond usual ignorance of the law and its procedures and precedents: Josef K. is not even aware of what it is the law here is accusing him of having done—and neither are we. By the end of the novel, however, we are left unsure as to whether his is the reliable point of view (if only because his struggles are so obviously futile). Kafka's ingenuity has been to slip under the reader's guard, to present his character in a way that makes him seem reliable, only then to undermine it all. In handling the ethical dilemmas the novel presents, we are forced by its author to work our way through the layers of entrapment, so that we can finally get some sense of the very ethical universe itself.

4. Trial and Imprisonment

We have seen that much of the "trial" of modern writing involves disorientation, misplaced or delusional agency, and a sense of entrapment in the very limitation of the narrative point of view. We can, in light of the above, now grasp how the novel has been framed, and in which respects it is indeed, a *trial*. At first, we might think that trial and imprisonment are unrelated. In this respect, however, we need to understand the special nature of imprisonment in Kafka's thought, and how nearly all levels of restraint placed upon him *also* concern the "trial" itself. Josef K., strangely, is neither imprisoned behind bars nor held in chains. This is not to say his imprisonment is not palpable and without effect. Quite the contrary, it *does* have effects, and these work on a number of levels. In brief, his form of "imprisonment" is constituted by (1) an arrest; (2) a series of court demands made upon him; (3) a variety of soft sanctions and social hostility and disapproval; (4) an apparent inability to communicate in the language of his interrogators; (5) the processes of judgement themselves require K. to perform in ways to which he is profoundly unaccustomed—and his own personality in this sense becomes the thing that limits his performance; and (6) his freedom—but not his personal liberty—is restricted. We can now look at each of these in a little more detail.

The first layer of trial and of imprisonment is *physical*. When we consider law and justice, we tend, as readers to think immediately of the physical manifestations of these things. In the *Trial*, indeed, we do see these things. There are police, there are officials of the court, and there is even a police station. Many television shows never get beyond this level of trial and imprisonment. We are informed at the outset of the novel, and at the same time as the protagonist himself is informed, that Josef K. is under arrest. The physical cage of the gaol, however, is hardly central to the story, and as we see later, the courthouse itself is hardly imposing. The entrapment of the protagonist does take place on this level, but Kafka's plot analyzes its workings and legitimacy at every point of the protagonist's decline.

If the level of imprisonment that is physical is one that works by startling him physically—in his bed, and eventually by executing him—the second level concerns the way he is forced to change his behavior in response to *official demands*. These are obscure, but recurrent—and the first of them opens the text itself. It may seem strange to think of demands as being restrictive, yet it only takes a moment's reflection on the nature of bureaucratic work-worlds to see how this might be so. Throughout the novel, we know that K. is monitored, his movements traced and assessed, his case considered.

A third level of imprisonment concerns the way the *society* around him responds to his arrest. He gains no support from those around. He is watched with keen interest, but we have the sense that most are glad that he is the one being taken away, and not them. Social approval and disapproval are powerful forces, and can be even more restrictive—and judgemental—than any court of law.

The fourth level of imprisonment—and of trial—concerns the way language *works,* or rather, *fails to work*. The failure here concerns the failure of communication itself. Witness the opening scene: " 'Who are you?' asked K., half-raising himself in bed. But the man ignored the question, as though his appearance needed no explanation" (T 1953, 7). The communication fails, and the imprisonment begins. In this exchange, language fails to communicate even the most basic information: What is he on trial for? Who is accusing him? Why? How might he defend himself? To whom should he speak? When, near the end of the terrible ordeal, he is in church, we see that Josef K. cannot even follow the advice offered by a priest. In this sense, we are reminded over and over again of his misunderstandings of the system, of his inability to hear advice, and, in his turn, of his ability even to present his case for trial. We see, at this level, how imprisonment in language, and his very failure to break though these bonds condemns him, and is indeed integral to the trial itself.

The fifth level of imprisonment, and indeed of trial, forces Josef K.—and his reader—to think about *"performance"* in the actual trial itself. Josef K.

is told to be "far more reticent" in his comments (T 1953, 19). In a host of observations through the book, we see Josef K.'s personality being assessed, even as we as readers form our assessments. The assessment is made through a myriad of small events as he misjudges his performances, as he is defiant when he should comply, compliant when he should stand resolute. As we watch with growing dismay, of course, we cannot be sure that we ourselves would perform any better than he does.

The sixth level of imprisonment/trial is the subtlest, and yet most obvious of all. It concerns the *disjunction between freedom and liberty*. Josef K. is led to the station, where he is told that he is under arrest, but this is not quite as he imagines it to be. He is sharply informed that "You have misunderstood me. You are under arrest, certainly, but that need not hinder you from going about your business" (T 1953, 21). This imprisonment is quite different from the usual kind. He is not going to be restricted physically. Yet things from now on are going to be anything but normal. One of the interesting disjunctions in *The Trial* is that K. retains, right until the end, every liberty, but no freedom whatsoever. Indeed, this supplies the basis for one interpretation of the ethical order of the novel. If we take this dimension as the end point of the novel, then we could contend that the "trial/imprisonment" of the protagonist is a case of free will being assessed, of his acute failure to act in a personally principled way, and a condemnation as a result of the fact that he does not exercise his liberty in a way deserving of freedom.

There is, perhaps, a further level of trial and imprisonment. It concerns the very structures of human sociality in the modern world themselves (these are derivative perhaps of the third point above). We flag these in advance, but will handle their detail later. For now, we observe only that it is not necessary for Josef K. to be a morally innocent man to be tried and found innocent of criminality. For this to happen, a social structure that requires scapegoats has to be in place, and in such a context, *any* candidate could be chosen, and *anyone* could be found guilty of just the same kinds of behavior as those exhibited by Josef K.

5. Guilty?

We open the ethical universe of this novel by posing a very simple question: *is Josef K. guilty?* In 1975, the Australian scholar Eric Marson showed just how prismatic the possibilities of interpretation of *The Trial* might be. In a compellingly argued (and strongly text-based) exegesis, he contends that most readers of Kafka's *Trial*, and indeed his work as a whole, miss this key point: Josef K. is guilty. To the obvious retort that it seems tough to be sentenced to death for a crime that is never made manifest, Marson contends that this is exactly the logic of Kafka's grim utopian visions, ideas that are even more obvious in his view in the *Penal Colony*.

Let us take the usual departure point of most readers of Kafka's work. One factor that has misled countless English, and it would seem, even German, readers of *The Trial* is, in fact, its widely cited and memorable opening sentence: "Jemand mußte Josef K. verleumdet haben, denn ohne daß er etwas Böses getan hätte, wurde er eines Morgens verhaftet" (T 2008, 3);[7] [Someone must have been telling lies about Josef K., for without having done anything wrong he was arrested one fine morning (T 1953, 7)]. There are linguistic clues that we shouldn't make any preemptive conclusions about K.'s guilt or innocence. The German formulation "mußte" usually signifies an observation offered by a protagonist, not a narrator—and the subjunctive "hätte" reinforces this. Speirs and Sandberg contend, on the basis of this, that the recognition that Kafka, even in this opening sentence, is speaking from the perspective of K. removes at least one possible misprision: "we are not reading the story of a man who is arrested despite the *fact* that he is innocent, but rather the story of a man who *maintains* that he has been wrongfully arrested."[8] But as the authors themselves conclude, "this is not the end of the problem, however."

For Marson, it is perfectly obvious that once rereadings of the above kind are conducted, we need to revise our initial impressions of our central character. Marson sees the central problem of culpability of *The Trial* in the repeated demonstrations of Josef K.'s selfishness. At all stages, he contends, the novel shows this, and it is most striking in his utter "self-concern exemplified by Josef K.'s behaviour to his mother," a woman who makes few demands on her son, and even those it seems, he chooses not to fulfil.[9] For Marson, the courtesy with which Josef K. is treated is not evidence of a wider Arendt-style banality of evil, but rather, of the fact that Josef K. is so myopic that he never takes hold of any of the many opportunities the court presents to him to save himself. These, in Marson's view, and in keeping with the third level of imprisonment we detailed in the preceding section, are directed toward making Josef a better person, a more humble person, and one who is more self-aware.[10]

Josef K. is also portrayed as superior and snobbish, faults that are shown in his treatment of subordinates,[11] and more important still, in his inability to see that an imposing building (which he expected the court to be) is not the same thing as true justice. Josef K. believes too much in appearances, according to Marson, and as he puts it, gets everything wrong at every turn:

> Readers...follow and adopt Josef K.'s opinions more or less at face value that the court in the novel is worthless and wrong, not so much because it executes K. but because it is unpretentious and has its existence in the dirty and musty attics of slum dwellings. Now it can be shown easily enough

that K. is a young man very easily impressed by externals, and it can also be shown that most of his opinions of the court are wrong.[12]

For Marson indeed, the misreading is part and parcel of Josef's culpable shallowness, selfishness, and snobbery. He may not deserve to die in this nonfiction world of ours, but he does in the Kafka world of fiction and does so simply because he is not just guilty, but is also utterly recalcitrant. Marson suggests the court does occasionally make mistakes—and these are shown precisely because it then sets about rectifying them. In this view, the novel appears as an exploration of the modern psyche, which in the person of Josef, Kafka finds wanting. The ruthless pursuit of his criminality—located in his inner being as it were—then appears as a logic, a grim utopia indeed. The fantasy Kafka offers when read this way is one of a certain figuration of Judaeo-Christian judgement, in which the *real and inner guilt* of the person is first revealed and then punished.

Marson's interpretation has advanced the intellectual debate about this novel from the typical initial reader-response that the "figural narrative situation" (as Stanzel terms it) generates. Marson's reasons for going beyond the initial sympathy a reader feels for a character through whom the events are focalized are indeed sound. Yet there is no reason to cease our interpreting once we find a range of reasons for critiquing Josef's behavior. Quite the contrary in fact, given that, as readers, we have an ongoing—and ultimately well founded—intuition that if he is not completely innocent, then his guilt such that it is, is unexceptionable. Once we raise this as a problem, however, an entirely new order of problems presents itself, and these are what we seek to resolve in the remainder of our chapter.

6. Orders of Possible Guilt

If we hold the hypothesis that Josef K. is himself guilty in abeyance for a time, we may raise other possibilities of which there are at least two.

Perhaps, first of all, "the apparatus" is guilty. For all the reasons Marson gives concerning perspective, we as readers do tend to read it this way, and the weight of historical interpretation certainly lies here. If we adopt the view that Josef has—and as readers, we must, at least provisionally—then this reading is a staging post on the way to any other reading. But if this common reading is correct, then it will have to be given an adequate basis, and considerable specification of "the apparatus" will need to be supplied. This basis, we believe, is to be found in another apparent alternative ordering of the ethical world of the novel: the issue of victimhood itself.

Second, perhaps the behaviors of all concerned—including those of Josef K—are what lead to guilt being ascribed (rather than shown). "Guilt" in this sense would actually be a secondary issue, and *we as readers would not even need to form a judgment*. We could pose this in terms of two related questions: (1) why are we so prone in our reading of this book, *hermeneutically*, to see K. as innocent, or at the very least as a kind of *victim*? And, more basically, (2) what historical conditions and philosophical presuppositions have conspired to make the very question of K.'s guilt or innocence a central interest? In respect of both questions, it is not a matter of setting them aside, for they are indeed essential. Rather it is a matter of *understanding* their import.

In our consideration of how these issues criss-cross one another, we do not need to avoid the dimensions of modernity's emergence in the present century (still less to question whether or not these stories are some sort of outward expressions of Kafka "working through his issues") in order to appreciate the sociohistorical context in which *The Trial* was written. Suffice to say that Kafka wrote into that moment in which Europe was sliding inexorably toward fascism, an historical shift whose consequences for victimhood—and its perception—are hard to overstate.[13]

Keeping all these things in mind, let us deal with each briefly, in order, and see how both of the hypotheses we advance in this section interrelate and might be supported. Our contention is that, despite his vanity and arrogance, Josef K. does indeed present to us as a *victim*, but in a sense that we wish to redefine. That is to say, he is a victim in the strict theoretical sense that he is subject to a victimage mechanism, in Girard's version of that term. "Victims" in this sense are not necessarily *innocent*, but rather, their guilt, if present, is unexceptional. Given that Josef K. is often regarded as "everyman"—or as Camus would have it, "like everybody else"[14]—it would hardly serve to demand of him a moral rectitude unknown among other ordinary humans. Not only is he a victim, however, he is—in all the senses we have invoked so far—a *modern victim*.

7. Josef K. and Job

Many commentators writing on Kafka make preliminary observations concerning Kafka's Jewish background. We believe this vein of criticism needs to be taken more seriously, as it supplies good reason to question the prevailing orders of interpretation of the novel (though not, as we shall see, of the sound intuition of the general reader that there is nothing unexceptionable in Josef's guilt compared with our own, as readers).

Let us begin with a letter from Gershom Scholem to Walter Benjamin, written in 1931:

> I advise you to begin any inquiry into Kafka with the Book of Job, or at least with a discussion of the possibility of divine judgment, which I regard

as the sole subject of Kafka's production [worthy of] being treated in a work of literature. These, you see, are in my opinion also the vantage points from which one can describe Kafka's linguistic world, which with its affinity to the language of the Last Judgment probably represents the prosaic in its most canonical form.[15]

Scholem was neither the first nor the last to situate *The Trial*—or Kafka's work more generally—in the context of a biblical, indeed Jewish, idiom. As early as 1929, Margarete Susman argued that no oeuvre better models Job's wrangling with God better than did Kafka's. Max Brod's biography made similar arguments eight years later—as have Harold Bloom, Martin Buber, Northrop Frye, and George Steiner, among others. But what does the parallel amount to, if it exists at all?[16]

In itself, the shift to a study of victimage and Judaism has *not* led critics instantly to rethink the terms of guilt proposed by Marson. Quite the contrary: Stuart Lasine has written a thoughtful series of articles on certain biblical themes in Kafka's work. Lasine affirms that the Book of Job affords a particularly useful hermeneutic frame through which *The Trial* can be examined—indeed that the latter "affirms the same set of moral values [as] Biblical law."[17] In other words, for Lasine, where Job is ultimately, and rightly, vindicated by God, K.'s grisly end equally reflects divine justice: "K. is held accountable by the court and is punished in much the same way that God tries the guilty in the Hebrew Bible."[18] Hence, despite its theological mode, Lasine's thesis resembles in interesting ways that of Eric Marson's.

To press his case, Lasine draws on the work of René Girard, whose reading of this book figures Job as a scapegoat of his community. Girard's reading of the Book of Job fits into his broader theory of a "victimage mechanism" as being at the center of conventional culture—and biblical texts as the primary historical force by which this mechanism of culturally unitive acts of collective violence is (and continues to be) demythologized. For Girard, the Book of Job offers a prime example of the way in which certain biblical texts invert the relationship between victims of collective violence and persecuting communities. In this sense, the Book of Job is an immense *psaume* in that it depicts the unrelenting persistence of an accused person justifiably asserting their innocence; Job's "friends" constitute the persecuting community in their insistence that Job's misfortunes reflect his culpability.[19]

Girard himself has noted (although he has not himself analyzed) the parallels between the Book of Job and Kafka's narratives, especially with regard to the way in which those accused can become mimetically entangled in the accusations such that they themselves begin to doubt their own innocence.[20] Lasine argues that the parallels simply serve to differentiate in a radical way the moral character of the two protagonists: "At every point Job and K. mark opposite poles of moral behavior and attitude in relation to others. This opposition extends to their status as *scapegoats*. While Job may well be the community's failed scapegoat, as Girard contends, for Lasine, K. merely adopts the pose of victim in order to evade his personal responsibility towards others."[21] For Lasine, indeed, the conclusion is inescapable: where Job is rightfully vindicated, "Kafka's novel investigates and punishes K. according to the Biblical concept of divine administration of justice."[22]

It is as much his evident moral failings as his inability to learn from them that brings K. to his violent end. Even more than this, Lasine sees K. is not only not a scapegoat, but is actually himself part of the mob, displaying the "same tendency to twist the facts to fit his theories that characterizes Job's *friends*, rather than Job himself."[23] Like Marson, Lasine goes to great lengths to catalogue K.'s moral shortcomings: his "motivated ignorance of himself";[24] his inability to "abandon the pose of detached spectator"; his unwillingness to examine his past; his attraction to a married woman; his willingness to "raise his hand against poor children"; his rejoicing "at the idea of his enemy's ruin";[25] his lack of concern about the sufferings of others, and so on.[26] Much of this is hard to counter; moreover, Lasine's already-comprehensive set of shortcomings could be supplemented with many others.

In our view, however, Lasine has missed one of the most essential aspects of scapegoat theory. We can pose this as a question: is it really the case that no questions beyond that concerning K.'s virtue, or lack of it, are sufficient (although perhaps necessary), to determine his status as a scapegoat? This seems to assume that scapegoats can be characterized in terms of a sort of primordial ontological innocence. *Ergo*, given his evident moral weakness, K.'s fate is precipitated by none other than K. himself, and is in perfect accord with conceptions of Biblical justice. Moreover—surprisingly in our view—Lasine takes his analysis a step further, suggesting that K.'s inability "to recognize that what the court does is *a function of K.'s own assumptions and his refusal to be personally accountable for his thoughts and deeds.*"[27]

Irrespective of whether this is an accurate representation of "biblical justice," scapegoats do not have to be *innocent* to be scapegoats. In our view, a person's status as a scapegoat cannot be determined simply by an examination of his or her moral qualities. In structural terms, a scapegoat is determined by a capacity to unite a community whose polarization around him or her generates, or promises to generate, social unanimity—a person or group whose lynching or banishment functions to generate all communal senses of the esprit de corps following acts of collective violence.[28] That is to say, the designation of an individual, or a group, as a "scapegoat" is not primarily *morally*, but *anthropologically* determined.[29] In our view, therefore, Josef K.'s primary error does not reside in his inability to be "personally accountable," to exercise some moral agency, but in his evident delusion that he is an *agent at all*.

Indeed, in the light of a truly anthropological theory of scapegoating, we contend that it makes better sense to preserve the shape of Lasine's analysis while flipping the indictment of K. on its head. As a perceptive reader of Girard, Lasine would presumably be sensitive to the fact that the world depicted in the novel offers numerous examples of what Girard would call a "crisis of distinctions" or "sacrificial crisis": of mutable symbols, widespread symmetries of identity, and blurring of cultural distinctions. During his first interrogation by the court, those he thought to be members of the audience, dispersed in the court, each according to their judgment of him, on closer inspection turn out to be colleagues, each with a "stiff and brittle" beard and "little black eyes" (T 1953, 56). K. sees that each wears an identical badge, the same badge as worn by the Magistrate himself (56). It is hard to not characterize this as a depiction of an accusatory community, a sign of—among other things—widespread cultural degeneration. In *The Trial*, the institution ostensibly *most* concerned with justice, the law courts, represent but a veneer of due process, and one that is both thin and brittle, as we see when an orgasmic "shriek" interrupts K.'s testimony and a "little circle" forms around the participants, the gallery spectators "delighted that the seriousness which K. had introduced into the proceedings should be dispelled in this manner" (55).

If this is indeed a court of "divine justice," then one has to ask what kind of deity is involved. Unable to find desired information about the machinations of the court—and based on information provided by the manufacturer—K. seeks out the court painter, Titorelli. This man, a confidant of many of the judges of the court, possessed of "considerable insight" into its workings, is enveloped in a burlesque of urban decay and decrepitude—of shifting shadows, "deafening din," and "sludge oozing about slowly on top of the melting snow" (T 1956, 150–1). K. stood before the painter and before his very eyes, the image of justice being painted transformed, such that it "no longer suggested the goddess of Justice, or even the goddess of Victory, but...a goddess of the Hunt in full cry" (T 1956, 163).[30]

It is important to call attention to the fact that K. is a socially isolated bachelor who lives in a room in a boarding house. His authority extends only to his underlings and his customers at the bank. In victimary terms, K. presents an ideal admixture of vulnerability and power. After all, a victim needs to be in some radical sense vulnerable: victims are people *without community*—so that their lynching or banishment is not avenged—and powerful enough for the act of victimage to be sufficiently cathartic. In this context, K. surely doesn't stand a chance against the "goddess of the hunt."

8. Modern Victimhood

According to Martin Parker, *The Trial* is an example of a genre he calls "the organisational gothic," a literary and filmic excursions into the horrors of bureaucratic rationality *in extremis*. We will supplement—and modify somewhat—this reading by contending that *The Trial* offers us a portrait of a peculiarly modern form of victimhood, that occurring within the context of oppressive and amoral forms of bureaucratic rationality. Kafka's work captures in a particularly vivid way the anxieties that the modern citizen feels in the powerful but absurd machinations of bureaucratization: a series of processes whose rationale and procedure are almost as opaque to those who are its functionaries as those being manipulated by it.[31] Suffused with a stark but sometimes comic pessimism, Kafka's work offers a cultural critique analogous to Max Weber's image of the "iron cage" of bureaucracy.[32]

Weber realized that the expansion of bureaucracy involves the danger of an inflexible, technically ordered, and dehumanized social order.[33] For Weber, bureaucratization represents one face of modern "rationalisation," of the widespread application of "rational calculation" to social institutions and processes.[34] But we should understand what this *means*. Malcolm Warner has argued that "in Kafka's work, the workings of bureaucracy are...far from 'rational'."[35] But this is not what "rational" means for Weber; "rationalization" isn't a synonym of "reasonable-ization," but names the way in which social institutions become increasingly constituted by rigid regimes of rules that prescribe the way particular practical or pragmatic ends are to be achieved. As an example of modern automation, these procedures operate largely independently of any exercise of judgement.[36] In the modern world at least, it is not always easy to distinguish the so-called rational or logical from the absurd. Camus argues that *The Trial* is indeed predicated on a certain *"excess* of logic."[37] Likewise, Kafka saw bureaucracy as somehow "springing straight out of the origins of human nature."[38] There are few institutions more bureaucratic than banks.

It is not the bank, however, that is the main source of K.'s troubles, but the law. Why might this be? We could survey some possibilities. Perhaps the law, according to the genre demands of the "organisational gothic," serves as a site of focus because modern bureaucracies are ultimately underwritten and structured by the diverse applications of legal rationality. For Weber, modern forms of social power are exercised through impersonal processes, and their legitimacy specified in terms of *legality*.[39] Perhaps there are other reasons why the law is the privileged site of oppression in much of Kafka's work. Milan Kundera writes of the characteristic form of victimage in the twentieth century under the sign of "the tribunal," a term he borrows from *The Trial*:

> Tribunal: this does not signify the juridical institution for punishing people who have violated the laws of the state; the tribunal (or court) in Kafka's sense is a power that judges, that judges because it is a power; its power and nothing but its power is what confers legitimacy on the tribunal.... The trial brought by the tribunal is always *absolute*; meaning that it does not concern an isolated act, a specific crime (theft, fraud, rape), but rather concerns the character of the accused in its entirety.[40]

Kundera's assertion that "the tribunal" does not denote "the juridical institution" is perhaps overly restrictive; it may be truer to say that it need not necessarily denote the juridical institution. Anthropologically speaking, we could argue that modern courts represent an advance over premodern and tribal forms of "justice" because they are structured by the presence of a "transcendent," neutral judiciary; this insertion of a "disinterested" third party breaks the symmetry of oppositions and so lessens the risk that the retributive act will become endlessly reciprocated—in other words, a blood feud.

To be sure, like all forms of social transcendence, the authority underwriting a legal trial is not forever. And in certain political formations, as well as during episodes of cultural disintegration or "sacrificial crises," the judiciary risks simply becoming another player in a scene of ongoing, contagious violence. The image of society that Kafka gives in *The Trial* is one of overriding social decay, where officials seem to possess only nominal authority and superiors never appear, where distinctions between social actors, even in the courts become effaced. In these kinds of situations and their political correlates, legal machinery becomes simply a locus of absolute power, its legitimacy residing in power alone.

We can now put the two layers of interpretation together: this is a novel that simultaneously condemns the Weberian structures of legal and other apparatuses in our society and also does so in terms of victimage mechanisms. Ours is a double claim: *The Trial* represents a portrait of modern victimhood, with the adjective carrying the same weight as the noun. It is *modern* insofar as the judiciary, or the particular form of it represented in the novel, is a distinctly modern institution;[41] it is a portrayal of victimhood insofar that it depicts a process of collective or unanimous victimage. Let us be clear. In *The Trial*, we witness the travails of a man who is arrested and charged with an offence that he cannot be informed about—a man who can find no advocates to act on his behalf—and subject to a system whose impersonality and opacity cannot be overcome, whose relentless operation results in him being taken to a quarry by two men and killed "like a dog" (T 1956, 251).

9. Conclusion

With the closing of the novel, we arrive at the closing of our argument. In discovering the victimary structure of the book, in finding indeed that Kafka is actually analyzing this structure, we are returned to the possibility that the first reading of the novel offers—the deep intuition that the system itself is deeply and ineliminably guilty. For all the harsh humor of this text at its unfortunate protagonist's expense (and Marson and Lasine, surely, have correctly divined this dimension of the work), the abiding humanity of the work and the wellspring of its perennial appeal lies in the fact that we can all of us relate personally to the struggles of this mean-spirited, but ever-so-modern, man. If he stands condemned, surely so do we all—and by the very processes of victimage that we ourselves participate in on a daily basis.

Shortly before the knife plunges "deep into his heart," K. glances up to see a "flicker of light" on the top story of a house adjoining the quarry; a window flings open, and "a human figure, faint and insubstantial at that distance and that height, leaned abruptly far forward and stretched both arms still farther. Who was it? A friend? A good man? Someone who sympathized? Someone who wanted to help?" (T 1956, 250). There is left open, once again, the possibility—or perhaps, more accurately, an insinuation—of help, but this help, we now realize, will come too late. The agonising last scene underlines the extent to which K. is without an advocate; at the mercy of a system whose rules he always only comes to know after the fact—if at all—we readers come to finally understand, even if K. himself never does, that his agency in this sorry affair has been delusional.

Unlike victimage in the sense that Girard has analyzed it, the sacrificial violence depicted in *The Trial* operates through an intricate series of displacements determined by modern "rationalisation"; instead of an angry mob, we have a bureaucratically dispersed series of actors, each "doing their duty." Opposition to K. is both unanimous and evenly distributed through a network of seemingly arbitrary series of actors, processes, and demands. This is to say that in *The Trial*, bureaucracy functions like a mob in that no one person can be singled out as responsible for K.'s death. Yet, as with the other writers of this disturbing era, we cannot ourselves avoid a certain sense of responsibility. If K. is indeed pursued by "the god of the hunt in full cry," it is worth reminding ourselves that such a "God" (or devil) may escape our attention because it seems to be characterized more by inanity than insanity (T 1953, 163). As a narrative depicting profane violence struggling to sacralize itself through institutional "due process," Kafka presents us with what might be called, to mangle Hannah Arendt, the banality of divinity.

Notes

1. The Book of Job 9: 20–2.
2. Sheldon S. Wolin, *Politics and Vision* (London: Allen and Unwin, 1961), 354.
3. This was a world with a felt sense of decline, witnessed in the extraordinary flowering of the small group of Secessionist painters (Klimt, Schiele) whose ornamental sense was accompanied by a more or less strong sense of inner decay (Klimt's elaborate tableaux may have been beautiful, but some, such as his Judith painting, had ghoulish dimensions; Schiele's images are confronting, even today). Vienna was also home to psychoanalysis, in the work of Sigmund Freud, whose pages drip not just with a negative view of human motivations, but also, with images of cities from past times (his lines on archaeology are particularly striking in this respect, as are his accounts of the buried city of Rome). These images are not presented for their own sake, but rather to show how civilization is itself a veneer, how histories lie buried literally beneath our feet—and also, within our psyches—see Sigmund Freud, "Civilisation and its Discontents," *The Standard Edition of the Complete Psychological Works of Sigmund Freud*, Vol. 23. (London: Hogart, 1964), 69.
4. See for instance, Robert Musil, *The Man Without Qualities,* trans. E. Wilkins and E. Kaiser (London: Picador, 1979), 306–16.
5. In *Narrative Fiction: Contemporary Poetics* it is put thus: "In so-called "third person centre of consciousness" (James' *the Ambassadors,* Joyce's *Portrait*), the centre of consciousness (or "reflector") is the focalizer, while the use of the third person is the narrator." (Shlmoth Rimon-Kenan, *Narrative Fiction: Contemporary Poetics* [London: Methuen, 1983], 73.) In Kafka's case, even this seems a bit inadequate, as we feel the narrator-role itself is contaminated by the constriction of vision.
6. Franz Stanzel, *A Theory of Narrative,* trans C. Gödsche (Cambridge: Cambridge University Press, 1984).
7. We thank Dimitris Vardoulakis for his observations on this sentence.
8. Ronald Speirs and Beatrice Sandberg, *Franz Kafka* (London: Macmillan, 1997), 68.
9. Eric Marson, *Kafka's Trial: the Case Against Josef K.* (St Lucia: University of Queensland, 1975), 45–46.
10. Ibid., 50 and 71.
11. Ibid., 53 and 56.
12. Ibid., 10–11.
13. J.P. Stern has compared the court in *The Trial* with those in the Third Reich. (J.P. Stern, "The Law of *The Trial,*" in *On Kafka: Semi-Centenary Perspectives,* ed. Franz Kuna [London: Elek Books, 1976], 29–35.)
14. Albert Camus, *The Myth of Sisyphus,* trans. Justin O'Brien (London: Penguin, 1955), 116.

15. Gershom Scholem, *Walter Benjamin: The Story of a Friendship*, trans. Harry Zohn (New York: New York Review of Books, 2001), 216.

16. If it were simply a matter of formal stylistic or syntactic homologies it would at least get us beyond the often facile psychoanalytic adumbrations of Kafka's work—of tying the often repeated motifs of his novels and short stories to his family drama, particularly his fraught relationship with his father (for instance, Derek Jones and Graham Handley *The Modern World: Ten Great Writers* [London: Channel Four Publications, 1988], 22; also see Anthony Storr *Dynamics of Creation* [London: Penguin, 1972], 76–80.) For different reasons, Dostoevsky has been subject to the same kind of hermeneutic taming—by making either the characters or the author himself some kind of paradigmatic case study of psychopathology. Although offering putative "explanations" of the literary object, such theoretical ruses act only to distance this work, and perhaps our implication in it. It might be worth considering what René Girard has said—that Dostoevsky might provide a more adequate account of so-called psychoanalytic phenomena than Freud can offer with regard to Dostoevsky's novels. (Girard, 36–60; Cf. Christopher Fleming, *René Girard: Violence and Mimesis* [Cambridge: Polity, 2004], 12–16 and 32–40.) As suggestive as Scholem's comments are, he develops them no further—and despite Benjamin's positive reaction to Scholem's letter, his own development of the religious themes in Kafka's work owe more to the Kabbalah and the concepts (and literature) of "Aggadah" and "Halakhah"—of Talmudic, Midrash, and legal sources respectively—than straightforwardly *biblical* ones. (Cf. Scholem, *Walter Benjamin: The Story of a Friendship*, 221.) Even Camus talks of Kafka's novels as "a theology in action." (Camus, *The Myth of Sisyphus*, 114.)

17. Stuart Lasine, "The Trials of Job and Kafka's Josef K.," *The German Quarterly* 63.2 (1990): 187.

18. Ibid.

19. For a summation of Girard's reading of the Book of Job, see Fleming *René Girard: Violence and Mimesis*, 121–3.

20. René Girard, *Job: The Victim of His People*, trans. Yvonne Freccero (Stanford, CA: Stanford University Press, 1987), 127.

21. Stuart Lasine, "The Trials of Job and Kafka's Josef K.," 187 (our emphasis).

22. Ibid., 191. In another essay, Lasine compares K. with Balaam, the "wicked" prophet from the Book of Numbers who "chooses to go down the wrong path for the wrong reasons, and is therefore rightfully led to punishment and death." (Stuart Lasine, Kafka's *The Trial.*" *The Explicator* 43 [1985]: 22–23.)

23. Stuart Lasine, "The Trials of Job and Kafka's Josef K.," 187.

24. Ibid., 188.

25. Ibid., 189.

26. Ibid., 190.

27. Ibid., 187 (our emphasis).

28. Indeed, the persecution of certain criminals—or criminal classes—involves both legal culpability *and* scapegoating. In debates about punishment, advocates of "restorative justice" have criticized retributivists not for advocating the punishment of innocent people, but for the way in which retributivism involves the scapegoating of the (legally) guilty.

29. We are not suggesting that there is not an "ethics" to anthropological inquiry. See Fleming and O'Carroll (2003, 2005).
30. Note also that in *The Illiad*, Artemis—the goddess of the hunt—wreaked revenge on Oeneus who did not sacrifice to her by sending the Calydonian Boar.
31. Walter Benjamin, "Letter to G. Scholem, 1938," in *Correspondence*, Vol II (Paris: Aubier, 1980), 248. Weber often uses the image of bureaucracy as a kind of "machine." (Max Weber, *Protestant Ethic*, 121; *Economy and Society* lix.) Camus argues that many of Kafka's characters are "inspired automata." (Camus, 118.)
32. Martin Parker, "Organisational Gothic," *Culture and Organization*, 11.1 (2005): 159–60.
33. Max Weber, *The Protestant Ethic and the Spirit of Capitalism*, ed. Peter Baehr, trans. Gordon C. Wells (London: Penguin, 2002), 121; and *Economy and Society: An Outline of Interpretive Sociology* (Berkeley: University of California Press, 1978), 289.
34. Ibid., lix.
35. Malcolm Warner, "Kafka, Weber and Organization Theory," *Human Relations* 60.7 (2007): 1025.
36. Max Weber, *The Theory of Social and Economic Organization*, trans. A. M. Henderson and Talcott Parsons (New York: Oxford University Press, 1947), 115; *From Max Weber*, ed. and trans. H. H. Gerth and C. Wright Mills (New York: Oxford University Press, 1974), 293–94.
37. Camus, *The Myth of Sisyphus*, 116.
38. Richard Heinemann, "Kafka's Oath of Service: 'Der Bau' and the Dialectic of Bureaucratic Mind," *PMLA* 111.2 (1996): 256.
39. Max Weber, *From Max Weber*, ed. and trans. H.H. Gerth and C. Wright Mills (New York: Oxford University Press, 1974), 299; cf. P. Lassman, "The Rule of Men Over Men: Politics, Power and Legitimation," ed. S. Turner, in *The Cambridge Companion to Weber* (Cambridge: Cambridge University Press, 2000), 91.
40. Milan Kundera, *Testaments Betrayed: An Essay in Nine Parts* (New York: Harper Collins, 1995), 227.
41. Even so, we do not go as far as Ronald Gray does in asserting that *The Trial* particularly concerns the Austrian legal system of the early twentieth century.

CHAPTER THREE

KAFKA AND DERRIDA *BEFORE THE LAWS*

Howard Caygill

What if the "man from the country" of Kafka's *Before the Law* was not so much seeking to enter the law as to leave the country? That he was an emigrant who did not succeed in becoming an immigrant, but through some accident, of birth, of timing, was held at the border? Such a change of interpretative orientation, from an entry to an exit narrative, might shake not only the understanding of Kafka's *Before the Law* and its place in his authorship, but also many of the issues surrounding the relationship of philosophy, law, and literature raised and intensified by Derrida's reading of this text. To change the sense of *Before the Law*, to see it as a fable of failed exit rather than failed entrance puts at issue many of questions provoked by this text and the nature of the law that seems to be its obscure object. It makes of the text a story of accidental exodus, where the inability to surmount an aporia or blockage generates the phantasmal quest for salvation and the law.

Kafka's short narration of the encounter between the man from the country and the guardian of the entrance to the law and the commentaries it has provoked are characterized by extreme interpretative profligacy. The story itself exists in four versions and was published three times during Kafka's lifetime, as well as posthumously with Kafka's own commentary as part of the culminating vicissitudes of Josef K. in *The Trial*. It has been justly described as "belonging certainly among the most-interpreted parables of our century, perhaps is *the* parable of the century—comparable in its universal applicability to Andersen's story 'The King's New Clothes'—*the* parable of the nineteenth century."[1] Its status as *the* parable of the twentieth century is inseparable from its alleged narration of the deferred entrance to the law, from the story it would tell of the tension between the universality of the law and the singularity of any entrance to it. It has intrigued not only scholars and philosophers but also entered popular culture through the framing role given to it in Orson Welles' adaptation of *The Trial*. It was also the occasion for one of Derrida's most intense inquiries into the relationship between literature and philosophy, an investigation itself appearing in three versions: first as a seminar in the 1980–1981 series dedicated to the theme of "respect" pursued through readings of Kant and Freud, then as a lecture to the Royal Philosophical Society in London in 1982, and finally as Derrida's contribution to the 1982 Colloque de Cerisy on the work of Jean-François Lyotard, published in the proceedings as "Prejuges: Devant la Loi."[2]

Derrida's first reading of *Before the Law* in the seminar interrupts and augments the bipolar movement between Kant and Freud that is the signature of his series of seminars on respect.[3] It emphasizes the themes of failed penetration and *coitus interruptus*, of the fictional aspects of the law, repetition, and the notions of guarding and height. The emergence of Derrida's *Before the Law* from the matrix of the seminars is significant for several reasons. It accounts for certain emphases and details, such as the emphasis on the nasal hair of the guard that is carried over into subsequent versions from the seminar, but it also highlights the persistence of Kantian structures in the organization of the published text. These include the classic problem of relationship between action and law, the references to hypotyposis, but above all the use of the table of judgments from the three critiques to organize Derrida's reading of *Before the Law*.

Perhaps the most significant outcome of the reading of *Before the Law* in the seminar is its performative interruption of a line of philosophical argument by a work of literature. The seminar on *Before the Law*—the last before the Christmas vacation—broke the sequence of philosophical readings that preceded and succeeded it, and seems to have provoked further reflection on the question of the relationship between literature and philosophy. The performance of the interruption of philosophy by literature in the seminar is thematized in the two subsequent versions of *Before the Law*. The law of philosophical exposition respected until the seminar on *Before the Law* is suspended in the face of the literary exception, prompting a testing and a reinvention of the protocols of philosophical reading.

The predominantly Kantian matrix of the reading of *Before the Law* is evident in Derrida's reliance upon the table of judgments to organize his reading of the literary text. The patterning of judgments and categories according to their quantity, quality, relation, and modality that characterized all three of Kant's critiques is evoked in Derrida's four "axiomatic trivialities" or presuppositions before the reading of the text. These are its *quantity* or "identity, singularity and unity," its authorship or *quality*, the literary *relation* that binds together the events of the text, and the "title" or *modality*, by which is meant the ways in which the text presents itself to us or we find ourselves stood before it. The "axiomatic trivialities" that a literary text has an original identity, an author, a narrative, and a title add up to a consensus or (Kantian) *sensus communis* to which Derrida both appeals and announces his intention to "undermine." These conditions of possibility of a literary text are rooted in "our community of subjects participating on the whole in the same culture and subscribing in a given context, to the same system of conventions."[4] However, this subscription is not simply a matter of consensus, but is ultimately guaranteed by law; thus literature is sheltered by a system of laws and guardians, before which and before whom Derrida must stand before gaining entrance. His strategy, however, seems to differ from that of the "man from the country" who also finds himself before the law in search of a title: instead of being arrested by the law, Derrida seeks to "undermine" the laws before which he must stand, to seek an indirect entrance.

Derrida's readings of *Before the Law* gather parerga as they appear, changing the text even where its letter remains unchanged. It itself undermines the first axiomatic triviality that the identity of a text is in some sense stable. The seminar text is carried over wholesale into the London *Before the Law* but set within the frame of the question of philosophy and literature; this "version" is in turn is carried over into the third appearance of the text in *Prejuges Devant la Loi,* within the frame of the question of judgment. In *Before the Law,* Derrida commences his reading of Kafka's text by referring back to the seminar; he says in London, in 1982, that his reading "is coloured by a seminar during which, last year, I thought I had teased out this story of Kafka's."[5] Yet the reading is not so much accomplished through the chromatic filter of the previous seminar as through the wholesale citation of the seminar but filtered by the specific demands of the second reading. And this was a reading undertaken within the irony of a quasi-Hegelian struggle for recognition: he thought he had "teased out" the story, had made its meaning emerge, only to realise that the story had "laid siege to my attempt at a discourse on the moral law and respect in the Kantian sense of the term."[6] The besieger becomes the besieged, the metaphor of the siege pointing to the insistent presence of the grail narratives and the notion of a quest in the second and third appearances of *Before the Law.*[7] The man from the country also lays siege to the law, but in a harsh irony Kafka has the Doorman give a lowly stool to the man from the country on which he can sit and spend his entire life hopelessly "besieging" the law. In the event, Kafka's text seems less to ravage and break down the walls of Derrida's attempted discourse on the moral law than to sit to one side of it and wait.

While refraining from relating the "details of this struggle" in the spirit of a grail narrative, Derrida moves straight to a description of some of the salient points of the siege. The first concerns Kantian hypotyposis—the symbolic presentation of the moral law: the law "never shows itself but is the only cause of that respect."[8] The second is the introduction of "narrativity and fiction," and with this historicity, "into the very core of legal thought." As a coda, Derrida also refers to two additional motifs, height and guarding, all adding up to "A space, then, in which it is difficult to say whether Kafka's story proposes a powerful, philosophical ellipsis or whether pure, practical reason contains an element of the fantastic or of narrative fiction."[9] This space of indecision is corroborated by Kafka's story, which narrates the collapse of the assumptions of universality and singularity surrounding the law, and points to the ways in which inaccessibility generates narrative, perhaps even the narrative of the law.

Derrida's framing of the reading of *Before the Law* culminates in the Kantian question of whether law and the literary object share "conditions of possibility," conditions that are very close to the "philosophical ellipsis" of the idiom of the law. When delivering the third, Cerisy *Before the Law*, Derrida introduced this particular "colouring" of the Kafka story as the second of two "programmes" or "destinations" that "marked" the reading of the text. The first is identified in Lyotard's description of the "pragmatic of Judaism" and the "meta-law" expressed in the injunction "be just" and its requirement that each time it is necessary to decide what it means to be just. With this, the understanding of *Before the Law* as pointing to a philosophical ellipsis as a condition of the possibility for law and fiction is supplemented by the further understanding of the text as an exploration of the problems generated by what is described as a specifically Jewish injunction to "be just." Yet it is also more than this, since the second programme of the Cerisy repetition of *Before the Law* secretly—this is perhaps a secret between Lyotard and Derrida—aligns the text with Kafka's contemporary story *In the Penal Colony*. The performative self-destruction of the *Apparat* in that story is staged around the inscription of the condemnation "be just" on the body of the officer/executioner. We have to do then with two self-destructive machines involved with the law, the doorway, and the Apparat, both emerging from the same period of Kafka's authorship, the autumn following the outbreak of the First World War.

If we return to the table of categories and focus on the first—the question of the identity of the text—it is possible to confirm and intensify Derrida's intuition that *Before the Law* has no definitive identity, but changes according to its modality, to where and how it appeared. His full citation of it at the outset of each of his three readings contributes to the already complex history of reframing the text, summoning it to appear before and yet also within his text. Derrida immediately puts into question the presupposition that this text has an identity "which we hold to be unique and self-identical, to exist as an original version incorporated in its birthplace within the German language."[10] Yet it becomes very quickly clear that this text for Derrida was born at least twice. One of the main lines of argument concerning the "difficulty with literature" experienced by the "man from the country" depends on the different circumstances in which the text appeared, above all the text Derrida imagines having been written in 1919 (referring to the appearance of *Before the Law* in the collection *A Country Doctor*).[11] However, the text Derrida imagines having been written in 1919 had already been published in two very different settings in 1915 and 1916, appearances that are left unmentioned by Derrida and that complicate his argument considerably. The text was in fact born four times, but Derrida's attention is focused upon the relationship between the 1919 text in *A Country Doctor* and the version related and commented upon by the prison chaplain toward the end of *The Trial*.

Attempts to determine the genesis of *Before the Law* must confront problems with chronology since the composition of the *The Trial,* begun in the autumn of 1914 and abandoned early in 1915, locates the version with commentary before the version without it. The version embedded in the narrative of *The Trial* with elaborate commentary was written five years before Derrida's own assigned date of composition in 1919. In the latter version, it is shorn of its commentary and embedded in a series of stories clustered around the theme of failed exits.[12] We shall see that it had a complex history of publication as a text severed from *The Trial* even before its appearance in 1919.

If we move to Derrida's conclusion, his attempt to shut the door on *Before the Law*, we see him engaged in the effort to "judge that this text belongs to 'literature'" through an epoche of the parable. He proposes to "subtract from this text all the elements which could belong to another register (everyday information, history, knowledge, philosophy, fiction and so forth—anything that is not necessarily affiliated with literature)"[13]. At the end of this *epoche*, he finds at work in the text "an essential rapport with the play of framing and the paradoxical logic of boundaries, which introduces a kind of perturbation in the 'normal' system of reference, while simultaneously revealing an essential structure of referentiality. It is an obscure revelation of referentiality which does not make reference, which does not refer, any more than the eventness of the event is itself an event."[14] The "obscure revelation" involves the event or "singular performance" after which the man from the country asks his final question:

> ' "Everyone strives after the law" said the man, how is it then, that in all these years no-one except me demanded entrance?" The Doorman understood that the man was already at his end, and, in order to reach his failing

hearing, shouted at him: "No one else could have entered here, for this entrance was meant only for you. I am now going to close it."

This is the point at which for Derrida "the singular crosses the universal, when the categorical engages the idiomatic, as literature always must. The man from the country had difficulty in grasping that an entrance was singular or unique when it should have been universal, as in truth it was. He had difficulty with literature."[15] It is also the Kantian difficulty of hypotyposis, or specifically that kind of hypotyposis that Kant contrasts with symbolism, namely schematism, to which he devotes a section of the *Critique of Pure Reason* that shows the relationship between universal categories and singular intuitions, but it is one which becomes sharply evident before the plurality of *Before the Laws*.

Derrida moves on to *The Trial* in a spirit of counterproof. "We find there the *same* content differently framed, with a different system of boundaries and above all without a proper title, except that of a volume of several hundred pages. From the point of view of literature, the same content gives rise to a completely different work."[16] What constitutes the difference is neither form nor content, but "the movements of framing and referentiality." Literature *is* this movement, one described by Derrida referring to *Before the Law* as a "strange filiation, a metonymic interpretation of each other, each becoming a part that is absolutely independent of the other and each time greater than the whole; the title of the other."[17] Here Derrida moves rapidly from the category of quantity to that of modality—from the plurality of the text to the title. He shows how each version of the text is the "condition of the possibility" of the other, in some sense entitling the other version. While the specific condition of possibility of literature is the "power to make the law," this depends on the prior condition "that the text can itself appear *before the law* of another, more powerful text protected by more powerful guardians."[18] The mode of appearance of literature is governed by a canon protected by guardians.[19] In the case of *Before the Law*, the doubling of the text generates "a powerful ellipsis" in that the text appeals to itself, it is its own law but is also necessarily other to itself.

Kafka's text itself is more than one: *Before the Law* appeals to itself, offers a commentary upon itself. Its plurality puts into question its quality as a text written by a single author and also its internal relation or narrative: the internal narrative differs according to whether it finds itself at the end of *The Trial* or between the stories "An Old Page" and "Jackals and Arabs" in the collection *The Country Doctor*. The quantity of the text or its identity is determined not only by its title, or modality, but also its relation: how its narration is shaped by where it stands and what it borders. The experience of Josef K. in *The Trial*, who after hearing the story is told by the Priest that he is "nowhere near" the main doorway, reorients the narration of the man from the country who has at least found the door. Kafka's text then "tells us perhaps of the being-before-the-law of any text. It does so by ellipsis, at once advancing and retracting it. It belongs not only to the literature of a given period, inasmuch as it itself is beyond the law (which it articulates), before a certain type of law. The text also points obliquely to literature, speaking of itself as a literary effect—and thereby exceeding the literature of which it speaks."[20] The exemplary character of *Before the Law*—both in the sense of what it narrates, its "relation" as the unworking of a singular law, and its modality or appearance before the law of itself in another version—consists in the way that it resists belonging to a field, but "is the transformer of the field." Potentially it not only transforms the field but can also swallow it up. It opens a *mise-en-abyme* within the text and between the texts. *The Trial* says Derrida "would therefore have already have set up a *mise-en-abyme* of everything you have just heard, unless *Before the Law* does the same thing through a more powerful ellipsis which itself would engulf *The Trial,* and us along with it."[21] Derrida turns at this point to the quotation of *Before the Law* in *The Trial* and what he calls the "structural possibility of this *contre-abyme*," which he distances from chronology "even if, as we know, it is only *Before the Law* that Kafka will have published, under this title, during his lifetime."[22] The movement between *Before the Law* and the "*Before the Law*" incorporated in the *The Trial* exceeds chronology, but what happens when we confront this structural possibility and its complex metonymic movement with the existence of three *Before the Law*s?

These three versions are the same text, but as we have learnt from Derrida they are also different by virtue of being situated in very different frames. Their existence complicates even further the already almost unbearably complex scenario of *mise-en-abyme* and *contra abyme* set in motion by Derrida between *Before the Law* and "*Before the Law.*" *Before the Law* itself is already plural, with very different framings, thus inviting an historical inquiry into its modality or various appearances.[23] The text was first published in 1915 in the culturally specific circumstances of the Prague Independent Jewish weekly journal *Self-Defence* (*Unabhängige judische Wochenschrift Selbstwehr*), to which Kafka was a subscriber.[24] The circumstances of this first publication seem to force a relaxation of Derrida's scruples regarding the "elements which could belong to another register" cited above. For *Selbstwehr* was dedicated to forging a Jewish national identity, wagering upon the cultural unity of Eastern and Western Judaism and contributing to the debate around the definition of Zionism. The first publication of *Before the Law* thus took place within the context of a debate about Jewish national identity and the character of Zionism.

While the publishing circumstances of the first *Before the Law* might invite a reading of the text within a Zionist register, an even more specific context might also be conjectured. During the period when Kafka was writing *The Trial*, and hence *Before the Law*—the Autumn of 1914—the aspirations for a united Jewish identity entertained by *Selbstwehr* were challenged by a refugee crisis in Prague. Jewish refugees from the Galician front placed increasing pressure on the resources of the Jewish community to support them, resulting in the issue of an official decree banning them from entering into the city. The refugee problem, debated in the pages of *Selbstwehr,* resulted in the closing of the gates of Prague to the men and women from the country. The guardians were not so much guarding the law as the economic situation and the established privileges of the Prague Jewish community.[25] The first *Before the Law* is thus placed within the general context of the invention of Jewish national identity and the specific context of the period of public reflection (1915) following the perceived failure of the first real test to the notion of Jewish national unity. Its composition was in all probability contemporary with the Decree of the Ministry of the Interior closing the city to refugees.

The fable of a man from the country prevented by a guard from entering the gate in this context assumes multiple valences. One of these, consistent with Kafka's writing of this period, is sardonic irony: The man from the country as a refugee encountering inhospitality and interpreting the guard and the obstacle to his entry in terms of a forbidden law rather than a forbidden territory. Finding himself before a guarded door was an accident, this was the singularity of the door; the man from the country found himself in the predicament of not being able to exit nor enter, the retelling of this predicament in terms of an individual barrier to a universal law would come later. The law was a story told to make sense of the accident of being the wrong person at the wrong place at the wrong time.

The second *Before the Law* appears in very different circumstances, those of the German language literary avant-garde. Published in Kurt Wolff's Leipzig-based *Almanach neuer Dichtung: Vom jüngsten Tag,* it appears with full literary credentials as a work of an avant-garde writer. Here *Before the Law* most closely approximates the literary text that Derrida will set in relation to "*Before the Law*" in *The Trial.* Its subsequent appearance in the 1919 *A Country Doctor* is complicated by its place among fables of escape and misrecognition. Kafka's plans for the order of stories in the collection fluctuated during the summer of 1917, with *Before the Law* shifting within the broader constellation of stories. These shifts provoke a change in the identity of the story itself. In the first plan from February 1917 it is located between "A Dream" and "Fratricide," that is, following the story of the burial fantasy of Josef K. and preceding the expressionist story of a murder; between a fantasy of death and the act of murder. In the April 1917 list, *Before the Law* still follows "A Dream," which is now the opening story of the collection, but is followed by "An Imperial Messenger"—one of the more explicit narratives of failed exit that make up this collection of failed exits. By July/August 1917, it has moved again, now finding itself between "Ein altes Blatt," the story of the closing of the palace doors against the nomads, and "Jackals and Arabs," one of Kafka's fables of messianic misrecognition.

These placings and replacings of the text may be considered as virtual versions of *Before the Law*, showing how Kafka undertook a commentary upon it by means of placing (*Setzen* in German) it beside other stories. In the February *Before the Law,* readers would encounter it in the context of fables of imagined and actual death, pulling its narrative toward the death of the man from the country. In the April list, it is located before the narration of the fantasy of a singular message sent by the emperor, a message whose arrival is thwarted by the impossibility of the messenger exiting from the palace, a blockage paralleling the predicament of the man from the country unable to exit from the country before the gates of the law. In the final version, *Before the Law* follows a story of the attempt to defend the palace door—the viewpoint of the guard—and a fable of messianic misrecognition, where the desire of the jackals to escape the Arabs provokes inappropriate and laughable messianic fantasies with respect to the traveller. In the final version, *Before the Law* appears as the inverse of the guard's predicament—as the point of view of the nomad/man from the country seeking entry to a guarded space—as well as a fable of how deprivation provokes religious fantasy, of the law or of the Messiah. This order is perhaps closest to the *Selbstwehr* appearance of the text in the context of closing the gates of Prague and the predicament of the men and women from the country held outside the gate.

What is certain is that the 1919 text that Derrida takes as his point of departure is already shot through with citations of itself, is already plural. This would not come as a surprise to him and indeed confirms his thesis by complicating it. The category of quantity is already at play in the various versions, published and planned, of *Before the Law*. And according to these contexts, the quality (authorship) and relation (narrative) of the texts are also negotiable. The author of a story for *Selbstwehr* is different from the author of a story for the *Almanach neuer Dichtung*, who is in turn different from the author of *A Country Doctor*, who is different from the author of the unpublished novel *The Trial*. In terms of relation or the internal order of the text, the "same" narrative is different in *Selbstwehr* than in the *Almanach neuer Dichtung* than it is according to its place in the list of contents of *A Country Doctor*. And finally the modality, already complex in Derrida's reading across *Before the Law* of *A Country Doctor* and "Before the Law" of *The Trial,* is raised by several powers of complexity. The ellipsis of *Before the Law* works itself through in diverse literary, political, cultural, and historical contexts. The play of *mise-en-abyme* and *contra abyme* that Derrida finds exemplary in *Before the Law* is itself mise en abyme, and the arrival at an original text ever more deferred.

In one of his concluding statements, offered in the disingenuous mode of apology, Derrida confesses that: "This has hardly been a scene of categorical reading [*peu categorique*]."[26] In fact it was literally categorical, the "risked glosses," "multiple interpretations," "posed and diverted questions," "abandoned decipherings" and "intact enigmas" all taking place (*Gesetzt*) according to the table of categories (a procedure explicitly thematized in *The Truth in Painting*). These are the set of accusations (categories) that Derrida lists as having silently organized the specific accusations, acquittals, defences, praises, and comparisons. In the Cerisy version, the list is interrupted by the name of Jean-François Lyotard—"a commencer par Jean-François Lyotard"—recalling the theme of "be just" and then followed by the allusion: "This scene of reading seemed to concern itself around an insular story. [Cette scene de lecture semblait s'affairer autour d'un recit insulaire.]"[27] The island in question may be *Before the Law* considered in isolation from the rest of Kafka's work, but it might also refer to Kafka's island story *In the Penal Colony.* Here the encounter of individual, law and guilt is purely accidental, and issues in an accident, one that happened during the inscription of the law transgressed by the technician of the Apparat, namely "be just."

Notes

1. Aage A. Hansen-Love, *Vor dem Gesetz,* in *Franz Kafka: Romane und Erzählungen,* ed. Michael Muller (Stuttgart, Reclam: 2003), 146.
2. Jacques Derrida, "Prejuges: Devant la Loi," in Jacques Derrida et al., *La faculté de juger,* (Paris: Les editions de minuit, 1985), 87–139.
3. A transcript of these lectures is available in Derrida's archive at UC Irvine in Box 15 Folder 9.
4. Jacques Derrida, "Before the Law," in *Jacques Derrida: Acts of Literature,* ed. Derek Attridge (London: Routledge, 1992), 184.
5. Ibid., 190.
6. Ibid.
7. The mobilization of the grail narratives and the citation of Roger Dragonetti's work *La vie de la letttre au Moyen Age (le conte du Graal)* in the second and third versions, while ostensibly contributing to an argument for multiple authorship, also sets the key for reading Kafka's text as a quest narrative, with the law serving as the grail.
8. Derrida, "Before the Law," 190.

9. Ibid., 191.
10. Ibid., 185.
11. "This was before Kafka wrote *Vor dem Gesetz* (1919)." (Ibid.,192.)
12. For an analysis of *A Country Doctor* see my "Kafka's Exit: Exile, Exodus and Messianism" in *Aesthetics and the Work of Art*, eds. Peter de Bolla and Stefan H. Uhlig (Basingstoke: Palgrave Macmillan, 2008).
13. Derrida, "Before the Law," 213.
14. Ibid.
15. Ibid.
16. Ibid.
17. Ibid.
18. Ibid., 214.
19. "(author, publisher, critics, academics, archivists, librarians, lawyers and so on)." (Ibid.)
20. Ibid., 215.
21. Ibid., 217.
22. Ibid.
23. I am indebted to Hartmut Binder's *"Vor Dem Gesetz": Einführung in* Kafkas *Welt* (Stuttgart-Weimar: Verlag J.B. Metzler, 1993), for some of the details of its publishing history.
24. *Selbstwehr: Unabhängige judische Wochenschrift*, 9th year, n.37 (7 September 1915). For analyses of the cultural and political location of *Selbstwehr* and the nature of its Zionism see Hartmut Binder, "Franz Kafka and the Zionist weekly *Selbstwehr" Leo Baeck Institute Yearbook* 12 (1967): 135–48; and Scott Spector, *Prague Territories National Conflict and Cultural Innovation in Franz Kafka's Fin de Siecle* (Berkeley: University of California Press, 2000),160–168.
25. See Reiner Stach, *Kafka: The Decisive Years*, trans. Shelley Frisch (Orlando Harcourt Inc, 2005), ch. 33 "The Return of the East," 484–492: "In late 1914 *Selbstwehr* carried a statement by the Relief Action Committee of the Jewish that said, 'we implore everyone with human compassion to help.' But by the time just half of the needed donations had been collected, the number of newcomers had doubled again, and the community had no choice but to report to the Bohemian governor that their funds were depleted. On January 18, 1915, a decree from the ministry of the interior closed the city to refugees.'"
26. Derrida, "Prejuges," 134.
27. Ibid., 135.

PART II
RECONCEPTUALIZATIONS OF KAFKA'S CAGES

Chapter Four

Kafka's Cage

John Mowitt

Silence is all of the sound we don't intend. There is no such thing as absolute silence. Therefore, silence may very well include loud sounds and more and more in the twentieth century does. The sound of jet planes, of sirens, et cetera. For instance now, if we heard sounds coming from the house next door, and we weren't saying anything for the moment, we would say that was part of the silence, wouldn't we?... But I think electronics now are essential and I think this is what makes rock and roll so interesting.[1]

As the preceding epigraph makes plain, the Cage of my title is John Cage, the US composer, mycologist, and unintentional, certainly reluctant, aesthetician who died in 1992. Although previously linked to Kafka by Deleuze and Guattari,[2] this odd pairing calls for more than the passing attention they direct to it, and this despite the fact that the problem of how to enter the burrow (*der Bau*) of Kafka's work explicitly concerns them. What justifies this attention is the way the silence that defines the relation between these two monsters of the twentieth century (to my knowledge despite Cage's interest in Kierkegaard, he had nothing to say of Kafka who, as is well known, was an attentive reader of Kierkegaard), the way this silence can be heard to address heated questions that bear on the sociology of culture in general and the status of music within critical or "new" musicology in particular. At issue is less the matter of "expression" (dear to Deleuze and Guattari) and more what here will be referred to as "inscription," that is, the process through which music—both as a musicological construct, and as a performance practice—can be said to belong to its moment, to its time and place. Because much of what passes for "new" under the new musicological sun bears precisely on this process—the contention, variously stated, that the extramusical influences the properly musical (and vice versa)—the amplification of Kafka's Cage promises to agitate these turbulent waters. Moreover, because the legacy of Adorno looms large over these distinctly disciplinary depths, due in part to the way his "negative dialectics" reconceived inscription so as to include the cultural negation of society within this process, his construal of music as both concept and practice deserves to be put in play. And this despite the fact that he appears to have been silent about what will serve as the textual matrix of these remarks, Kafka's parable, "*Das Schweigen der Sirenen*" [the silence of the sirens].[3]

What is here referred to as amplifying Kafka's Cage encounters numerous obstacles, some of which demand preliminary comment. I will restrict myself to three: influence, music, and method.

With regard to the first, how precisely are we to understand the influence that Kafka had upon Cage given that the latter appears to have been unaware—except in the most general, "culturally literate" sense—of the former? Or, to make things interesting, how might we make sense of the way in which Cage may have influenced Kafka, a writer who died when Cage was 12 years old? Such questions beg one to recognize that influence and inscription share a family resemblance. Specifically, the former might be said to derive from, or otherwise depend upon the latter, in that if one holds that cultural artifacts are decisively inscribed in a temporal sequence, a historical chronology, then the matter of influence becomes a question of knowledge: given that x preceded y, is there evidence that x mattered to y? Sooner or later, the question of knowledge comes to be dominated by the authority of priority, what in an earlier theoretical vocabulary was summarily dispatched in the word "origin." Missed in this temporal reduction of inscription is precisely the conflicted intricacies of space, the various locations—both subjective and geographic—from within which chronology is not simply lived, but contested. Revolutions generate new calendars seeking to unfold in their own time.

Here it seems crucial to invoke the epistemological scandal of what Freud called *Nachträglichkeit* [afterwardness]. Perhaps influence occurs unconsciously, not simply in the sense of happening involuntarily, but in the sense of happening "belatedly," that is, after the fact, where "fact" refers to a temporal prior that only assumes its priority in the remote wake of its passing. In effect, from another scene. While one might exemplify what happens to influence under such circumstances by appealing to Foucault's concept of discourse, where a "frame of intelligibility" can be said to condition any number of otherwise unrelated enunciative possibilities, more fecund is the recognition of what Althusser called "structural causality" behind Lacan's oft-repeated contention that Freud *anticipated* Saussurean linguistics. Key here is not simply the way "structural causality," as an elaboration and refinement of the Freudian concept of "over-determination," obviously derives from the contact, at once personal and professional, between Lacan and Althusser, but the way Althusser's concept urges us to stay focused on the problem of inscription, a focus perhaps first urged upon us by Frederic Jameson in the methodological introduction to *The Political Unconscious*. What "structural causality" definitively complicates is the concept of reflection, that is, the model of spatial inscription that grasps it as an extension of *mimesis*, wherein the molecular structure of realism—the thing and its representation—becomes *mutatis mutandis* the means by which to think the relation between society and culture. Under such constraints even modernism, often set opposite realism (especially by Jameson), becomes a realism, in effect the theoretical centerpiece of Georg Lukács' still resonant reading of Kafka in "Franz Kafka or Thomas Mann" from 1956. Against this, "structural causality" does not simply invert the priority of the thing and its representation, society and culture, but rather it underscores the spatiotemporal intricacy of cause and its many avatars, notably of course, determination when used to describe the relation between society and culture, especially when projected onto the orthodox architecture of the *Bau* and the *Uberbau*, base, and superstructure. What Althusser understood is that the intricacy of cause at the level of consciousness, that is, at the level of the subjects of history, is what Lacan had properly formulated through the concept of the unconscious-structured-like-a-language. This is precisely why Lacan could write to Althusser while reading "On the Materialist Dialectic" from the summer of 1963: "Your article—I'm reading it. It fascinates me, and I discover my questions in it."[4] Not only might this be thought to confirm a fragment of intellectual history, but it bears testimony to the very question of "influence" as it arose within the event of their friendship. "I discover my questions in it."

Again, what stands out here is the complication of causality, not just what in certain circles goes by the term, "presentism," that is, the somewhat diffused critique of historicism that insists that we, in the present, can never know the past on its own terms. Rather, at the core of this complication stands something of a "black box," that is, the site of what is at bottom a relation by which, put in historical terms, the first and the last lose their ordinal simplicity. Indeed, relation is the not so secret passageway that allows influence and inscription to communicate. In that spirit, influence will be deployed here as the means by which to entertain the notion that Kafka thought Cage's silence for him, but only once Cage had, in effect, returned the gesture. By referring to the silence that defines the relation between these two men, I hope both to say something within and about silence while rendering immediately pertinent the procedure, undertaken here, of their pairing.

Music. Perhaps the most obvious place to turn for Kafka's final word about music is *"Josephine die Sängerin oder das Volk der Mäuse"* [Josephine the singer, or the mouse folk], a tale recently bent by Mladen Dolar to the task of salvaging the postdeconstructive voice. As its title signals immediately, through the ambiguously conjunctive "*oder*" [or], the tale relentlessly complicates what is to be understood by singing. Is it really piping (*pfeifen*)? Whistling? A relation? In what is certainly the most sustained consideration of the strictly musical implications of this tale, John Hargraves is quick to point precisely to this difficulty as it is contained in the term, *pfeifen* [piping], which is strictly antithetical in the Freudian sense, that is, it can mean both performing and booing.[5] Under these circumstances, the question of what precisely counts as music is likewise thrown into radical doubt, not in the sense of whether it can be made the object of a judgment of taste, but in the sense of whether we can formulate the frame of intelligibility within which its ontological character can be specified. Kafka's tale seems preoccupied with achieving precisely this effect. Responding to a biographical impulse, Hargraves explores this difficulty in the wake of the well-known diary entries where Kafka proclaims, at one and the same time, his "unmusicality" and his belief that music can only be understood by the "unmusical," proposing that music for Kafka thus becomes a metaphor for a "latent metaphysical force at work behind the foreground of human existence."[6] This claim is what motivates Hargraves's titular appeal to silence, an appeal that, in the end, he does very little with except to provide musical expression with a rather familiar depth, one whose precise contours are defined by no fewer than four disciplines: philosophy (metaphysical force), linguistics (metaphor), art history (foreground), and psychoanalysis (latency). All the same, Hargraves succeeds in attuning our ears to the problem of the unmusical in Kafka, urging us to recognize that music is precisely at stake when it does not otherwise appear to be in question. Thus, instead of bemoaning the fact that, compared to Broch and Mann, Kafka offers "infrequent instances of examples of music" one needs to craft a reading of Kafka that responds to the call of the unmusical, to the resonant deficiency of music.[7]

Method. In his much read review of Max Brod's study of Kafka, Walter Benjamin with a cruel precision honed by desperation, detailed the costly paradoxes of Brod's reading, perhaps most memorably accusing his text of displaying "a fundamental contradiction between the author's thesis and his attitude."[8] Here, as Réda Bensmaïa has argued, Benjamin berates Brod for an error we too risk, namely that of, as Benjamin had earlier put it, "missing the point of Kafka's works."[9] Not simply a misreading, but a betrayal. After establishing that Brod's misinterpretation is animated by a variant of Pietism, Benjamin insists that the pious misinterpretation is one that either systematically avoids the irksome distractions of psychoanalysis and dialectical theology, or succumbs to them without resistance. Alas, the promise held out by such an observation—that of properly engaging psychoanalysis and dialectical theology and thus getting Kafka right—is not fulfilled in Benjamin's own commemorative essay on Kafka, an outcome summarized and distilled in Adorno's bitter methodological precaution: "Each sentence says, 'interpret me,' and none will permit it."[10] And although Adorno in his "Notes on Kafka" goes to some length to establish the startling solidarity between Kafka and Freud (both recognize the Ego as a "mere organizational principle"), his doubts regarding the hermeneutics of dialectical theology are unequivocally stated.[11] Through such a method, and here Adorno offers his assessment of the failure of his friend's essay, Benjamin succumbs to myth, even if knowingly. While this might suggest that Adorno's reading lands comfortably on the side of psychoanalysis, it does not. Aware that it is precisely Kafka's "literalness" that pushes him out ahead of Freud, Adorno urges that Kafka be read as an allegorist (here reviving one of Benjamin's signature constructs), not of the sort to be found in Goethe, but rather as one who recognizes that the literal and the figural are, as it were, worlds apart. In this Adorno prepares to align himself with the very "textualism" now widely held to have superseded him.

Does this then bring one to a true *aporia* (impasse) in methodological reflection on the challenges posed by Kafka's texts? Can we truly navigate the channel between the Scylla (who strikes from above) of theology (whether dialectical or not), and the Charybdis (who sucks from below) of psychoanalysis, especially without benefit of Circe's fateful counsel? Adorno's recasting of this channel as the space of secular allegory contains a suggestive appendix. For him, Kafka's relation to Freud is realized not only in his radicalization, his literalization of the critique of the Ego, but also, and more importantly, in their shared struggle to snatch "psychoanalysis from the grasp of psychology."[12] Precisely because Adorno associates this gesture with the Kafkaesque impulse to push beyond metaphor to flesh, in effect, to reaffirm the so-called seduction theory, it would appear that the space of secular allegory, that of letter and spirit, is understood to be active within and along the disciplinary "zone" (as Adorno names it) between psychoanalysis and psychology. Decisive here is the rather unsettling notion that Kafka's texts operate to scramble disciplinary frontiers, that they deploy what Derrida once called, the "law of genre," not merely within the field of the literary—are his texts "novels," "stories" or even "meditations"?— but on or against all that the literary fronts upon. Including, of course, music. Which, as if buffeted by Poseidon's *ressentiment*, sends us back to the question of how to read for the musical, or to up the ante, the musicological in Kafka's texts? The preceding discussion of Hargraves's analysis has already indicated the heading of such a reading, but without yet clarifying the matter to which we have returned, that of inscription.

If "*Das Schweigen der Sirenen*" is the appropriate text upon which to focus such a reading this is in no small part due to the decisive role played by Book 12 of *The Odyssey* in Adorno's thinking about Enlightenment culture in general and music in particular. The reading of the Sirens episode occurs in the first chapter of *Dialectic of Enlightenment*,[13] setting the stage for the more extended treatment of *The Odyssey*[14] in Chapter Two, a treatment wherein "enchantment" (*Verzauberung*) emerges as the term shared by and thus (con)fusing myth and enlightenment. Forgive me if I do not rehash this well-known discussion, choosing instead to foreground two elements: the motif of inscription and that of music. With regard to the first recall that Adorno and Horkheimer concentrate our attention on the dialectical interplay between Ulysses and the crew. Each follows one of two escape routes: Ulysses fetters himself in order to open his ears; the crew seals its ears shut in order to work. Taken together, the two escapes map the contradictions of class society wherein domination becomes, both within and between subjects, the precondition for aesthetic experience, the lived encounter with the sonic beauty of the Siren's song. As Adorno and Horkheimer are keen to stress, the point is not that one class has access to the beautiful while the other does not, but that both classes engage aesthetic enjoyment as a compensation for the constraints imposed upon them by the social order they inhabit. The nature and scale of these constraints are certainly different—although Adorno and Horkheimer have been charged with abandoning "class analysis"—but key is the proposition that the dialectical tension between art and society arises from yet overarches the social division of class. Thus, art bears the inscription of the social order in its essentially compromised isolation from it, an account of inscription that takes reflection theory to its very limit in proposing that art reflects society in refusing to reflect it. How one thinks "cause" here is obviously a vexed issue and its stands at the heart of what Adorno sought to articulate as a "negative" dialectic.

The Homeric episode centers on song and in that sense would appear to sound the motif of music blatantly. Clearly though, the ease with which Adorno and Horkheimer pass from a discussion of singing to art in general suggests that music is the means by which to think the modern incarnation of the contradiction between art and society, in general. My colleague Richard Leppert, across the pages of *Essays on Music*, has made it difficult, if not impossible to ignore such a claim.[15] Be that as it may, the specifically musical character of the episode, when conceived in the broad framework of aesthetics, effectively leaps out in Adorno's words, written half a decade before the exilic collaboration with Horkheimer: "Complaints about the decline of musical taste begin only a little later than mankind's twofold discovery, on the threshold of historical time, that music represents at once the immediate manifestation of impulse and the locus of its taming."[16] This, the opening sentence of Adorno's blistering reply to Benjamin's "The Work of Art in the Age of its Technological Reproducibility,"[17] segues within the space of a few pages to Book 3 of *The Republic* where Socrates recommends banning soft and excessively sorrowful musical modes from his state, a gesture suggesting that "the threshold of historical time," is precisely the abyss thought by Adorno and Horkheimer to conjoin the mythic past and the enlightened future. Moreover, the dialectical interplay between the manifestation and taming of impulse is what the two men find, in effect, allegorized in the Sirens episode. In this sense, the episode is centrally about music and its fate. But this should make us all the more attentive to the locus of silence in the episode. It resides in the experience of the crew, an experience found at the opposite end of the apian chain from the "honey sweet" voice of the Sirens, that is, in the "sweet wax of honey" shutting the holes in their heads to this voice. Although the point escapes the authors of *Dialectic*, it would appear that Homer seeks here, at the very core of a telling on/off binary (open/close; hear/not hear; succumb/survive etc.), to locate the dialectical interplay of beauty and domination but now staged as the relation between humans and animals. No wonder the bees are abandoning us. Silence then, to use a term put in play by Adorno and Horkheimer, is "entwined" with music, not sound, but music as the locus of the manifestation and taming, the domesticating, of impulse, a taming here understood in the Nietzschean sense of the "breeding" fundamental to the very production of the human itself. But how precisely is one to think the "entwinement" of music and silence? Is this a matter of appreciating, at the level of musical notation, the function of the rest, or, at the level of jazz performance the function of "sitting out?" Is silence simply a matter of not playing?

The disciplinary reflections with which my preliminary remarks concluded invite additional questions. Is entwinement, perhaps, another avatar of the "zone" between psychoanalysis and psychology, or between philosophy and nonphilosophy, say musicology? Is silence a name for and thus a means by which to think what acts within this zone without succumbing to its topographic protocols? By linking silence and the unintentional, Cage points us precisely in this direction, for intention might well be read as the *Forschungstrieb* [research drive] (as Freud would put it) of a discipline. And, it is surely not by accident that the thinker of disciplinary reason, Michel Foucault, when in *The Hermeneutics of the Subject* lectures he comments upon the Sirens episode in *The Odyssey*, zeroes in on the acutely pedagogical significance of outmaneuvering the passivity of listening.[18] In any case, a version of this disciplinary puzzle is one of the many disturbing challenges put before us by Kafka's parable, *"Das Schweigen der Sirenen."*

Pending whatever transformation of the Brod organized Kafka canon results from combing the remains found in the late Esther Hoffe's apartment, "*Das Schweigen*" is preceded in the *Gesammelte Schriften* (vol. 5) by what would qualify as an "allegory of reading." Literally two entries before appears "*Von den Gleichnissen*"[on parables] in which Kafka, certainly in Brod's mind, provides something like a key for the sketches, aphorisms, and parables that surround it. Adorno cites, in support of his appeal to the enabling concept of allegory, Benjamin's discussion of parable in "Franz Kafka," reminding us that, like Scylla and Charybdis, this metacritical mouthful stands like an ordeal, a test, on the way into one's reading of Kafka.[19] Although the closing line, quoting the first of two interlocutors, "*Nein, in Wirklichkeit; im Gleichnis hast du verloren*" [no in reality, in parable you have lost], would appear to support Adorno's championing of "literalness" (parsing *Wirklichkeit* as actuality or reality), the more striking feature of the parable is the way it revisits the philosopheme, deployed repeatedly within the West from Plato to Heidegger, of "uselessness." Consider, for example, the way the parable on parables takes up the theme of "use." "*Viele beklagen sich, dass dei Worte der Weisen immer wieder nur Gleichnisse seien aber unverwendbar im täglichen Leben, und nur dieses allein haben wir*" [many complain that the words of the wise are always merely parables and of no use in daily life, and this is the only life we have]. Kafka's insistence that daily life is the only one we have later effects a collapse between the unusable—the transcendental hallmark of philosophy—and parables as such. Not only do philosophy and parables share the quality of lacking use, but Kafka's repudiation of an actuality outside or above daily life suggests that philosophy uses its expository recourse to parable to blur the ordinary, lived distinction between uselessness and the rule of the wise. The parable stands thus revealed as the alibi of philosophic domination. Kafka, as the consummate gadfly, asserts that if we really wanted to go where philosophers are pointing, to the "*sagenhaftes Drüben*" [fabulous beyond] we would have already left. Clearly we don't. But what kind of "key" is one that stresses—in a paradoxically philosophical register—its lack of utility? Strictly speaking, it is an inadequate key, as we shall see.

Surviving then the ordeal of the test of "*Von den Gleichnissen*," one passes to the Sirens, counseled to read the parable—qua parable—not simply as an alibi, but as a site wherein a certain disciplinary friction produces the available light, that is, as a site within which the questions, "is there (not what is, but is there) philosophy?" and, "is it about domination?" are insistently posed. As intimated above, the fact that silence arises here will prove instructive, and the task of figuring out how to "read" the already read, will prove essential to receiving these instructions.

"Beweis dessen, das auch unzulängliche, ja kindische Mittel zur Rettung dienen können" [proof that inadequate, even childish methods, can save us].[20] Thus begins the parable. It reads, oddly, as something of a *quod erat demonstrandum*, a conclusion, as if the whole parable is an example of philosophy in reverse, perhaps even capsized. What is demonstrated? That inadequate, even childish methods (*kindische Mittel*) can save us (Kafka uses here the German *Rettung* which has the strong theological resonance of salvation, not simply rescue). His stress on the "*unzulängliche*" [inadequate] would suggest that here too he wishes to agitate the matter of the uselessness of philosophy by pressuring the relation between Ulysses and what Plato in Book Six of *The Republic* called the "true pilot." What brings this into contact with the figure of the child, or the quality of childishness, appears to be the Schillerean notion of *die Naïve* [the naïve, as opposed to the sentimental] that is, the fact that in heading out to confront the Sirens Ulysses deploys a variant of the purely infantile fantasy: if I close my eyes, and I can't see the other, the other can't see me, or, restated in the proper sensory register, if I plug the ears of my crew, then I will be able to hear what I am not to hear, giving no sign—in the extreme case, shipwreck—that I am indeed hearing what I am not to hear. To clarify in what sense this method is "inadequate" requires that the arc of the parable be sketched in.

It is comprised of six paragraphs followed by an "appendix" (*ein Anhang*). In the first, Kafka reconstructs Ulysses's preparation for the encounter with the Sirens. Taking extreme, even ridiculous precaution he both plugs his ears *and* binds himself to the mast. As if to draw out the vital symmetry between Circe (who is never mentioned) and the Sirens, the paragraph introduces a preemptive aural complication in the encounter through the figure of hearsay. Which is more risky, hearsay or singing? In stressing Ulysses' "*unshuldiger Freude über seine Mittelchen*" [innocent joy over his little stratagem],[21] Kafka places the child of the founding premise/conclusion at the helm. The first paragraph concludes with what will turn out to be an avatar of the lexical and conceptual driver of the parable, the slippery preposition "*entgegen*" [toward, out to].

The second paragraph, in justifying the title assigned to the parable, opens with perhaps the most brilliant "oh shit" line in the European canon: "Nun haben aber die Sirenen eine noch schrecklichere Waffe als den Gesang, nämlich ihr Schweigen" [now the Sirens have still a more fearsome weapon than their singing, namely, their silence].[22] Immediately, we sense that Ulysses is ill prepared, that, in effect he has been betrayed by everyone, by Circe who thus becomes a *femme fatale*, all those who might have counseled him and, of course, he is betrayed by his own naïve self-confidence. We also vividly see, and this is an issue agitated to great effect in Blanchot's reading of the episode (about whom more later), that this is not Homer's Ulysses.[23] As if to stress this the paragraph contrasts the respective dangers of singing and silence from the vantage point of a future wherein reports of Ulysses' exploits have become legend. Some may have survived the Siren's song, but no one or nothing "*irdisches*" (earthly) can endure their silence. Crucial here is the insistence throughout on "*ihr Schweigen*," not silence, in general (whatever that might be) but the silence of the Sirens, that is, the silence that takes the place of a singing too beautiful to endure.

The third paragraph presents the scenario of the failed encounter. It unfolds as if the Sirens intended to sing, but don't. Their silence comes not as the decisive well-aimed blow, but mysteriously. Do they recognize and respond to his tactic of sensory deprivation (with ears plugged he could hear neither their silence nor their song), or does his "*Anblick der Glückseligkeit*" [look of bliss] so stun them that they forget to sing? Either way, the third paragraph casts silence as reactive, stripped of unambiguous intentions.

The fourth paragraph extends the "preemptive complication" of the first down into the sonic enigma of silence itself. "Odysseus aber, um es so auszudrücken, hörte ihr Schweigen nicht, er glaubte, sie sängen, und nur er sei behütet, es zu hören" [but Ulysses, if it can be so expressed, did not hear their silence, he believed they were singing and only he did not hear them].[24] Crucial here is the entwining of the perception of a singing that *is* silence, an event so singular as to cast doubt on its communicability, and the metalinguistic gesture of, "if it can be so expressed," where the "use" (or "uselessness") of parabolic expression arises as the means by which to point at the limits, not simply of a certain code (in this case German), but of a frame of intelligibility within which hearing falls unthinkably *between das Schweigen* and *den Arien*, the arias echoing in the mere gestures of singing. As if to sear this predicament into an image, the paragraph concludes with Ulysses sailing out of range of the Sirens, his eyes fixed on a distance set opposite their singing faces (the implication being that the Sirens were lip synching to a tape that malfunctioned), a distance nearer to the danger they represented than he could grasp.

The fifth paragraph exploits the structure of what Lacan would call extimacy to effect a pivot, a conceptual whirlpool. Now it is Ulysses who plays the siren. He does not, of course, sing. Instead he looks resolutely ahead. The Sirens, who have already forgotten to sing, now forget everything and seek only to fall within his gaze, Ulysses' Gaze (*pace* Theo Angelopoulos). They seek what Kafka calls his "*Abglanz*," the light reflecting from his two great eyes. Crucial here is the sensory *agon* of the eyes and the ears especially as it might herald an encounter between two frames of intelligibility.

The sixth paragraph is only two sentences. In this paragraph, Kafka propounds a theory of consciousness, suggesting that had the Sirens possessed consciousness, the pivot wherein they fell within the gaze of the other would have destroyed them. Needless to say, the temptation of a psychoanalytic reading, indeed a Lacanian one at that, is nearly irresistible. To succumb to it, however, is not only to restore the seductive (the *verführerisch*, the misleading) invulnerability of the Sirens in hermeneutic guise, but it is to fill in the very figure of the channel between dialectical theology and psychoanalysis we are struggling to chart. As if to remind us of this, the second sentence is utterly perfunctory, Adorno would say, "literal": "So aber blieben sie, nur Odysseus ist ihnen entgangen" [so they remained as they had been, all that happened is that Ulysses escaped them].[25] Thus, read philologically the paragraphs prior to the appendix tack from *entgegen* to *entgangen* [escaped] from set out to meet to elude, toward and away.

The appendix moves, as if to gut everything, to restore the *metis* of Ulysses by suggesting that even his blissful face was nothing but a knowing way, a bluff. He thus reduces the gods to poker players with weak hands. At the same time, Kafka here restates the "uselessness" of the parable noting, in the tone of an afterthought, that "Es wird übrigens noch ein Anhang hierzu überliefert" [an appendix to the foregoing has also been handed down].[26] In effect, oh, and by the way, we also already know that it might have been otherwise. This *too* is part of the myth. As if to underscore the way this laces and relaces back through all that has proceeded, the last word of the paragraph and of the parable is "*entgegengehalten*," a term used to characterize the cunning use of Ulysses' shield to counter or oppose the Sirens and the gods, but one which, in the context of the parable (functioning if not like a rhyme-word, then certainly a thought-word) appears almost anagrammatic, as a collection of letters in which "*entgegen*" and "*entgangen*" are, as it were, "*gehalten*" or contained, caged.

If we right the parable, the Q.E.D. would follow here. Thus, in the foregoing sequence of major and minor premises, we learn that inadequate or childish techniques can save us; that Ulysses saved himself; therefore Ulysses probably used childish techniques. But what precisely were they? In the course of the six paragraphs and appendix, these techniques flicker by as if repeating the enigmatic exchange that concludes, "*Von den Gleichnissen*": parables can make parables of those who use them; isn't that a parable?; you're right; yes, but only in parable; no, in reality you are right, in parable you are wrong. A version of the Cretan's paradox. The Kafkan/Homeric paradox might be phrased: a child would prepare for battle only to misjudge the adversary; realizing this, the adversary would assume this to be a bluff and avoid drawing attention to the misjudgment hoping to exploit it later; baffled, the child would ignore and thereby eliminate the tactical difference between judgment and misjudgment (the weapons of song and silence) and simply proceed with belligerent confidence; likewise baffled, the adversary would misjudge the sign of confidence as a presentiment of victory and capitulate to the invincible child; after coming to terms, the child reveals itself to be the master of bluffing, capable, in effect, of making total adequacy look and sound exactly like utter inadequacy. Stated thus, the parable scuttles itself, showing that—if inadequacy and adequacy are indistinguishable—then inadequate means can indeed save us, in fact, we are always already saved. No sweat.[27]

Crucial here is the motor of the paradox, that is, the circumstance under which the inadequate and the adequate become the same without thereby being identical. Given the subject matter of the parable perhaps the decisive presentation of this structure occurs when Ulysses "hears" (his ears are plugged) the silence *as* song. This is a situation that conforms literally to what earlier I referred to as the "entwinement" of silence and music, indeed, I would suggest that the entire parable is designed to pose this problem and to invite speculation about it. This is why Kafka rewords Homer in precisely the way he does, displacing the Homeric locus of silence—namely the crew (there is no mention of them in *"Das Schweigen"*)—thereby resituating the conflict between freedom and necessity *within* the child and therefore between the child and the adversary. Moreover, if I have insisted upon the anagrammatic status of the last word, *"entgegengehalten,"* this is because the language of the parable is bound up in the problem it poses. The going toward, *entgegen*, and the going past, *entgangen*, are subsumed within the going nowhere, the counter or parry of the shield, *entgegengehalten*. This is not an evocation of fixity, but of a disquieting negativity, of a constitutive instability, as if the appendix in metabolizing the coming and the going hopes to draw attention to the nonrelation at the heart of relation, at the core of encounter. This would appear to be a radicalization of the Lacanian dictum—there is no sexual relation—one that in emphasizing the several and repeated ways that Ulysses and the Sirens, the child and the adversary, anticipate and misread one another critiques relation in general. Indeed, this critique of relation finds expression in the language of the parable, a circumstance perhaps predicted in the very name, Sirens, which derives from the Greek *seira*, or cord, binding, at once evoking the grip of their song, the physics of enthrallment, but at the same time evoking the strategy deployed by Ulysses to resist their power. Whether speaking of binding or entwinement, the parable frets beatifically over the relation that holds through release.

Marcel Detienne and Jean-Pierre Vernant add an important wrinkle here by reminding us that precisely to the extent that *metis*, the virtue or skill Ulysses was thought to embody, involved being able to slip through the fingers, the grasp, of one's adversary by turning its strength against it, not only does *metis* speak directly to the relation, the grasp that cannot hold, but it places a contest over types of knowledge at the core of Ulysses's encounter with the Sirens.[28] Of course, this is what Adorno and Horkheimer seek to emphasize in trying to situate the origin of philosophy in the abysmal shift from myth to enlightenment. But what Detienne and Vernant stress is that the contest over knowledge is itself subject to the wiles of *metis*, and that this must be kept in mind when thinking about Kafka's attention to the silent song. Again, what is accented in the parable is the silence of the Sirens, that is, *their* silence, as if what is crucial is precisely the contest of knowledges, the expectations simultaneously solicited and refused. Precisely because the Sirens' song is "known" to be fatal, Ulysses prepares for it. In attempting to outfox the fox, or, as Kafka posits, in being stunned by the inadequate preparation of the foxiest fox, the Sirens counter with an even more lethal weapon, one thought to fall outside the frame of intelligibility within which Ulysses's opening gambit was planned. And so on. The point is that the entwinement of silence and song puts in play divisions of knowledge that can be grasped (indeed?) as predisciplinary articulations of disciplinary reason, as if the parable through its fraught relation to philosophy, insists that such issues demand the reader's attention.

The question—what is silence, and how would we know?—is a question John Cage sought to answer in the early fifties. This is how he tells it:

> There is always something to see, something to hear. In fact, try as we may to make a silence, we cannot. For certain engineering purposes, it is desirable to have as silent a situation as possible. Such a room is called an anechoic chamber, its six walls made of special material, a room without echoes. I entered one at Harvard University several years ago and heard two sounds, one high and one low. When I described them to the engineer in charge, he informed me that the high one was my nervous system in operation, the low one my blood in circulation. Until I die there will be sounds. And they will continue following my death. One need not fear about the future of music.[29]

Regarded by many as the founding articulation of Cage's aesthetic theory, there is some doubt as to whether the reported event ever took place. According to Cage's biographer, David Revill, there were two anechoic chambers at Harvard, neither of which clearly matches Cage's description.[30] If one counts the hyperechoic chamber that Douglas Kahn notes was also at Harvard, then precisely where this encounter between Cage and silence took place is itself concealed in a black box. But this is as it should be. Cage sets out on a quest for silence, seeking reassurance that experimental music has a future. Instead of encountering silence, he encounters two sounds. In effect, in those two pitches what he encounters, what he hears, is the limit of his assumptions (his musicological or even acoustical knowledge) about the nature of silence, an encounter that obliges him to rethink both those assumptions and the entwinement of silence and sound. The issue here is less about the impossibility of silence faced with the embodiment of human listening, than it is about the way this missed encounter poses questions about the categories—including, less it pass unremarked, the category of the human subject—within which its possibility had been conceived. Strikingly, Cage segues abruptly from the sounds happening on either side of his death, to the "future of music." While, this is typically understood to have provided listeners, even if metaleptically, with the music for "4' 33'" (which Deleuze and Guattari find staged in "Descriptions of a Struggle"), that is, whatever ambient sounds happened while the keyboard of the piano was exposed during the four "movements" of the piece, more important here is to note the motif of "intention" sounded in the epigraph of this essay. When Cage says, as reported by Revill, "silence is not acoustic. It is a change of mind. A turning around,"[31] he is gesturing directly at the way acoustics, a particular interdisciplinary field of knowledge, gives form to our intentions such that one might go about "making" silence precisely by defeating echoes. "Turning around" here does not presumably mean changing direction or rotating one's head. It means troping, it means changing the way knowledge informs our intentions. It means catastrophe. That Cage was motivated by Robert Rauschenberg's blank canvasses, his "mirrors of the air," would strongly suggest that both men understood clearly the challenge they were posing to the frame of intelligibility within which either painting or music had been understood.

It is especially telling that in light of this, as my epigraph has it, Cage heard sirens in the silent field of the unintended. What this underscores, aside from an intriguing etymological genealogy, is that what Kafka grasped, and Cage takes from him—a relay that took place, as I have noted, in silence—is that silence is less "entwined" with song, or music, than it names, however inadequately, what escapes in or as the nonrelation, the channel, *between* sound and what no longer is even its opposite. This is what Derrida appears to have been driving at when he titled a decisive chapter of *Speech and Phenomenon*, "The Voice that Keeps Silent," a text that was always more about philosophical ideology than it was about the faculty of speaking.

Let me then approach the musicological aspect of *Dialectic of Enlightenment* from a different angle. Signposting this approach are two essays of Jean-François Lyotard from the early 1970s—"Adorno as the Devil" (*diavolo* in the original, as if to emphasize the Italian cover for his

Jewish, Wiesengrund, identity), and "Several Silences"—both pieces that, as the second title suggests plainly, engage the work of John Cage. Both were written during the period of Lyotard's career where he, like so many others, was concerned to weigh in on the encounter between Marx and Freud. *Libidinal Economy* where, in his chapter on "the tensor," he provides his own reading of Ulysses, dates from this period. However, unlike many of his compatriots concerned with this encounter, Lyotard was distinctive in paying keen attention to its German articulation. It thus comes as no surprise that as he moved to articulate its aesthetic implications, he found himself face to face with Adorno. In "Adorno as the Devil" and "Several Silences," this face-off occurs in and around the musicological inflection of Adorno's aesthetic theory.[32] The argument unfolds a bit differently in each case and since the evaluation of Cage's significance changes accordingly, my comments will proceed *in seriatum*.

"Adorno as the Devil" asks to be read as a theoretical and political challenge to the evaluative distinction drawn by Adorno between Stravinsky and Schönberg in *The Philosophy of New Music*. Lyotard's point is not to reverse this evaluation—to delineate what might be either salvaged or championed in Stravinsky's "poetics of music"—but to challenge the musicological implications of the terms deployed to advance it. At issue, simply put, is the critical force of *Kritische Theorie* [capitalized to evoke "critical theory" as a school or tendency] a matter, given the enormous import Adorno now has for the "new musicology," of considerable note. As the title implies, Lyotard seeks to establish the ultimately theological character of Adorno's position, showing that his investment in the redemptive power of the negative obliges Adorno, not to ally himself with the devil (Lyotard regards this as the failure of Mann's presentation of the matter in *Doktor Faustus*), but to fulfill the satanic function in a struggle over meaning that is fundamentally Judeo-Christian in character. Sounding a theme then making its rounds on the Parisian scene, Lyotard worries over the capacity of philosophy to think negativity outside the box of the socio-discursive conditions of philosophy, including—perhaps especially including—a philosophy impatient with merely interpreting the world as opposed to changing it. Crucial here is *Kritische Theorie*'s account of the subject, an account hampered by an all too reasoned assessment of the significance of Freud. Stated within the concerns of *The Philosophy of New Music* this now somewhat dated line of criticism takes the form of showing that Schönberg's dodecaphonic serialism is, at best, the sonic articulation of the satanic function, and thus precisely the spectral lure for Adorno's musicology. Schönberg as siren.

Cage becomes urgently relevant because through him Lyotard shows what Adorno misses by posing the problem in terms of an opposition between Stravinsky and Schönberg and the social tendencies their compositions are said to "represent." The issue is not whose music is more or less progressive, but what is understood by *music* and who controls this? Lyotard is aware that Adorno recognizes that progressivism cannot be adjudicated without *some* account of musical substance, but for Lyotard Cage represents a more fecund probing of the theoretical and political matters at stake. Because of its obvious connection with the unintentional, and therefore a distinctly post-Freudian subject, Lyotard places strong emphasis on Cage's embrace of the aleatory, even going so far as to organize the form of his own exposition as if dictated by procedures derived from the *I Ching*. This gesture underscores what Lyotard perceives as the practical continuities between composing the new music and theorizing within range of music so composed. While this heightens attention to the musicological problematic, Lyotard seems content to do little more with Cage here than to posit his work as nondiabolical, as post-Judeo-Christian. Unequivocally he sides with Cage, who famously—to cite the title of his interviews with French musicologist Daniel Charles—declared himself to be "for the birds," and against himself, that is, their cages.

Doubtless this terseness is due to the fact that the year before, in "Several Silences," Lyotard had developed more thoroughly, but also more critically, what Cage brought to musicological and philosophical reflection on the nature of music. In turning explicitly to the question of silence, he writes:

> When Cage says: there is no silence, he says: no Other holds dominion over sound, there is no God, no Signifier as principle of unification of composition. There is no filtering, no set blank spaces, no exclusions: neither is there a work anymore, no more limits #1 [the element or quality deemed to be musical] to determine musicality as a region. We make music all the time, "no sooner finish one than begin making another just as people keep on washing dishes, brushing their teeth, getting sleepy and so on: noise, noise, noise. The wisest thing to do is to open one's ears immediately and hear a sound before one's thinking has a chance to turn [it] into something logical, abstract, or symbolical."[33]

Here Lyotard's impatience with the Frankfurt School's concept of the subject complicates his own embrace of psychoanalysis, by pointedly challenging the work of *L'Ecole freudienne* and Lacan's concepts of the Other and the Signifier in particular. Striking though is his alignment of Cage's concept of the silence that isn't one, with the absence of the Other, here conceived under the broad heading of the undisclosed location of the signifier, followed by a citation in which Cage stresses the urgency of listening for sounds *before* they are recognized, that is, before they come to belong to a frame of intelligibility in which they signify. As he says elsewhere in the essay, "A sound [*son*] is a noise [*bruit*] that is bound [*lié*]."[34] While one might wish to insist upon a distinction between the symbolical and the symbolic, what leaps out in Lyotard's formulation is the relation between the Other and the discourse within which sounds assume their musical character. Silence points deliberately at the before or the between of discourses charged with monitoring what Cage here calls "noise, noise, noise," and thus also at the limits of the psychoanalytical Other. In drawing attention to this aspect of Cage's thought, Lyotard thankfully spares us from the "new age" Cage, that is, the riddling sage content simply to still the mind through Zen-like paradoxes.

Nor, however, is Cage spared from criticism. Specifically, Lyotard picks up on Cage's concept of the body in the latter's account of the anechoic chamber, arguing that what he and Adorno share is a phenomenological notion of the body, "a body that composes." He goes on to argue that this body filters and binds, drawing attention if only terminologically to the fact that the body matters not in and of itself but from within a field of practices that includes a set of lived assumptions about who or what makes sounds. In this sense, music generates, as a horizon of sense, the body that enjoys sending and receiving it. Against this, Lyotard appears to invoke something like "true" silence, that is, what Cage filtered out of his anechoic experience namely, the death drive. Invoking the authority of Freud, he declares that "the death drive is never heard, it is silent."[35] However, as if to immediately parry a misreading Lyotard links the silence of the death drive with both the Paris Commune of 1871, and the student uprising of May 1968, making it obvious that two exceedingly noisy events—events, as he says, "we did not hear coming"—took place in, or perhaps as, the silence of the death drive.[36] Again, this field of associations shifts death away from mortality toward limit, or closure; away, in effect, from death to drive although not as modeled on the compulsion to repeat, but on something like the compulsion to repeat differently, to break down.

Running with the point, Lyotard moves to justify his title, "Several Silences," by proliferating silences. In in doing so he reinforces the import attached by Kafka to "their [the Sirens'] silence." Two of the most resonant are the silence of analysis (which he subdivides into the silence of the imaginary, the silence of the symbolic, and the silence of the analyst) and the silence of *Kapital* (a term left in German presumably to conflate Marx's text and its object). Ostensibly developed to radicalize Cage—wouldn't there be as many silences as there are frames of intelligibility, and in not seeing this aren't you, all protestations to the contrary notwithstanding, just being a musician?—this series of silences blatantly underscores the question of limit, of break, of closure, drawing direct attention to the deployment of silence as a way to think, a way to conceptualize what passes through the channel between say, dialectical theology and psychoanalysis, or say between philosophy and musicology, or, for that matter, between the singing the Sirens withheld and the silence Ulysses took for their singing.

Blanchot in "Ars Nova" from *The Infinite Conversation* pursues a similar line, although his touchstone is not that of silence, but that of the work and the space of its absence (a motif, by the way, put to work differently in Foucault's later treatment of madness as "the absence of work").[37] Despite this, what emerges unmistakably in the alignment of Blanchot and Lyotard is the question posed to Adorno as to whether he has risen to the actual challenge posed to musicology by the new music. Although Blanchot does not link "Ars Nova" to "The Song of the Sirens" section of *The Book to Come*,[38] a not so hidden, or hidden in plain sight, passageway allows the essays to correspond. In both texts, Blanchot places the accent on the absence of the work, although in his reading of the episode from Homer, he insists: "that enigmatic song is powerful because of its defect."[39] As if extending his hand through this passageway toward us, Blanchot invites us to see that it is precisely the concept of music generated in Horkheimer and Adorno's reading of Homer that supports his philosophy of the new music, in short, the championing of Schönberg with whom, in the interest of full disclosure, Cage briefly studied. Perhaps because Blanchot's accents fall where they do, Cage does not however come up. But the defect in the Sirens' song, a defect he formulates with a knowing glance at Kafka's parable—"The Sirens, it seems, they did indeed sing, but in an unfulfilling way,"[40] touches on their silence in a manner that Lyotard helps us to hear as "Cagey," that is, as a deft and cunning move against a certain musicological construal of the musical work. Is this not what Blanchot is gesturing toward in the opening of "Encountering the Imaginary," when he characterizes the island of the Sirens as the place where music "had itself disappeared more completely than in any other place in the world"?[41]

In silence then, something has been passed between Kafka and Cage. If music is indeed best grasped (a decisively polyvalent verb in this context) by the unmusical, by the one approaching music from the outside, and if this slippery grasp, this seizure of the nonrelation at the heart of relation, is what is expressed in the elusive silence taken for song in *"Das Schweigen,"* then what has been thought there, precisely to the extent that it rhymes conceptually with what Cage understands by the domain of the unintended, anticipates the deployment of silence in Cage's aesthetic theory. *"Das Schweigen"* is Kafka's Cage, its bottled message of musicological critique, unfolding (think here of Benjamin's contrast between the flower bud and the paper boat) on the disserted shore of a different discourse, one set adrift in the recesses of an anechoic chamber some twenty years later. Perhaps it is in this sense, if not specifically with regard to this example, that Benjamin, in his radio lecture on *Beim Bau der Chinesischen Mauer*, not only characterizes Kafka as "prophetic," but later reads "*Das Schweigen*" as prophesy, as an utterance possessed by what it cannot yet imagine, a "token of escape."[42]

But what then of inscription? At issue here is how one situates music, and it is plain that Adorno's extraordinary contribution to this intellectual task is his ability to think the specificity of music—what Lyotard calls the apparatus, "*le dispositif*," that is music[43]—while not simply connecting it to social history, but grounding its new incarnation in capitalist modernity. Crucial here is the logic of negative dialectics wherein, through the motif of negativity—and expressly the residue that survives the negation of negation—an irreducible structural instability is placed at the contact point between the apparatus of music and the social process. In his own pass over these troubled waters, Lyotard is content to make the following observation:

> To produce a surface as appearance is to produce surface as a site of inscription. But imagine that the Renaissance had not invented or re-invented appearance in painting, music, architecture, politics: that there would be no general theatricalization. Then there would have been no surface as a site of inscription, even the category of inscription would be impossible [...]. One has to think the primary processes on this side of generalized theatricalization and inscription, as connections and transformation of either influx or flux, without ever being able to decide what is active or passive in the connection. Thus, without inscriptibility and without surface.[44]

Aside from reminding us that perhaps we are asking the wrong question, that is, a question that in its very language has conceded the matter prematurely, what does this really tell us about the problem of situating art in its social or historical context? It tells us that the effort to do so has a history. It tells us that the category of inscription belongs to this history. And it tells us that appearance construed as the surface of a depth, in effect, "theatricalization," is the template put in circulation by this history. That the alternative, modeled on Freud's account of the primary processes where the agency of connectivity is undecidable hardly clarifies things, only underscores the paradoxical and ultimately feckless character of Lyotard's formulation. Doesn't the claim that the category of inscription belongs to history beg the question: what does "belong" mean in such a sentence? Or, formulated even less charitably, given that Lyotard is writing in the wake of the Renaissance in what sense doesn't the category of the "primary processes" belong to this same history? It merely locates reality in a depth that is pure surface. Put differently, while Lyotard's quarrel with Adorno over the political meaning of Schönberg is compelling on its own terms, the implications of this quarrel for the question of inscription are at best unclear.

But perhaps here the silence that falls between Cage and Kafka is instructive. If it makes sense to deploy the notion of the "black box" as a way to approach this silence, this is because the "black box" in framing the point of contact at the core of inscription simultaneously raises the problem of causation. What happens to the influx such that a certain flux results? For Adorno, and here his Marxism trumps his Hegelianism, society must cause art to repudiate it. Schönberg embodies a progressive politics because his music is determined to hate tradition properly, not just thematically, but down to the most fundamental musical parameters. But it is determined to do this. As Lucien Goldmann might say—and he and Adorno famously quarreled—Schönberg's consciousness formed within the "world view" organized by the situation of a nonorganic intellectual caught up within the forward stumbling of late modernity. In fact, however, rare is Adorno's recourse to a formulation like, "In the eyes of the Viennese composer, coming from a parochial background, the norms of a closed, semi-feudal society seemed the will of God" from his late essay on Schönberg.[45] More typical is his recourse to precisely what Engels in his remarkable 1893 letter to Franz Mehring, concedes as having been neglected in his and Marx's account of ideology, namely, "the formal side, the ways and means" by which ideological contents come about.[46] In Schönberg's case where, as Adorno insists, content consistently risked succumbing to procedure, such an emphasis might seem so immanently derived as to have been foretold. Moreover, one might legitimately argue that Max Weber in "The Rational and Social Foundations of Music," specifically through the concept of "rationalization" had already secured a rich sociological, and to that extent "causal," account of musical form, its ways and its means. So is Adorno's centrality within critical musicology due simply to the fact that he composed string quartets and that he wrote prolifically, and beautifully on music? This is necessary but not sufficient.

Even if we concede the legitimacy of critiques such as those of Lyotard or Blanchot we do run up against, perhaps even aground upon, the remainders, the as yet unassimilated aspects of Adorno's struggle with inscription. Once one folds reason, and by extension rationalization, into the dialectic of enlightenment, that is, once one situates the terms of one's own analysis within the troubled process they seek to analyze, then the explanatory force of a concept like "determination" (the hold, the grip, of the *Bau* on the *Uberbau*, society on music) is checked, not neutralized, but profoundly and intractably challenged. Is Adorno not drawing attention to the theoretical and political opportunity generated here when in the methodological section of the introduction to *Philosophy of the New*

Music, he inveighs against both reducing music to the status of an "exponent of society," and the error of "applying" philosophical concepts to either music or society? While it is clear that neither tendency thinks adequately the inscription of an unsettling negativity, it should also be noted that here Adorno is repeating the motif of wresting psychoanalysis from psychology, that is, he is drawing attention to fact that the disquiet of negativity is bound up with a conflict within disciplinary reason between, in this case, sociology and philosophy. This points less at the problem of what can be said about music once we recognize it as inscribed within the social process, and more at the fact that coiled up within this problem is the problem of the "knowledges" that stand to be authenticated by prevailing in the struggle to produce the concepts by which one account of social determination versus another might be thought to hold sway. Put differently, what Adorno has come to represent is a properly "nonvulgar" sociology of music, as opposed to a philosopher of Marxism who urges those of us concerned with the latter to recognize that the very nature of Marxism is at stake in making sense of music. Adorno himself had trouble recognizing, much less sustaining this, failing to see in his dismissal of the "crafty naïveté" of mass culture, precisely what Kafka "heard" in the silent song of the Sirens. For in the end, what slips through the *mano a mano* of philosophy and sociology is the silence *of the Sirens*, that is, the naming of a held release where a different way of knowing—not the irrational, not unreason and emphatically not Hegel's "cunning of reason"—works, however absently, its charms. This silence, the one that forms along the disciplinary frontiers that establish yet limit both our intentions and our expectations, is where *metis* is called for. Answering this call means wondering aloud, and with frequency, whether we have the right concepts for thinking everything from influence to determination, whether, in the end, we have missed what Benjamin had the temerity to call the point. One might say that Bataille was certainly onto something when he observed that Kafka, as if anticipating the tendentious query published by *Action* (a postwar French Communist weekly) "Should Kafka be burned?"— weighed in, as it were, in advance by instructing Brod to do precisely that. Doubtless, although no reference is made to "*Das Schweigen*," this is what leads Bataille to characterize Kafka, not simply as childlike, but of all writers "the most cunning."[47] It is from within Cage's echoless chamber, I will propose, that we hear how faintly yet forcefully this observation bespeaks Cage's and Kafka's "unmusical" challenge to musicology. For if music sets the high water mark of the *Uberbau*, then critical musicology must commit itself to the task of reworking, if not Marxism per se, then the critical practice that engages the social order over which music contemptuously yet vainly soars.

Notes

1. John Cage in conversation with Michael Zwerin from the *Village Voice* (January 6, 1966) as printed in *John Cage*, ed. Richard Kostelanetz (New York: Penguin, 1970) 161–67.

2. See Gilles Deleuze and Félix Guattari, *Kafka: Toward a Minor Literature*, trans. Dana Polan (Minneapolis: University of Minnesota Press, 1986), Chapter One.

3. Franz Kafka, "*Das Schweigen der Sirenen,*" in *Gesammelte Schriften*, Vol 5, ed. Max Brod (New York: Schocken Books, 1946).

4. Louis Althusser, *Writings on Psychoanalysis: Freud and Lacan*, eds. Olivier Corpet and François Matheron, trans. Jeffrey Mehlman (New York: Columbia University Press, 1996), 151.

5. John A. Hargraves, *Music in the Works of Broch, Mann, and Kafka* (Rochester: Camden House, 2002), see the chapter titled "Kafka and Silence."

6. Ibid., 162.

7. Ibid.

8. Walter Benjamin, *Selected Writings*, Vol. 3, ed. Michael Jennings, trans. various (Cambridge, MA: Harvard University Press, 1999–2002), 317.

9. Walter Benjamin, *Selected Writings*, Vol. 2, ed. Michael Jennings, trans. various (Cambridge, MA: Harvard University Press, 1999–2002), 798.

10. Theodor W. Adorno, "Notes on Kafka," in *Prisms*, trans. Samuel and Shierry Weber (Cambridge, MA: Massachusetts Institute of Technology University Press, 1981), 246.

11. Ibid., 251.

12. Ibid.

13. Theodor W. Adorno and Max Horkheimer, *Dialectic of Enlightenment*, ed. Gunzelin Schmid Noerr, trans. Edmund Jephcott (Palo Alto, CA: Stanford University Press, 2002).

14. Homer, *The Odyssey of Homer*, trans. Richard Lattimore (New York: Harper Colophon Books, 1967).

15. Richard Leppert, ed., *Essays on Music: Theodor Adorno*, trans. Susan Gillespie (Berkeley: University California Press, 2002).

16. Ibid., 288.

17. In *Writings*, Vol. 3.

18. Michel Foucault, *The Hermeneutics of the Subject: Lectures at the Collège de France 1981–82*, ed. Frédéric Gros, trans. Graham Burchell (New York: Palgrave Macmillan, 2005), 335.

19. Benjamin's own fragment, "On Proverbs" might also have attracted Adorno's attention, but did not. In it, Benjamin develops the notion of a constitutive gap between proverbs and experience, picking up nicely on Kafka's rewrite of cunning through the juridical formulation *noli me tangere* conceived as the prosopopeial self-presentation of the proverb. Or, as M. C. Hammer put it: "can't touch this."

20. Kafka, "*Sirenen,*" 97.

21. Ibid.

22. Ibid.

23. Lars Ilyer, in philosophy at Newcastle-on-Tyne has written exhaustively on this material and in ways that invite immediate comparison with what I

am arguing with regard to Kafka. (Lars Ilyer "Blanchot, Narration and the Event," in *Postmodern Culture* 12:3 [May 2002]: 25–48.)

24. Kafka, "*Sirenen*," 97–98.
25. Ibid., 98.
26. Ibid.
27. Under the general heading of "*Berichtigungen alter Mythen*" Brecht has revisited this Homeric episode as well. (Bertolt Brecht, *Gesammelte Werke in acht Bänden* [Berlin: Suhrkamp Verlag, 1967], 207.) He too casts doubt on whether the Sirens sang, but by emphasizing the class politics of the episode, asking the reader whether one should believe Ulysses's account of the encounter. Like Adorno and Horkheimer, he recognizes that at stake in the myth is precisely the question of the nature of art, but true to the politics of *engagement* Brecht calls up the specter of the grumbling crew members who take some small consolation in knowing that the Sirens would never waste their art on someone eager to enchain himself precisely in order to dominate others. Brecht, as one might expect, draws attention to Kafka's "correction" of the myth, but stresses that current events have rendered it less convincing. See, on the entire project of "myth correction" as taken up by Brecht and Kafka, Frank Wagner, *Antike Mythen: Kafka und Brecht* (Wurzburg: Königshausen und Neumann, 2009).
28. Marcel Detienne and Jean-Pierre Vernant, *Cunning Intelligence in Greek Culture and Society*, trans. Janet Lloyd (Sussex: Harvester Press, 1978), 21.
29. John Cage, *Silence* (Middleton: Wesleyan University Press, 1961), 8.
30. David Revill, *A Roaring Silence John Cage: a Life* (New York: Arcade Publishing, 1992).
31. Ibid., 164.
32. Jean-François Lyotard, "Adorno as the Devil," trans. Robert Hurley, *Telos* 19 (spring 1974): 127–137.
33. Jean-François Lyotard, *Driftworks*, ed. Roger McKeon, trans. various (New York: Semiotext(e), 1984).
34. Ibid., 92. It is worth noting that this distinction between noise and sound, where the former is, as it were, more raw and less cooked, appeals to noise five years before its systematic deployment by Jacques Attali in his political economy of music, *Noise*. (Jacques Attali, *Noise: The Political Economy of Music* [Minneapolis: University of Minnesota Press, 1985].) For what it is worth, Attali's interest in Cage, although sustained, is less philosophically and politically rich than one finds in Lyotard in that he seems content to group him among various "representatives" of the era of what he calls "composing," and this despite the fact that his concept of "heralding" (in the end not really different from Adorno's invocation of the utopic) is clearly concerned with, as Jameson notes, the problem of inscription.
35. Lyotard, *Driftworks*, 91.
36. Ibid.; translation modified.
37. Maurice Blanchot, *The Infinite Conversation*, trans. Susan Hanson (Minneapolis: University of Minnesota Press, 1993).
38. Maurice Blanchot, *The Book to Come*, trans. Charlotte Mandell (Palo Alto, CA: Stanford University Press, 2003).
39. Ibid., 5.
40. Ibid., 3.

41. Ibid.
42. Benjamin, *Writings*, Vol. 2, 799.
43. Lyotard, *Driftworks*, 94.
44. Ibid., 98; translation modified.
45. Adorno, *Prisms*, 151.
46. Lee Baxandall and Stefan Morawski, eds., *Marx and Engels on Literature and Art*, trans. Baxandall and Morawski (Saint Louis: Telos Press, 1973), 99.
47. George Bataille, *Literature and Evil*, trans. Alistair Hamilton (New York: Urizen Books, 1973), 85.

CHAPTER FIVE

"THE FALL IS THE PROOF OF
OUR FREEDOM": MEDIATED
FREEDOM IN KAFKA

Dimitris Vardoulakis

The Primacy of Imprisonment

In *Totality and Infinity*, Levinas proffers a radical critique of philosophy
from the ancient Greeks to Martin Heidegger. This consists in questioning the assumption that philosophy starts with the question, "*ti esti*" or
"what is." The question of existence inevitably leads to totality, that is, to
a structure that eliminates difference because it seeks to subsume alterity to the subject's representations. According to the tradition that asks
"what is?" the ideal of human fulfilment is freedom. Conversely, Levinas
proposes a sense of imprisonment that is more primary than freedom. The
suspicion against freedom and the attempt to find a productive sense of
imprisonment bind Levinas to Kafka.[1] A complex sense of imprisonment
traverses Kafka's works, from Gregor Samsa's confinement in his room in
the *Metamorphosis*, to the land-surveyor's entrapment in the village seeking
access to the castle, to Josef K.'s generalized imprisonment in a city where
everyone judges him as guilty in the *Trial*. By focussing on imprisonment,
Kafka converses with philosophy, if not directly, at least on a conceptual
level that engages polemically with the idea that freedom is the goal of
human existence.

Two points are indispensable in grasping the primacy of imprisonment. First, the opposition to freedom will be profoundly misunderstood
if imprisonment is confined to the empirical. According to Levinas, it is
the presence of the Other, as a formal structure, that makes it impossible to
assert one's freedom. Or, as he puts it in *Totality and Infinity*, "My freedom
does not have the last word; I am not alone."[2] The Other is more primary
than the subject's existence. Hence, the recognition of an unsurpassable
alterity incompletes every attempt to totalize knowledge. The radical

critique of ontology and epistemology entails the ethicopolitical conclusion that the Other imprisons the subject: "The *moral* relation with the Master who judges me subtends the freedom of my adherence to the true."[3] The Other masters the I, imprisonment is more primary than freedom. "[The Other] reveals himself in his lordship."[4] So, the sense of mastery or lordship of the Other is not a straightforward imprisonment. The Other limits the self. But Levinas is not referring to specific prisons, these are not particular limits. It is, rather, that the Other necessitates a sense of limitation, delimitation, or imprisonment. But unlike a "real" prison, the limits here are not brick and mortar walls. The limits, rather, figure as the presentation of the otherness of the Other. The limits are porous or permeable.

Second, the sense of imprisonment that arises from the Other's mastery does not entail the complete eradication of freedom.[5] Levinas, rather, evades a humanist or logocentric sense of freedom, which is characterized by opposing freedom to imprisonment, by positioning freedom as completely separate to imprisonment. "My freedom is...challenged by a Master who can invest it," promises Levinas, envisioning this investment as a different form of relation, one that is implied in ontology even if it is not usually recognized as such.[6] As an illustration, Levinas refers to Gyges, a shepherd who, according to Plato, discovered a ring that made him invisible, and used this power to kill the king, marry the queen, and install himself in the throne.[7] "Gyges position involve[s] the impunity of being alone," that is, the sovereign illusion of a subject that is free from being judged, as if it were limitless, as if it were the impersonation of justice.[8] Such a freedom is "an-archic," that is, without a law, groundless and unable to lead to discourse—it is silent.[9] Yet it still presupposes alterity: "The silent world is a world that comes to us from the Other.... This silence is not a simple absence of speech; speech lies in the depths of silence like a laughter perfidiously held back."[10] The real absence of freedom consists in the idea that one can be free. This is an imprisonment in the illusion that one can be free alone, invisible to others like Gyges. Conversely, it is possible to seek a freedom *from* such a sense of freedom. This is a freedom that is always conditioned, mediated, limited—it is never an absolute freedom, it is always a freedom from or an "exit" as the ape says in Kafka's "A Report to an Academy." It manifests itself as laughter in the face of the illusion of limitless freedom, or its obverse, a steadfastly limited imprisonment. Thus laughter is the effect through which the two aspects of the primacy of imprisonment—mediated freedom and the porous limits of imprisonment—are presented.

Such a laughter that destroys the egoist sense of freedom reverberates throughout Kafka's works. Laughter is an effect of the humanist conceptualization of a complete separation between freedom and imprisonment—that is, an effect of understanding freedom as limitless and hence of denying the primacy of imprisonment. This explains the different instances and types of imprisonment in Kafka's writings. All these Kafka cages are required in order to present the "an-archic" freedom in Levinas' sense, that is, a freedom that harbors the illusion that it is the opposite of imprisonment. This separation is graphically presented in "The Nature Theatre of Oklahoma," the last chapter of *Amerika*. This is a unique moment in Kafka's work. When Karl Rossmann arrives at the Nature Theatre, he seems to achieve absolute freedom—indeed, this is the single scene in Kafka approximating redemption or an admission to heaven. For such an absolute freedom to be represented, Karl Rossmann had to arrive to America like a convict in a penal colony, quickly to be rejected by his uncle, and then to be ensnared in one situation after another. From this gigantic prison that spans the continent, Karl Rossmann escaped to the Nature Theatre where everyone was absolutely free—one could even choose the name they could join under, and Karl Rossmann decided to join as "Negro" (A 1962, 286/2002, 409).[11] So, even though the Nature Theatre may appear as an exception in Kafka's work, it is conceptually indispensable for an understanding of its dialectical opposite, absolute imprisonment. This has also been observed by Walter Benjamin:

> "I imitated because I was looking for an exit, and for no other reason," said the ape in his "Report to an Academy." This sentence also holds the key for the place of the actors of the Nature Theatre. "Right here" they must be congratulated, since they are allowed to play *themselves*, they are freed from imitation. If there is in Kafka something like a contrast between damnation and salvation, it has to be searched for entirely on the contrast between the world theatre and the Nature Theatre.[12]

If there is a possibility of salvation in Kafka, this is can only happen because his characters find themselves encaged. An absolute, "an-archic" freedom requires a "fallen" world—what Walter Benjamin calls the "world theatre" that in his essay on Kafka is described as dominated by the holders of power and mythic law.[13]

And yet the scene of salvation represented by the Nature Theatre with its complete lack of restrictions or limits is not without irony. A laughter about the ontological possibility of such a free state is larking perfidiously. After the completion of the recruitment for the Nature Theatre and a festive meal, the new recruits take the train to Oklahoma completely unencumbered, without even any luggage (A 1962, 296/2002, 416). On the carriage, Karl Rossmann is initially excited with his friend Giacomo, riding "carefree [*sorgenlos*]" across America (296/416). Soon, however, their conversation dries up and the interaction with the other passengers, also actors of the Nature Theatre, becomes uninteresting. Suddenly, the landscape outside appears captivating:

> Everything that went on in the little compartment... remained unnoticed in front of what one could see outside [*Alles was sich in dem kleinen... Coupé ereignete, verging vor dem was draußen zu sehen war*].... [B]road mountain streams appeared, rolling in great waves down on the foothills and drawing with them a thousand foaming wavelets, plunging underneath the bridges over which the train rushed; and they were so near that the breath of coldness rising from them chilled the skin of one's face [*der Hauch ihrer Kühle das Gesicht erschauern machte*]. (297–8/ 418–9; translation modified)

These are the last words of the chapter on the Nature Theatre as well as the conclusion of the novel. Without forewarning, a single sentence announces that the members of the Nature Theatre, those who have been liberated and have reached absolute freedom, appear boring, while the landscape outside becomes fascinating. Even more emphatically, the final metaphor of the text referring to the stones' breath suggests that the mountains are animated whereas the actors are petrified, they are frozen in a kind of rigor mortis. Whence the unexpected petrification of the newly freed actors? As it will be argued, this reversal is crucial in Kafka's presentation of the primacy of imprisonment over freedom. For the moment, it suffices to note that Kafka is making a similar point to Levinas. A sense of freedom presupposes a sense of imprisonment. From that point of view, absolute freedom and absolute imprisonment cannot sustain their separation. Instead, they transpire to be the obverse sides of the same coin. They both lead to the same result: a loss of embodiment, the eradication of singularity.[14] Gyges' invisibility and the actors' petrification belong to the same ontological category.[15]

As already intimated, laughter in Kafka is an effect of the complete separation of freedom and imprisonment—in other words, an effect of the denying mediated freedom and imprisonment's porosity. But this also means that the complete separation of freedom and imprisonment is necessary for laughter to figure. The various cages of *Amerika* are *not* liquidated in the absolute or "an-archic" freedom of the Nature Theatre of Oklahoma. Such a freedom is an illusion. The new recruits of the Nature Theatre are no more free than stones, inanimate matter for which the question of freedom cannot even arise. Their freedom leads to silence, to invisibility—and Kafka mischievously laughs with them as he turns his gaze to the animated nature outside the train window. It is this laughter, as it will be argued, that allows for a recuperation of the singularity and embodiment that the Kafka characters lose in their search for freedom.

The destruction of limitless or absolute freedom in Kafka's works does not merely require a demonstration of the philosophical weight of Kafka's prose, as if a political message were separable from the literary work.[16] It rather requires to show, firstly, that imprisonment is more primary than freedom in Kafka, while noting that this does not eliminate freedom but radically reworks it so that freedom and imprisonment are not governed by a relation of absolute separation. It requires, secondly, to show how the primacy of imprisonment makes possible a notion of embodiment so that the singularity of the subject is not squandered in the promise of a future redemption nor in the illusion that one is already precluded from such freedom. It requires, finally, to identify the effect of the primacy of imprisonment—an effect that is discernible in Kafka's laughter and it is the literary quality of his work, and hence can only be discovered through a close reading.

For such a close reading, the texts chosen are "A Report to An Academy" and "A Fasting Artist." This is not an arbitrary choice. They both present the separation of freedom and imprisonment, which is necessary for laughter to figure in such a way as to present the primacy of imprisonment. The separation of freedom and imprisonment moves in opposite directions in the two short stories. Whereas in "A Report to An Academy" the ape is imprisoned seeking freedom, in "A Hunger Artist" the artiste feels free in his cage while abstaining from nutrition only for this freedom to dissolve in a sense of imprisonment. Nevertheless, despite the different directions of the relation between freedom and imprisonment in the two short stories, it will be instructive to discover that they both lead to disembodiment and the loss of singularity. The laughter in the face of this loss will figure as the effect of the separation of freedom and imprisonment, thereby asserting the primacy of imprisonment and the affirmation that singularity cannot be eliminated.

Regaining the Power to Say "One"

"A Report to an Academy" relates the story of an ape, Red Peter, who is captured in Africa, transported by boat to Europe and who relinquishes his animal nature in order to escape the cage where he is held as captive. Starting from a sense of absolute imprisonment, an idealized freedom is presupposed. Freedom and imprisonment are completely separated. Such a presupposition of freedom is, however, nothing but a ratiocination, or the operation of reason, characteristic of the human. The animal can only achieve freedom, if it already thinks as a human. It can only escape to the human nature, if it is already trapped in human nature, imprisoned in a nature other than its own. This creates a double movement throughout

"A Report to an Academy." Initially, imprisonment is seen as a deplorable state from which the ape seeks to escape. The ideal toward which the ape strives is freedom. But the second movement reveals that this striving is already a human characteristic, so that in striving for freedom the ape is already trapped in a different nature, resulting in the loss of the ape's embodiment.

The title, "Ein Bericht für eine Akademie," registers this double movement. It does so through the ambivalence of whether the "ein" and "eine" are indefinite articles or numerical adjectives. Is it *"a"* report to *"an"* academy, or *"one"* report to *"one"* academy, or *"one"* report to *"an"* academy, or *"a"* report to *"one"* academy? An animal can only desire something specific, while the human can yearn for abstract ideals such as freedom. Just as a dog could only say "I want this one bone in front of me," the transcendence of animality can be indicated by the ability to say "I want a something" not necessarily now, but as a general, abstract proposition. So long as Red Peter speaks in numerical adjectives, he remains tied to the animal desire that is linked to the here and now. His escape from the cage has not been accomplished. The movement of the short story is from the adjectives to the indefinite articles that show the human capacity for abstract thought and ratiocination. Red Peter's report wants to suggest that he no longer says "one" report to "one" academy, but rather "a" report to "an" academy. And yet, the use of the indefinite article means that Red Peter is encaged in a nature that is not his own, he is trapped in human nature. There is, on the one hand, the desire to escape from imprisonment in order to find freedom, but, on the other hand, the fulfilment of that desire presupposes the entrapment in a different nature, which is an even more pervasive or sinister form of imprisonment than the cage Red Peter had found himself in. It is more pervasive or sinister because Red Peter thereby loses his embodiment, he is trapped in the abstraction of the indefinite, he puts himself in the cage of reason. Kafka traces this movement throughout the short story and ultimately shatters this cage through the figuration of laughter.

The pivotal term around which the whole report is structured is "Ausweg," meaning exit or way out. As Red Peter explains, when he found himself trapped in the cage on the ship's deck, he realized that he needed to copy the manners of his human captors in order to join them outside the cage. Thus the imitation was not an end in itself. "There was no attraction for me [*es verlockte mich nicht*] in imitating human beings; I imitated them because I was looking for an exit [*einen Ausweg suchte*] and for no other reason" (RA 1995, 257/2002, 311; translation modified). Red Peter says that it was not alluring to him—he had no uncontrollable, animal desire—to imitate the humans. His only goal was to find an exit. "No, freedom was not what I wanted [*Nein, Freiheit wollte ich nicht*].

Only an exit: right or left, or in any direction.... To get out, to get out! [*Weiterkommen, weiterkommen!*]" (253–4/305; translation modified). Even though Red Peter says that "I did not think it out in this human way [*Ich rechnete nicht so menschlich*]," still the structure of the sentences that describe his conception of the exit unmistakably indicate that in his cage he was already thinking like a human (255/307). It is not only that he is searching for *an* exit, any kind of exit, an exit with an indefinite article, nor is it not only that he can conceptualize the play-acting of being human as the means to the goal of achieving such an abstract exit that suggest he has already been calculating like a rational human.[17] Further, this exit is conceived as a "weiterkommen," that is, as a movement away from the cage but also as a progress, as a bettering of one's state through calculation. Thus, Red Peter can only assert that he was looking for *an* exit so long as he was already human in some way. There is an absolute separation between the animal and the human that corresponds to the absolute separation between imprisonment and freedom—the ape is locked up in the cage while the humans are free outside. Red Peter strives to become human in order to find himself in the space of freedom outside the cage. He thereby renounces his singular being in the world. His being is now an imitation, a calculated hypocrisy.

At the same time, in a remarkable passage, Red Peter denies that this hypocrisy, necessary so as to appear as—so as to *be*—human and to escape the cage, leads to anything that resembles human freedom. Although he steps outside the cage to join the humans, his exit and human freedom are categorically different:

> I fear that perhaps one does not quite understand [*man nicht genau versteht*] what I mean by "exit." I use the expression in its fullest and most popular sense. I deliberately do not use the word "freedom." I do not mean the great feeling [*große Gefühl*] of freedom on all sides. As an ape, perhaps, I knew that [*Als Affe kannte ich es vielleicht*], and I have met men who yearn for it. But for my part I desired such freedom neither then nor now. (RA 1995, 253/2002, 304)

He rejects explicitly the "great feeling" of limitless, unconditioned freedom—"freedom on all sides." That's the freedom desired by mankind but experienced concretely by apedom. Even though Red Peter can grasp what a human in the abstract ("*man*") can or cannot understand, his rejection of that great feeling differentiates him from the humans. But this is not merely to assert that the sense of freedom is different for humans and apes. It further enacts a *reversal* whereby the exit that the ape is searching for appears more primary than the freedom the humans are yearning for. In other words, the reversal halts the oscillation of the two movements—human or animal, free or captured—that can be found in "A Report to an Academy."

This reversal is configured as laughter. Red Peter continues immediately after the previous citation:

> In passing: may I say that all too often men are betrayed by the word freedom. And as freedom is counted among the most sublime feelings, so the corresponding disillusionment can be also sublime. In variety theatres I have often watched, before my turn came on, a couple of acrobats performing on trapezes high in the roof. They swung themselves, they rocked to and fro, they sprang into the air, they floated into each other's arms, one hung by the hair from the teeth of the other. "And that too is human freedom," I thought, "self-controlled movement." What a mockery of holy Mother Nature! Were the apes to see such a spectacle, no theatre walls could stand the shock of their laughter. (RA 1995, 253/2002, 304–5)

The apes' laughter is directed against the humans. Red Peter says that the humans' idea of freedom—that is, the idea of freedom of those whose manner of thinking he has adopted in order to find his exit—is laughable. This is a laughter that Red Peter directs against Kafka as well—or, maybe Kafka directs that laughter against his fellow humans—given that the scene described by the ape resembles the scene from the short story "Up in the Gallery." Even though Kafka often uses scenes from the circus or variety theaters, still this resemblance is significant given that "Up in the Gallery" was published as the third story in the collection *A Country Doctor* that also contains "A Report to an Academy" as its concluding story. The two-paragraph story presents two different scenes of acrobatics, one of abjection and the other of exaggerated sublimity, that deeply affect a spectator. An ape could never be affected like that because it does not yearn for such lofty or great feelings of freedom on all sides. If there is such a freedom, the animal has already tasted it. Limitless freedom is a concrete reality for the ape. Therefore, it finds the human attempts at grasping such a freedom idealizations and futile, even ludicrous. So, even though Red Peter can only look for an exit if he is—and the "is" is ontologically strong here—already a human, his rejection of freedom indicates a position that is more primary than the human, or, more accurately, a position that is more primary than the human understood as completely separate from the animal, and human freedom as completely separate from imprisonment. The ape's exit requires the passage through the human but is, at the same time, the enactment of a reversal figuring as the laughter that destructs the illusion that governs the human ideal of freedom.

Deleuze and Guattari arrive at a similar conclusion about the laughter in Kafka: "Only two principles are necessary to accord with Kafka. He is an author who laughs with a profound joy, a *joie de vivre*, in spite of, or because of, his clownish declarations that he offers like a trap or a circus. And from one end to the other, he is a political author, a prophet of the future world."[18] Kafka's laughter and the political import of his writings are inextricable. Deleuze and Guattari explicitly address this connection in "A Report to an Academy" as a line of flight: "for Kafka, the animal essence is the way out, the line of escape, even if it takes place in place, in a cage. *A line of escape and not freedom.*"[19] This line of escape or exit is indeed a freedom irreducible to an idealized notion of freedom that is positioned as solely human as well as completely separated from imprisonment. But the idea of the reversal expressed as Kafka's laughter can be better articulated by slightly reformulating Deleuze and Guattari's assertion about Red Peter: the animal essence is the way out, the line of escape (not simply "even if" but more emphatically) *only because* it takes place in place, in a cage. In other words, the ape has to be captive in order to search for the exit. The ape has to traverse the separation of freedom and imprisonment as well as the separation of the human and the animal, it has to pronounce the humanizing indefinite articles—"a" report to "an" academy. The ape has to humanize itself and thereby lose its singularity and embodiment, lose its animality.[20] Only by going through this terrain that allows for a conception of an idealized freedom, or what Levinas calls "an-archic" freedom, is it possible to show that there is something more primary, namely, a freedom understood as *Ausweg*. This exit or way out is not absolute, it is not unconditioned. In fact, it can only be an exit *from*, a way out *from*—a freedom *from*. Without the cage, such a sense of mediated or conditioned freedom is impossible. When the reversal is registered in the form of laughter, the ape can reclaim the numerical adjective— "one" report to "one" academy. But regaining the capacity to say "one" no longer refers to a single entity standing on its own. Starting from within the cage, the ape pronounces the indefinite article "a," it passes through the human, it includes the other. So, the ability to revert back to the "one" also asserts that imprisonment is more primary than freedom.

The Other's Laughter

The term "Hungerkünstler" was not unusual in Kafka's days. As Peter Payer has shown, hunger artists performing exhibitions were common in Central Europe.[21] The most famous of these exhibition hunger artists was Giovanni Succi, whose career was the direct inspiration for Kafka's short story.[22] The successor of these exhibition artists is David Blaine, who, in September 2003, enclosed himself in a transparent cage next to the Thames and abstained from food for forty-four days. Alongside the exhibition artists, fasting has a venerable history in religion. The religious significance of severe food depravation is profound.[23] For instance, the Orthodox Hesychast movement of the fourteenth century used techniques that included fasting in order to achieve *theosis* or deification.[24] There are, of course, physiological reasons why fasting leads to visions.[25] Regardless, those who can sustain themselves without nutrition for a long period of time exercise an unmistakeable fascination. Whether they are thought to experience a vision of the divine, or whether their exhibition has a "pulling" power, the hunger or fasting artist is regarded as moving beyond the humanly possible, and consequently as a venerable individual endowed with special powers. Kafka's Hungerkünstler treads on the line between the exhibition hunger artist and the fasting saint.[26] What is absent in Kafka's story is the fascinated gaze of others on the Hungerkünstler. Instead, it is the artiste himself who exhibits an unwavering self-belief in his practice—in his greatness—all the while remaining oblivious both to whether he is performing a religious or commercial function, or whether this is recognized by others. He regards himself as most free when he is alone in his cage, unhindered in his abstinence.

Even though the cage with the iron bars is a common object in "A Report to a Academy" and in "A Hunger Artist," still it functions in different ways. In the former, the cage indicates a sense of absolute imprisonment from which the ape seeks to escape. In the latter, the cage is *the* site of freedom for the artiste. The hunger artist is happy in his cage, "paying no attention to anyone or anything" (HA 1995, 268/2002, 334). And his "happiest moment [*am glücklichsten*]" was when those watching him overnight to make sure that he ate nothing were served "an enormous breakfast" in the morning (269/336). This instils in him a sense of superiority. It is as if he is apart from his fellow men. He is the only one who is happy and free in his cage. Indeed, he is so separated from the others that, in reality, he is "the sole completely satisfied spectator of his own fast" (270/337). Thus, although "A Report to an Academy" presents the cage as enforcing complete imprisonment, and "A Hunger Artist" as leading to freedom and happiness, still the two share an important common characteristic: both require a clear-cut separation between freedom and imprisonment. As already shown, it was that separation that characterized the humanist tradition that sought the fulfilment of human existence in freedom. As Levinas argued, however, the fulfilment of this ideal can only lead to the loneliness and silence of "an-archic" freedom. The hunger artist fulfils this image—his freedom belongs to the same category as the invisibility of Gyges and the petrification of the actors of the Nature Theatre.

Through Levinas' description of the presupposition of the Other in "an-archic" freedom, it was possible to argue for the primacy of imprisonment over freedom. Absolute freedom can never be actualized because it is impossible to sustain the separation between freedom and imprisonment. The border collapses though the intervention of the others. This effect is registered in this short story through the commercial aspect of fasting: "The longest period of fasting was fixed by the impresario at forty days, beyond that term he was not allowed to go, not even in great cities, and there was good reason for it, too. Experience had proved that for about forty days the interest of the public could be stimulated by a steadily increasing pressure of advertisement, but after that the town began to lose interest" (HA 1995, 270/2002, 337–8). As an exhibition artiste, his freedom is conditioned by the audience's interest. This exasperates the hunger artist. "He had held out for a long time, an illimitably long time, why stop now, when he was in his best fasting form, or rather, not yet in his best fasting form?" (271/338–9). He wanted his fasting to be "beyond what is possible to conceive [*ins Unbegreifliche*]" since his fasting abilities were limitless (*denn für seine Fähigkeit zu hungern fühlte er keine Grenzen*) (271/339). It is this desire toward the inconceivable and the limitless that, on the one hand, separates him from the other humans, raising him to a higher physicospiritual level, and, on the other hand, impedes him from fully enjoying his status given the externally imposed commercial restrictions.

The waning of public interest in exhibitions of fasting was, consequently, a relief for the hunger artist. The public represent an other that figures merely as a constraint, a contingent limitation. Seeking a contract with the circus that allowed him to fast indefinitely, the artist thought that he was on his way to greatness. It was immaterial that the circus management did not put him at the centerstage of the orchestra, since ultimately his quest was not commercial but spiritual: he wanted to fast beyond the limits of reason. The scene of freedom that takes place in the circus recalls "Up in the Gallery" as well as the reference to the acrobats in "A Report to an Academy." In both these cases, the sublime, great feeling of freedom is represented in the orchestra. This, of course, would have provoked the boisterous laughter of the apes. But the hunger artist's mission was no longer to exhibit his achievement for all to see. Instead, it was a personal quest, and the audience going past his cage on the way to the menagerie was only an added bonus. The hunger artist was left there to fast alone, without hindrances, without limits.

And yet, the Kafkaesque laughter can again be heard, and it is once more the effect of the absolute freedom, the effect of the separation between freedom and imprisonment. A long time passes and the hunger artist is forgotten. One day, the circus personnel notice the cage. Poking in the straw, they discover the hunger artist's emaciated body and they ask him surprised whether he is still fasting. With hardly any strength left, the hunger artist whispers: "'Forgive me, everybody'" (HA 1995, 276/2002, 348). This is not a message to the onlookers. It is, rather, a soliloquy. The hunger artist admits to himself that he has failed to achieve a feat that is beyond human reason and that transcends the limits of fallen human existence. This failure is *not* due to his imminent demise. Rather, it is because "'I have to fast, I can't help it... because I couldn't find the food I liked. If I had found it, believe me, I should have made no fuss and stuffed myself like you or anyone else'" (277/348–9). It is not merely the death following this admission that robs the hunger artist of his embodiment. He had lost his body long before that. The reason is that, instead of a spiritual quest that would have allowed him to transcend the other humans and reach a higher level of happiness and freedom, in fact the hunger artist was determined by a baser instinct—revulsion for food. Even though he presents fasting as a higher human quality, he is in fact trapped in an animalist desire—a desire that says "I don't want this *one* food, nor this *one*, and so on." His fulfilment of complete freedom was the loss of his human body in the body of the animal, the other that can never be spiritually enlightened and free. The reversal that was discovered in "A Report to an Academy" operates here as well. The hunger artist's greatest moment of liberation was in fact his most profound moment of submission. The hunger artist is neither a performer, nor someone who fasts for religious transcendence. Instead, he is someone who has lost this human embodiment in the other, the animal body, a body like the panther's, who occupies the cage after the hunger artist's death.

The laughter in "A Hunger Artist" is different from the laughter in "A Report to an Academy." The ape's laughter consists in that it has traversed human freedom, escaped from the cage, and regained its embodiment in being able to say "one" again. The initial position within imprisonment allowed him to return there after it destroyed the human illusion that imprisonment is completely separate from freedom. The hunger artist, on the contrary, starts from a position of freedom. His cage is his paradise, the equivalent of the stage of the Nature Theatre of Oklahoma. And, like the actors of the Nature Theatre, the hunger artist has no means of escaping. His actions to enhance his freedom in fact push him further into a state of disembodiment, the loss of his singularity in the inconceivable and the limitless. Unlike the ape, the hunger artist does not have a chance, because the prison of freedom is stronger than the prison of an actual cage. Correspondingly, the laughter in the two stories is different. In "A Report to an Academy," the reversal leads back to imprisonment, albeit changed, an imprisonment that is more primary than freedom. Consequently, the laughter there is mischievous, exuberant, celebratory—this is a *joyous* laughter and it is a *joyous* reversal.[27] In "A Hunger Artist," the reversal does not lead back to the cage and the illusion of spiritual freedom. Instead, it leads to the other, the animal that is excluded as unspiritual, as unworthy of the grand quest that the artiste sets for himself. It is through the other that laughter figures:

> The panther was missing nothing. The food he liked was brought him without hesitation by the attendants; he did not seem to miss his freedom even once [*nicht einmal die Freiheit schien er zu vermissen*]; his noble body, furnished almost to bursting point with all that it needed, seemed to carry freedom around with it too [*dieser edle... Körper schien auch die Freiheit mit sich herumzutragen*]; somewhere in his jaws it seemed to lurk; and the joy of life [*die Freude am Leben*] streamed with such ardent passion from his throat that for the onlookers it was not easy to stand the shock of it. (HA 1995, 277/2002, 349; translation modified)

The freedom of the panther consists in being content within its own "noble body." The freedom that it holds in its jaw is also a smile at the previous occupant of the cage, whose body was held captive by an illusion of freedom. Just as in the end of *Amerika* that which by definition lacks freedom, the inanimate matter, the stone, is suddenly animate and it is as if it grins to the petrified actors of the Nature Theatre, similarly also here it is the other—the animal that is content in its own body so long as the body is fed—that grins to the hunger artist. The laughter that results from an initial position of freedom is more delicate, less discernible, because Kafka cannot find here the redeeming quality of reverting back to the cage. This is a *lugubrious* laughter since the reversal does not lead back to singularity.[28] Still, even though the hunger artist fails to gain his singularity, the laughter is still related to it, since it is registered on the face of the panther in a cage, where freedom is neither missed nor absent. This is the laughter of the Other that the hunger artist sought to suppress but did not manage to.

Effect as Means

The primacy of imprisonment appears in Kafka as an effect. *Discursively*, the effect is the establishment of the primacy of imprisonment over freedom. This entails that Kafka rejects two related positions. First, that imprisonment can be reduced to the empirical and hence given steadfast limits—for instance, the walls of the cage that the ape is placed in. Second, that freedom can be limitless—for instance, the freedom of restrictions for the actors of the Nature Theatre or the unhindered fasting of the hunger artist. To put this the other way, the primacy of imprisonment establishes, first, that the borders of imprisonment are porous—the ape is not freed when it steps outside the cage—and, second, that freedom is conditioned or mediated, it is always a freedom *from*—for instance, freedom from the entrapment of the ape in human nature or the freedom of the panther from the unrestricted freedom of the hunger artist. Discursively, these two perspectives from which the primacy of imprisonment can be understood could be summed up by saying that they designate the freedom *from* humanist freedom. This is a mediated or conditioned freedom.

Textually, the effect is the laughter that arises as a response to humanist freedom. Denying the primacy of imprisonment entails that imprisonment and freedom are seen as opposites that are completely separate. However, this separation cannot be sustained. The ape is not free when he starts acting out as a human, nor is the hunger artist free when he enacts his instinctual revulsion to food. Kafka's texts sustain for as long as possible the illusion that freedom and imprisonment can be separated. As a result, the laughter in his texts is easily overlooked. But to notice that laughter is to recognize the political significance of his writings. In other words, it is to recognize that the textuality of Kafka's prose is inextricable from the discursive issue of the primacy of imprisonment.

The question then arises: If the primacy of imprisonment, both discursively and textually, is enacted as an effect, then, what's the cause of that effect? It is here that Kafka provides a Spinozist answer in the dialogues that were recorded by Janouch:

"Accident is the name one gives to the coincidence of events, of which one does not know the causation. But there is no world without causation. Therefore in the world there are no accidents, but only here..." Kafka touched his forehead with his left hand. "Accidents only exist in our heads, in our limited perceptions. They are the reflection of the limits of our knowledge. The struggle against chance is always a struggle against ourselves, which we can never entirely win."[29]

Just like Spinoza, Kafka proposes a certain determinism by saying that there are no accidents. But the main point is, rather, that, just as accidents are "in our heads" so is also the chain of causes and effects. Final causality is merely a human fiction. Conversely, to "struggle against chance" means to struggle against the egoism of the self that looks for final causes—causes whose aim is, for instance, to lead to "an-archic" freedom. The cause for Kafka, as for Spinoza, is immanent, that is, it is only present in its effects that consist in the struggle against the self's representations.[30] In other words, the primacy of imprisonment is ungrounded. It is not even a concept to the extent that it cannot be fully defined. Instead, it appears only as the destruction of its opposite—as the destruction of limitless freedom.

And yet, this destruction is productive, since it gives rise to freedom *from* the humanist notion of freedom.

The productive aspect of the primacy of imprisonment entails that the effect figures as a means. It is the discursive means whereby mediated freedom arises and the literary means that structures the textuality of Kafka's works. At this point, the notion of the reversal attains its full significance. The reversal is crucial for two reasons. First, it allows for—it is the means for—the unfolding of the relations of the primacy of imprisonment as an effect. These are formal relations, they concern ways that freedom and imprisonment relate to each other. They are relations between neither existent entities nor concepts. It is the *task of criticism* to unfold these relations and the relations are potentially singular to every text—or, rather, to every critical reading of the text. Two such types of relations have been discussed, and many more could be discovered through a textual analysis of Kafka's short stories. The first reversal discussed above showed that the ape imprisoned within the cage could find an exit only so long as it was already a human and hence already joined the men outside his cage. But this humanization of the ape is reversed through the way that the ape laughs at the illusion of unlimited freedom. The second reversal started in the same setting—a cage—but from a different position, since the hunger artist is contending to be happy and free in his cage. In fact, however, the hunger artist was trapped in an instinctual revulsion that made a mockery of his spiritual quest for limitless freedom. The laughter here is registered through the panther who replaces the hunger artist in the cage and who is truly happy and content in its own body, it feels free so long as it is well-fed. The first aspect of the reversal, then, allows for an interaction between the discursive and the textual elements of the text so that the text becomes a story—it acquires a meaning.

Second, the reversal allows for—it is a means of—the *possibility of judgement*. Judgement depends upon the presupposition of the Other, or recognizing the primacy of imprisonment. This depends on whether singularity has been attained. In the case of the ape, for instance, the starting point of imprisonment enabled Red Peter to traverse the position of the human and its imprisonment in limitless freedom in order to regain the power to say "one." That power consisted in finding again his own singularity. Conversely, the hunger artist was lost in the limitless space of freedom as he envisaged it alone in his cage. He shunned the baser drives, such as the commercial aspect of his exhibitions, in favor of a spiritual quest. At the end, however, it was only the panther who retained its embodiment in the cage and who could grin for the fate of the cage's previous occupant. A final but significant note is required here. The reversal can allow for judgement about whether singularity is retained because the judgement is related to the effect of the primacy of imprisonment. As such, singularity or embodiment cannot possibly be understood either as a collapse to the empirical—that's the notion of imprisonment as limited—nor as an abstraction—that's the notion of limitless freedom. Singularity is the way that the empirical and the limitless are held in a productive and yet unresolvable suspension. They are mediated, they condition each other, they are formed *from* the possibility that neither usurps the other. Thus, the possibility of judgment and singularity are tied up with mediated freedom.

Kafka was fully aware of the power of the reversal in general and of its importance for the development of a notion of freedom in particular. For instance, in the *Conversations*, Kafka says to Janouch: "'Men can act otherwise. The Fall is the proof of their freedom.'"[31] Kafka does not believe in salvation—or, more accurately, he deconstructs the idea that there is a limitless freedom where one can be free alone. Rather, freedom can take place only within the fallen world, the world where the individual is imprisoned within his or her own body. It is possible to talk about freedom only by asserting this primacy of imprisonment in the world. This is a thought that cannot possibly be reduced to an existential pessimism without defacing it, as it is also shown from its corollary: "'Anyone who grasps life completely has no fear of dying. The fear of death is merely the result of an unfulfilled life. It is a symptom of betrayal.'"[32] This recalls Spinoza again, Proposition 67 of Part IV of the *Ethics*: "A free man thinks death least of all things, and his wisdom is a meditation of life, not of death." Freedom is understood in contrast to both the actual fact of empirical death and the fear of a death that would have spurred the establishment of the space without fear, a space of absolute freedom. Freedom is the attainment of singularity so long as freedom is understood as mediated by this dual impossibility—an impossibility that figures in Kafka's cages.

Notes

1. For another attempt to bring Kafka in conversation with Levinas, see Laura Stahman, "Franz Kafka's 'The Burrow' as Model of Ipseity in Levinasian Theory," *Mosaic*, 37.3 (2004): 19–32.
2. Emmanuel Levinas, *Totality and Infinity: An Essay on Exteriority*, trans. Alphonso Lingis (Pittsburgh, PA: Duquesne University Press, 1969), 101.
3. Ibid.
4. Ibid.
5. The fear that the privileging of alterity would make freedom disappear is recorded in the philosophical tradition as the accusation of determinism against Spinoza. Despite Levinas' seeming dismissal of Spinoza, they share a lot in common as Hent de Vries has shown in "Levinas, Spinoza, and the Theologico-Political Meaning of Scripture," in eds. Hent de Vries and

Lawrence E. Sullivan, *Political Theologies: Public Religions in a Post-Secular World* (New York: Fordham University Press, 2006), 232–48. See also the last section of the present chapter for parallels between Kafka and Spinoza.

6. Levinas, 101.

7. Cf. Plato, *Republic*, trans. Paul Shorey (Cambridge, MA: Harvard University Press, 2003), 359d–360a. For an account for the two most famous but very different versions of the Gyges story, see Gabriel Danzig, "Rhetoric and the Ring: Herodotus and Plato on the Story of Gyges as a Politically Expedient Tale," *Greece & Rome*, 55.2 (2008): 169–92.

8. Levinas, 90.

9. Ibid.

10. Ibid., 91.

11. Alexis de Tocqueville, in a well-known passage, describes American sovereignty as a space of absolute freedom similar to the Nature Theatre: "[Americans] govern themselves, so weak and restricted is the part left to the administration, so much does the administration feel its popular origin and obey the power from which it emanates. The people rule the American political world as God rules the universe. They are the cause and the end of all things; everything arises from them and everything is absorbed by them." *Democracy in America: Historical-Critical Edition of De la démocratie en Amérique*, ed. Eduardo Nolla, trans. James T. Schleifer (Indianapolis: Liberty Fund, 2010), p. 97.

12. Walter Benjamin, "[Notes on Kafka]," *Gesamelte Schriften* eds. Rolf Tiedemann and Hermann Schweppenhäuser (Frankfurt a.M: Suhrkamp, 1991), 2.3: 1262. For a discussion of how this idea operates in Benjamin's essay on Kafka, see my *The Doppelgänger: Literature's Philosophy* (New York: Fordham University Press, 2010), ch. 5.

13. Walter Benjamin, "Franz Kafka: On the Tenth Anniversary of his Death," in *Selected Writings*, ed. Michael W. Jennings et al. (Cambridge, MA: Belknap, 2001), volume 2, 794–818.

14. Heinz Politzer suggests that at the end of the *Amerika* Karl Rossmann "has lost his name and will never more be heard of." Politzer then goes on to link this idea of the original title of the novel, *Der Veschollene*: "From now on the nameless one will be what he always was in Kafka's mind, *Der Verschollene*." (Politzer, *Franz Kafka: Parable and Paradox* [Ithaca, Cornell University Press, 1966], 162.)

15. One could possibly ask the following question here: How far does actually the similarity between Kafka and Levinas go, given that Levinas would understand the Other only as human? The question essentially asks whether Levinas' notion of the ethical actually remains trapped in humanism. It can be argued, however, that it is a profound misunderstanding of Levinas to ask whether the Other is human or nonhuman. Instead, the Other is the "Jewish" challenge to the "Greek" question of existence. Therefore, one should not try to define the Other as such and thereby ontologize or totalize it—one cannot ask whether the Other is human or nonhuman—but one should rather seek to explore the formal relations that arise when the "Jew" and the "Greek" come face to face. Cf. Jacques Derrida, "Violence and Metaphysics: An Essay on the Thought of Emmanuel Levinas," in *Writing and Difference*, trans. Allan Bass

(London: Routledge, 2002), 97–192. Although I cannot examine these issues in any detail here, the implicit argument is that such a notion of relationality is really what binds Kafka and Levinas.

16. This is what Theodor Adorno calls the "deadly aesthetic error": "Kafka's works protected themselves against the deadly aesthetic error of equating the philosophy that an author pumps into a work with its metaphysical substance. Were this so, the work of art would be stillborn: it would exhaust itself in what it says and would not unfold itself in time. To guard against this short-circuit, which jumps directly to the significance intended by the work, the first rule is: take everything literally; cover up nothing with concepts invoked from above. Kafka's authority is textual." ("Notes on Kafka," in eds. Samuel and Shierry Weber, *Prisms* [London: Neville Spearman, 1967], 247.) As I will argue, Kafka's textual authority figures as laughter.

17. In other words, the notion of play-acting effects the separation between the animal and the human, since it is only humans who are meant to have hypo-critical abilities.

18. Gilles Deleuze and Félix Guattari, *Kafka: Towards a Minor Literature*, trans. Dana Polan (Minneapolis: University of Minnesota Press, 1986), 41.

19. Deleuze and Guattari, 35.

20. Marthe Robert provides illuminating insights on Kafka's humour by departing from a comparison with *Don Quixote* in *The Old and the New: From Don Quixote to Kafka*, trans. Carol Cosman (Berkeley: University of California Press, 1977). Robert argues that "quixotism" is the drive to relate literature to the real, the correlation of work and life that characterizes modernity. She further identifies the connection between humour and imitation as one of the way that this quixotism is carried out: "Like those insects who protect themselves against their nearest and strongest enemies by a mimetic ruse, quixotism apes the manner, tone, and gestures of its anonymous adversary, whose indifferent, self-interested or simply lazy conformity it perceives on all sides." Robert compares Cervantes's creation to Kafka's land-surveyor in *The Castle*, but this description of imitation is even more apt to Red Peter. The ape's imitation is related to life so long as freedom is an issue that has to do with "our" world. Robert continues: "Here, however, the tactic of simulation is not only a defensive consideration, it is a formidable weapon." (Ibid., 27.) Imitation exposes that which is imitated and ultimately dismantles or deconstruct it. Red Peter imitates the human desire for freedom in order to show its absurdity. But this absurdity can only be demonstrated if the ape imitates the humans, if the ape appears to have humanized itself.

21. According to Walter Vandereycken and Ron van Deth, in 1926 there were six simultaneous performances by hunger artists in Berlin. (*From Fasting Saints to Anorexic Girls: The History of Self-Starvation* [New York: New York University Press, 1994], 88.) See also Peter Payer, *Hungerkünstler in Wien. Eine verschwundene Attraktion (1896–1926)* (Vienna: Sonderzahl, 2002).

22. See Astrid Lange-Kirchheim, "Nachrichten vom italienischen Hungerkünstler Giovanni Succi: Neue Materialien zu Kafkas *Hungerkünstler*," *Freiburger literaturpsychologische Gespräche: Jahrbuch für Literatur und Psychoanalyse* 18 (1999): 315–40.

23. See Vandereycken and Deth, *From Fasting Saints to Anorexic Girls*, 14–32; for the Jewish tradition specifically, see Eliezier Diamond, *Holy Men and Hunger Artists: Fasting and Asceticism in Rabbinic Culture* (Oxford: Oxford University Press, 2004).

24. For Gregory Palamas, the major defender of Hesychasm, see John Meyendorff's classic *A Study of Gregory Palamas* (Bedfordshire: Faith Press, 1974, 2nd ed.). For a description of the techniques of the movement, see Kalistos of Diokleia, "Praying with the Body: The Hesychast Method and non-Christian Parallels," *Sobornost*, 14.2 (1993): 6–35.

25. Aldus Huxley, for instance, provides an explanation why extreme fasting came to be associated with mystical experiences: "By reducing the amount of available sugar, fasting lowers the brain's biological efficiency and so makes possible the entry into consciousness of material possessing no survival value. Moreover, by causing a vitamin deficiency, it removes from the blood that known inhibitor of visions, nicotinic acid. Another inhibitor of visionary experience is ordinary, everyday, perceptual experience. Experimental psychologists have found that, if you confine a man to a 'restricted environment,' where there is no light, no sound, nothing to smell and, if you put him in a tepid bath, only one, almost imperceptible thing to touch, the victim will very soon start 'seeing things,' 'hearing things,' and having strange bodily sensations. Milarepa, in his Himalayan cavern, and the anchorites of the Thebaid followed essentially the same procedure and got essentially the same results. A thousand pictures of the Temptations of St. Anthony bear witness to the effectiveness of restricted diet and restricted environment." (Aldus Huxley, *The Doors of Perception* [London: Penguin, 1959], 74, and cf. 118–9.)

26. Contrary to the Muirs' translation, Kafka never talks of a "professional" hunger artist.

27. This is not to say, of course, that every instance when the starting point is imprisonment would necessarily lead to this joyous reversal. A case in point is Josef K. in *The Trial*. Josef K. has his chance to let the joyous laughter reverberate at the end of the dialogue with the priest in the Cathedral. However, he fails to grasp the comical implications of concluding the conversation by saying "Die Lüge wird zur Weltordnung gemacht." I develop this argument in my contribution to the volume *Kafka and Philosophy*, edited by Brendan Moran and Carlo Salzani (forthcoming). But the point is that a typology of laughter in Kafka is not exhausted in the distinction between a joyous and what I will call in a moment lugubrious laughter. See also note 28.

28. As I indicated in note 27, the typology of laughter in Kafka is not exhausted in the distinction between a joyous and a lugubrious laughter. There is a third, major category that I cannot discuss here in detail but I would like, nevertheless, to outline briefly. It is characterized by a hysterical or surface laughter that is reminiscent of farce. One of the best examples of this laughter are the histrionics of the soldier and the condemned man "In the Penal Colony." In general (although this point needs a careful reading of Kafka's texts), this kind of laughter is only associated with secondary characters. That's why Walter Benjamin is correct in this essay on Kafka to indicate that the secondary characters are outside the nexus of the world of law and the

Nature Theatre. Again, I hope to provide an analysis of this type of laughter in a later text.

An important work on this topic is Felix Weltsch's *Religion und Humor in Leben und Werk Kafkas* (Berlin: Herbig, 1957). Weltsch, who knew Kafka personally, stresses the importance of humor in understanding Kafka's work. Weltsch provides very astute analyses while remembering that humor was part of Kafka's personality. But there is a significant difference with the approach taken here. Weltsch identifies only one type of humour in Kafka. This is a serious humor that is related to religion ("es ist einer ernster Humor und deshalb gerade kann er in Kafkas Schaffen mir Religion verknüpft werden") (Weltsch, 79). The difference with the present approach is highlighted if one considers Weltsch's interpretation of the humour in "A Hunger Artist." For Weltsch, the humour consists in the chaotic string of reasons proffered for the fasting—as entertainment, as business, as means to admiration—which are resolved in the final explanation that the artiste was disgusted by food. According to Weltsch, this explanation reorders the crazy chaos of different reasons (Weltsch, 79). Such an interpretation sees the work as a self-subsisting entity, whose only connection to the "outside" is the notion of unity, that is, the religious impulse. Conversely, the interpretation of humor proposed here locates laughter and the connection to the "outside" in the way that unity—such as the unity of the ideal of freedom—is shattered. Whereas for Weltsch Kafka's humour consists in the reconstitution of a totality, for the present interpretation laughter is the effect of totality's impossibility.

29. Gustav Janouch, *Conversations with Kafka* (London: Derek Verschoyle, 1953), 55. I am quoting from Janouch's volume despite the doubts about their provenance. It is fascinating that in the conversations Kafka functions in a certain sense as Janouch's Other. From that point of view, the issue of whether the conversations are accurate transcripts is of secondary importance. I am also noting that the citations are to the first edition, but they can all be found in the second edition as well.

30. Cf. Kiarina A. Kordela, *$urplus: Spinoza, Lacan* (New York: SUNY, 2007).

31. Janouch, 65.

32. Ibid., 74.

CHAPTER SIX

"WORKFORCE WITHOUT POSSESSIONS": KAFKA, "SOCIAL JUSTICE," AND THE WORD *RELIGION*

Peter Fenves

Among the fragments to be found in Franz Kafka's octavo notebooks, there is a curious proposal for what appears, at first glance, to be a utopian community of dedicated workers. Unlike the surrounding fragments, the proposal is more akin to an historical or sociological document than a literary sketch or philosophicoreligious meditation. It stands out, above all, because of its odd officiousness, as if the insurance office from which Kafka had recently been released suddenly insinuates itself into his literary existence. Kafka called the fragment "Die besitzlose Arbeiterschaft," which I will henceforth translate, with some reservations, as "Workforce without Possessions."[1] *Arbeiterschaft* designates a body of workers, sometimes—but not necessarily—organized into a union. Unlike *workforce*, the German term does not imply stored-up labor power, which can be effectively applied to a given economic situation; rather, it suggests nothing beyond a collection of workers whose only commonality lies in the work they are called upon to perform, whether alone or in combination with one another. Probably written in February or March of 1918, "Workforce without Possessions" is neither a defense nor a critique of the October Revolution in Russia, the events of which Kafka seemed to follow with some degree of interest. Nor does it appear to have much in common with other socialist or communist programs, including those proposed under the banner of Zionism. Whereas Zionist collectives are, as the name itself indicates, related to Zion, the *Arbeiterschaft* Kafka envisages is capable of forming itself almost anywhere. It is true that the fragment includes "dates" among its short list of acceptable foodstuffs, and in this way points toward Palestine perhaps; but when the fragment actually poses the question "where?" there is no trace of this association: "there, where one can help, in abandoned districts, in poorhouses"—which scarcely sounds like Palestine circa 1918. Kafka then adds, almost as an afterthought, the word "teacher," without specifying whether the workers in question are supposed to be teachers or whether the workforce is to be located wherever the workers might find one. In any case, among the more compelling reasons to resist the temptation to view Kafka's sketch as a socialist or Zionist community is the presence of a state to which the workforce remains tenuously connected.[2]

And despite the fact that the fragment has been translated as "Brotherhood of Poor Workers," it has even less to do with brotherhood than with Zion.[3] The "working life" of its workers is, to be sure, "a matter of conscience and a matter of faith in co-humanity [*Mitmenschen*]," but nowhere is there any indication of fraternity or even only camaraderie. It would be similarly misleading—but doubtless less so—to represent the workforce as a revision or reiteration of another community of common humility, namely monasticism, particularly of the Franciscan kind, the emergence of which in the thirteenth century generated a complex and consequential discussion about the difference between owning things outright, which would be forbidden, and simply being permitted to use them. Only to a limited extent can the operations of the workforce be understood in terms of apostolic poverty: there is faith, to be sure, but only in "co-humanity," and there is trust, but only the trust in the relation through which a worker becomes a worker without possessions—or, in Latin, a language to which I will repeatedly return in this essay, a "proletariat." For, as Kafka emphasizes at the end of the first section of the fragment, which is placed under the title "Duties," the function of trust resides in making the mediation of the law superfluous: "The relation to the employer to be treated as a relation of trust, never demanding the mediation of the courts. Each job taken on to be brought to an end in all circumstances, except for grave considerations of health."

Thus ends the first section of the fragment, which is placed under the heading of "Duties." An enumeration of two corresponding "Rights" immediately follows. The proposal for the construction of the workforce is thus laid out in the form of a juridical document, in which the fulfillment of certain obligations secures corresponding rights, while the enjoyment of these rights generates the resulting duties. As the transitional clause unmistakably indicates, however, the duty into which the others issue is purely negative: in case of conflict, both parties are to refrain from seeking legal remedies. Conflict, specifically conflict that would prompt a worker to initiate a strike, must be avoided at all costs, and this obligation can be guaranteed under the condition that the workers always do what they have agreed to do, unless they are physically unable to do so, in which case the use of force would be both useless and impotent. In this way, the work-force puts the legal order out of work without supposing that either the law loses its binding force or the state withers away. The relation of trust between employer and worker is such that neither relies on an external and supposedly neutral power, namely the courts, to enforce the agreements. In term of Roman law, which Kafka studied for his law degree, every-thing involving the "workforce without possession" belongs to the sphere of private law.

But—and this is one of the crucial elements of the fragment—the right secured for the workers primarily consists in the opportunity to *stop* working. The first of the two rights limits the workday to six hours, more or less the amount of time Kafka worked in his capacity as insur-ance lawyer—"four to five," he adds "for corporeal work." The second specified right makes it possible for the worker to withdraw from work altogether: "During illness or inability to work because of age," workers are "to be taken up in state homes for the elderly and hospitals." Far from doing away with the state, then, the workforce is part of its welfare sys-tem. Any possessions that workers acquired prior to their inclusion in the workforce are to be given to the state for the "erection of hospitals and homes"—presumably the very homes and hospitals into which they retire as soon as they are completely unable to work. An abbreviated system of social security thus emerges. Even if the courts are prohibited from enter-ing into the relation of employer to worker, this relation is still established in conjunction with the state: "Council [*Rat*]," Kafka writes and then adds in parenthesis "(difficult duty) mediated with the government." Because the workforce is specifically not constructed as an independent mode of existence, sustained by feelings of fraternity, dedicated to either a god or an ethical ideal, serving as an inner-worldly image of salvation, it must enter into a mediated relation with something outside of its private-law sphere. If the workforce is dedicated to any principle, it is to working as little as possible—thus to the principle of laziness or lethargy, which can be recognized as such only if there is a just enough work as well. And the possessionless character of the workforce guarantees that its work will dis-appear as quickly as possible, leaving almost no memorial of what has been done. The only significant trace of work done by the workforce lies in its continued existence; but this, too, is limited, for, as the closing words of the fragment indicate, the *Arbeiterschaft* is to be given "one trial year."

Nowhere does Kafka specify what the workforce must accomplish in order for it to pass this test; but there is good reason to suppose the experi-ment is bound to fail. For, to put it bluntly, it is doubtful whether *anyone* could join the workforce—or at least join it as a matter of choice. The reason for raising this doubt can be found in the clause immediately preceding the note about the difficult duty of giving advice: "Provisionally, at least, exclusion of those who own their own businesses [*die Selbstständigen*], those who are married, and women." About the last two classes of persons, there is probably little to add; but with respect to the first one, the situation is not so simple. If "die Selbstständigen" ("small-business owners," "men of independent means," "those who stand by themselves") are prohibited from joining the workforce, its "work life" cannot be considered primarily a matter of conscience and faith but is, rather, rooted in extraneous circumstances and bodily needs. Perhaps it could still be said that the workers would choose to join the workforce but only if, in the same vein, it can be said of workers who are physically unable to work that they choose not to do so. For this reason, "die Selbstständigen" is probably not supposed to mean "persons of independent means" or "people who own their own businesses." But it is even less likely that it is supposed to mean those who "stand on their own" as a result of their unmarried status, for, if this were the case, then no one—neither a woman, nor a single man, nor a married man—can enter into the workforce. And there is no indication that it is reserved for children.

Given such considerations, it is clear that the fragment represents, for Kafka, an alternative to marriage: an institution in which a few middling men, "five hundred, upper limit," can be freed of their independence without at the same time falling into the intolerable position of the "family man" or "Hausvater." But this is not all that the fragment represents; it also, and more importantly, presents a social aggregate into which no one is born but to which no one can then choose to belong—no one, that is, who is indeed one, "he himself," a private person, whose independence is such that he can be identified and counted as one who either "stands" or "falls" on his own. In the context of the fragment, Kafka does not provide a name for the "one" or "no one" who is allowed to join; but he comes ever so close to doing so: in German, its name would be *der Un-selbstständige*, he who is "non-self-standing" or "non-independent" but is not therefore leaning on someone or something else. In other words, he—and for now at least, it must be "he"—who enters into the workforce is no longer the "he" who is recognizable from outside its sphere of operations. He becomes a worker pure and simple, and his principal occupation consists in doing as little work as possible, thus being as little "himself" as possible, and this littleness expresses itself in the condition of nonownership.

Working in a No-Man's-Land

All of this is predicated, however, on the presumption that "Workforce without Possession" is a proposal for a workforce without possession—a proposal, that is, which represents a blueprint for the construction of an as yet unrealized institution. The fact that the rules for membership are discouraging, to say the least, gives enough reason to suppose that the fragment may be something else as well. Even if it is difficult to view the text as a literary sketch or a philosophicoreligious meditation, it can still be seen as notes toward a critique of a literary work, where *critique* is understood roughly along the lines Benjamin outlined in his essay on Goethe's *Elective Affinities*: as the alchemical flame in which the work disappears; more prosaically, if still obscurely, as the disclosure of its "truth-content."[4] As it turns out, a work-in-progress with which Kafka became intimately familiar revolves around the institution of a workforce without possessions. Here is the voice of a certain character named Biber, who acts as the "teacher" for the narrator in the early chapters of a novel Max Brod was writing in the fall of 1917: "The land on which you are standing is holy land, for it is stateless."[5] The premise of the novel is that a world war continues indefinitely, creating an anti-state in the "no man's land" that separates belligerent parties. In this midst of this neutral zone, a community of workers is established under the leadership of a messianic figure named Dr. Askonas. Biber, one of his disciples, continues his pedagogical exercise: "You want an explanation? Now then: we are on terrain that no longer belongs to military command and which the civil authorities have not yet taken charge of. Years of war have laid everything to waste.... The key thing is that no one bothers about us. So there is really a tiny spot of land that is without war.... We who are without space live outside of time.... The crop is harvested. So we work, and live off of what we work on."[6]

Brod ultimately published his work-in-progress under the title of *Das große Wagnis* (The Great Risk). The title is drawn from a game that another character, a nurse named Ruth, invents for the purpose of teaching children that each and every choice they make is a great risk, for every choice is decisive. Children learn all kinds of things, Ruth explains to the narrator, who soon enough falls in love with her; they learn how to talk correctly, walk correctly, eat correctly, and so forth; but they are never taught how to *will* correctly. The game she constructs is meant to make up for this lacuna. A labyrinth-like board with numerous interconnecting cartons is its setting. Onto this board, there is placed a ball, which represents a prisoner in a well-guarded prison. The goal of the game is to get the ball out "into the open," *ins Freie*, which can be accomplished only with one swift, certain, and integral movement. The game involves a "great risk" because "there is one and only one chance for liberation." If the player hesitates, or makes a false move, "everything is lost."[7] Not only is this the rule of the game ("one chance only"), it is also the law of life, and especially, it should be emphasized, the law of married life. Ruth is a literary representative of the woman with whom Brod, already married to someone else, had recently become involved, and *The Great Risk* represents, among other things, a revision of *Elective Affinities*, in which the leap into the open—if it can be accomplished—is not only supposed to free one from martial conflicts but from marital ones as well: "indeed," Ruth tells the narrator, "the quick decision is the great risk.... There is no time for reflection.... My game is naked life."[8] Kafka responds specifically to this passage in a letter to Brod from November 1917: "If the rigor of this game is a self-torment and torment of the loved one, then I understand her; but if it is an independent conviction, which has no source in the circumstances of Ruth's life or yours, then it is a desperate conviction.... The whole thing is almost a war game, built on the famous idea of the breakthrough, a Hindenburg opportunity. Perhaps I misunderstand you," he adds with characteristic diplomacy, "but if there are not countless possibilities of liberation [*Befreiung*], particularly, however, possibilities in every moment of our life, then there is perhaps none at all." Even more diplomatically—to the point of disingenuousness perhaps—he concludes: "But I do really misunderstand you. The game is indeed permanently repeated; because of the momentary lapse, only the moment is lost, not everything."[9]

Two possibilities emerge from Kafka's critique of Brod's work-in-progress: either the risk of the game is small; or there is no risk at all, which is equivalent to asserting that there is no game, after all—or that the game is no game but is, in fact, "naked life," as Ruth says, even if she means something very different. Applied to the real risk, whose rules Ruth's game is supposed to reproduce for the sake of making its stakes accessible to children, this means: the "free state of Liberia"—which Biber identifies as "the true Eretz Yisrael"[10]—can be established whenever and wherever a no-man's land is discovered. A few months after expressing his misgivings about Ruth's game, in January 1918, more exactly, Kafka communicates to Brod his considered opinion of *The Great Risk*. As a literary work, it is of scant significance; in terms of what he calls the "social-intellectual" order, however, it is "a magnificent open word. It is perhaps nothing more than this statement, this leaping-aside-of-time [*dieses der-Zeit-an-die Seite-springen*]; but this, too, can be a great beginning. We [Kafka and Oskar Baum] spoke into the early evening about the novel as if it were an historical document that one used to prove this or that point. It was also this way with [Brod's earlier novel, *Castle*] *Nornepygge*, but then I was still too little touched by it."[11] Ruth's game is won when the ball is sprung from the board. Brod succeeds in his novel by springing aside time to the point where the meaning of *Zeit* (time) and *Seite* (side) are as close as the words themselves. Sideways time, as opposed to its rectilinear counterpart, then expresses itself in the possibility of a "great beginning," which has nothing to do with great risks but is, on the contrary, a matter of simple trust.[12]

Shortly before writing this summary comment, Kafka had tried to give Brod some advice about the conclusion to the novel, which would recount what happens to the "free state of Liberia" when it begins to disintegrate as a result of the fact that no work can get done without the application of physical force. Having abandoned their names—"Proper names are self-love, symbols of being alone," according to Biber[13]—the members of the Liberian community become so thoroughly identified with their work that they adopt the names of their jobs. Still, for want of any reason to work, they also stop doing so. The sole exception to this disorganized general strike can be found in the case of "The Waiter," who carries out his duties only because he has no choice, having been put into chains. At the end of the novel, as Liberia is bombed, the narrator tries to escape; but he is taken into custody, condemned as a traitor, and finally shot. According to Brod's diary, he finished the novel on Christmas day of 1917. Kafka, who apparently did not know that his friend had completed the novel, gives him the following advice in January of 1918: "It suddenly came to me, prompted by reading out loud [Ernst] Troeltsch's essay, that the positive conclusion of the novel really wants something simpler and closer than I had originally supposed, namely the erection of a church, a sanitarium [*Aufrechtung einer Kirche, einer Heilanstalt*], therefore something that will almost without a doubt come and is already being built around us in the same tempo as our collapse."[14]

The conclusion Kafka proposes can be considered "simple and close" for the simple reason that it is already enclosed in the novel. In one of its opening chapters, Biber had said—and here I am repeating myself: "The land on which you are standing is holy land [*heiliger Boden*]." In place of a "holy land" there emerges a "sanitarium" (*Heilanstalt*), which is unattached to any land. In terms drawn from Brod's novel, this means that the collapse of the "Liberian" experiment is no cause for despair, for the experiment can start up again; it was always only a beginning, indeed a "great beginning," and the church or sanitarium with which the novel should end—comparable to the ones that Luther ushered into existence, according to Troeltsch—would be the sign of a readiness to leap into a new Liberia, should conditions ever again prove favorable. *Contra* Ruth, then, everything is not lost—not even the novel, which, despite its literary decrepitude, survives as an historical document from which a discussion of contemporary political conditions can begin. But nothing is "gained" either, for the sanitarium into which Liberia folds is not a place into which one can simply enter or, more exactly, *choose* to enter. As the topic of Troeltsch's essay suggests, grace is required, and the erection of the *Heilanstalt* is predicated on the transformation of its meaning: "Grace is, according to the classical formulation of Melanchthon, no longer *medicina* but, rather, *favor*."[15] Troeltsch's own formulations, however, betray something different: not only does the term *Heilanstalt* suggest an institution in which medicines are dispensed; he also represents this new sanitarium as a universal claim that the rite of baptism turns into a possession.[16] If, however, the *Heilanstalt* were indeed to be a matter of *favor* rather than *medicina*, then it could be understood in precisely this manner: a sanitarium without medicine. Instead of being a "common wealth," this *Heilanstalt* would be predicated on the absence of possessions and would respond directly to the problem Troeltsch addresses, even if the problem can no longer be limited to that of "Luther, Protestantism, and the Modern World," to quote the full title of the essay Kafka read out loud to his friend Oskar Baum, who was sight-impaired.

"Workforce without Possession" can thus be seen as an elaboration on the suggestion that Kafka made for the conclusion of *The Great Risk*: it is something "positive," a church or sanitarium, the tempo of which corresponds the sideway-character of collapse. The fact that "Workforce without Possession" reads as though it were a "social-intellectual" statement goes without saying. Nor is it surprising that it represents something akin to a "night residue" of his day-to-day writing. Assicurazione Generali, the Trieste-based insurance company for which Kafka worked, like all insurance companies, sought to minimize risks. By calling his novel *The Great Risk*, Brod brings literature into relation with the insurance business. And Kafka replies in turn—by minimizing the risk of Liberia, if not altogether nullifying it, and by changing the idea of liberty, in turn. Added to this is the undeniable fact that the fragment in question reverses the work conditions into which Liberia falls: in the latter, no one works unless compelled to do so; in the former, work is always only a matter of "conscience." Above all, however, Kafka's advice concerning the conclusion to *The Great Risk* grants a degree of insight into the most puzzling dimension of the fragment: the apparent impossibility of anyone entering into the workforce voluntarily. It is not as though you or I are in a position to join the *Arbeiterschaft* simply by the fact that we are human beings, who are willy nilly defined by our ability to make choices; and despite the effort of commentators to associate the workforce with Zionism, their only evidence is a single word: "dates." The workforce arises out of the collapse of Liberia, with the result that the citizens of the latter—if "citizen" is the right word—enter into the former under conditions that it cannot be captured by terms such as "elective will" and "faculty of choice." The "free choice" is at odds with the "free state" of Liberia. This is already apparent in Kafka's critique of Ruth's game, which resolves into the proposition that there is always a possibility of liberation, and for this reason, there is no choice that secures this chance. "Advice" or "counsel" is a "difficult duty" for the same reason: it is not exactly that there can be *no* "choice," no choice of work, for example, or no choice of spouse, but the incompatibility between the faculty of choice and the state of liberation makes every choice "difficult," even when one kind of choice, that of a spouse, is excluded from the start. And what of the stateless condition of Liberia does the workforce retain, so that it can be understood as its continuation? Obviously and paradoxically, the absence of possessions, for this absence represents the lack of an administrative-juridical power in the space from which the workers come. For those who belong to the workforce, things always remain in the state of *res nullius* ("no one's thing"), to use Roman juridical language, and they do so precisely because they are themselves exponents of a *terra nullius* ("no one's land"), which is not so much destroyed—for how can space be destroyed?—as temporarily reoccupied. The workforce is therefore attracted toward those places where a utopian experiment is at the point of dissolving, leaving a "church" or "sanitarium" in its place: "There where one can help, in abandoned districts, poorhouses."

Taken from the Gold Coast

But Liberia, of course, is also the name of a real country. When Biber first utters this almost numinous name, he insists on this point: "You are in Liberia, my friend, the state of freedom. A Negro republic? No clue? The name came to us half in jest, but we found that it corresponded to one of our main principles, the principle of nonoriginality. We hate originality, and we persecute... paradox as our fiercest enemy."[17] Biber's lack of originality may be in this choice of names a reflection of Brod's own. To be sure, his friend never wrote about "Liberia," as far as we know; but Kafka had recently written and even published in the pages of Martin Buber's journal *Der Jude* a curious "report" that takes its point of departure from the region where Liberia was founded by former slaves of the United States: the Gold Coast of Africa, which, as the name suggests, is presumably also the source of great wealth. This, in any case, is the homeland of the ape that acquires the name Rotpeter and eventually composes "A Report for an Academy" (RA 1994, 234–45). The acquisition of this derivative name—about which Rotpeter is none too happy—coincides with his own acquisition, which, for obvious reasons, had to be original: he was a *res nullius* until he came under the dominion of the "firm of Hagenbeck," which presumably refers to the famous zoo-owner and impresario from Hamburg, who commissioned the transportation of indigenous Canadians to his zoo as items for display.[18] In the course of a hunting expedition, Rotpeter was shot twice: the first shot marked him; the second instantly— and one might say, magically—changed his status from *res nullius* to *res*

Hagenbeckeum. By aping his captors, he derives a corresponding and correspondingly derivative right, which culminates—this is the end of the "report"—in the acquisition of a semidomesticated chimpanzee either as spouse or as pet, or as both at alternative times, during the night as the former, during the daytime as the latter, in accordance perhaps (for this is scarcely clear) with his faculty of choice.

As for the "Liberian" character of Rotpeter's place of origin, it can be discerned from the following remarks, which can be read allegorically in any number of ways, so that readers may discover a way out of an interpretative impasse and, by so doing, produce a second-order allegory in which they themselves are comparable to the figure that their reading makes into something other than what he is, namely a marked and captured ape: "I had no way out," Rotpeter says, referring to his cage on board the ship, "but I had to procure one, for without it, I could not live. . . . I am afraid that one does not exactly understand what I understand by 'way out.' I use the word in its most usual and complete sense. I intentionally do not say 'freedom.' I do not mean this great feeling of freedom on all sides. As an ape I knew it perhaps, and I have met human beings who yearn for it. As concerns me, however, I demanded freedom neither then nor now." Much could be said here about Rotpeter's theory of freedom, especially since he adds: "By the way, with freedom one all-too-often deceives oneself among human beings. And just as freedom is counted among the most sublime feelings, so is the corresponding disappointment the most sublime." But commentary on this sublime passage, which reads as though it were a parody of Rousseau, or one of Rousseau's commentators, including Kant, would be largely beside the point if it did not remember the status of its writer: a possession, presumably still Hagenbeck's, whose "liberation," such as it is, changes nothing with regard to his status. Even the repetitive-perfomative character of his work remains the same. It is not as though, for Rotpeter, the "way out" and "freedom on all sides" are opposed *in general*—this is the point of Kafka's critique of the ball-game Ruth invents. The point is, rather, that Rotpeter's "way out" is also the way in which the Hagenbeck firm expresses *its* own "corporate" personhood: by granting a language to its possessions. Kafka probably never read the opening chapters of Marx's *Capital*, which discuss the language of commodities; but Rotpeter is the speaking possession *par excellence*.

As long as Rotpeter must be held in custody, the firm cannot demonstrate that it really possesses him, for this is in the nature of the juridical concept of possession. In order for something to be mine, I must be able to leave it, without it therefore returning to the condition in which it can legally become yours. Rotpeter passes from the state of physical detention to that of juridical possession by discovering a way out, which represents, in juridical terms, the way in—that is, the way into the sphere of private right as opposed to that of sheer physical force. Thus Rotpeter's own version of self-deception, which expresses itself in the following line of thought, broken as it is, even if the break is rarely recognized as such: "for Hagenbeck," Rotpeter says, speaking of the Hamburg firm as though it were a legal persona comparable to himself, "apes belong on the crate wall—well, so I stopped being an ape." The fictional voice of Hagenbeck reflects itself in the ape's own. Only insofar as Hagenbeck possesses things without actually detaining them does it actually possess them. Furthermore, only when the "firm of Hagenbeck" is personified can Rotpeter emerge as a person. And finally, only when Rotpeter discovers a way out of his detention is the Hagenbeck firm in a position to demonstrate its own freedom—a demonstration that is particularly important for a firm because its existence lies in the legal code. Hence the inconspicuous yet essential "also" in the following passage, which brings Rotpeter's meditation on freedom to a close: "Often, while waiting to start a vaudeville performance, I have watched some pair of acrobats rushing about on trapezes under the ceiling. They swung, they rocked, they leaped, they floated into each other's arms, one carried the other by clenching his hair in his teeth. 'This is also human freedom,' I thought to myself, 'autocratic motion!' You mockery of holy nature! No building would withstand the laughter of apedom at this sight."

The Case of Gracchus

About animals that have an *animus* to return, the Emperor Justinian authorizes the following formulation in his *Institutes*, which has provoked ridicule in more than a few commentators: "in the case of those animals which generally come and go, the rule has been endorsed that they are treated as yours so long as they have the mind to return [*animum revertendi habent*]. If they cease to do so, they also cease to be yours and are available to the first taker. And they are regarded as ceasing to have this intention when they abandon the practice of returning."[19] As numerous jurists have noted, including one under whom Kafka studied, Ludwig Pffaf, the discussion of acquisition of things belonging to no one, from which the above quote is drawn, occupies a disproportionately prominent place in the doctrine of acquisition, for it is relatively uncommon for such things to be acquired. Almost all acquisitions, and particularly those that call for legal remedies, derive from previous acquisitions. Even in the *Institutes* themselves, this disproportion attracts a brief notice: "if an island arises in the sea," Justinian explains, and immediately adds, "which is a rare occurrence," but then presses on: "it is open to occupation, for it is believed to belong to no one."[20] Despite their rarity, however, such occurrences deserve discussion, for they represent a fundamental juridical transformation: what was once outside the sphere of law enters into it, and a purely physical report, if such a thing could ever be produced, even by an ape, is insufficient for the assessment of the case under consideration. Less rare than the emergence of a new island out of the sea is the entrance of wild animals into the eyesight of hunters; but it nonetheless represents the very same thing: a chance for the sphere of right to expand into the wildness. Because of its relative frequency, the discussion of original acquisition—which gained renewed significance after 1492, for obvious reasons—is generally called the doctrine of *ferae bestiae*:

> Wild beasts, birds and fish, that is, all animals born on land or in the sea or air as soon as they are caught by anyone, forthwith become his, for what previously belonged to no one is, by natural reason, accorded to its captor.... The question was raised whether wild animals, which have been so that they could be captured, forthwith become yours. In the opinion of some, it is and is held to be yours at once, so long as you pursue it; but should you give up the chase, it is no longer yours and is again open to the first taker. Others held the view that it becomes yours only if you actually take it. We give authority to the second view, for many accidents may occur such that you do not take it.[21]

Among the many accidents that would interfere with the chase, one is paradigmatic, for it can be discerned in the word itself—an accident, namely, in which the hunter falls. Such is the case—or the fall—of a hunter whose fate Kafka explores in a series of contemporaneous fragments: a hunter who accidentally falls while chasing a chamois. As a wild goat, the chamois occupies an ambiguous juridical position, for, in general, goats are tame; a wild goat falls under the doctrine of *ferae bestiae* only under the condition that its wildness outpaces its goatness, as it were. As for the name of accident-prone hunter, Gracchus, commentators have often noted that it resembles the Latin word *graculus* (one "c"), from which the English word *grackle* derives and which translates into Czech as *kavka* ("jackdaw").[22] As support for this interpretation, which has been declared "authoritative," presumably because it has been repeated often enough, it is frequently noted that Kafka twice visited the town in which the first fragment is set, Riva del Garda, the second time on his way to a sanitarium, in which, as it happened, an Austrian officer shot himself. But Gracchus is a good name in its own right, indeed a very good name. Among the notable Gracchi, one in particular, Tiberius Sempronius Gracchus, made the name into a byword for radical social justice when he championed a set of agrarian laws, the famous *lex sempronia agraria*, which called for an unprecedented redistribution of large agrarian estates to possessionless Roman soldiers, who has recently fallen to the level of the urban proletariat.[23] These laws came into effect only as a result of what would later be called a "mass urban strike." And Tiberius was only the first of several Gracchi who committed themselves to the cause of radical social justice. So closely was the name Gracchus associated with this cause that it was applied to the last and most radical among the French revolutionaries, "Gracchus" Babeuf, who was executed in the so-called conspiracy of the equals.

The hunter Gracchus differs from other Gracchi even while he is unambiguously alive, for, as a hunter—as opposed to a soldier or farmer, to say nothing of a social reformer—he is out for himself, and apparently for himself alone. This aloneness is then eternalized as a result of his accident, which not only sends him into a region of indeterminacy but similarly affects the chamois he failed to capture: it, too, acquires an eerily ambiguous status. Something like the obverse of the Rotpeter-Hagenbeck scenario thus obtains: in one case, the corporation and the commodity collectively gain voice, as each reinforces the personhood of the other; in the other case, Gracchus and the chamois enter into a "no man's land." What this means for the chamois we don't know. What it means for the hunter is a little clearer: he is doubtless dead, but "to a certain extent" he is alive as well. Something of "The Waiter" in *The Great Risk* thus attaches itself to the Hunter Gracchus, insofar as both figures are attached to their work—one by a chain, the other by his name. As long as the hunter Gracchus remains the *hunter* Gracchus, according to the *old* doctrine of *ferae bestiae*—which Justinian annuls by imperial fiat in the passage quoted above—the chamois could remain his, since he at least had it in his sights when he fell; but since he is dead, he cannot complete the capture by taking the thing under his charge. And it is by no means out of the question that the old doctrine remains in effect, for, near the end of the second major fragment—which, incidentally, immediately issues into the first version of Rotpeter's report—it becomes clear that the accident took place in the fourth century, thus before Justinian's authoritative codification. It is therefore possible that the chamois is neither Gracchus's nor someone else's, and this neither-nor is equivalent to saying, in positive terms: here is a *res nullius* in an "objective" sense, that is, an object that under no conditions can be made into "my thing," regardless of how powerful the "I" becomes. The chamois could be "practically annihilated," to use Kant's telling phrase,[24] as long as Gracchus would remain practically (but only practically) annihilated as well. If, however, it is *possible* for one thing to be a *res nullius* in an "objective" sense, without a specific law barring the acquisition of the thing in question, then it becomes questionable whether anything can become one's own. An utterly non-possessable chamois, ever running about, as the insertion of "wilderness" into civilization, makes it impossible to determine with any degree of certainty the all-important lines that distinguish mine from thine. In light of this possibility, the hunter Gracchus, despite his initial aloofness, could be considered the most revolutionary Gracchi of all: Tiberius Gracchus only wanted to take land away from absentee owners of large latifundia and give it to destitute Roman soldiers; "Gracchus" Babeuf only wanted to make the people of his nation equal in terms of the goods they enjoyed; the fall of the hunter Gracchus, by contrast, inadvertently raises the possibility that no one can take possession of anything at all. Every "good" enters into the juridical state that characterizes the elusive chamois.

"Don't laugh!"—so says Gracchus in both of the major fragments where he appears. The second time, it is because he has just described himself as the patron saint of sailors, to whom the cabin boy anxiously prays during a troubling storm. The interlocutor denies that he ever laughed; but there is good reason for Gracchus to be suspicious, for what help could he be to anyone, even a lowly cabin boy, he who has been lying on a bark, doing nothing, "practically annihilated," for fifteen hundred years? To which one can add: unlike his namesakes, Tiberius and Babeuf, for example, he never did anything—not simply because he is a literary character (as if this were also not true, to some extent, of Tiberius and Babeuf, whose historical reality is not to be denied, of course, but whose Gracchian character largely derives from the literature of political historiography), not simply because of this but also, and especially, because he is not, to use an expression, "his own man." He is Kafka's man, or Max Brod's, to some extent (for Brod made into a public figure); more so, however, he is, or was, his patron's. And the conversation he conducts with an unnamed interlocutor almost addresses this very question— "almost" because at the precise point where this question would be inescapable, the interlocutor begins his own line of interrogation: "Gracchus, one request. Tell me briefly yet coherently [*kurz aber zusammenhängend*] how it actually stands with you." Gracchus, however, is interested in something else—something other than himself and his bewildering identity, for he is reflecting on the even more bewildering status of the "patrons." "Who is the patron?" the interlocutor asks, to which Gracchus replies, "the possessor of the bark," and immediately adds, "These patrons are outstanding human beings. Only I do not understand them." It turns out, moreover, that *his* patron, the one who possesses the bark, just died in Hamburg—which, of course, brings up the question whether or not the bark is possessed any longer, for, without a so-called will, the juridical relation of possession ceases with death, and so, too, presumably does that of patronage, even if the patron is a corporation like Hagenbeck. Beyond what Gracchus says about the patrons, the word itself reveals only so much about question at hand: the patron, derived from *pater*, of course, is the protector, the *Schutzherr*, and his protection is particularly appropriate in only a few contexts beyond that of informal and devotional relations, especially, however, in the context of sailing on the open seas, in which the captain of a ship is called its "patron," for he is there to protect the ship from hostile elements, both natural and human. When Kant personifies the land in his *Doctrine of Right*, he captures in a striking manner the relation of patronage: "if you cannot protect me, you cannot command me," the land says to its potential possessor, and Kant immediately adds in his own voice, "and this is how the famous dispute [between Grotius and Selden] about open and closed seas is to be resolved: the sea can be a state's as far as a cannon can reach."[25] This resolution goes beyond the elemental difference between land and sea: *whatever* one possesses can be heard to say—even if one understands as well as Kant that things do not speak, that personification is silent deception—"I will be yours as long as you protect me." With the death of their patron Gracchus and the bark are both in the same position: free, one could say, but also, in the same stroke, totally exposed.

Gracchus, for instance, is exposed to a foreign line of interrogation, which ironically revolves around his own identity: "As for the patrons, this is how things stand: originally, though, the bark belonged to no one [*Die Barke hat doch ursprünglich keinem Menschen gehört*]"—at which point the interlocutor interrupts Gracchus line of thought, asking for a "brief but coherent" account of himself alone. Nothing further is said about the patrons, at least in the texts available to us. Gracchus's statement begs for an explanation. How did the patron acquire something that originally belonged to no one? How did the bark change its status from no one's to someone's? The patron obviously did not "mix" his labor with the wood of the bark, to cite Locke's famous account of original acquisition,[26] and still more obviously, the patron did not gain possession by occupation: he lived in Hamburg, while Gracchus has occupied it for more than a millennium, much longer than the year or two prescribed by Roman law for *dominium* under the doctrine of *usucapion*. Despite all of this time, which would perhaps qualify the bark as a new island, especially since a millennium on the water is as nothing compared to the entire time it is destined to remain afloat, namely forever—despite all of this, the bark, this quasi-island, which bisects land and sea, is not Gracchus's. He is a patron, to be sure, but only a "patron saint" or *Schutzgeist*, to whom the cabin boy vainly prays: this is sheer fantasy, which stands in contrast to the reality of the relation of possession, which never accrues to him. If ever a *lex sempronia* was called for, even if it does not take the form of a *lex agraria*, it is in the case of the patron's bark. Little wonder that it is the focal point of Gracchus's attention: patrons enjoy a power though which they are able to acquire a *res nullius* without labor or occupation—a power that is as ludicrous as the protection Gracchus offers to the cabin boy during a stormy night on the sea. Just as the chamois draws Gracchus into a precipice, however, the interlocutor draws his attention away from the abyssal problem of "patronic" possession and directs it back toward his own ambiguous status—which suggests that the question of identity ("who am I, after all?") may be little more than a ruse that willy-nilly draws attention away from the kind of questions Gracchus had begun to raise: how on earth does so-called original acquisition come about? How did the bark fall into the hands of the patron? And what happens to it now that the patron is dead? "Only I do not understand them," Gracchus says of the patrons, after having praised them, and continues, "I do not mean their language, although, of course, often I do not understand their language either. But this is only by-the-by. In the course of centuries I have learned enough languages and could be the interpreter between ancestors and contemporaries. But the line of thought [*Gedankengang*] of the patrons, this I do not understand."[27] If, after more than a thousand years, Gracchus still cannot understand the patrons' line of thought, there is good reason to suppose that it cannot be followed under any condition. If the line of thought cannot be retraced, it is doubtful that it is indeed a matter of thought. On the contrary, the "line" may be an expression of "freedom" in the form of violence—and thus unjust.

No such conclusion can be drawn, however, at least not from the extent texts: there is not the slightest hint of injustice—in contrast to guilt, which Gracchus expressly denies. But there is no corresponding question of injustice in the case of his patron. Without the trace of injustice, even if only in the inarticulate form of anger, no movement can be generated that aims to restore the status quo ante: the way back to the original state of things, which would also be a way forward to a just order of possession, is blocked. All of the impasses that gather around the juridical doctrine of *res nullius* concentrate themselves into the image of the bark, which Gracchus's patron acquired, without a coherent rationale, but which cannot be seized for the very same reason: incoherence, the absence of a coherent "line of thought." The intensity of this concentration extends beyond the dimension of the doctrine that concerns the doctrine of *res nullius*, as it emerges in private law; it also encompasses the corresponding doctrine in divine law, which specifies the condition under which a things is put out of circulation for good: "Things belonging to no one are sacred things or religious things or sanctified things; for whatever stands under divine law is among no one's goods."[28] Of these three kinds of things, only the middle one can be created without public or pontifical approval: "Anyone can, by his own will, make a place religious, if he buries a corpse on his land."[29] The irony of this law is inescapable, for as soon as one acquires a piece of land, it can be made so that it is unjust for anyone to acquire it, including oneself.[30]

Despite the clarity of the law, which prompted some ghoulish decisions, its juridical status is difficult to establish. It is neither a doctrine of private law, the law of nations, nor natural right; and it could not be called a law of reason either, for there is no coherent "line of thought" that proceeds from the existence of a properly buried corpse to an obligation, imposed on everyone, to refrain from acquiring the portion of the earth's surface that lies above it. And the law under which something becomes *res religiosae* is not exactly "divine" either—at least not divine in the same sense as the laws governing *res sanctae* and *res sacrae*, which are expressions of state power and pontifical authority respectively. Anyone able to own a plot of land; anyone who is *sui juris*, "his own man," can, with the assistance of a corpse, remove a portion of land from intrahuman commerce. In this case, and this case alone perhaps, human-divine commerce, such as it is, has nothing to do with either public or priestly pronouncements but is mediated solely by the presence—if this word can be used—of a corpse that has duly come to rest. The law of *res religiosae* thus represents the reversal of the law of *ferae bestiae*; under the latter, something that belongs to no one becomes someone's; under the former, a special kind of thing, namely the land, which belongs to someone, becomes no one's. In the singular case of Gracchus, this law is potentially generalizable, for wherever Gracchus lands, under the condition this is with the permission of the landlord, for example, the burgomaster of Riva, a portion of the land over which he is lord becomes *herrenlos* ("lordless"), and to this extent, "religious"—only not religious in a sense that corresponds to a cult that places the things in its possession, or at least under its protection, at the disposal of its guardians, whether it be priests or pontiffs: "religious," therefore, only in itself.

Because he is not "his own man," the non-hunting "hunter Gracchus" can enter into the workforce without possessions. Or more exactly Gracchus anticipates whatever it is that would be permitted to enter into this workforce: someone who is, in some sense, also no one, or "no man," *kein Mensch*, to use his own term. Because he is no one, he attracts the kinds of questions his interlocutor poses: "Tell me briefly yet coherently how it actually stands with you." To the extent that he is no one, however, he can also be said to be the prior possessor of his patron's bark, for, as he says, it originally belonged to no one, *keinem Menschen*—which does not necessarily imply that, before it fell into the hands of the patron, it belonged to a god, not even to Bacchus, his paronym, whom he honors by drinking copious amounts of wine.[31] Gracchus makes the lands into which he is welcomed "religious," belonging to no one, and he does so in such a way that the relation of belonging cannot be mediated by a public or pontifical representative, who would determine its limitations. The relation is always only one-to-one, or one-to-no-one. And the relation proposed in "Workforce without Possession" can be understood accordingly: the employer, who is *sui juris*, stands in an immediate relation to the worker, who is there not in order to work, in which case he would be representing himself, but as a member of a workforce designed so that workers can work as little as possible. Call it "depersonalization" or even "alienation"—neither of these words captures the extent to which the workforce makes whoever enters it into a "no one" to which things originally belonged but which the members of workforce, its rights and duties being such as they are, cannot take for themselves but must, instead, leave as they are: theirs, to be sure, but only insofar as they refrain from taking them for themselves. The underlying job of the workers who, without allegiance to any ascetic ideal, decline to make things their own is not so much defined by what they do, mediated by a governmental or ecclesiastic body, still less by what they have, which is precious little, as by what they *make*, regardless of where they find themselves: they, as a group of Gracchi, make things "religious," wherever the lords of the land allow them to stay: "religious" not in the modern sense and perhaps not in the Roman sense but only in the sense of the sole mode of *res nullius* that can be created without the mediation of priests or pontiffs.

Notes

1. See Franz Kafka, *Gesammelte Werke in zwölf Bänden*, ed. Hans-Gerd Koch (Frankfurt a.M.: Fischer, 1994), 6: 221–23; all translations of the Kafka texts are my own.
2. For a brief discussion of the fragment in relation to Zionism, see Bill Dodd, "The Case for a Political Reading," in *The Cambridge Companion to Kafka*, ed. Julian Preece (Cambridge: Cambridge University Press, 2002), 139–140.
3. Franz Kafka, *Wedding Preparations in the Country and Other Posthumous Prose Writings*, ed. Max Brod, trans. Ernst Kaiser and Eithne Wilkins (London: Secker and Warburg, 1954), 119–20. Brod included the entire text, with little commentary, in his *Franz Kafka: A Biography*, trans. Humphrey Roberts (New York: Schocken, 1960), 84–85.
4. See Walter Benjamin, "Goethes Wahlverwandtschaften," in *Gesammelte Schriften*, eds. Rolf Tiedemann and Hermann Schweppenhäuser (Frankfurt a.M.: Suhrkamp, 1972-91), 1: 126.
5. Max Brod, *Das große Wagnis* (Leipzig and Vienna: Wolff, 1918), 59.
6. Ibid., 59–60.
7. Ibid., 100.
8. Ibid., 103.
9. Franz Kafka and Max Brod, *Eine Freundschaft*, ed. Hannelore Rodlauer and Malcolm Pasley (Frankfurt a.M.: Fischer, 1987–89), 2: 189.
10. Brod, *Das große Wagnis*, 59.
11. Kafka and Brod, *Eine Freundschaft*, 2: 227.

12. For an extraordinary exposition of the sideway character of time in Hölderlin's late poetry, see Werner Hamacher, "Parusie, Mauer. Mittelbarkeit und Zeitlichkeit, später Hölderlin," *Hölderlin-Jahrbuch* 34 (2004-5): 93–142.
13. Brod, *Das große Wagnis*, 66.
14. Kafka and Brod, *Eine Freundschaft*, 2: 220.
15. Ernst Troeltsch, "Luther, der Protestantismus und die moderne Welt," reprinted in *Gesammelte Schriften*, ed. Hans Baron (Tübingen: Mohr, 1925), 4: 213.
16. Ibid., 4: 208.
17. Brod, *Das große Wagnis*, 56.
18. See especially Nigel Rothfels, *Savages and Beasts: The Birth of the Modern Zoo* (Baltimore, MD: Johns Hopkins University Press, 2002).
19. Justinian, *Institutes*, eds. and trans. Peter Birks and Grant McLeod (Ithaca, NY: Cornell University Press, 1987), II, 1: 15. One of Kafka's professors in Roman law, Ludwig Pfaff, contributed to the reediting of Karl Ludwig Arndts von Arnesberg's famous *Lehrbuch der Pandekten* (Stuttgart: Cotta, 1886). Another of his law professors, Emil Pfersche, received his degree based on research into the law of interdicts, in relation to which the juridical concept of possession is defined.
20. Justinian, *Institutes*, II, 1: 22.
21. Ibid., 1: 11–12.
22. The fragments under consideration here can be found in Kafka, *Gesammelte Werke*, 6: 40–45 and 96–100. For a discussion of the Hunter Gracchus fragments that mentions the Gracchus family of ancient Rome, see Guy Davenport, "The Hunter Gracchus," *The New Criterion* 14 (1996): 27–35. The tradition in which the association with the Roman family is dismissed and replaced with an interpretation that emphasizes the grackle begins with Wilhelm Emrich's magisterial *Franz Kafka* (Bonn, Athenäum, 1958), 21. It is reiterated in Hartmut Binder, *Kafka Handbuch* (Stuttgart: Kröner, 1979), 2: 337, who discusses Kafka's desire, as a city-dweller, to be in the country, "Der Jäger Gracchus. Zu Kafkas Schaffensweise und poetischer Topographie," *Deutsche Schillergesellschaft* 15 (1971): 375–440.
23. Kafka would have been familiar with the story of the Gracchi from his schoolboy lessons in Latin, which probably included copious amounts of Livy's *History of Rome*. More importantly, as Joel Morris has detailed in an as yet unpublished paper, in 1916 Kafka read Samuel Lublinski's *Entstehung des Judentums*, which discusses the Gracchus family in conjunction with its critique of Roman civilization. According to Lublinski, the Romans, who thought of themselves as utterly distinct from the slaves whom they conquered, were unable to address "the social question," a failure made evident by the incompleteness of the Gracchian reforms; see Samuel Lublinski, *Entstehung des Judentums aus der antiken Kultur* (Jena: Diederichs, 1910), esp 43-44. Through the intercession of Max Brod Kafka also became familiar with Adolph Damaschke's *Bodenreform,* which includes two chapters about the land reform movements initiated by Tiberius Gracchus and Gajus Gracchus; see Adolph Damaschke's *Bodenreform: Grundsätzliches und Geschichtliches zur Erkenntnis und Überwindung der sozialen Not,* 4th ed. (Berlin: Buchverlag der "Hilfe," 1907), 227-39.

24. Immanuel Kant, *Gesammelte Schriften*, ed. Königlich Preußische [later Deutsche] Akademie der Wissenschaften (Berlin: Reimer; later, De Gruyter, 1900–), 6: 250; *Doctrine of Right* §2 in its original version, which some recent English editions of the text have altered. For further discussion of this paragraph, see my essay, "Marital, Martial, and Maritime Law: Toward Some Controversial Passages in Kant's *Doctrine of Right*," *Diacritics* 35 (2005): 101–120.

25. Kant, *Gesammelte Schriften*, 6: 265; *Doctrine of Right*, §15.

26. John Locke, *Two Treatises of Government*, ed. Peter Laslett (Cambridge: Cambridge University Press, 1960), 303–18.

27. Kafka, *Gesammelte Werke*, 6: 97.

28. Justinian, *Institutes*, II, 1, 5.

29. Ibid., 1, 6.

30. This "religious" law did not go entirely into oblivion. It is remembered here and there—as, for instance, in the central chapter of Goethe's *Elective Affinities*, where a dispute over the legality of turning a burial ground into parkland links the first part of the novel to the second.

31. For the suggestion that Bacchus is to be read in Gracchus, see Erwin Steinberg, "Three Fragments of Kafka's 'The Hunter Gracchus,'" *Studies in Short Fiction* 15 (1978): 307–17.

Chapter Seven

Kafkaesque: (Secular) Kabbalah and Allegory

A. Kiarina Kordela

> *To do justice to the figure of Kafka . . . one must never lose sight of one thing: it is the purity and beauty of failure. . . . There is nothing more memorable than the fervor with which Kafka emphasized his failure.*
>
> —Walter Benjamin[1]

Kabbalah

In his introduction to Franz Kafka's *The Trial*, George Steiner argues that it "embodies the particular techniques of . . . rabbinic hermeneutics," which make it "truly accessible only to those schooled in the labyrinth . . . of the rabbinic legacy."[2] This legacy, Steiner continues, "persists in parodistic or bastard guise in such current Judaic derivatives as Freudian psychoanalysis or Derridean deconstruction," which, like Kafka, are "heir to this methodology and epistemology . . . of 'unending analysis' (Freud's phrase)."[3]

Just like a dream is always mediated by the secondary process that "censor[s]" and "interpret[s]" the "absurdity" of the raw latent dream thoughts,[4] Kafka's work, too, is a series of "commentary and commentary on commentary."[5] Like the deconstruction of a text, any commentary or interpretation, far from being imposed on the Kafkaesque text from the outside, is both inherent and "unending," such that it will always already have been "read, *in the text*," as Derrida would put it, or will always already have been part of the original myth, as Lévi-Strauss would say, for whom Freud's reading of *Oedipus* "should be included among the recorded versions of the Oedipus myth" on the same level as Sophocles's version.[6] Though it is true that all textuality is an open, unlimited cage, some texts, the Kafkaesque included, seem to be privileged. For, even when, as Steiner writes, "set beside Kafka's readings of Kafka, ours are, unavoidably, feeble," and "the thought that there is anything fresh to be said of... *The Trial*" or any of Kafka's other works "is implausible," we do not give up reading in his work our writings.[7]

This by now canonical take on textuality and authorship echoes Kafka's own conception of the self, the author, and truth. As Stanley Corngold writes, stressing the importance Kafka lays on chance within empirical reality, "Kafka's 'self'... is a precipitate of the acts of chance that break off interpretation, and hence it is not a self."[8] Being "defined not by particular interests," Kafka's "self is precisely its lucid tolerance of whatever arises [chance] in the place where control, for the sake of mastery and reward, has been relinquished."[9] By bringing together Kafka and Nietzsche, whose self is traditionally associated with the issue of mastery (think of Nietzsche's "will to power"), Corngold concludes that after the intro-duction of the "New Nietzsche, the 'nomadic' Nietzsche of Deleuze and Foucault, Nietzsche's self" is read "as 'Kafkan': not as a maker of fictions but as itself a fiction, which would then have to be said to be constructed by chance," rather than by a further, mastering authorial self, on another (meta-)level.[10]

What I would like to argue, however, is that in Kafka the interplay between interpretation and self does not exhaust itself within the entrap-ments of fiction. Rather, the raison d'être of the Kafkaesque dialectic between interpretation or imaginary mastery and fictional self is to point to a Truth *beyond* itself—a Truth, which, albeit an effect of this dialectic, nevertheless transcends it as its *beyond*. In other words, the dialectic of fic-tion is also an open or porous (rib)cage that breaths Truth. (Indeed, one could see the Kafkaesque as the most sublime force against the highest peril of dialectical thought, the entrapment in the imaginary.)

Expectably, the Truth in question concerns the Law (epistemologi-cal or sociopolitical). As Steiner remarks, being part of the "kabbalistic" and "rabbinic legacy," Kafka "self-evidently... meditates on the law," the "essential concern of Talmudic questioning."[11] There is also plenty of evidence in both Kafka's texts and in ample Kafka scholarship that he perceived his writing as a "new Kabbalah." For instance, Malcolm Pasley identified in Kafka's manuscript of *The Castle* lines in which Kafka had inserted slashes dividing them into groups of ten letters, and which, cor-responding neither to the "logical" nor to the "rhythmic articulations" of the text, must be considered to have been meant to establish "esoteric meanings."[12] This chapter inserts in the same "kabbalistic" tradition other thinkers who have never claimed to perceive their writing as part of it, and regardless, of course, of whether or not they were Jewish. Here, *inclusion within the kabbalistic tradition* requires fulfilling *three criteria*. The first is the aforementioned "essential concern" with the law, and more specifically, the eternal law underlying any empirically given laws within the historical era determined by this law (a distinction that will be specified below). The second criterion derives from Kafka's own definition of the Kabbalah in his writings, as in the following oft-cited entry in his diaries:

"Pursuit," indeed, is only a metaphor [*Bild*]. I can also say, "assault on the last earthly frontier," an assault, moreover, launched from below, from mankind, and since this too is a metaphor [*Bild*], I can replace it by the metaphor [*Bild*] of an assault from above, aimed at me from above.[13]

"Metaphor" is the translator's word for "Bild," which literally means "picture" or "image," and as an adjective, as in the phrase "*bildlich reden*," means "to speak figuratively." In other words, Kafka is referring here not to metaphor in the more technical and narrow sense, as opposed to, say, metonymy, simile, allegory, parable, and all other specific forms of "speaking figuratively." In fact, since "Bild" is first of all the representation of something, Kafka' statement applies to all representation, which is by necessity always figurative, if by that we mean that it replaces the real thing with something other that represents it, as a "Bild" does. "Bild" points to a figurativeness more primary and fundamental than the common distinction between the "literal" and the "figurative" meaning of a word, and is thus presupposed even when we decide to read Kafka literally. This passage exemplifies the "Kafkan metaphor"—as, in Corngold's words, a "chiasm" or "rhetorical technique of arbitrary substitution and reversal"—which expresses and performs the arbitrary essence of all representation.[14] Kafka's text continues to assert that "[a]ll such writing" that reflects on and reveals its own arbitrariness and reversibility of metaphors as it performs them, "is an assault on the frontiers [*Grenze*]," and "if Zionism had not intervened, it might easily have developed into a new secret doctrine, a Kabbalah."[15] Thus, the kabbalistic tradition includes all writing that attempts to reveal, through its performance of and reflection on arbitrary substitutions and reversals between words, an eternal law.

To arrive at the third criterion required for a comprehensive definition of the Kafkan Kabbalah, I invoke once again Steiner who has pointed out that Kafka's "Judaic perception" is concerned not with "the language of the Adamic [which] was that of love" but with "the grammars of *fallen* man [which] are those of the legal code."[16] Kafka's law pertains exclusively to a post-lapsarian mankind. Importantly, for Kafka, this fall occurred when mortality was bestowed not on man but on God. As Maurice Blanchot puts it, "it is a dead transcendence we are battling with" in Kafka's work—the transcendence of a dead law or God embodied, for instance, in the "dead emperor the functionary represents in 'The Great Wall of China,'" or "the dead former Commandant" of " 'The Penal Colony.' "[17] In Kafka, transcendence is a function that "is present because it is not there"; "dead" or absent, it is "even . . . more invulnerable, in a combat in which there is no longer any possibility of defeating" it.[18] Kafka's vision is concerned with the law of the secular man, for whom God is dead, and yet, for that matter, all the more invincible.

With the addition of this third criterion, it becomes conspicuous that Jacques Lacan is another member of this kabbalistic tradition, as he extensively critiqued the common (post-)Nietzschean (or vulgar atheist) assumption that the "death of God" introduces a liberating force in human history, by arguing that far from entailing that "everything is permitted," "God is dead" means precisely that "nothing is permitted anymore."[19] So invincible is this secular dead God that Lacan could not resist stating that the "true formula of atheism" is "God is unconscious."[20] The secular law is a dead, yet invulnerable, transcendence, which is the object of a specifically secular metaphysics, designated by the term Kabbalah. (Kabbalah is intrinsically atheist and secular—in the true, nonvulgarized, sense—and, by that token, decisively non-secular*ist*.)

To clarify now the distinction between eternal law and empirical laws, it follows from the above that one can speak of eternal law only in a historically specific sense; that is, it designates the unlimited range of the validity of a law within one and the same *limited*, yet overarching, historical era—a given socio-economico-cultural configuration—such as, in our case, the era of secular capitalist modernity in whose various concrete formations we live roughly since the seventeenth century, and which some day will come to pass. In other words, both the eternal law and the empirical laws are historical; the former as the transcendental precondition of the historical era in question, the latter as the empirically possible manifestations of the former law. While all empirical laws rely on some fiction—they are, as we say, culturally, socially, and, in short, ideologically constructed— the transcendental or eternal law presupposed for their functioning lies beyond fiction, albeit only its effect. It is their logical presupposition. The transcendental law, therefore, relates to the empirical laws in the same way as the death drive—Freud's term for the *beyond* the pleasure principle— relates to the pleasure principle. As Gilles Deleuze puts it, commenting on the "pleasure principle" and its "not homogeneous" "*beyond*":

> What we call a principle or law is, in the first place, that which governs a particular field; it is in this sense that we speak of an *empirical* principle or law. Thus we say that the pleasure principle governs life universally and without exception. But there is another and quite distinct question, namely, in virtue of what is a field governed by a principle; there must be a principle

of another kind, a second order principle, which accounts for the necessary compliance of the field with the empirical principle. It is this second-order principle that we call transcendental.... [The death drive is] not the exception[] to the [pleasure] principle but...its '*foundation*.'[21]

Truth or the transcendental law is this residue, this second-order principle *beyond* all empirical laws, which, while not homogeneous with the empirical truths or laws (which are fictitious), is *not* their exception but their foundation. Take the law of relativism: "everything is relative" or "everything is fictitious"; for this law to apply universally, a further second order law must be its foundation, namely, the law that the statement itself—"everything is relative"—is itself *absolute*; for if it is not, then some empirical laws or truths may be absolute. But by recognizing the absoluteness of this law, one ceases to be relativist, just as the law remains unknowable to a true relativist. It is due to this relation that we can say without contradiction that the law or Truth is unknowable *and* that fiction points to it. Except that, as we shall see below in the context of the Kafkaesque revision of Cartesian doubt, this relation is not a matter of a simple shift between being inside and outside the given (ideological) field. (It is for the same reason that psychoanalysis asserts that the sheer recognition of the causes of the symptom does not suffice for its removal.)

The Kabbalah examines the *beyond* of a cage (an empirical field) that allows it to function as a confining cage while simultaneously opening it up. Kabbalistic thought, therefore, drastically differs from the widespread, uncritical, postmodern wholesale embracement of relativism or cultural constructivism as a closed cage with no transcendental foundation.[22] Accordingly, the key task of Kabbalah is to formulate the relation between empirical laws and their transcendental precondition, the Law(s), thereby opening up the conditions for sustaining or undermining them. And the Kafkaesque is a specific logic through which one can practice Kabbalah.

In addition to Lacan, Immanuel Kant, and Walter Benjamin are some of the major figures of this Kabbahlistic legacy on whom I draw below in order to formulate the various logics of the Kafkaesque. Like Kafka, these thinkers are concerned with the eternal laws governing a series of specifically secular phenomena intrinsically linked to the signifier—be it the law, as in Kafka; the transcendental preconditions of reason, as in Kant; the subject (as the subject of the signifier), as in Lacan's case; or, in Benjamin's case, allegory (as the logic of the secular signifier).[23] Though scarcely referenced here, mention is due to the two cardinal figures that laid the ground of Kabbalah, and whose theories tacitly subtend the present argument: Baruch Spinoza and Karl Marx. Beyond their shared concern with the law—Spinoza, with the eternal laws of substance (by which is meant both thought and matter), and Marx with "the eternal laws of commodity-exchange"[24]—they were also the first to conceptualize in monistic terms the relation between the positive and the negative, from truth and false (as in Spinoza) to success and failure or crisis (as in Marx).[25] Central to the Kabbalah, monism lies, as we shall see below, also at the heart of the Kafkaesque.

Taming the Tiger (Kafka's Critique of Reason)

The Kafkaesque concern with the eternal law is pronounced most succinctly in Kafka's short stories known as "paradoxes." Here is the paradox of "The Tiger."

> ONCE A TIGER was brought to the celebrated animal tamer Burson, for him to give his opinion as to the possibility of taming the animal. The small *cage* with the tiger in it was pushed into the training *cage*, which had the dimensions of a public hall; it was in a large hut-camp a long way outside the town. The attendants withdrew: Burson always wanted to be completely alone with an animal at his first encounter with it. The tiger lay quiet, having just been plentifully fed. It yawned a little, gazed wearily at its new surroundings, and immediately fell asleep.[26]

Initially, we are given an opposition—wild versus tamed—but at the end of the story, we encounter a set of terms—being plentifully fed, yawning, gazing wearily, and falling asleep—which, even as, strictly speaking, they do not necessarily *denote* the state of being tamed, *associate* it.[27] This technique of semantic displacements confers on the text its notorious air of absurdity, so indispensable to the Kafkaesque mode of articulating the eternal law.[28] And in this case, the law could be formulated as follows: If the law is that everything must be tame, and hence that everything wild is tamable, then, one way or another, everything finds itself in a tamed state, regardless of the actual events that take place in the realm of experience. For if the law depended on the particular empirical circumstances, it would not be unconditional.[29] The Kafkaesque is concerned not with the succession of events that lead from state A to state B—all of which remain confined within the cage of fiction—but with the transcendental law that makes it necessary that state A leads to state B no matter what events may have occurred between the two. The redoubling of cages in Kafka's parable mirrors this redoubling of the L/law: several laws may allow for this or the other chance events to occur in the "small cage with the tiger," but these laws have their foundation on the Law of the large "training cage."

All this amounts to saying that in the Kafkaesque universe empirical reality, the succession of events between the given initial and final states, is resolutely unknowable or uninterpretable. But although it may be true of this, and other, stories that "the chance moment that breaks off interpretation" is (the tiger's) "all-pervasive fatigue,"[30] I would suggest that Kafka is capable of effecting this interpretative breakdown through any state, up to and including the quasiopposite exuberance of life, as it springs out, for instance, at the end of *The Metamorphosis* (in the "good figure" of Samsas' daughter), or "The Cell" (the freely moving body of the narrator), or "The Hunger Artist" (the shockingly free, joyful, and insatiable "noble body" of the panther). The crucial point is not so much what prevents interpretation but what is prevented from being interpreted, namely, empirical reality as a series of causes and effects.

To stress the point, the final term in the arbitrary displacement—be it fatigue and even death or insatiable and exuberant life, sexuality, and animality—is the stand-in for a break in interpretation, and hence for a demolition of both fiction and the self. Truth, then, must lie outside the interpretation of experience, but not for that matter out of reach. For the claim itself that empirical reality is not cognizable *is* itself a claim to truth—in fact, to the Truth regarding empirical reality.

So far the Kafkaesque advances two truths that we could call Kafka's shibboleths: first, that the law functions unconditionally, and, second, that empirical reality is not cognizable. That the law functions unconditionally means above all, to recall Blanchot's reference to a "dead transcendence," that it is not (and must not be) grounded. Doubting "that the emperor was descended from the gods" lies far from "doubt[ing] the emperor's divine mission" and that he "was our rightful sovereign." The doubt of the emperor's "divine descent," "naturally, did not cause much of a stir; when the surf flings a drop of water on to the land, that does not interfere with the eternal rolling of the sea, on the contrary, it is caused by it."[31] It is not the divine descent of the emperor that is the ground for his authority; rather it is his authority that is the ground for our doubting his divine descent. This is the Kafkaesque version of the notorious Cartesian doubt: the sole ground of the secular law is our own doubt thereof.[32]

Regarding the relation between the first and second truths, their presupposed distinction between unconditional law and empirical reality expresses a credo central to the Talmudic tradition, often attributed to the "Maharal of Prague," the Renaissance Humanist Rabbi Judah Loew ben Bezalel (1512–1609), and most revered and influential spiritual lieder of Kafka's Jewish Ghetto. Scholars have pointed out the relevance to Kafka's thought of the Rabbi's paradoxical teachings, according to which there are two powers: a "horizontal" or "human" power that accounts for sciences and all other products of human creativity, including tolerance, and which doubts the other, "vertical" or "divine" and utterly nontolerant, absolute, power, which holds humanity in total disregard.

We can hear the echoes of this Talmudic cosmodicy and theodicy in one of the most representative philosophers of the Enlightenment, Immanuel Kant, whose investigation into "pure reason" famously led him to its "antinomies" or "paradoxes." Kant's distinction between the "horizontal" and the "vertical" cuts instead between "appearance" and the "thing-in-itself" (i.e., the thing regardless of how it appears to humans). Since we can know the world only as it appears to us, we cannot ever know anything about the thing-in-itself. Whence follows that the two fundamental categories through which we perceive the world, time and space, "are nothing existing in themselves and outside of my representations."[33] Corollary to the first is Kant's further distinction between the understanding, which "refers to experience so far as it can be given," and reason, which aims "at the completeness" or "absolute totality of all possible experience [which] is itself not experience" but a "transcendent" concept, such as the *totality* of the world or of experience.[34] The task of reason is to form a totality out of all experience, and, because this is impossible, reason necessarily fails. Bringing together the two distinctions, it follows that insofar as reason fails to cognize the totality of all experience, then this totality is a thing-in-itself—something that escapes reason's grasp.

Moreover, Kant stresses the fact that this failure of reason occurs in two ways. This owes to the fact that there are two aspects in which reason examines the totality of experience: the limits of this totality in time and space, and its boundaries in terms of the causal relations that determine it. Kant calls the first aspect "mathematic," as it involves the addition of temporal or spatial parts, and the second "dynamic," as it examines the causal dynamism governing the totality. In both cases, reason arrives at antinomic conclusions (or so it seems).

Beginning with the dynamic antinomy, when it inquires into the causality determining the totality of experience, reason is forced to admit as equally true both: the thesis that "causality in accordance with laws of nature is not the only one from which all the appearances of the world can be derived;" rather, "[i]t is also necessary to assume another causality through freedom in order to explain them"; *and* the antithesis that "there is no freedom, but everything in the world happens solely in accordance with laws of nature."[35] Next, however, Kant surprises us by proceeding to show that the "falsehood" of the dynamic antinomy "consists in representing as contradictory what is compatible," that is, far from being mutually exclusive, the thesis and the antithesis of this (after all only ostensible) antinomy are compatible.[36] For, Kant continues, while "natural necessity" and "freedom" might appear to be incompatible, "if natural necessity is referred merely to appearances and freedom merely to things in themselves, no contradiction arises if we at the same time ... admit both kinds of causality"; "natural necessity" (i.e., determinism) can "attach to all connections of cause and effect in the sensuous world [appearances], while freedom can be granted to the cause which is itself not an appearance (but the foundation of appearance)," i.e., the thing-in-itself qua the first and final cause of appearance—what the Maharal would call "divine" power.[37]

In short, on the one hand, there are definite laws governing the causal relations of everything within the realm of appearances or experience—what for Kant is accessible to human cognition—while, on the other hand, the realm of the thing-in-itself—what for him is not accessible to cognition—is marked by one absolute Law: freedom.

* * *

In Kant's scheme, we can see a secular formulation as much of the Talmudic doctrine as of the Calvinist credo that "some men . . . are predestinated unto everlasting life, and others foreordained to everlasting death," depending exclusively on "His [God's] mere free grace and love, without any foresight of faith or good works" on the part of the men condemned or redeemed.[38] In Max Weber's renowned commentary, God's "grace is the sole product of an objective power, and not in the least to be attributed to personal worth."[39] Grace is another word for God's absolute freedom from anything humans may be, do, or know—it is the Law that applies to *the* thing-in-itself, God. This is the logically necessary conclusion following from the reasoning, in Weber's succinct summary, that:

> To assume that human merit or guilt play a part in determining [humans'] destiny would be to think of God's absolutely free decrees, which have been settled from eternity, as subject to change by human influence, an impossible contradiction.[40]

To avoid the "contradiction" one must assume both: On the one hand, that human destiny is determined from eternity" by some absolute Law (Grace)—one's redemption or condemnation is irrevocably foreordained. On the other hand, that grace—the sole first and ultimate cause of the choice between the two—is absolutely free (which necessarily also means absolutely unknowable).

All that is still needed to secularize entirely the Calvinist credo is to include within the realm of human experience the permanence of the soul or afterlife, where the final condemnation or salvation takes place. Sure enough, Kant writes:

> Life is the subjective condition of all our possible experience; consequently we can only infer the permanence of the soul in life, for the death of man

is the end of all experience that concerns the soul as an object of experience.... The permanence of the soul can therefore only be proved...during the life of man, but not, as we desire to do, after death.[41]

It is because of this inclusion of afterlife within the empirical life that Calvinism, even as it makes salvation only radically arbitrary but not impossible, ultimately does not lie far from the Talmudic universal condemnation of humanity. For, as Weber remarks, Calvinism amounts to a shift from the "Father in the heaven of New Testament, so human and understanding," to an absolutely "transcendental being, beyond the reach of human understanding"; and this new doctrine of "extreme inhumanity" in turn brought about a shift in consciousness accompanied by "a feeling of unprecedented inner loneliness of the single individual."[42] With Calvinism and more generally Protestantism—Weber's capitalist religious denomination *par excellence*—the modern individual emerged out of a process in which

> no one could help him. No priest, for the chosen one can understand the word of God only in his own heart. No sacraments, for though the sacraments had been ordained by God for the increase of his glory, and must hence be scrupulously observed, they are not a means to the attainment of grace, but only the subjective *externa subsidia* of faith. No, Church, for...the membership of the external Church included the doomed. They should belong to it and be subjected to its discipline, not in order thus to attain salvation, that is impossible, but because, for the Glory of God, they too must be forced to obey His commandments.[43]

Weber's vociferous evocation of the desolate state of the individual vis-à-vis this unforeseen preclusion of salvation unmistakably echoes Kafka, logically and rhetorically alike: the accused must obey the disciplines of the law not in order to attain salvation (final acquittal), which is impossible, but because for the Glory of the Law, they too must obey Its commandments. The painter Titorelli in *The Trial* resounds as much the rabbi's as the priest's teachings: having accepted to "write down on a sheet of paper an affidavit of [K.'s] innocence," Titorelli continues his dialogue with K., while both the possible kinds of acquittal and the judges judging the affidavit proliferate, to come to the conclusion that, if the affidavit is approved by many judges, then the next

> Judge is covered by the guarantees of the other Judges subscribing to the affidavit...and though some formalities will remain to be settled, he will undoubtedly grant the acquittal to please me and his friends. Then you can walk out of the Court a free man." "So, then I am free," said K. doubtfully. "Yes," said the painter, "but only ostensibly free, or more exactly,

provisionally free. For the Judges of the lowest grade, to whom my acquaintances belong, haven't the power to grant a final acquittal, that power is reserved for the highest Court of all, which is quite inaccessible to you, to me, and to all of us. What the prospects are up there we do not know and, I may say in passing, do not even want to know. (T 1992, 158)

Even if the prospects "up there" could ever amount to releasing K. as a truly "free man" once and for all, this remains entirely irrelevant to the life that is "accessible" to us and in which there are at best ostensible or provisional acquittals. Calvinism does not exclude the possibility of a definite acquittal, but it does exclude it as far as the life "accessible" to us is concerned, which, at least since Kant, includes our afterlife. (Needless to say, this universal condemnation is nothing other than the illusion into which secular humanity can slip in the face of the radical failure of the law to be known.) Thus, "dead transcendence" merges the Judaic and Protestant traditions to the point of indiscernibility, yielding to the dogma of what we may call the secular denomination. It remains a question whether the latter has increasingly become the large "taming cage" encompassing all other "small cages" of so-called denominations and religions.

*   *   *

But, as the reader may have noticed, even as the Maharal of Prague, Kant, and Weber may all offer a kind of matrix for mapping the Kafkaesque attitude toward secular salvation, there remains a conspicuous deviation between Kafka and Kant's dynamic antinomy. Namely, while for Kant experience is subject to "natural laws" (determinism), so that the laws governing particular experiences are theoretically knowable, Kafka raises experience—including particular experiences, not just the totality of experience—to the level of the thing-in-itself by rendering it unknowable. Kafka performs a kind of explosion of immediate experience in such a way that the particular, concrete, humanly perceptible experience—e.g., how can a tamer tame a tiger?—behaves like the totality of experience, which is itself no experience but a transcendental concept, and which, as such, neither can be known nor does it occur in time and place—something which, again, explains the Kafkaesque, oft perceived and expressed, impression of absurdity. To account for this aspect of the Kafkaesque, we must now turn to Kant's other antinomy, the mathematic.

When reason examines the totality of experience in terms of its limits in time and space, it is initially misled to admit as true both the thesis that "the world has a beginning in time, and in space it is also enclosed in boundaries," and the antithesis that "the world...is infinite with regard to both time and space."[44] What reason momentarily forgets here is that, to repeat, space and time are categories of appearance (representation), not of the thing-in-itself. Since the question raised here concerns from the outset the limits of the world in time and space, the only possible referent of the word "world" in our question is not the world-in-itself but the world as appearance. Hence, Kant concludes, in the case of the mathematic antinomy, both "the thesis and the antithesis... are false."[45] But the lesson of all this for Kafka evidently is that the above is true not only of the totality of experience but also of any particular, entirely accessible experience, since *any* experience is experienced through the categories of time and space. Hence, any experience whatsoever can be known only as experience (our representation of the experience in time and space) and not as a thing-in-itself; in short, particular experience is as unknowable *in itself* as is the totality of experience. This is why Kafka can, as we saw in the context of the dynamic antinomy, treat any particular experience as the totality of experience (i.e., as a thing-in-itself beyond the dimensions of time and space), and thus as unknowable.

The sole object our representations can cognize are our representations. Indeed, Kant too, arrives at the conclusion that, while the mathematic antinomy may tell us nothing about the world-in-itself, it offers us access to epistemological knowledge, that is, knowledge about our knowledge of the world. In Kant's words, "I cannot say the world is *infinite*... nor will I say that it is *finite*"; instead, "I will be able to say... only something about the rule in accord with which experience... is to be instituted and continued," thereby determining the "magnitude (of experience)."[46] In other words, even if the thesis and the antithesis of the mathematic antinomy are false ontologically, they are true epistemologically. In this case, we are facing a true antinomy: the thesis and the antithesis, while both logically true, are mutually exclusive: our *experience* of the world has *and* has not limits in time and space.

In conclusion, we can know nothing about the world-in-itself (Law), though we can know it as appearance, but then we only arrive at mutually exclusive truths about this appearance.[47] Which is why all representation (and interpretation) fails.[48] The obscure meanders of the Kafkaesque reveal with glaring clarity that knowledge is the struggle to formulate the relation between an unknowable and unconditional law and mutually exclusive interpretations of experience. Kafka's own work, lending itself to all possible interpretations, forms an exemplary specimen demonstrating the point.[49] And, possibly, so did his life and death, at least according to Milena Jesenska's obituary words: "[Kafka was] a man condemned to regard the world with such blinding clarity that he found it unbearable and went to his death."[50]

Albeit unique, Kafka's failure is not singular. Marked by, shifting, and amplifying both the dynamic and the mathematic failures, "the circumstances of this failure are manifold."[51]

The Penal Marriage

All this amounts to saying that only what is experienced not as a coercive imposition (law) but as one's own immutable (or at least irresistible) destiny can function as the Law. If Kafka's fiction makes this point directly, his diaries and letters are an equally lengthy and convoluted exposition of the same point, but *ex negativo*: when a law *is* experienced as an external imposition, then it lacks the quality of the unconditional and can, more or less, easily be infringed.

Thus, Kafka's diaries oscillate between two unequal forces: the imperative to marry and the impossibility not to write (even if on some days writing appears impossible and the right words keep failing him).

The duty to marry, and its the preparatory step, engagement, are cast in terms of a moral-legal code and metaphors borrowed from the penal system:

> And despite all this, if we, I and F., had equal rights, if we had the same prospects and possibilities, I would not marry. But this blind alley into which I have slowly pushed her life makes it an unavoidable duty for me, although its consequences are by no means unpredictable. Some secret law of human relationships is at work here.[52]

Or:

> Was tied hand and foot like a criminal. Had they sat me down in a corner bound in real chains, placed policemen in front of me and let me look on simply like that, it could not have been worse. And that was my engagement.[53]

Hence, there is "Kafka, the writer," but never "Kafka, the husband."[54]

The Cage on Trial

The entire epistemological possibility of *The Trial* is predicated on the collapse of the distinction between empirical realm and unconditional transcendental law. Joseph K.'s fatal error, quoting again Corngold, lies in his having been "[f]rom the beginning...determined on conducting his case in the...accustomed light" "of personal experiences," as a result of which the "interpretative decision that K. makes" invariably "proves to be fatal."[55] Focusing on a deleted passage from *The Trial*, which, as Clayton Koelb observes, "introduces a sharp distinction between the Law and the law," Corngold argues that Kafka's deletion is "evidence of the importance... of merging the two orders," the transcendental and the empirical, "in the consciousness of Joseph K."[56] K.'s approach, then, is an allegory of the severest interpretative error on the part of the reader in the face of the Kafkaesque. It would be fatal to wonder whether the animal-tamer tamed the tiger, or, whether K. was rightfully accused.

Are we to come then to the conclusion that even if fiction is an open cage, a gateway to truth, guilt and condemnation nevertheless constitute the hermetically closed cage from which ultimately nothing can escape? Upon his execution at the very end of The Trial, K. comments on his own death with the words: "Like a dog!" And the novel, albeit otherwise unfinished, seals itself with the legendary words: "it was as if the shame of it must outlive him" (T 1992, 229). Are we to conclude that, with God's death, not even death provides an escape out of the cage of guilt? Such a conclusion would be more fatal than K.'s own errors.

But before scrutinizing further The Trial's ultimate line, I would like to spell out three intertwined relations that generally mark the Kafkaesque cage, including The Trial.

First, there is no entrance into this cage. Like the bewildered voice exclaiming "How did I get here?" introduces itself as always already trapped in "The Cell,"[57] Joseph K., being introduced as already "arrested," is from the outset always already trapped in the hands of the law (T 1992, 1).[58] "Admittance to the law" is denied to "the man from the country" also because, always already and unbeknownst to him, it "was intended" exclusively "for [him]" (213 and 215). The reality of the Kafkaesque cage has always begun prior to the text's beginning.

Second, so long as one looks for an exit, there is none. Even physical death is not the way out of being treated "like a dog!," for even after Joseph K.'s execution, "the shame of it must outlive him" (T 1992, 229).

The first two are presupposed for the third principle: finally, even as—if not precisely because—there is neither entrance nor exit, one is outside the cage. "The Cell" presents us with a partly austere world behind whose doors there is nothing but "a dark, smooth rock-face... extending vertically upwards and horizontally... seemingly without an end," and partly with an the opulent, albeit equally hermetic "royal apartment." Yet, these two parts do not form a whole; as the narrative voice abruptly informs us: "that was not all."[59] Leaping to a new paragraph, Kafka concludes his paradox by exclaiming a one-liner: "I do not have to go back again, the cell is burst open, I move, I feel my body."

This mere recognition that whatever is given to experience is never all is what extricates us from the cage of empirical reality and its habits, while we inhabit it. The Kafkaesque is that paradoxical cage one can be confined in only by being outside of it, and vice versa. [Note, of course, that "vice versa" implies also that when we assume that we are free we may actually be encaged. This may be the true meaning of the Hegelian master–slave dialectic and of our contemporary lives in hegemonic liberal democracies, to whose logic the Kafkaesque may offer us the key.]

How does Kafka's text construct such a paradoxical cage? To return to *The Trial*'s finale, how can the text's final judgment—"it was as if the shame of it must outlive him"—burst open the cage of guilt? It does so in two ways.

First, the narrator tells us explicitly that "it was *as if* the shame of it must outlive him" [es war, *als sollte* die Scham ihn überleben]—a statement that directly negates the affirmative status of the state described. The power of this grammatical form—"as if" [als (ob) + Konjunktiv II]—has been exhaustively elaborated in the writings of Jeremy Bentham, Freud, Octave Mannoni, Lacan, and beyond.[60] It is the formulation encapsulating what Freud called fetishism: "I know the mother does not have a penis but I act as if she did."[61] So, when the narrator tells us that "it was *as if* the shame of it must outlive him" it is in order precisely to indicate that in truth the shame of it *does not* outlive him, that it is rather a fetishistic illusion to assume that it does—this being the illusion that entraps its victim in guilt.

Second, we do not know who, if anybody, is this naïve observer who falls into the pitfall of this fetishistic illusion. Is there anyone among the characters who misses the subtle, yet decisive, self-denial of this "as if," and who instead believes that the shame indeed outlives K? And even if there is no such naïve observer, who is the observer who knows all of the above? (That is, that the shame does not outlive K. *and* that his dying like a dog is capable of producing the fetishistic illusion that it does.) Is it the gaze of his executioners, K.'s himself, or the narrator's? If we do not know the answer to these questions, we also do not know with whom we identify when we attribute *any* meaning to this statement. Are we placed in the position of the wardens, the victim, the comparatively impartial narrator, or some other character? And even if we were capable of deciding whose gaze it is, we would still not know whether this gaze sees in this final line the ulti-mate affirmation *or* negation, or simultaneous fetishistic affirmation and grammatically entailed negation, of the triumph of shame.

The Trial's closing statement is not an exception. The text begins with the eminent supposition that "[s]omeone *must* have been telling lies," soon turns to "the old lady opposite, who *seemed* to be peering at [K.] with a curiosity unusual even for her," to pass then to the "man" who, due to his "suit," "*looked* eminently practical, though *one could not quite tell* what actual purpose it served," then to the sounds of the "next room" where "it rather sounded *as if* several people had joined in"—and as we increasingly become prone to identify all these gazes as K.'s, K. enters the next room, as we are approaching the end of the second page, and the narrator startles us: "... there was a little more free space than usual, yet *one did not perceive that at first*" because of the "man who was sitting at the open window reading [like us] a book" (T 1992, 1–2; emphasis mine). If one did not perceive that at first because of his distraction by the unexpected man, then it cannot be K. who perceived it.

This permeative uncertainty thwarts our desirous quest for knowledge regarding the given empirical reality, as nothing aids us in deciding for or against depicted appearances. If we nevertheless succumb to the temptation of blindly deciding for either, then we do not know with whose gaze we identify—i.e., we do not know who we are. The Kafkaesque eliminates the self, with its imaginary identifications, while sustaining (a thus impersonal) desire at its maximum capacity, as a sheer potentiality that can never be actualized. Thus it points to the truth of both the self and desire. The truth about guilt follows from them.

Allegoric Salvation

Benjamin argued that ever since the emergence of baroque allegory, it is only "in the triumph of matter" that salvation can be expected.[62] Under these circumstances, the "allegorically significant is prevented by guilt from finding fulfillment of its meaning in itself."[63] This arraignable predicament may not be specific to secular thought, since "allegory itself was sown by Christianity," insofar as its doctrines maintained that "not only transitoriness, but also guilt should seem evident to have its home in the province of idols and of the flesh" (matter).[64] But the crucial (secular) break occurred when, "[f]rom the seventeenth century onwards," as Peter Harrison puts it, "nature was increasingly divested of its symbolic meanings," so that natural occurrences could no longer function as "signs and symbols of transcendental truth" and, hence, of "revealed theological truths."[65] Losing this ability, the Word—what Foucault designates as the theocratic "ternary" sign—yields to the secular word—the "binary" sign. While the "ternary sign" was based on "the similitudes" which, due to their divine origin and guarantee, "link the marks to the things designated by them" in an "organic" way, the secular "binary sign" arrives after "the destruction of the organic," which rendered the link between marks and things arbitrary.[66] This view that deprived nature of its ability to bear any transcendental or theological significance, as Benjamin writes, inevitably "brought down nature with it," so that it eventually became a "mute, fallen nature," incapable of revealing any meaning.[67] Henceforth, with its "tendency to silence," in which nothing can "be named," nature offers itself at best "only to be read...uncertainly by the allegorist, and to have become highly significant thanks only to him."[68] Ever since, the thus "mute creature is [still] able to hope for salvation through that which is signified," but the latter can be only arbitrarily "picked up from [the] fragments" of matter by the allegorist.[69]

At the very moment when matter becomes mute, allegory takes up the insatiable task of making sure that "[w]hatever it picks up, its Midas-touch turns it into something endowed with significance."[70] But, if divinity refuses to speak through nature, then all significance and, hence, anything spiritual, must be the product of devil. In this process, the "absolute spirituality, which is what Satan means, destroys itself in its emancipation from what is sacred," and all that remains is a "soulless materiality." The "purely material and [the] absolute spiritual are the poles of the satanic realm" that thought and knowledge have come to become.[71] This process brings with it a reconfiguration of guilt: If humans are enticed to knowledge, it is because "Satan tempts"; it is "He [who] initiates men to knowledge," and this in itself "forms the basis of culpable behavior."[72] Guilt becomes the basis of the allegorist's consciousness that knows that it is not God who speaks through things, *a fortiori*, that things do *not* speak, and that if *he* makes "soulless matter" speak, this is due to his satanic temptation. With this secular rendition of the primal sin, "[in] the very fall of man the unity of guilt and signifying emerges" yet again, but this time "as an abstraction."[73] For now, "good and evil are unnameable, they are nameless entities," as are God and Satan.[74] Thus, like the reader of Kafka, the allegorist knows neither the meaning of things nor the gaze that, nevertheless, makes him pick up this and not some other meaning. In Benjamin's stunning conclusion, since it can know nothing,

[a]llegory goes away empty-handed. Evil as such, which it cherished as enduring profundity, exists only in allegory, is nothing other than allegory, and means something different from what it is. It means precisely the nonexistence of what it presents.[75]

And in time, "[k]nowledge, not action," will become "the most characteristic mode of existence of evil," as this "passion" for finding significance in matter "did not remain confined to the age of the baroque" but is rather "all the more suitable as an unambiguous indication of baroque qualities in later periods" and "a more recent linguistic practice."[76] By the time of modernism, the allegoric principle has been crystallized so that "[k]nowledge of evil...ensues from contemplation" and must therefore, as Kafka's work testifies, be "the opposite of all factual knowledge."[77]

Essentially, allegory amounts to "'nonsense' (*Geschwätz*), in the profound sense in which Kierkegaard conceived the word," as "the triumph of subjectivity and the onset of an arbitrary rule over things"—the two conditions at "the origin of all allegorical contemplation."[78] For, if allegory means the nonexistence of what it presents, then the demolished self of the Kafkaesque allegory is a roundabout way of restituting "the triumph of subjectivity" through precisely "an arbitrary rule over things," an arbitrary series of signifying displacements and substitutions. "Subjectivity, like an angel falling into the depths, is brought back by allegories, and is held fast in heaven, in God."[79]

Expanding this logic beyond the demolition of the self and its corollary resurrection of redeemed subjectivity, it follows that the paradox of the Kafkaesque lies in its prerogative to bring about liberation and salvation only through a passionate and obstinate preoccupation with confinement and condemnation. That's the consequence of an evil that does not exist but in allegory and means the nonexistence of what allegory presents. This is one way of understanding Adorno's assertion that the Kafkaesque "expresses itself not through expression but by its repudiation, by breaking off."[80] Self-rebutting expression results from the fact that "one of the strongest impulses in allegory" is its inherent tension between two apparently contrary tendencies: "an appreciation of the transience of things, and the concern to rescue them for eternity."[81]

Like religion, therefore, allegory is the source of both guilt and redemption. Accurately Kafka describes his "whole literature," as Mark Anderson remarks, as an activity "*in place* of organized belief" or "a *Form des Gebetes*, a 'form of prayer.'"[82] Yet, as both Benjamin's and Kafka's Kabbalism indicate, there is an irreducible difference between Biblical and secular allegories, due to their distinct places of enunciation: God, and guilty allegorists, with their dubious, arbitrary significatory operations. So, due to their humble origin, even as "Kafka's writings are by their nature parables[,]...it is their misery and their beauty that they had to become *more* than parables. They do not modestly lie at the feet of the doctrine," for "[t]hough apparently reduced to submission, they unexpectedly raise a mighty paw against it."[83] The promise of secular salvation is enunciated by a voice of irreverent arrogance, at once submissive and revolutionary.

Parable: The Allegorical Not-All

In a discussion of allegory, we cannot omit Kafka's own allegorical instructions regarding practicing allegory. These are most succinctly offered in his parable "On Parables," or rather, "*Von den Gleichnissen*" (OP 1985, 359)—a term that, like "Bild" (whose meaning, "image," *Gleichnis* can also have), Kafka uses to designate not any specific literary trope or genre (distinct from, say, fable or allegory) but the general practice of establishing conceptually, by whatever rhetorical means, a comparison or analogy between two (or more) states of affairs, so that when speaking of the one, one can be understood as (also) speaking of the other(s).[84] In the specifically Kafkaesque mode of *Gleichnis*, rhetoric is employed to obtain the overall conceptual structure that defines it.

Kafka's *Gleichnis* on *Gleichnissen* initially appears to be predicated on the opposition between reality or "daily life" and "parables" (*Gleichnissen*), which constitute the unreal or lofty realm of philosophy. In response to the complaint presented in the first paragraph by an initial narrative voice that apparently represents daily life—"that the words of the wise are always merely parables and of no use in daily life"—the following dialogue ensues:

> Why such reluctance? If you only followed the parables you yourselves
>   would become parables and with that rid of all your daily cares.
> *Another said*: I bet that is also a parable.
> *The first said*: You have won.
> *The second said*: But unfortunately, only in parable.
> *The first said*: No, in reality: in parable you have lost.
>
> (OP 1979, 158)

If we follow the apparent logic of the text, then its meaning seems to be that, having "won," that is, having recognized the first interlocutor's invitation (to follow the parables as a means of becoming oneself a parable and get rid of daily cares) as itself a parable, and hence, as something useless to daily life, the second interlocutor decides to ignore entirely the parables and to go about busing with daily life—hence the first interlocutor's final statement: "No, in reality: in parable you have lost." In this reading, Kafka seems to hail "daily life," if not as the sole reality, at least as the sole reality worth considering, while discarding philosophy and the general use of "parables": a blatantly non-Kafkaesque reading, if not for any other reason, simply because of its clear-cut oppositions.

Now let us reread the text through Benjamin's afore-described account of allegory. Let us begin with the passage that Kafka's *Gleichnis* explicitly designates as a "*Gleichnis*": "Why such reluctance? If you only followed the parables you yourselves would become parables and with that rid of all your daily cares." If the function of a *Gleichnis* is to present something other than what it does, then this something other is the impossibility of getting rid of daily cares by following parables; on the contrary, in its allegoric self-negation, the statement asserts that following parables safeguards our remaining within our daily life. Hence, far from being about some "fabulous yonder," parables *are* about daily lives; the two realms supplement one another, so that only by thinking parabolically can one gain wisdom about daily reality.

This conclusion exposes the matter-of-factual statement of the initial narrative voice—in which parables can only "set out to say merely that the incomprehensible is incomprehensible" whereas "the cares we have to struggle with every day" are a "different matter"—as yet another parable. For that statement presents something different than what is actually the case: an illusory severance of reality from parable. Whence the "also" [*auch*] in the second interlocutor's statement: "I bet that is also a parable"—only if the statement of the initial voice was a parable can the next statement, by the first interlocutor, be *also* a parable. It follows that reality and parable are so intrinsically intertwined that it is impossible ever to free oneself of either: one cannot dwell in reality without the means of parables, just as one cannot deal with anything else but reality when one employs parables. Thus we shift from the initial or ostensible opposition between reality and parable to a situation in which liberation from reality is possible only within our confinement in reality—*but* now reality is expanded to include parable as one of its constitutive parts, as the realm of failure (illusion) presupposed for winning (obtaining Truth) in reality.

(Mis-)recognizing, through this "also," that the second interlocutor has understood that both, the single exaltation of either daily life or lofty wisdom, are parables, the first interlocutor admits: "You have won." The narrative strategy at this point consists, on the one hand, in the sudden and unexplained shift of the first interlocutor—who had been advocating the escape away from daily life—from the position of not knowing to that of knowing (both what the true relation between reality and parable is, and how parables operate, i.e., by representing what does not exist). And on the other hand, in the fact that, by contrast, the second interlocutor remains trapped in ignorance, and responds: "But unfortunately, only in parable." (Evidently, he had carelessly spit out that "also," without himself being aware of its significance.) But undistracted, the first interlocutor persists in his knowing position, and objects that, on the contrary, in parable he lost—since with his "also" he presented the extent state of affairs, rather than what does not exist—and, hence, through this failure in parable he won in reality.

In this of all *Gleichnissen*, meant to explicate *Gleichnis* itself, Kafka pedagogically demarcates the (first) part of the text that obeys the cardinal rule of *Gleichnis*—self-negation—to set it apart from the rest of the text— the statements to be taken at face value. The latter part is the constitutive internal exception of *Gleichnis*, that is, the precondition required for the statements of the first part of the text to negate themselves (if they did not, the statements of the second part could not be taken at face value, and vice versa). The entire allegorical text is thus a not-all set, since it includes within itself both its members (the self-negating statements) and its exception (the nonnegateable statements), which is presupposed for the rest of the members to negate themselves.[85] Which is why allegory is not to be reduced to a sheer self-negation; the "something different from what" any allegory represents is not just the opposite of what it presents.[86] Yet, to this must be added, as Deleuze stresses, the precondition of any symbolic structure, namely the indispensable element that prevents the two parts of the set—the "regular" members and their exception—"from simply reflecting one another" in a purely imaginary relation.[87] What follows the line "that is also a parable" is not the mirror image, positive or negative, of what precedes it. "On Parables" obtains its symbolic structure through the element "also"—"seen" (by the one interlocutor) and not "seen" (by the other), it "belongs to no series" and, while it has "no double," it "is nevertheless present in both" series (of statements by the two interlocutors and of the statements in each of the two parts of text).[88] Thus, "On Parables" is *allegory*—a not-all set consisting of self-negations and their presupposed internal exception, without the one part mirroring the other by dint of a supernumerary element that traverses both.[89]

Allegory, thus, brings to relief two major philosophical formulations that, from the two ends of secular modernity, subtend its logic. On the one hand, Spinoza's dictum that "truth is the standard both of itself and of the false";[90] and, on the other hand, Lacan's comment on "the profound ambiguity of any assertion":

> [I]t is as establishing itself in, an even by, a certain lie, that we see set up the dimension of truth, in which respect it is not, strictly speaking, shaken, since the lie is itself posited in this dimension of truth.[91]

Kafkaesque and Perversion

As mentioned in an earlier footnote, one of the ways of obtaining textually a not-all set is the prevention of the set of narrative gazes from becoming fully identifiable. This lacking ultimate gaze, whose presence would close the not-all set, is the gaze pertaining to a dead transcendence. It is omniscient (capable of telling the truth) only by being ignorant and impotent (telling lies). It is a gaze that can be omniscient only at the cost of being no one's gaze, being the gaze of "an Other witness, the witness Other than any of the partners"; only in this way is "the Speech that it supports... capable of lying, that is to say, of presenting itself as Truth."[92]

Encountering this haunting Kafkaesque gaze, we may be overtaken by the temptation to take it upon ourselves, to embody it, and thus let our own gaze become the ultimate arbitrator of the meaning of the presented reality—appealing, in our helplessness, to any means that could aid us, including, not least, sources that are not in the text. We can be led to this fallacy if we forget that the gaze of dead transcendence is the gaze of a "witness Other than any of the partners"—which include both those in the text and us, the readers. If we let this happen, we enter the realm of perversion.

As Lacan puts it, there is "a dialectic of the eye and the gaze," which is operative in "what every organ determines, namely, duties."[93] The eye obediently follows the dictations of the gaze due to "the pre-existence to the seen of the given-to-be-seen"—i.e., what can be seen and what not.[94] The eye sees only what the gaze forces it to see...exceptionally what it allows it to see. The spatial distribution between these two functions is that "on the side of things, there is the gaze...things look at me, and yet I see them,"[95] or, in Žižek's paraphrase, "the eye viewing the object is on the side of the subject, while the gaze is on the side of the object."[96] This is the reason why, when being given to see (or hear, or sense in any way) this or the other thing, we always wonder (at least until our imaginary interprets the gesture): The Other is showing or "saying this to me, but what does he want?"[97] So it is that everything we perceive never has an unambiguous meaning, and external reality always reserves a degree of mystery.

In exceptional cases, however, this "normal" distribution of functions can be inverted, so that we, the subjects, become the direct bearers of the gaze, and thus objectified. This is the case in pornography, in which, as Žižek writes, "instead of being on the side of the viewed object, the gaze falls into ourselves, the spectators, which is why the image we see on the screen contains...no sublime-mysterious point from which it gazes at us. It is only we who gaze stupidly at the image that 'reveals all.'"[98] In other words, as Žižek writes, "pornography's perversity does not lie in the fact that "it...shows us all the dirty details"; perversity "is, rather, to be conceived in a strictly formal way," as the structure that forces "the spectator" or reader "a priori to occupy a perverse position," the position of a gazing object rather than a viewing subject.[99] This is why neither pornography is always perverse (it can exude much mystery when, for instance, studied as part of cultural analysis) nor perversion is always pornographic. Replacing the Other's gaze with ours perverts the Kafkaesque.

It is then quite ironic that the more Kafka's work repels such approaches as *ad hominem*—psychologizing or otherwise—interpretations, the more they swarm around it. (How many times have we been told that K. is accused because Kafka felt personally guilty?) Like in the face of a gory or obscene scene, we avert our eyes from the petrifying gaze of dead transcendence, we change direction and run after the shelter of some safer gaze, intimate enough to know what we do not—and to tell the truth without lying. The shelter is the trap.

"Alas," said the mouse, "the whole world is growing smaller every day. At the beginning it was so big that I was afraid, I kept running, and I was glad when at last I saw walls far away to the right and left, but these walls have narrowed so quickly that I am in the last chamber already, and there in the corner stands the trap that I must run into." You only need to change your direction," said the cat, and ate it up.[100]

Notes

1. Walter Benjamin, "Some Reflections on Kafka," in *Illuminations*, ed. Hannah Arendt, trans. Harry Zohn (New York: Schocken, 1969), 144–145.
2. George Steiner, introduction to *The Trial*, by Franz Kafka (New York: Schocken, 1992), ix.
3. Ibid.
4. Sigmund Freud, *The Interpretation of Dreams*, trans. James Strachey (New York: Avon Books, 1998), 528.
5. Steiner, ix.
6. Jacques Derrida, *Of Grammatology*, trans. Gayatri Chakravorty Spivak (Baltimore, MD: The Johns Hopkins University Press, 1976), 159; Claude Lévi-Strauss, *Structural Anthropology*, trans. Claire Jacobson and Brooke Grundfest Schoepf (New York: Basic Books, 1963), 217.
7. Steiner, vii and ix.
8. Stanley Corngold, *Franz Kafka: The Necessity of Form* (Ithaca, NY: Cornell University Press, 1988), 160.
9. Ibid., 160–161.
10. Ibid., 163.
11. Steiner, ix.
12. Malcom Pasley, "Zu Kafkas Interpunktion," *Euphorion* 75:4 (1981): 474–490 and 490.
13. Franz Kafka, *The Diaries of Franz Kafka, 1914–1923*, trans. Martin Greenberg (New York: Schocken, 1949), 202 (January 16, 1922).
14. Corngold, 155.
15. Franz Kafka, *Diaries, 1914–1923*, 202 (January 16, 1922).
16. Steiner, ix.
17. Maurice Blanchot, *The Work of Fire*, trans. Charlotte Mandell (Stanford, CA: Stanford University Press, 1995), 7.
18. Ibid., 7.
19. Jacques Lacan, *The Seminar of Jacques Lacan Book XVII: The Other Side of Psychoanalysis*, ed. Jacques-Alain Miller, trans. Russell Grigg (New York: Norton, 2007), 199–200.
20. Jacques Lacan, *The Seminar of Jacques Lacan Book XI: The Four Fundamental Concepts of Psychoanalysis*, ed. Jacques-Alain Miller, trans. Alan Sheridan (New York: Norton, 1981), 59.

21. Gilles Deleuze, *Masochism: Coldness and Cruelty* (New York: Urzone, 1989; New York: Zone Books, 1994), 112–3.

22. It is also in this sense that Kafka's work, albeit increasingly canonized as "major literature," is today even more minor than it was in modernism. Here I am referring of course to Deleuze and Félix Guattari's characterization of Kafka's work as "minor literature." (Gilles Deleuze and Felix Guattari, *Kafka: Toward a Minor Literature*, trans. Dana Polan [Minneapolis: University of Minnesota, 1986].)

23. Though we shall return to Benjamin's allegory below, let us already note that it is because Benjamin's account of baroque allegory is an analysis of the secular signifier in general that several theorists were able to show that his theory provides a formal analysis of secular discursivity, including its modernist and postmodernist variants. Influential in this regard was the work of Christine Buci-Glucksmann who argued that modernist and postmodernist theories and literatures constitute a "baroque paradigm," as defined by Benjamin, marked by allegorical style, the overlap of aesthetics and ethics, and so on. (Christine Buci-Glucksmann, *Baroque Reason: The Aesthetics of Modernity*, trans. Patrick Camiller [London: Sage, 1994].) Major thinkers whose work presupposes the same position include Gilles Deleuze, Jacques Derrida, Fredric Jameson, Philippe Lacoue-Labarthe, Jean-François Lyotard, Paul de Man (and with an emphasis on the relation of allegory to mourning and melancholia), Judith Butler, Cathy Caruth, Shoshana Felman, Julia Kristeva, Dori Laub, Julia Reinhard-Lupton and Kenneth Reinhard, and Juliana Schiesari.

24. Karl Marx, *Capital: A Critique of Political Economy*, Vol. 1, intro. Ernest Mandel, trans. Ben Fowkes (London: Penguin Books, in association with New Left Review, 1990), 301.

25. For more on this monistic relation, as well as the interrelations among Spinoza, Marx, and Lacan, and the relation between thought (signifier) and being, see A. Kiarina Kordela, *$urplus (Spinoza, Lacan)* (Albany: SUNY Press, 2007).

26. Franz Kafka, *The Basic Kafka*, intro. Erich Heller (New York: Washington Square Press: Pocket Books, 1979), 184.

27. Here it must be added that even the question as to whether the tiger is indeed tamed or just behaves like tamed is irrelevant, for the Kafkaesque espouses the Pascalian principle that there is no difference between being something (e.g., a true Christian, as in Pascal's own example) or behaving like one (going to church, praying, etc.), since by acting as if one believed the belief becomes real. (Blaise Pascal, "The Wager," in *Pensées*, trans. A. J. Krailsheimer [London: Penguin, 1995], §418–26; 121–27.)

28. Gerhard Neumann calls the later term that comes to replace the initial element in this arbitrary chiasm the "foreign, analogous term," which does not perform a reversal of neither identical or synonymous nor antonymous or oppositional (e.g., untamed–tamed), but rather introduces "analogous," yet "foreign" or displaced, terms (untamed–sleeping). This rhetorical trope allows for the "gliding paradox," so characteristic of Kafka's (ostensibly) illogical texts. (Gerhard Neumann, "Umkehrung und Ablenkung: Franz Kafkas 'Gleitendes Paradox,'" in *Franz Kafka*, ed. Heinz Politzer [Darmstadt: Wissenschaftliche Buchgesellschaft, 1973], 459–515.) The culminating, as well as typical, such "foreign, analogous term" in the Kafkaesque is of course

the animal. For the animal is neither identical or synonymous nor antonymous or oppositional to the human. In terms of the structuralist Greimasian square, and borrowing from James H. Kavanagh's application of it on Ridley Scott's film *Alien*, while the machine is nonhuman, and the alien antihuman (i.e., kills humans), the cat (whom the otherwise ruthless female protagonist saves toward the end of the film at the risk of her life) is non-antihuman—neither a machine, nor a hostile alien, but that part of humanity that reconfirms its humanity. (James Kavanagh, "Feminism, Humanism and Science in *Alien*," in *Alien Zone: Cultural Theory and Contemporary Science Fiction Cinema*, ed. Annette Kuhn [London: Verso, 1990], 73–81; and A. J. Greimas and F. Rastier, "The Interaction of Semiotic Constrains," *Yale French Studies* 41 [1968]: 86–105.) The difference between *Alien* and Kafka's work being that in the latter the animal as the "foreign, analogous term" of the human reveals the inhumanity of humanity. Furthermore, the Kafkaesque non-antirelation of the "foreign, analogous term" to the human—the fact that the human is an animal, yet an animal is not a human but is required for humans to grasp their inhumanity—is what makes it possible, and postulates, to read Kafka's works simultaneously as "parables," as Benjamin argues, and, as Adorno counterargued, literally, or "as the contrary of metaphor," as Deleuze and Guattari maintain. (Benjamin, *Illuminations*, 144; Deleuze and Guattari, 22.) As Henry Sussman writes, "The Burrow"—a text that, going beyond *The Metamorphosis*, brings to the limit Kafka's experimentation with the animal-principle—marks "an end to Kafka's writing…a culmination of its exploration into the limit disclosed in the process of metaphor…bespeaking the same duplicity, illusoriness, impenetrability, and limit characteristic of the literary text" itself. (Henry Sussman, *Franz Kafka: Geometrician of Metaphor* [Madison: Coda Press, 1979], 150.) What else can this limit be than precisely the overlap of metaphor and its "contrary," the literal or the "kill[ing]" of all metaphor, all symbolism, all signification, no less than all designation"? (Deleuze and Guattari, 22.)

29. Hence the fact that Kafka's thought is marked, in Corngold's words, by a radical "indifference to the concerns of a practical, world-mastering, empirical consciousness." (Corngold, 160.)
30. Ibid., 159.
31. Kafka, "The Emperor," in *Basic Kafka*, 183.
32. This is also the principle of ideological interpellation. As Žižek has argued in his critique of Althusser via Kafka, if the "ideological belief in a Cause" is possible it is only insofar as there is a radical doubt, "a residue…of traumatic irrationality and senselessness sticking to" the ideological call; for *"this leftover, far from hindering the full submission of the subject to the ideological command, is the very condition of it;* it is precisely this non-integrated surplus of senseless traumatism which confers on the Law its unconditional authority." (Slavoj Žižek, *The Sublime Object of Ideology* [London: Verso, 1989], 43; see also Louis Althusser, "Ideology and Ideological State Apparatus (Notes Towards an Investigation)," in *Lenin and Philosophy and Other Essays*, trans. Ben Brewster [New York: Monthly Review Press, 1971], 127–186.) The function of Kafka's "mysterious bureaucratic entity (Law, Castle)" lies in emphasizing the fact that the Kafkaesque subject is interpellated precisely insofar as

it "does not understand the meaning of the call of the Other." (Žižek, *Sublime Object*, 44.)

33. Immanuel Kant, Prolegomena to Any Future Metaphysics That Will Be Able to Come Forward as Science, trans. James Ellington (Indianapolis: Hacket, 1977), 82, §52c.
34. Ibid., 70, §40.
35. Immanuel Kant, *Critique of Pure Reason*, ed. and trans. Paul Guyer and Allen W. Wood (Cambridge: Cambridge University Press, 1998), 484–85, B472/A444–B473/A445.
36. Kant, *Prolegomena*, 83, §53.
37. Ibid., 84–85, §53.
38. The *Westminster Confession*, chapter III, no. 3 and 5; as cited in Max Weber, *The Protestant Ethic and the Spirit of Capitalism*, trans. Talcott Parsons (Mineola: Dover Publications, 1958), 100.
39. Weber, 101.
40. Ibid., 103.
41. Kant, *Prolegomena*, 76, §48.
42. Weber, 103–4.
43. Ibid., 104.
44. Kant, *Critique*, 470–71, B454/A426–B455/A427.
45. Kant, *Prolegomena*, 82, §52c.
46. Kant, *Critique*, 526 and 528; A520/B548, A523/B551 (Kant's parenthesis).
47. Consequently, only what transcends the categories of time and space can be unconditional. Nowhere else perhaps in Kafka's writings is the necessarily transcendental and supratemporal status of the Law indicated as explicitly as in "The Great Wall of China," in which time, conceived as a succession of countable parts in an irreversible continuum, is forcefully twisted into a whirlpool. Reread particularly the last four pages, starting with: "The Empire is immortal, but the Emperor himself totters... " ("The Great Wall of China," in *Basic Kafka*, 75–80.) Through a series of temporal anastrophes, a sort of perpetual loop of spatiotemporal somersaults, the text replaces time and space with something that cannot be called their opposite—if by that is simply meant the absence of time and space—but a beyond of time and space presupposed as their foundation, dead, and hence more invulnerable. In the concluding paragraph, the Law's necessary dependence on this (a)spatio-temporal attitude is admitted with apologetic triumph: "This attitude then is certainly no virtue. All the more remarkable is it that this very weakness should seem to be one of the greatest unifying influences among our people; indeed, if one may dare to use the expression, the very ground on which we live. To set about establishing a fundamental defect here would mean undermining not only our consciousness, but, what is far worse, our feet." (Ibid., 79–80.) Here we meet again the principle of ideological interpellation. Only the "very weakness" to arrive at the Truth about the world, and our necessary reliance on (imaginary/ideological) interpretations, allow us to constitute meaningful realities and thus obtain the "greatest unifying influence among our people." (If we listen to Benjamin, the Law of a post-lapsarian humanity behaves no differently than Kafka's own: "once he was certain of eventual failure, everything worked out for him *en route* as in a dream." [Benjamin, *Illuminations*,

145.]) The necessity of the failure of the Law (as a precondition for its effectivity) is also the morale of the priest's conclusion at the end of the parable which condenses *The Trial*, that "man muß nicht alles für wahr halten, man muß es nur für notwending halten [it is not necessary to accept everything as true, one must only accept it as necessary]" (T 1998, 270; T 1992, 220). We may of course recall here the words attributed to Hobbes: *"autoritas, non veritas, facit legem* [authority, not truth, makes the law]." But Kafka's wording not only foregrounds the Law's disregard of, or more precisely, repulsion to any legitimate ground, such as logical justification, but also reflects the Law's tautological self-grounding (i.e., failure or lack of ground) by means of a rhetorical loop: the (re)appearance of the words "man muß...für...halten [one must take or hold as (true, or, necessary)]"—or, in the English translation, the reappearance of the word "necessary"—at the beginning and the end of the phrase (T 1998, 270). It is precisely through rhetoric and the performative function of language—the medium necessary for formulating the legal system—that the fundamental paradox of the Law's ungroundedness carries on to empirical laws. Klaus Mladek attempts to draw the attention of legal scholars to this arbitrary and tautological self-grounding of the laws by arguing that, contrary to "a particular liberal legal tradition that sees laws themselves as grounded in reasonable origins and a certain communitarian fantasy of communal values," and which "dependably ignores the force and antagonism of the law," in truth laws are grounded on nothing but their own textual "narratological-performative *making* of authority and criminality," that is, the arbitrary "complexities of writing, violence and interpretation," with their "profound complicity among grammar, thought and judgment." (Klaus Mladek, "Gotta Read Kafka: Nine Reasons Why Kafka Is Crucial for the Study of the Law," *Studies in Law, Politics, and Society* 31 [2004]: 89–117, 98 and 89.) Finally, let us note the striking analogy between the law and capitalist economy, insofar as both are based on failure. As Marx stresses, for far from being undermined by its failures or crises, "the mechanism of the capitalist production process removes the very obstacles it temporarily creates" (Marx, *Capital*, 770). Evidently, Kafka would subscribe not to what is known as Possibility Theories, "in which general crises occur if and when there is a certain conjunction of historically determined factors," but to the Necessity Theories, which are "based on the...law as the expression of an intrinsic dominant tendency...in which the periodic occurrence of general crises is inevitable...because these are built-in mechanisms within capitalist accumulation which adjust capacity to effective demand, and...keep wage increases within the limits of productivity increases." (Tom Bottomore, ed., *A Dictionary of Marxist Thought*, 2nd ed. [Oxford: Blackwell, 1991], 161 and 164.)

48. In this regard, Kafka appears to advance *avant la lettre* Fredric Jameson's thesis about postmodern global capitalism "whose mechanisms and dynamics are not visible...and therefore stand as a fundamental representational problem." What we mistake for adequate representations of this unknowable world, and "[a]ll of the terms that lie to hand[,]...are already figural, already soaked and saturated in ideology," our imaginary interpretations. (Fredric Jameson, *The Geopolitical Aesthetic: Cinema and Space in the World System*

[Bloomington: Indiana University Press, and London: British Film Institute, 1992], 2.) This, as we shall see below, is of course not the end of Jameson's argument.

49. Crucially, the cause of this interpretative plethora lies not in any linguistic difficulty. In this regard, Neumann rightly questions the linkage of Kafka's work with expressionism, as is advocated, for instance, by Gerhard Kurz, *if* by expressionism we mean the destruction of the "semantic, grammatical, or syntactic structure" of a text, which clearly is not what the Kafka's text performs. Rather, not unlike Kant, it "pursu[es] conventional thought processes" with "extreme meticulousness...in order to reach the point where they collapse" and where "something" else "leaps forth, which Kafka...calls 'genuine life.'" (Neumann, 486, 474, and 508; see also Gerhard Kurz, *Traum-Schrecken: Kafkas literarische Existenzanalyse* [Stuttgart: Metzler, 1980].)

50. Milena Jesenka, "An Obituary for Franz Kafka," in Jana Cerna, *Kafka's Milena*, trans. A. G. Brain (Northwestern University Press, 1993), 179.

51. Benjamin, *Illuminations*, 145. Kafka's antinomic representation of the world constitutes thus the epitomic contrast to "mythical thought" which, as Lévi-Strauss has shown, "always progresses from the awareness of oppositions toward their resolution." (Lévi-Strauss, 224.)

52. Franz Kafka, *The Diaries of Franz Kafka, 1910–1913*, trans. Joseph Kresh (New York: Schocken, 1948), 296 (August 14, 1913).

53. Franz Kafka, *Diaries, 1914–1923*, 42 (June 6, 1914).

54. It is another question whether Kafka's coercive conception of conjugal ties, as well as his debasement of sex (the "disease of the instincts," as he called it), account for his quasi-caricaturist female characters, such as the "compassionate sister" in *The Metamorphosis*, who, as Vladimir Nabokov remarks, far from possessing a depth of subjectivity, is stereotypically fashioned after the literary pattern of "the domineering...strong sister of the fairy tales." (Vladimir Nabokov, "Franz Kafka: The Metamorphosis," in *Lectures on Literature*, ed. Fredson Bowers [San Diego: Harvest/HBJ, 1982], 271.)

55. Corngold, 221–222.

56. Clayton Koelb, "The Deletions from Kafka's Novels," *Monatshefte* 68 (Winter 1976): 365–372; Corngold, 222 and 222, n. 28.

57. Franz Kafka, "The Cell," in *Basic Kafka*, 183.

58. Regarding *The Trial*'s first sentence—"Jemand mußte Josef K. verleumdet haben, denn ohne daß er etwas Böses getan hätte, wurde er eines Morgens verhaftet" (T 1998, 1)—we may also add that the narrator begins by positing, without any certainty ("must..." [mußte...]"), a possible, active, past perfect cause ("must have been telling lies [mußte...verleumdet haben]") for the postpositive, first past-tense, passive event (K.'s arrest: "was arrested [wurde...verhaftet]"). In other words, K.'s reality has begun not only prior to the beginning of the text but also prior to the narrator's interpretative activity regarding K.'s pretextual reality. As Corngold remarks, since the "narrative" in *The Trial* "begins not with the first event of the plot"—"he was arrested"—"but with a first interpretation of the event"—"Someone must have been telling lies about Joseph K."—K.'s "ordeal would have to have a beginning before it has been preread" and interpreted by the narrator. (Corngold, 223; T 1992, 1.)

59. Franz Kafka, "The Cell," in *Basic Kafka*, 183–184.
60. See Jeremy Bentham, *Theory of fictions*, ed. C. K. Ogden (London: Kegan Paul, Trench, Trubner and Co., 1932); as well as Jacques Lacan, *The Seminar of Jacques Lacan Book VII: The Ethics of Psychoanalysis 1959–1960*, ed. Jacques-Alain Miller, trans. Dennis Porter (New York: Norton, 1992), 12; for my elaboration on Lacan's reading of Bentham's "fictitious" in relation to Freud, see Kordela, 168 n. 39; Hans Vaihinger, *The philosophy of "as-if,"* 2nd ed., trans. C. K. Ogden (New York: Harper and Row, 1924); Octave Mannoni, *Clefs pour l'imaginaire ou l'autre scène* (Paris: Seuil, 1969), particularly the chapter "Je sais bien, mais quand meme..."
61. Sigmund Freud, "Fetischismus," in *Gesammelte Werke*, ed. Anna Freud (London: Imago; Frankfurt a.M.: Fischer, 1999), XIV, 311–17.
62. Walter Benjamin, *The Origin of German Tragic Drama*, trans. John Osborne (London: Verso, 1977), 227.
63. Ibid., 224.
64. Ibid.
65. Peter Harrison, "Miracles, Early Modern Science, and Rational Religion," *Church History* 75:3 (September 2006): 493–510, 500.
66. Michel Foucault, *The order of things: An archaeology of the human sciences*, trans. anon (New York: Vintage, 1970), 42. Because by "allegory" Benjamin means the secular "binary" arbitrary sign, he differentiated it above all from the symbol, which, as Ferdinand de Saussure notes, "is never wholly arbitrary" but is rather characterized by "a natural bond between the signifier and the signified," as is evident, for instance, in the "symbol of justice, a pair of scales, [which] could not be replaced by just any other symbol, such as a chariot." (Benjamin, *Origin*, 68.)
67. Ibid., 224.
68. Ibid., 224–5.
69. Ibid., 227 and 216–7.
70. Ibid., 225.
71. Ibid., 230.
72. Ibid., 229.
73. Ibid., 233–4. This "unity of guilt and signifying," is insinuated in Walter Sokel's suggestion that the narrative mode of *The Trial* is to be described by the term *"Zweisinnigkeit* (divided perspective)," as the coexistence of two "narrative tracks," in which "the narrator [who] wants [K.] to confess his guilt" is the "counterpoint to Joseph K.'s strategies of affirming his innocence." (Walter Sokel, "The Trial," in *Deutsche Romane des 20. Jahrhunderts: Neue Interpretationen*, ed. Michael Lützeler [Königstein: Athenäum, 1983], 110.) Corngold makes the link between guilt and writing more explicit by stating that, since the narrator "too is unable to identify the offence of which K. is guilty... [t]he only possibility of enriching his perspective is... to read it 'allegorically' (*andeutungsweise*), as pointing beyond the contrary assertion of guilt by a guilty narration to an act of verbal composition," so that what the narrator "refers us to [is] a being who, unlike Joseph K., writes" (Corngold, 224).
74. Benjamin, *Origin*, 234.
75. Ibid., 233.
76. Ibid., 229–30.

77. Ibid., 233.
78. Ibid.
79. Ibid., 235.
80. Theodor W. Adorno, *Prisms*, trans. Samuel and Shierry Weber (Cambridge: The MIT Press, 1997), 246.
81. Benjamin, *Origin*, 223.
82. Mark Anderson, Kafka's Clothes: Ornament and Aestheticism in the Habsburgh Fin de Siecle (Oxford: Clarendon Press, 1992), 6.
83. Benjamin, *Illuminations*, 144.
84. In other words, in the present text I use "allegory," "parable," and "simile" interchangeably, and all are to be differentiated only from "symbol." In this respect my reading fully complies with Adorno's: "The two moments [of the comparison] are not merged, as the symbol would have it, but yawn apart and out of the abyss between them blinds the glaring ray of fascination. Here too, in its striving not for symbol but for allegory, Kafka's prose sides with the outcasts, the protest of his friend [Max Brod] notwithstanding. Walter Benjamin rightly defined it as parable" (Adorno, 246).
85. Such "paradoxical" or "extraordinary sets" (e.g., a set containing itself as its own member) were first observed in mathematics by Dmitry M. Mirimanoff and others, and were undesirable because, as the development of modern set theory showed, they undermined mathematics altogether. For this reason, John von Neumann and others introduced an "axiom of restriction" that ruled them out. (See also Georg Cantor, Adolf Fraenkel, and Ernst Zermelo, eds., *Gesammelte Abhandlungen mathematischen und philosophischen Inhalts* [Vienna: Springer, 1990]; and Kurt Gödel, *Consistency of the Continuum Hypothesis* [Princeton, PA: Princeton University Press, 1940].) By contrast, (post-)structuralist theory largely draws on such sets. For Marx's pioneering analysis of capital in terms of the not-all set, see Kojin Karatani, *Architecture as Metaphor: Language, Number, Money*, ed. Michael Speaks, trans. Sabu Kohso (Massachusetts: The MIT Press, 1995), the chapter "Money," 67–71; and, also in relation to both the Kantian antinomies and Lacan's application of set theory, see Kordela. In literature, there are various ways to confer on a text its not-all structure or allegoric form. If the *Gleichnis* on *Gleichnissen* does so by treating part of its statements as its internal exception, *The Trial*, for instance, relies on its aforementioned unidentifiable gaze. The latter shares the same logic as Deleuze's "out-of-field" in cinema, which confers on film its "non-totalizable" or not-all "relation." (Gilles Deleuze, *Cinema 2: The Time—Image*, trans. Hugh Tomlinson and Robert Galeta [Minneapolis: University of Minnesota Press, 1995], 279; see also Gilles Deleuze, *Cinema 1: The Movement—Image*, trans. Hugh Tomlinson and Barbara Habberjam [Minneapolis: University of Minnesota Press, 1991], particularly "Chapter One.")
86. Allegory, therefore, shares the same logic as Freud's negation (*Verneinung*), under the precondition that we understand that the term does not mean a sheer negation. For in defining negation Freud did not conclude with the statement: " 'You ask who this person in the dream can have been. It was *not* my mother.' We emend this: so it *was* his mother." Rather, taking this example as his point of departure, Freud infers: "It is just as though the patient had said: 'It is true that I thought of my mother in connection with this person, but

I don't feel at all inclined to allow the association to count.... That is something I would rather repress.' A negative judgment is the intellectual substitute for repression.... By the help of the symbol of negation ["No"], the thinking process frees itself from the limitations of repression and enriches itself with the subject-matter without which it could not work efficiently" (Sigmund Freud, "Negation," in *General Psychological Theory* [New York: Collier, 1963], 213–214.) Which is to say, far from concluding at the moment of the negative judgment, the "achievement of the function of judgment only becomes feasible...after the creation of the symbol of negation has endowed thought with a first degree of independence from the results of repression." For only then can judgment deduce that it is nothing other than "a recognition of the unconscious on the part of the ego [that] is expressed in a negative formula," given "the fact that in analysis we never discover a 'No' in the unconscious" (Ibid., 217). The unconscious *lives* unalloyed the antinomy that consciousness can bear only by means of the symbol of negation which negates the one of the two antinomic statement, thereby conferring on consciousness a first degree of independence from the results of repression. The truth lies neither in the thesis nor in the antithesis of the antinomy, but in the acceptance of both as the first plateau toward a Truth that takes both as its standards. For a clear and astute presentation of negation as a properly Spinozian syllogism, see Robert Pfaller's piece, where he also shows that the standard (Hegelian) misunderstanding of negation as a self-negation endowed with transformational powers leads to the misleading and dubious assumption that in order not to be in any form of confinement, including ideology, it would suffice to acknowledge that 'I am in confinement' or "'I am in ideology.'" (Robert Pfaller, "Negation and its reliabilities: An empty subject for ideology?" in *Cogito and the unconscious*, ed. Slavoj Žižek [Durham: Duke University Press, 1998], 235.) The problem with this rationale is not only that it performs "an imaginary transgression" but that "even the wish of transgression within it is imaginary," craving only our entrapment. (Ibid., 236.) This is due to the fact that the "Hegelian solution...presupposes topologically that the only transgression of certain spaces is a negative transgression; that the only beyond of a closed space is an empty beyond" or that "what limits the positive" is "something negative." By contrast, "the Spinozian principle" of monism indicates "that something can only be limited by something else that is of the same nature," namely, also "positive." (Ibid., 234.) If we want to arrive at a space beyond our "daily cares," we do not endeavor to do so by going "*hinüber* [over there]" conceived as an unreal empty space that stands for the opposite of "the only life we have."

87. Gilles Deleuze, "How Do We Recognize Structuralism?," trans. Melissa McMahon and Charles J. Stivale, in *Desert Islands and Other Texts 1953–1974*, ed. David Lapoujade (Los Angeles, CA: Semiotext(e), 2004), 183.

88. Ibid., 184.

89. Here we can compare formally Kafka's work to another mode of German-speaking modernist literature that also criticized the bourgeois life of capitalist modernity. Illustrious examples of this movement include Frank Wedekind's *Lulu* and Arthur Schnitzler's *Reigen*. Its approach could be called "criticism via phenomenal replication," insofar as it exposed the empirical reality of

capitalist incessant exchangeability by replicating it hyperbolically (a strategy later popularized further by Andy Warhol). A recurrent topos in this literature was prostitution, explicit or implicit, as its ideal limit is the reduction of desire to an act repeatable between theoretically infinite exchangeable bodies (and money), a principle that stages commodification on the level of human sexuality. Through this trope, authors cynically exposed the homology between capitalist exchange and modernist desire, which, as Freud was simultaneously discovering, was hysteric, requiring the perpetual sliding of its object. Kafka's criticism, by contrast, proceeds by "transcendental replication." Allegory in particular lends itself to this form of criticism, as it stages a central transcendental structure of capitalism: its not-all character, insofar as capital is the internal exception of the set of all commodities, being both their exclusive measure *and* a member of the set of commodities (as capital, too, is bought and sold, for instance, by credit companies). (See Marx, particularly "The Commodity," 125–77; and, again, the aforementioned chapter in Karatani.)

90. Baruch/Benedict de Spinoza, "Ethics," in *The Collected Works of Spinoza*, Vol 1, ed. and trans. Edwin Curley (Princeton: Princeton University Press, 1985), 408–617, 479; part II, prop. 43, schol.
91. Lacan, *Four Fundamental Concepts*, 138. Which is why, to return to the earlier footnote on Jameson, in the face of particularly this by definition "unmappable system" of the postmodern "world order," "[a]llegory...fatally stages its historic reappearance...(after the long domination of the symbol from romanticism to late modernism)." To be sure, "[n]othing is gained by having been persuaded of the...verisimilitude of this or that...hypothesis" offered in our arbitrary allegories, "but in the intend" or "the desire" to "hypothesize...therein lies the beginning of wisdom," for it is only through our lies, our illusory interpretations of the world, that its Truth can be pointed to. (Jameson, 2–4.)
92. Jacques Lacan, *Écrits: A Selection*, trans. Alan Sheridan (New York: Norton, 1977), 305.
93. Lacan, *Four Fundamental Concepts*, 102.
94. Ibid., 74.
95. Ibid., 109.
96. Slavoj Žižek, Looking Awry: An Introduction to Jacques Lacan through Popular Culture (Massachusetts: October Books, 1991), 109.
97. Lacan, *Four Fundamental Concepts*, 214.
98. Žižek, *Looking Awry*, 110.
99. Ibid., 110.
100. Franz Kafka, "A Little Fable," in *Basic Kafka*, 157.

Chapter Eight

The Ethics and Beauty of *The Trial*: Kafka's Circumscription of Failure

Ross Shields

A work of art always involves encircling the Thing.

—Jacques Lacan[1]

Franz Kafka's *Trial* doesn't end. Despite Max Brod's attempt to produce a finalized version out of the unorganized manuscript, there is an irreducible incompleteness about this novel that persists beyond the final pages. Witness the following dialog between the protagonist, K. (reading, for a moment, the author into his hero), and a nameless priest:

> "Do you realize your trial is going badly?" asked the priest. "It seems that way to me too," said K. "I've tried as hard as I can, but without any success so far.... "How do you imagine it will end," asked the priest. "At first I thought it would surely end well," said K., "now sometimes I even have doubts myself. I don't know how it will end. Do you?" (T 1999, 212)

K. expresses the inconclusiveness of *The Trial* succinctly with the following words: "Assuming the trial ever comes to an actual conclusion, which I greatly doubt" (59).

For those not convinced by such interpretive textual substitutions, the sentiment that *The Trial* was a failure is made clear in the intentions of the author himself. I refer, of course, to Kafka's famous (and famously neglected) request that his unpublished work be burned unread. Critics for once agree on this point...with, that is, the necessary qualifier that this failure—the failure of *The Trial* to be written—is precisely the precondition of its beauty and force. This is what leads Gilles Deleuze and Félix Guattari to contend "[e]ach failure is a masterpiece,"[2] following Walter Benjamin's thesis: "To do justice to the figure of Kafka in its purity and its peculiar beauty one must never lose sight of one thing: it is the purity and beauty of a failure."[3]

Two questions arise. The first concerns the relation of what we will provisionally call the content of *The Trial*—the loosely defined themes of justice, law, freedom, and imprisonment—to its incomplete form. This might be expressed as follows: How can a *Trial* without end be articulated alongside the dialectics of innocence and guilt that have traditionally *demanded* a final judgment, whether juridical or analytical? What *Prozeß* lacks an *Urteil*? The second question is more properly aesthetic, or, better yet, is to be posed at the intersection of aesthetics and ethics—the sphere of beauty: What lends beauty to Kafka's masterpiece of a failure?

* * *

Adopting K.'s angle of incidence to *Trial* and *Castle*, I will take an *oblique* approach toward Kafka's corpus—that is, via the contours and relations sketched in a gesture parallel to and contemporaneous with Kafka's writing, namely, the psychoanalytic corpora of Sigmund Freud and Jacques Lacan, Oedipus and Antigone. Following Deleuze and Guattari's thesis that Kafka effects "an Oedipalization of the Universe," I will examine how Kafka's body of work reflects and refracts such distinct series as those composing, on the one hand, the legal body, and on the other, the sexed and desiring body of psychoanalysis.[4]

We are clearly descending here on the problematic of sublimation, which will offer an entry point to Kafka's text. Lacan offers two definitions of sublimation that are relevant to the study of Kafka. His first is culled from Freud:

> [T]he transformation of the sexual instinct into a work in which everyone will recognize his own dreams and impulses, and will reward the artist for having given him that satisfaction by granting the latter a fuller and happier life—and for giving him in addition access to the satisfaction of the instinct involved from the beginning.[5]

Lacan puts the second in terms closer to his own: "[Sublimation] raises an object... to the dignity of the Thing"[6]—terms that will require a brief gloss.

The contours of Oedipus' corpus, the coordinates of the male position of enunciation (which we will eventually find replicated on the textual level in *The Trial*), are in fact defined by the separation of this transcendent Thing (*das Ding*)—the mother figure in Freud's first formulation of Sophocles's infamous triangle. As Lacan writes:

> The world of our experience, the Freudian world, assumes that it is this object, *das Ding*, as the absolute Other of the subject, that one is supposed

to find again. It is to be found at the most as something missed. One doesn't find it, but only its pleasurable associations. It is in this state of wishing for it and waiting for it that, in the name of the pleasure principle, the optimum tension will be sought.[7]

This radical separation of the first object of desire is a product of the castrating cut of the signifier. Always already immersed in language, the subject has no direct access to the Thing in itself, which is raised to the transcendent plane. Desire is motivated by this original tension, as its subsequent objects will be chosen with a mind to replace the irreplaceable Thing:

> [The Thing] will be there when in the end all conditions have been fulfilled—it is, of course, clear that what is supposed to be found cannot be found again. It is in its nature that the object as such is lost. It will never be found again. Something is there while one waits for something better, or worse, but which one wants.[8]

This "something" is the imaginary object of desire—the semblance—substituted for the Thing. Because no object of desire can live up fully to the *jouissance* (signifying both "enjoyment" and "orgasm") promised by the Thing, the subject is always left wanting. This is the paradox at the heart of male subjectivity: Desire is always at bottom desire for the Thing, while the transcendent separation of the Thing guarantees the impossibility of full satisfaction—of an uncastrated or absolute *jouissance*—thus perpetuating an always unsatisfied desire. If the subject is chained to the Thing and its semblances, it should be recognized that this chain—a chain of signifiers, a prison-house of language—is a presupposition of the male position of enunciation, and that the castrating prohibition of an unlimited or "free" *jouissance* is a necessary condition of the metonymic sliding of (his) desire.

Through a synthesis of the two definitions of sublimation (the manifestation of desire in art; the object raised to the dignity of the Thing), it would now be easy to claim that Kafka offers a powerful substitute satisfaction for the lost Thing through his sketch of the castle at the top of the hill and in the image of the final judgment—guilty or innocent—promised by K.'s trial. In K.'s struggle to reach his Thing, might we not recognize our own "dreams and impulses"? Sublimation in Kafka would then consist in the artistic raising of a transcendent Thing out of the mundane objects of his narratives.

And yet, it is precisely this conclusion that we must resist. Herein lies the importance of Deleuze and Guattari's interpretation—that they manage to trace the movement in Kafka's text away from the male position and toward the female: "An unlimited field of immanence instead of an

infinite transcendence."⁹ The gap of infinite transcendence that separates the male subject from his Thing erupts in their reading, revealing
an unlimited field of immanence between the subject and the void of her
desire. If "Kafka attempts to extract from social representations assemblages of enunciation...and to dismantle these assemblages," it should be
understood that these assemblages of enunciation are modes of the male
position of enunciation (determined in psychoanalysis not by biology but
by the resolution of the Oedipal scenario), and that their dismantling lays
the necessity of this subjectivity bare in its contingency, thereby opening
up the possibility of an Other position of enunciation, that of feminine
jouissance.¹⁰ This movement from transcendence to immanence, supremely
illustrated in Kafka's *Trial*, is the protracted explosion of the transcendent
and stale dialectics of guilt and innocence—an ethical event that constitutes the specific beauty of Kafka's failure.

The Thing About Kafka

The play of transcendence and immanence permeates Kafka's architecture—in the courtrooms of *The Trial* and in the village at the foot of *The
Castle*. The image of a transcendently elevated judge, "about to spring up
any moment in a violent and perhaps wrathful outburst to say something
decisive or even pass judgment," separated from a defendant, "probably to
be thought of as at the foot of the stairs," gives way to an indefinitely proliferating series of contiguous law offices and attics, each leading into the
next (T 1999, 104). It is this logic, recognized by Deleuze and Guattari,¹¹
that opens the atelier of the painter, Titorelli, onto the offices of the court
(thought by K. to be only on the opposite side of the town):

> "What do you find so surprising?" he asked, himself surprised. "Those are
> the law court offices. Didn't you know there were law court offices here?
> There are law court offices in practically every attic, why shouldn't they be
> here too? In fact my atelier is part of the law court offices too, but the court
> has placed it at my disposal." (164)

The bridge of immanence crosses the gulf of transcendence even more
strikingly as K. approaches the castle, revealing anything but the expected
monolith: "Keeping his eyes fixed upon the Castle, K. went ahead, nothing else mattered to him. But as he came closer he was disappointed in
the Castle, it was only a rather miserable little town, pieced together from
village stone" (C 1998, 8).¹²

The architecture of the two novels alone suffices for the gradual realization that desire permeates every aspect of law: "where one believed there was
the law, there is in fact desire and desire alone.... The law is written in a porno

book."[13] Concomitantly, in both novels the network of often sexual relations developed by K. with supporting female characters (girls, washerwomen, landladies, barmaids, et al.) takes on more importance than the clusters of directly influential officials and judges—as, for example, when K. dismisses his lawyer, Huld, while maintaining relations with Huld's nurse. According to K.: "Women have great power. If I could get a few of the women I know to join forces and work for me, I could surely make it through. Particularly with this court, which consists almost entirely of skirt chasers" (T 1999, 213). K.'s desire, on the other hand, motivating in turn the desire of these supporting actresses, is from the start directed toward the resolution of his trial, a sentiment expressed to Huld: "I'm convinced it's necessary to intervene much more actively in the trial than has been done to this point" (187).

Obversely, the court, which depends on a transcendent legitimacy for its efficacy, denies the omnipresence of desire: "'You seek too much outside help,' the priest said disapprovingly, 'particularly from women. Haven't you noticed that it isn't true help'" (T 1999, 213). This statement should, of course, be read against a later utterance from the same priest (the prison chaplain): "I belong to the court" (224). By presumptuously assuming a disinterested stance toward K., the law negates its relationship to desire, its immanence: "Why should I want something from you," says the priest to K., "The court wants nothing from you. It receives you when you come and dismisses you when you go" (224). Titorelli too seeks to uphold the inaccessibility and density of the *Trial*: "Judges on the lowest level, and those are the only ones I know, don't have the power to grant a final acquittal, that power resides only in the highest court, which is totally inaccessible to you and me and everyone else" (158). Even lawyers with influence, who "stand incomparably higher in rank above the petty lawyers than those do over the despised shysters," are inaccessible: "I don't know who the great lawyers are, and it's probably impossible to contact them" (179). While this presumed objectivity is necessary for maintaining the law's transcendent relationships with its subjects, it is a façade that crumbles upon reflection. The concluding line of the very parable, "Before the Law," read to K. by the priest—the story of a man seeking, but denied, entrance to the law—illustrates this point, indicating the dependency of the law on its subject: "No one else could gain admittance here, because this entrance was meant *solely for you*. I'm going to go and shut it now" (217; my emphasis). The plane of immanence extends in both directions. The court is at least as bound to K. as K. is confined by his trial.

* * *

As Lacan notes, "[T]he question of the realization of desire is necessarily formulated from the point of view of a Last Judgment."[14] But if the verdict sought initially by K. is elevated to the dignity of a Thing, what are we to make of the fact of its deferral? Of the impossibility of a final acquittal? Lacan continues: "[M]an fashions this signifier and introduces it into the world…in the image of the Thing, whereas the Thing is characterized by the fact that it is impossible for us to imagine it. The problem of sublimation is located on this level."[15] Indeed, Kafka is a master of such sublimations. *But*, if Kafka raises his castle to the dignity of the Thing, it is only to bring it down again in the deconstructive gesture that characterizes his work. This is because Kafka does not produce an *image* of the Thing—a subli- mated surrogate required by the male position of enunciation—but rather sketches the limits of its impossibility. Kafka does not write the judgment, but writes *around* it, circumscribing the very failure of any representation of the Thing from which the thematic material of *The Trial* derives.[16]

Were K. to reach the castle or receive a sentence, this would undoubt- edly prove devastating for his subjectivity and would entail the destruction of his desire. His death drive would in this way obtain directly its lethal object, the Thing. Again in Lacan's words: "Try to imagine what 'to have realized one's desire' might mean, if it is not to have realized it, so to speak, in the end. It is this trespassing of death on life that gives its dynamism to any question that attempts to find a formulation for the subject of the realization of desire."[17] Much interpretation errs on this point, assuming that K. seeks his final judgment. It should rather be insisted that, deeper than K.'s conscious desire to be judged, K. *desires to desire to* be judged. K.'s desire is predicated on the impossibility of its consummation—any actual admittance to the space of the transcendent would spell the death of his desire, as well as the immediate end of the novel. This is why Kafka could not complete any of his three novels: His failure is a necessity imposed by the form required for their content. Kafka's work fails as an act of artis- tic sublimation. Or better still, the artistic sublimation in Kafka's work fails—the image of the transcendent Thing collapses onto the plane of immanence under the scrutiny imposed by K.

K. does not therefore enter, but rather goes around the locus of the Thing—and as he circumscribes it, gradually shifts his position of enuncia- tion to the female mode, as the once erect castle is shown to consist of a col- lection of shacks, and as an apparently mighty judge is revealed to be "just another examining magistrate," "so small he's almost tiny" upon inspection (T 1999, 106). According to Leni, a lover of K. and nurse of his lawyer, "he had himself stretched out that way in the painting, since he's ridiculously vain, like everyone here" (106). The shift in enunciation, from male to female, reveals therefore the anamorphosis involved in the painting of the judge— the image of authority is laid bare as nothing more than a signifier "orga- nized around emptiness."[18] If it is true that all art involves circumscribing the

Thing—a point at which Heidegger and Lacan concur—then there exists no better image of this than K.'s initial attempt to reach the castle:

> So he set off again, but it was a long way. The street he had taken, the main street in the village, did not lead to the Castle hill, it only went close by, then veered off as if on purpose, and though it didn't lead any farther from the Castle, it didn't get any closer either. K. kept expecting the street to turn at last toward the Castle and it was only in this expectation that he kept going. (C 1998, 10)

K.'s trajectory around the castle is parallel to the course taken by his desire around its Thing. Kafka goes beyond the male logic to the extent that the expectations of reaching the Thing at the center of the field of desire are gradually disappointed, and to the extent that the position of enunciation of the text changes to accommodate this perception.

Trajectories of Guilt

The trajectory of K.'s desire gives new meaning to the saying, to "move . . . in legal circles" (T 1999, 101). Unlike the male concern of penetrating the depths of the Other, the female position of enunciation takes an entirely different stance toward *jouissance*, one exemplified by the figure of the mystic: "they experience it, but know nothing about it."[19] *The Trial* and *The Castle* might be read as the gradual dawning of the epiphany: *jouissance* is experienced, the Thing is present in its effects, but nothing is or can be known about it. Nevertheless, in circumscribing this x the mechanisms and power structures that have grown up around it are gradually exposed. This means that the *effect* of the final judgment is certainly experienced by K., though it may exist only in its function as an ideal focus or logical singularity.[20] In the same way, the central castle affects life in the surrounding village. In the words of Giorgio Agamben: "in Kafka's village the empty potentiality of law is so much in force as to become indistinguishable from life. The existence and the very body of Joseph K. ultimately coincide with the Trial; they become the Trial."[21] Both K.'s gradually accept their Thing as a central void around which desire is organized.[22] It becomes then for K., "less a question of presenting this image of a transcendental and unknowable law than of dissecting the mechanism of an entirely different sort of machine, which needs this image of the law only to align its gears and make them function together."[23] The K. of *The Castle* even goes so far as to nearly forget his desire to reach the castle, instead becoming increasingly absorbed in the relations of everyday life and desires in the village.

A discussion of his legal options with the painter Titorelli sketches the possible positions of enunciation K. can take with respect to his case: "I forgot to ask first what sort of release you want. There are three possibilities: actual acquittal, apparent acquittal, and protraction" (T 1999, 152).

In "purely formal terms" actual acquittal is described as follows: "[T]he files relating to the case are completely discarded, they disappear totally from the proceedings, not only the charge, but the trial and even the acquittal are destroyed, everything is destroyed" (T 1999, 158). Note the similarity of actual acquittal to losing the trial—in the words of K.'s uncle: "Do you want to lose this trial? Do you know what that means? It means you'll simply be crossed off" (94). Actual acquittal is then analogous to the direct attainment of the Thing, to *jouissance* insofar as it "implies precisely the acceptance of death."[24] In the limit case of actual acquittal, proof of innocence merges with its dialectical opposite, the death sentence imposed by a conviction.

Apparent acquittal represents on the other hand the oscillation between the two poles of guilt and innocence. While actual acquittal is as impossible to achieve as *jouissance*—Titorelli tells K.: "I never saw a single actual acquittal"—apparent acquittal corresponds to the male position of enunciation (T 1999, 153-154). According to Titorelli:

> [T]he charge against you is dropped for the moment but continues to hover over you, and can be reinstated the moment an order comes from above.... There is no further change in the files except for adding to them the certification of innocence, the acquittal, and the grounds for the acquittal. Otherwise they remain in circulation; following the law court's normal routine they are passed on to the higher courts, come back to the lower ones, swinging back and forth with larger or smaller oscillations, longer or sorter interruptions.... Someday—quite unexpectedly—some judge or other takes a closer look at the file, realizes that the case is still active, and orders an immediate arrest. (158–159)

Apparent acquittal maintains the transcendent relation of inaccessibility between the condemned and the final verdict. The verdict never arrives, but neither does an actual acquittal—the condemned is arrested one day and released the next, as his desire takes a parallel course of death (desublimation from Thing to object) followed by rebirth (resublimation from object to Thing). The thesis and antithesis of the juridical dialectic (freedom and guilt) are not sublated as in actual acquittal, but are rather reified as two extremes between which the legal subject oscillates.

The third possibility offered by Titorelli offers an alternative to both the sublation and the oscillation of guilt and innocence, pointing to the female position of enunciation:

> [P]rotraction is when the trial is constantly kept at the lowest stage.... The trial doesn't end of course, but the defendant is almost as safe from a conviction

as he would be as a free man.... The trial must be kept constantly spinning within the tight circle to which it's artificially restricted. (T 1999, 160–161)

Deleuze and Guattari consider K.'s gradual acceptance of protraction (an alternative to the transcendent oscillation between guilt and innocence of apparent acquittal) as a victory of the immanent model over the transcendent: "the whole story of K revolves around the way in which he enters more deeply into [protraction].... He thereby leaves the abstract machine of the law that opposes law to desire, as body is opposed to spirit, as form is opposed to matter, in order to enter into the...mutual immanence of a decoded law and a deterritorialized desire."[25] If the trial is kept "constantly spinning within the tight circle to which it's artificially restricted," is it not clear that protraction recommends the circumnavigation of the Thing while abandoning the illusion that the Thing can ever be reached? Indeed, this realization dawns on K. later in his discussion with Titorelli: "'Both methods [i.e., protraction and apparent acquittal] have this in common: they prevent the accused from being convicted.' 'But they also prevent an actual acquittal,' said K. softly, as if ashamed of the realization. 'You've grasped the heart of the matter,' the painter said quickly" (161). The usual dialectics of innocence and guilt, freedom and confinement, are side-stepped in the case of protraction, lending credence to K.'s remark to an inspector: "Then being under arrest isn't so bad" (17).

Protraction thus serves as the juridico-political reflection of Lacan's strongest statement against phallic *jouissance*, his ethical imperative: "[T]he only thing one can be guilty of is giving ground relative to one's desire."[26] The logic of this maxim, linking transcendence to immanence, is expressed in spatial terms in the following extract from Kafka's "Advocates":

So if you find nothing in the corridors open the doors, if you find nothing behind these doors there are more floors, and if you find nothing up there, don't worry, just leap up another flight of stairs. As long as you don't stop climbing, the stairs won't end, under your climbing feet they will go on growing upwards.[27]

The trial will never progress beyond its initial stage, as desire will never develop into its end and death. By prolonging desire indefinitely, protraction offers one formula for resisting the inevitable coming-up-short with respect to *jouissance* encountered by the male subject.

*   *   *

The central question of *The Trial*—is K. guilty?—takes on here a significance beyond the usual dialectic of guilt and innocence: Does K. give ground relative to his desire? Perhaps one answer could be found in the words of K.: "I'm guiltless or at least not quite as guilty as they thought" (T 1999, 29). Guilt*less* to the extent that K. pursues his desire, as when K. dismisses his lawyer "in accord with [his] desires" to become more involved in his trial (184). *Guilty* to the extent that he gives ground, as when K. allows a student to carry away (literally) the object of his desire (the washerwoman): "K. followed them slowly; he realized that this was the first clear defeat he had suffered at the hands of these people" (64).

In turn, the question—"is K. guilty of having given ground relative to his desire?"—can be reformulated by looking at Lacan's "definition of a hero" (whom Lacan aligns in his seminar on ethics with the female position): "someone who may be betrayed with impunity."[28] Lacan writes:

> Something is played out in betrayal if one tolerates it, if driven by the idea of the good—and by that I mean the one who has just committed the act of betrayal—one gives ground to the point of giving up one's own claims and says to oneself, "Well, if that's how things are, we should abandon our position; neither of us is worth that much, and especially me, so we should just return to the common path." You can be sure that what you find there is the structure of giving ground relative to one's desire.[29]

To be betrayed with impunity is not, however, the same as tolerating the act of betrayal. To tolerate a betrayal implies giving up, as it were, one's ground. To be betrayed with impunity is rather to hold this ground despite the facticity of the betrayal. The ethical hero, rather than accepting such a betrayal, fights for her case. Her path is anything but "common." The hero occupies a paradoxical position—she is betrayed, a position that *usually* results in giving ground to one's desire, but she is not guilty. She has maintained her desire after its death or collapse. The hero thus refuses to accept the betrayal with which her story begins—the arrest of desire. If the paradox of the male position of enunciation has been shown to consist in desiring the inaccessible Thing, then the paradox of the female position of enunciation—the ethical subject—can be stated as follows: *Having recognized the emptiness of the Thing, she nevertheless maintains her desire.*

The Trial begins, in fact, with such a betrayal: "Someone must have slandered Josef K., for one morning, without having done anything wrong, he was arrested" (T 1999, 3). Whether K. is a hero, whether he may be betrayed with impunity, will be the crux on which his guilt hangs: Does K., having been betrayed to the court, give ground relative to his desire? A counter example (not of an anti- but of a nonhero) will be found in the hallway of the law offices among the figures of the defendants who had submitted petitions for acquittal months ago and are now waiting for an answer, "backs bowed and knees bent, [standing] like beggars in the street"

(69). The verdict for these men has already arrived—they have given up on their desire, they are guilty. Protraction is one strategy employed by K. to avoid this fate and to maintain his desire with respect to the final judgment: "The trial doesn't end of course, but the defendant is almost as safe from a conviction as he would be as a free man" (160). By protracting his trial, K. remains "guiltless or at least not quite as guilty" with respect to his desire.

Beauty and the Second Death

And yet protraction hardly seems to do justice to the heroic (female) position of enunciation. Is Block, another client of Huld who has according to the lawyer "gained a good deal of experience and knows how to protract a trial," a hero? (T 1999, 96). Huld continues: "But his ignorance far outweighs his cunning. What do you think he would say if he were to learn that his trial hasn't even begun yet, if someone were to tell him that the bell that opens the trial still hasn't rung" (196–197). Does K. fare no better in protracting his trial than Block or the defendants in the halls of the law court offices? The man from the country in the parable, "Before the Law" would appear to be deftly protracting his case. Should we consider him a hero? Does the female position of enunciation amount to no more than biding one's time at the entrance to the law?

The error of the man from the country consists in not recognizing that, by sitting *outside* the law he is already in fact *inside* the law, just as K. enters the law at the moment of his arrest. The warning of the doorkeeper is then but one more attempt to maintain the illusion of objectivity and transcendent separation of the Thing:

> If you're so drawn to it, go ahead and try to enter, even through I've forbidden it. But bear this in mind: I'm powerful. And I'm only the lowest doorkeeper. From hall to hall, however, stand doorkeepers each more powerful than the one before. The mere sight of the third is more than even I can bear. (T 1999, 216)

Because the man believes he is outside the law, he can do nothing to forward his case, choosing instead to sit "for days and years" like the men in the law court offices (216). The tragedy of his story is that it is only when the man is "nearing his end" that he recognize that he is already inside the law—that the gate was "meant solely for [him]," and that the law and its subjects are equiprimordial (217). Taking K. as its hero, the female position of enunciation would plug its ears with wax, ignore the silent protestations of the gatekeeper, and walk through the open door of the law—recognizing as it does so that the shortest distance between two points often takes the shape of a circle, and that entering the law only continues the subject in her concentric path around its final verdict. If arrest—the entrance to the space of the law—can be equated with the collapse of the male subject's desire, it should be noted that this is only K.'s first death—the death of Oedipus—and that this death is the first step toward the ethical ideal of the classical hero of Lacan's female position of enunciation: Antigone.

To be sure, the death of Oedipus prefigures Antigone's second death. These two deaths must be distinguished from one another to avoid confusion. If the first death is the fate of the male position of enunciation (the collapse of desire), the second death represents the limit against which the hero nevertheless maintains her desire.[30] Antigone, buried alive, occupies this space between two deaths, the purview of the hero. Like Antigone, K. dies with his accusation—but, and unlike the man from the country, his death, his entry into the law, is recognized as such from the beginning. K. is divorced at the start from his everyday intrigues and enters the space of the law. His desire is cut off from its goals: K. no longer pays his weekly visit to the waitress, Elsa; he gives up his responsibilities at his job to the executive vice president.[31] What distinguishes K. from the other figures in the law court offices, however, is that despite his death, despite the collapse of his everyday desire and his recognition of this collapse (the men from the hallway are in denial on this point), K. maintains a desire that is no longer predicated on the semblance of the Thing. K. recognizes, in the first stages of his trial, the "senselessness of the whole affair," the void at the center of desire, the absence of the final judgment, and the impossibility of actual acquittal, but nevertheless presses onward (T 1999, 50). The space, traversed in the course of protraction, between two deaths is then not merely the space of the accused—a purgatory between freedom and confinement—but the locus of knowledge reached upon recognizing the imaginary status of the transcendent dialectic of freedom and guilt. K.'s desire is arrested; his Thing doesn't hold up to scrutiny; yet he refuses to give ground to that desire—acting henceforth and for the duration of the novel in the absence of a cause.

"The beauty effect," writes Lacan, "derives from the relationship of the hero to the limit."[32] Beauty is the phenomenon associated with Antigone, with the hero approaching the limit of the second death:

> The true [second] barrier that holds the subject back in front of the unspeakable field of radical desire that is the field of absolute destruction, of destruction beyond putrefaction, is properly speaking the aesthetic phenomenon where it is identified with the experience of beauty—beauty in all its shining radiance, beauty that has been called the splendor of truth. It is obviously because truth is not pretty to look at that beauty is, if not its splendor, then at least its envelope.[33]

If Antigone represents one such hero—"nothing is more moving...than the desire that visibly emanates from the eyelids of this admirable girl"—K., I would argue, is a good contender for another.[34] As K. approaches the emptiness of his final verdict, both his beauty and the beauty of the text increase exponentially. The closer the novel approaches this *real* void of the absent Thing, the failure at the center of Kafka's work, the greater and more painful the beauty becomes. Recalling Benjamin's description of the particular beauty of Kafka—"the purity and beauty of a failure"—we can now add: Kafka's beauty is not the beauty of the failure of the male position of enunciation to get off, as it were, the hook—but rather the beauty of the failure of the feminine position of enunciation, the beauty reached in approaching the limit of the Thing.

Beauty also functions on the diegetic level—as noted by Fräulein Bürstner: "The court has a strange attraction, doesn't it?" (T 1999, 29). The curious fact of K.'s attractiveness might be explained by his own position between two deaths. A lawyer explains this phenomenon to K. with the following words:

> If you have an eye for that sort of thing, defendants are indeed often attractive. It is of course remarkable, in a sense almost a natural phenomenon. It's clear no obvious change in appearance is noticeable once a person has been accused.... The defendants are simply the most attractive. It can't be guilt that makes them attractive, for—at least as a lawyer I must maintain this—they can't all be guilty, nor can it be the coming punishment that renders them attractive in advance, for not all of them will be punished; it must be a result, then, of the proceedings being brought against them, which somehow adheres to them. (184–185)

It is not K.'s guilt that makes him attractive—on the contrary; his beauty is a product of his position between two deaths, having proceedings brought against him, having been betrayed. As long as K. does not loose sight of his trial and of his desire, this beauty will not diminish. That beauty indicates proximity to the Thing qua void might also elucidate the radiance of the law at the end of the parable figure's life: "And yet in the darkness he now sees a radiance that streams forth inextinguishably from the door of the Law" (216). A radiance, moreover, that is only perceived when the man from the country asks his final question and recognizes the law in its pure, empty form.

If "[t]he appearance of beauty intimidates and stops desire," then the hero between two deaths represents no more than the position of enunciation capable of maintaining desire in the face of beauty.[35] To be betrayed with impunity is then to maintain desire after the first death—to pass beyond without guilt. K. has died but has not given up his desire—he is condemned but, to the extent that he has not given ground relative to his desire, not guilty (though by no means innocent). While the first death involves the transgression of a boundary, the second death approaches a limit. Here I am referring to the Kantian distinction: "bounds...always presuppose a space existing outside a certain definite place and inclosing it; limits do not require this, but are mere negations which affect a quantity so far as it is not absolutely complete."[36] The topological difference between boundaries and limits is best illustrated in the following passage from *The Castle*—part of a conversation between K. and the sister of Barnabas, K.'s messenger and contact with the castle:

> [Barnabas] enters offices, but those are only a portion of the total, then there are barriers and behind them still more offices.... You shouldn't imagine these barriers as a fixed boundary.... There are also barriers in the offices that he enters, those are the barriers he crosses, and yet they look no different from the ones he has not yet crossed, so one shouldn't assume from the outset that the offices behind those other barriers differ significantly from the ones Barnabas has already been in. It is only during those bleak hours that one thinks so. And then one's doubts increase, one is defenseless against them. (C 1998, 174–175)

The "barriers he crosses" may be distinguished from the "other barriers" to the true offices of *The Castle* (the site of the real Thing) as boundaries from limits. Barnabas's work in the castle puts him beyond the first death—having already transgressed the boundary. Of the real limit he has heard only rumors that are believed during the "bleak hours" that signify the agony and beauty of feminine *jouissance*. The step that Barnabas is unable to make is to recognize that behind these "other barriers"—properly speaking, limits—the offices of the castle are radically empty. The path traversed by K. in the pursuit of his desire is not, as first intimated, a circle, but rather a spiral, asymptotically approaching but never reaching the limit/void of the Thing. In circumscribing and approaching this lack "buried at the center" of the field of desire, Kafka's stories derive their beauty (see Appendix).[37]

"The beauty effect is a blindness effect,"[38] and as K. approaches his second death the beauty of the impossible contact with the real thing becomes blinding: "With *failing sight* K. saw how the men drew near his face, leaning cheek-to-cheek to observe the verdict. 'Like a dog!' he said; it seemed as though the shame was to outlive him" (T 1999, 231; my emphasis). This passage is, however, ambiguous: K.'s failing sight, unlike that of the man from the country in the parable, catches no glimmer of the radiance of the law. His last words, moreover, recall a previous passage from *The Trial*:

> So the lawyer's methods, to which K., fortunately, had not been long enough exposed, resulted in this: that the client finally forgot the entire

world, desiring only to trudge along this mistaken path to the end of his trial. He was no longer a client, he was the lawyer's dog. If the lawyer had ordered him to crawl under the bed, as into a kennel, and bark, he would have done so gladly. (195)

"Like a dog!," indicates that the path along which K. leads his executioners is as mistaken as that of the client mentioned above. This path would then seem *not* to represent the actual trajectory of K.'s desire, to which he has given as much ground as he traversed in walking to the quarry. Alongside beauty, Lacan holds shame to represent a second barrier preventing "the direct experience of that which is to be found at the center of sexual union [i.e., the Thing]."[39] The fact of the shame outliving K. then indicates that the limit of the second death is still very much intact. K. fails to maintain the protraction—but at least, with this gesture, *The Trial* ends...

* * *

Or at the least it stops being written. Even if K. is unable to abandon all semblances of the Thing, seeking in the last pages of the novel, "the judge he'd never seen...the high court he'd never reached," the text of *The Trial* is smarter, cutting off with the contingency of K.'s death and the senseless verdict—the "final judgment [that] comes unexpectedly from some chance person at some random moment" (T 1999, 231 and 197). Fragmentary and incomplete, *The Trial* itself comes to take the place of the "absolute Other of the subject" it initially set out to circumscribe. By allowing the void of the Thing to overtake the borders of the novel form, Kafka's failure—K.'s betrayal—assigns the following task to the reader: to desire, read, write, and act in the absence of *The Trial*.

Appendix

I have superimposed here three topologies (three corpora): the schema of the two deaths, the architecture of *The Trial*, and the relation of freedom and confinement implicit in the novel. The three trajectories of guilt offered to K. by Titorelli are to be read through the literal terrain of one onto the allegorical body of another. Protraction is interesting, from a mathematical viewpoint, in that its monistic course is defined solely by the intermediate space (that of the accused), feeling the tug of its extremes only as a satellite feels the pull of the gravitational bodies around which it circles:

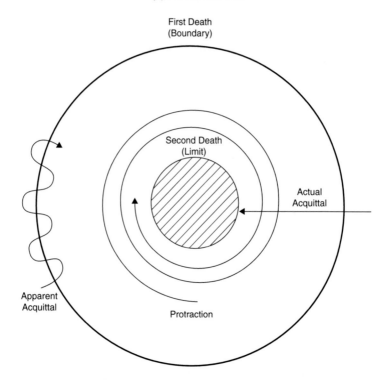

Notes

1. Jacques Lacan, *The Seminar of Jacques Lacan Book VII: The Ethics of Psychoanalysis*, ed. Jacques-Alain Miller, trans. Dennis Porter (New York: Norton, 1992), 141.
2. Gilles Deleuze and Félix Guattari, *Kafka: Toward a Minor Literature*, trans. Dana Polan (Minneapolis: University of Minnesota Press, 1986), 39.
3. Walter Benjamin, "Some Reflections on Kafka," in *Illuminations*, ed. Hannah Arendt, trans. Harry Zohn (New York: Schocken, 1968), 144–145.
4. Deleuze and Guattari, 10.
5. Lacan, *Ethics*, 200.
6. Ibid., 112.
7. Ibid., 52.
8. Ibid.
9. Deleuze and Guattari, 51.
10. Ibid., 46.
11. See ibid., 73.
12. See ibid., 8.
13. Ibid., 49.
14. Lacan, *Ethics*, 294.

15. Ibid., 125.
16. Applying a Barthean distinction, Kafka's text is one of bliss (*jouissance*): Opposed to the text of pleasure (*jouir*), which "contents, fills, grants euphoria," the text of bliss (what Deleuze and Guattari term "minor literature") "imposes a state of loss...brings to a crisis [the reader's] relation to language.... With the writer of bliss (and his reader) begins the untenable text, the impossible text." (Roland Barthes, *The Pleasure of the Text*, trans. Richard Miller [New York: Hill and Wang, 1975], 14 and 22.)
17. Lacan, *Ethics*, 294.
18. Ibid., 136.
19. Jacques Lacan, *The Seminar of Jacques Lacan Book XX: Encore; On Feminine Sexuality, The Limits of Love and Knowledge,* ed. Jacques-Alain Miller, trans. Bruce Fink (New York: Norton, 1999), 76.
20. See Lacan, *Ethics*, 315–316.
21. Giorgio Agamben, *Homo Sacer: Sovereign Power and Bare Life*, trans. Daniel Heller-Roazen (Stanford, CA: Stanford University Press, 1998), 53.
22. In Lacanese: K. learns to approach the Other (designated "A" for the French *Autre*) not as the *petit objet a* qua cause of desire, but as the signifier of the barred Other (S($\bar{A}$)). (See Lacan, *Encore*, 71–83.)
23. Deleuze and Guattari, 43.
24. Lacan, *Ethics*, 189.
25. Deleuze and Guattari, 52.
26. Lacan, *Ethics*, 321.
27. Franz Kafka, "The Advocate," trans. Tania and James Stern, in *The Complete Stories* (New York: Schocken, 1983), 451.
28. Lacan, *Ethics*, 321.
29. Ibid.
30. While the field of desire traversed by Deleuze and Guattari may extend limit*less*ly outwards, the very real limit at its center should be recognized as such. Deleuze's object = x or empty square might be seen to play a similar role. (See Gilles Deleuze, *The Logic of Sense*, ed. Constantin V. Boundas, trans. Mark Lester [New York: Columbia University Press, 1990], 66-73.) "Center" here in no way implies a static center, but one that circulates throughout the novel, always postponed, deferred, and one step ahead of K.
31. It is perhaps significant that K. works in a bank, given that, according to Lacan, the boundary of the first death involves the crossing out of the sphere of goods into the aesthetic sphere. K. leaves the economic sphere of exchange for the aesthetic sphere of beauty. (See Lacan, *Ethics,* 218–230.)
32. Ibid., 286.
33. Ibid., 216–217.
34. Ibid., 281.
35. Ibid., 238.
36. Immanuel Kant, *Prolegomena to Any Future Metaphysics That Will Be Able to Come Forward as Science*, ed. James W. Ellington, trans. Paul Carus (Indianapolis: Hackett, 2001), 86; §57.
37. Lacan, *Ethics*, 209.
38. Ibid., 281.
39. Ibid., 298.

PART III
PERFORMATIVES OF KAFKA'S CAGES

CHAPTER NINE

KAFKA'S FATAL PERFORMATIVES:
BETWEEN "BAD CONSCIENCE"
AND BETRAYED VULNERABILITY

Karyn Ball

Kafka was a realist after all.

—Georg Lukács

[There is p]lenty of hope... only not for us.

—Franz Kafka

I begin in a space between bars—two expressions of futility snatched from the lore surrounding the figures of Georg Lukács and Franz Kafka. It is well known that the Hungarian Marxist remained a party loyalist long after it was fashionable and that he notoriously privileged realist literature over its "decadent" modernist other because the latter was unable "to grasp the totality of social relations."[1] After his arrest by the Communist Party in 1956, when he was "deported, locked up in a castle and held without trial in Romania," Lukács was prompted to rethink his aesthetic allegiances while confronting Iron Curtain governmentality.[2]

Kafka putatively rejects the prospect of hope "for us" in the context of a February 28, 1920 exchange with Max Brod, quoted in his 1937 biography. After declaring that, "[w]e are nihilistic thoughts that came into God's head," Kafka dismisses the Gnostic premise that humans are a "radical relapse of God's"; however, when Brod queries him about hope outside our world, Kafka's smiles as he responds: "Plenty of hope—for God—no end of hope—only not for us."[3] The ubiquitous citations of this response excise God to accentuate its bleakness, yet from Brod's account, it would seem Kafka did not profess that evil is irredeemably intrinsic to the world. Though the current order cannot be transformed through human agency, God's endless hope might (in the future) overturn past and present suffering.

With their respective contexts eclipsed, my juxtaposition of these quotations evokes a paradox: If Lukács prizes realist literature for its ability to weave an "expressive totality" that indicates the departure point for a revolutionary transformation of (proletarian) consciousness, then what does such a totality look like when Kafka the decadent modernist is reborn as a realist? Realism coincides with modernism and thereby reproves Lukács at the uncanny moment when his political disillusionment becomes "fantastic" in Tzvetan Todorov's sense by blurring the figurative and the referential. In fantastic literature, the dogmatic persistence of an apparently irrational perception inverts the regnant certainty of natural laws and the rationality of consensually recognized norms. Yet Todorov also argues that this genre synecdochically condenses the effect of all literature as it "bypasses the distinctions of the real and the imaginary, of what is and of what is not."[4] "For writing to be possible," Todorov contends, "it must be born out of the death of what it speaks about; but this death makes writing itself impossible, for there is no longer anything to write."[5] Ultimately, then, "[t]he nature of literary discourse is to *go beyond*—otherwise it would have no reason for being; literature is a kind of murderous weapon by which language commits suicide."[6]

In appearing to annihilate its own condition of possibility, fantastic literature anticipates Jacques Derrida's prototypical deconstructive strategy of illuminating the performative contradictions in intellectual lineages that equivocate metaphysical binaries. A performative contradiction manifests itself when an argument enacts the problems it targets, a hypocrisy that becomes "fatal" when it destroys a text's authoritative "force" as a measure of its capacity to command belief. Imploded authority corrodes the promise of wisdom that an argument projects, along with the potential to move readers and critics beyond the circumstances that the latter condemn.[7]

In connecting Lukács and Todorov by way of Derrida here, I am proposing that Kafka's "realism" calls upon readers to attest, not to the prospect of revolutionary consciousness, or to its impossibility and hopelessness, but to a chasm that opens where the conditions for hope might have been, but have yet to emerge (perhaps). This paradox invites us to conjure hope in the same aporetic form and futural tense that Derrida in "The Force of Law" attributes to justice as "the experience of what we are unable to experience," that is to say, "an experience of the impossible."[8] Because justice is always to come, and this unforeseeable future will negate the injustice that preceded it, deconstruction draws its force—its unquenchable longing and infinite obligation—from an experience of inadequation between the calculability that governs law and the incalculability that keeps open an unfulfilled appeal to justice. If a petition for justice is never granted in the present, because justice is divided from law as Derrida infers, then Kafka's fatal performatives might be read as formalizing this aporia. Kafka's fiction permits readers to witness the hope of going beyond hopeless circumstances somehow sustaining itself in a universe that ceaselessly confirms the irremediability of despair. My question, then, is how Kafka's texts enunciate and transcend a frustrated longing for justice.

I. The Cage of "Bad Conscience"

Derrida's commentary on the "mystical foundation of authority" stipulates that the law is divided by the impossibility of guaranteeing its legitimacy as a means through a just end. By insisting that any contingent decision based on a declaration of "the facts" is, at the same time, *promising* a justification that might not arrive, Derrida underscores the proleptic desire at the heart of law that blurs the boundary between constatives and performatives in scenes of judgment. The overflowing of the performative proves "fatal" if it precipitates a recognition that "truth" must be made (and remade) and that justice has no horizon of expectation.[9] To the extent that it brings about this recognition, deconstructive legal criticism vexes the quasireligious presumption that law naturally operates on behalf of a preconsensual contract reiterated by sociocultural and economic structures. The law's moral-authoritative force derives precisely from the structural *iterability* of this presumption, which is misconstrued as a sign of foundational integrity.

In the course of enumerating "Nine Reasons Why Kafka Is Crucial for the Study of Law," Klaus Mladek agrees with Derrida that force "is the engine of law" that realizes itself "by creating criminals, lawbreakers and deviants."[10] Mladek criticizes "a particular liberal legal tradition that sees laws themselves as grounded in reasonable origins and a certain communitarian fantasy." This fantasy disavows "the force and antagonism of the law," which Mladek identifies with its "narratological-performative *making* of authority and criminality."[11] Casting Kafka in the role of Derrida's mentor permits Mladek to read the Prague writer's fiction as continually performing the violent complicities between "grammar, thought and judgment" that underlie legal justifications, the law's authority, and its bureaucratic apparatus.[12] Kafka's characters grapple with the fragile if not arbitrary relationship between sociojuridical norms and moral values in a universe wherein even the need to justify a death sentence has been sloughed off like an atrophied limb. Hence, the lesson Kafka proffers to critical legal scholars is "that judgments are fictions in the fantasy-realm of words," which is to say that, "'judgment can only be true about the word, but not in itself.'"[13]

While graphing judgment "as a grammar of punishment and pain," Mladek's Kafka "does not shy away from exposing the sexualized, sado-masochistic underpinnings of power and authority."[14] If judgment and punishment appear to assume a "foundation," then it solidifies in his protagonists' masochistic internalization of the moral necessity the law so overtly lacks.

The theses on sadomasochism that Mladek gleans from Kafka recall Nietzsche's staging of "bad conscience" as the instinct-mutilating precipitate of promising, memory, debt, guilt, and punishment. The emergence of "bad conscience" coincides with what Nietzsche refers to as the "internalization of man" to describe the systemic impact of a guilt-punishment matrix. Internalization not only inhibits the outward discharge of "all those instincts of wild, free, prowling man," but also inverts them *against man himself.*[15]

> The man, who, from lack of external enemies and resistances and forcibly confined to the oppressive narrowness and punctiliousness of custom, impatiently lacerated, persecuted, gnawed at, assaulted, and maltreated himself; this animal that rubbed itself raw against the bars of its cage as one tried to "tame" it; this deprived creature, racked with homesickness for the wild, who had to turn himself into an adventure, a torture chamber, an uncertain and dangerous wilderness—this fool, this yearning and desperate prisoner became the inventor of the "bad conscience." But thus began the gravest and uncanniest illness, from which humanity has not yet recovered, man's suffering *of man, of himself*—the result of a forcible sundering from his animal past, as it were a leap and plunge into new surroundings and conditions of existence, a declaration of war against the old instincts upon which his strength, joy, and terribleness had rested hitherto.[16]

Nietzsche's vision of "bad conscience" begins as a potentially creative and destructive will to power that is systematically denatured into a *jouissance*-saturated loathing for the animal within. Bad conscience is exacting: It spurs a pernicious guilt for an unremittable debt, promotes internalized surveillance, and rationalizes a petty scrutiny of others to ensure that no one forgets his obligations and no one enjoys herself *too much*. The badly conscientious subject renounces freedom in exchange for a promise-regimented soul that imprisons the body, to borrow Michel Foucault's phrasing, figured here as a repudiated *inner animal* rubbing itself raw against the bars of its own cage.

As is well known, the first section of Nietzsche's "Second Essay" introduces man as an animal bred to make and remember promises so as to "stand security for *his own future.*" To demystify this system, Nietzsche counterintuitively praises forgetting as a force of *"robust* health" that the faculty of memory abrogates in rendering man *"calculable, regular, necessary,* even in his own image of himself."[17] This modern dread of forgetting a promise mobilizes a spiteful mnemotechnics that functions like the "marvelous apparatus" from Kafka's "In the Penal Colony" to inscribe the prisoner's crime in his skin as it slowly executes him. Mladek's analysis of Kafka follows Nietzsche in decrying the inability to forgive as a symptom of a society in which "the fabric of all institutional memory and operationality" is permeated with bad conscience as the implicit grammar of juridical judgment.[18] If forgiveness requires forgetting, then it should permit "the erasure of the punishable deed from the files of bureaucratic memory,"[19] yet Kafka's texts markedly withdraw the prospect for such an absolution. It is in this respect that Kafka's fiction exposes the mechanics of situations in which the restorative powers of self-forgetting are withheld or, worse still, turned against those who need them most.

Nietzsche's caged animal metaphor for bad conscience brings to mind two of Kafka's stories in particular, "A Report to an Academy" and "A Hunger Artist." Both stories unfold in and around scenarios of forced or voluntary internment in cages, which serve as barred theaters of self-discipline for spectators and readers. A salient motif in Kafka's fiction, animals stand in for the lost vitality humans grieve as a cost of rationalization and discipline, and, when read side by side, these stories inversely comment on the consequences of forgoing the bestial pleasures of self-forgetting.

On the motif of Kafka's animals, Peter Stine observes, "that they betoken a vulnerable self escaping the coercion of a modern world in which social organization is fate."[20] This trope structures a captured ape's humanization through imitation in "A Report to an Academy." The fatal performatives that make up "A Report" evoke a continuum between the nonvoluntary-instinctual and the voluntary-rational registers of reaction in a manner that renders the "freedom" of a reasoning consciousness indiscernible.

As if he would reiterate Nietzsche's Second Essay, Red Peter locates the beginning of his capacity for memory on the decks of a Hagenbach steamer, in a "three-sided cage nailed to a locker" that comprises the fourth side. The ape recalls that "[t]he whole construction was too low for me to stand up in and too narrow to sit down in." He is forced to squat with his "knees bent and trembling all the time." In an oddly conditional tone, he conjectures that "probably for a time [he] wished to see no one, and to stay in the dark, [his] face was turned toward the locker while the bars of the cage cut into [his] flesh behind." Our reporter's conditionally retroactive "wisdom" exposes the intrusive influence of a "human" bad conscience that upholds suffering as a rite of initiation: "Such a method of confining wild beasts is supposed to have its advantages during the first days of captivity, and out of my own experiences I cannot deny that from the human point of view this is really the case" (RA 1971, 252).

To escape an intolerably cramped locker, Red Peter *instinctively* mimics a calm rationality. The self-preservative impetus of this mimicry freights the notion of free will that underlies conventional understandings of "rationality," thereby rendering his belated articulation of it "fatal." This instinctually driven performance becomes still more undecidable when he heralds it as the masterpiece of a "fine clear train of thought, which [he] *must have constructed somehow* with [his] belly, since apes think with their bellies" (RA 1971, 253; my emphasis). The serpentine temporality of the ape's sentences catalyzes the aporetic effect of this mind-body paradox:

> The calmness I acquired among these people kept me above all from trying to escape. As I look back now, it seems to me I must have had at least an inkling that I had to find a way out or die, but that my way out could not be reached through flight. I cannot tell now whether escape was possible, but I believe it must have been; for an ape it must always be possible. With my teeth as they are today I have to be careful even in simply cracking nuts, but at that time I could certainly have managed by degrees to bite through the lock of my cage. I did not do it. What good would it have done me? As soon as I had poked out my head I should have been caught again and put in a worse cage; or I might have slipped among the other animals without being noticed, among the pythons, say, who were opposite me, and so breathed out my life in their embrace; or supposing I had actually succeeded in sneaking out as far as the deck and leaping overboard, I should have rocked around a little on the deep sea and then been drowned. Desperate remedies. I did not think it out in this human way, but under the influence of my surroundings I acted as if I had thought it out [*Ich rechnete nicht so menschlich, aber unter dem Einfluß meiner Umgebung verhielt ich mich so, wie wenn ich gerechnet hätte*]. (RA 1971, 254–255/1998, 143)

While narrating the emergence of his "human" memory from animal sentience, the ape contrives fantastic syntaxes that continually split the temporality of his ability to make decisions. Markers of time (*now, then, at that time, today*), in tandem with modal verbs alternating from one clause to the next between the present, past, and conditional past tenses undercut the shift he reconstructs from "animal" instincts to "human" will. The ape seemingly addresses his past animal-being as well as his audience in charting what he *must have thought* had he been the creature capable of reason at the moment he deploys it. The empirically minded reporter recognizes the dire circumstances that determined his need to take action in a syntax that (impossibly) reminds us of our reporter's bestial embodiment in the same breath with which he subjunctively evokes the performative disposition of human rationality. We learn that despite its "as-if" freedom, reason cannot avoid instinctively and, thus, *nonvoluntarily* responding to threats to survival. He performs his way out of a cage, not because he *desires* freedom but because he *must* survive. With a twist of Jewish-messianic fatality, the speaker will nevertheless reckon with the open horizon of justice: "No one promised me that if I became like them the bars of my cage would be taken away. Such promises for apparently impossible contingencies are not given. But if one achieves the impossible," the ape explains, "the promises appear later retrospectively precisely where one had looked in vain for them before" (RA 1971, 255).

Humanity is equated with bad conscience as this eager disciple pays his dues by masochistically adoring his torturing master: "[S]uch a student of humankind no human teacher ever found on earth," Red Peter exclaims (RA 1971, 256). Yet "[t]o the sorrow of my teacher, to the greater sorrow of myself," he cannot hide his "disgust" [*Abscheu*] at the smell of schnapps, which he mentions three times in a single sentence: "I would lift the bottle, already following my original model almost exactly; put it to my lips and—and then *throw it down in disgust, utter disgust*, although it was empty and filled only with the smell of the spirit, *throw it down on the floor in disgust*" (256; my emphases). The threefold repetition of *disgust* is redoubled in the German by Kafka's recourse to *Abscheu*, which evokes the act of shying away. Along with the exact repetition of "throw it down in disgust," the dash between two instances of *and* marks an additional hesitancy in the ape's recollection of his fledgling attempts at human adaptation. Such redundancies might lead us to wonder why this particular memory stutters so conspicuously. The effect is to derealize the criteria that decide evolutionary hierarchies, since apes instinctively "shy away from" alcohol, a learned taste among humans, and yet the capacity for disgust is exclusively attributed to the latter.

Despite his failure, the ape's diligence inspires him to perform the requisite closing gesture: to rub his belly "most admirably and to grin" (RA 1971 256–257). The master nevertheless punishes the disciple for incompletely assimilating a ritual:

> Far too often my lesson ended in that way. And to the credit of my teacher, he was not angry; sometimes indeed he would hold his burning pipe against my fur, until it began to smolder in some place I could not easily reach, but then he would himself extinguish it with his own kind, enormous hand; he was not angry with me, he perceived that we were both fighting on the same side against the nature of apes and that I had the more difficult task. (257)

In excusing his teacher's cruelty, Red Peter succeeds where he otherwise fails: His incipient bad conscience lauds the hand that beats him, and thus demonstrates that he has internalized the necessity of punishment as a means of redressing fault.

Though he has replicated this last most challenging step, the ape clings to certain tokens of his former life including the "scar made by a wanton shot" that memorializes his violent capture. When one observer takes Red Peter's "predilection" for pulling down his trousers to reveal this scar to visitors as proof that his "ape nature is not yet under control," his fantasies instinctively stoop toward role-reversing vengeance: to see the "unscientific hand" of this writer "have its fingers shot away one by one." Despite this fantasy, the ape declares that "[e]verything is open and aboveboard; there is nothing to conceal." It is the shot that was "wanton," and not Red Peter's inclination to expose his wound before anyone he likes. The ape, by his own account, is merely being scientific, for "when the plain truth is in question, great minds discard the niceties of refinement" (RA 1971, 251–252). Our informant's perverse objectivity thus magnifies the rickety edifice of scientific detachment, which collapses so readily into an all-too-human fascination with his voluptuous red scar.

Red Peter rejects the imposition of this delicacy, even as his own language brims with rhetorical flourishes and elliptical repetitions—an excessive mimicry that belies his liminality. The ape's "precocious preciosity" and "overcarefulness of style" effects the demeanor of a parvenu "to Western culture, pleased with, but not yet quite sure of, himself."[21] His exhilarating feats might compensate for his insecurity, but on a formal level, they spotlight the performativity of knowledge. He takes lessons from five teachers "all at once by dint of leaping from one room to the other" (RA 1971, 258). Ape agility enables him to "leap" manically from one lesson to the next, whether he learns anything or not. Despite such successes, he manages to reach only "the cultural level of an average European. In itself, that might be nothing to speak of, but it is something insofar as it has helped [him] out of [his] cage and opened a special way out for [him], the way of humanity [*und mir diesen besonderen Ausweg, diesen Menschenausweg verschaffte*]" (RA 1971, 258/1998, 147). The doubling of *Ausweg* [escape] in this sentence renders it paradoxical, for if a "special" escape entails becoming human, then perhaps it is not an *Ausweg* in any true sense, and certainly *not for us*. The reporting "I" must modestly acknowledge that there "was nothing else for [him] to do, provided that freedom was not to be [his] choice" (1971, 258). "Ach, man lernt, wenn man muß" (1998, 146).

Red Peter has fought his way "through the thick of things" ["*ich habe mich in die Büsche geschlagen*"] (RA 1971, 258/1998, 147), an idiom he manifestly savors. The elliptical phrasing of his proclamation that, "[o]n the whole, at any rate, [he] has achieved what [he] set out to achieve" fatally underlines its own empty referentiality. Despite a "bright future," his report nevertheless carries an almost embarrassed admission: "When I come home late at night from banquets, from scientific receptions, from social gatherings, there sits waiting for me a half-trained little chimpanzee and I take comfort from her as apes do [*und ich lasse es mir nach Affenart bei ihr wohlgehen*]. By day I cannot bear to see her; for she has the insane look of the bewildered half-broken animal in her eye; no one else sees it, but I do and I cannot bear it" (259/147). To his credit, our informant does not repudiate his *Affennatur*; he distinguishes himself from his models and his audience by steadfastly avowing instincts that trouble his performance. Though he seeks solace from a half-domesticated chimpanzee, her "insane look" painfully refracts his "homesickness for the wild" and the ambivalence of his ascent on a species hierarchy that confined him in a torturously narrow cage but also provided a means of escaping it.

Concluding his report, he disingenuously represents himself as beyond judgment: "In any case, I am not appealing to any man's verdict [*Urteil*]. I am only making a report. To you also, honored Members of the Academy, I have only made a report" (RA 1971, 259/1998, 147). This empty gesture seems to grant the report a status in its own right *prior to* the expectations of his addressees and the official context of its enunciation; by simultaneously denying and announcing its rhetoricity as a subject-constituting performance, this gesture places the report's authority in abeyance. The question remains: *what* is a human who disavows his interest in the judgments of others? Certainly, if the academy does not render a verdict, Kafka's readers will if we can.

Red Peter's ambivalence contrasts starkly with the hunger artist's uncompromising aversion against animal enjoyment. Kafka's artist meekly accepts his internment near a menagerie, but quietly seethes with envy toward his animal colleagues who "distract" his audience from a full appreciation of his ascetic artistry. The self-denying artist is continually depressed by the signs of bestial self-forgetting—"the stench of the menagerie, the animals' restlessness by night, the carrying past of raw lumps of flesh for the beasts of prey, the roaring at feeding times" (HA 1971, 275). Despite his envy and revulsion, he does not complain, since "he had the animals to thank for the troops of people who passed his cage, among whom there might always be one here and there to take an interest in him" (275–276).

The cage in "A Hunger Artist" is not a prison, but a theater and a protective enclosure that preserves the protagonist's capacity to fulfill a self-made promise to fast endlessly to his heart's content without interference. Yet as his life seeps away, this sacrifice is canceled out, which renders his performance literally fatal ("nothing could save him now"). He simply fasts "on and on, as he had once dreamed of doing," but "no one, not even the artist himself, knew what records he was already breaking" (HA 1971, 276). A protruding ribcage renders the bars of his cage redundant and announces the prison his soul has become as he conflates renunciation with self-sovereignty. Meanwhile, the novelty of his self-discipline recedes into tedium: "People grew familiar with the strange idea that they could be expected, in times like these, to take an interest in a hunger artist, and with this familiarity the verdict went out against him.... The fine placards grew dirty and illegible, they were torn down; the little notice board telling the number of fast days achieved, which at first was changed carefully every day, had long stayed at the same figure, for after the first few weeks even this small task seemed pointless to the staff" (276). Readers who ask whether art requires an audience must content themselves with a concluding confession that equivocates the story's premise: In the end, his "art" is *non*voluntary, since he would have eaten if he could have found the food he likes.

After the artist dies amidst the straw lining the circus cage, the overseer replaces him with a panther, distinguished, above all, by his sinuous vitality:

> "Well, clear this out now!" said the overseer, and they buried the hunger artist, straw and all. Into the cage they put a young panther. Even the most insensitive felt it refreshing to see this wild creature leaping around the cage that had so long been dreary. The panther was all right. The food he liked was brought him without hesitation by the attendants; he seemed not even to miss his freedom; his noble body, furnished almost to the bursting point with all that it needed, seemed to carry freedom around with it too; somewhere in his jaws it seemed to lurk; and the joy of life streamed with such ardent passion from his throat that for the onlookers it was not easy to stand the shock of it. But they braced themselves, crowded around the cage, and did not want ever to move away.

The artist never forgets himself (as panthers do), and he dies from his relentless compulsion to pay off a self-contracted debt, a Pyrrhic victory on behalf of his art's dissipating aura. At this historical moment, however, even a lethal extreme of self-denial bores spectators who perform bad conscience without artistic pretenses. These dilettantes seek lively distractions from their own abjection regimes. Kafka's antithesis of a deformed will to power is the "joy of life" streaming with "ardent passion" from the jaws of a cat who would, quite naturally, love to devour them all.

II. The Cage of Betrayed Vulnerability

In naming expressionism Kafka's "authentic horizon," Theodor W. Adorno already sees from the window of his room at the "Hotel Abyss" what Lukács belatedly concedes in Romania—that Kafka inverts the

Hungarian Marxist's aesthetic politics in prefiguring a totalitarian universe that is "far too implacable to have sanctioned any kind of aesthetic realism."[22] In Kafka, "[t]he historical verdict is the product of disguised domination, and thus becomes integrated into the myth, that of blind force endlessly reproducing itself. In the latest phase of this force, that of bureaucratic control, he recognizes the earliest stage; its waste-products become pre-historical." By transposing these waste products into archetypes, Kafka reveals a horror more profound than the disintegration of individuality. "History becomes Hell in Kafka," according to Adorno, "because the chance which might have saved was missed."[23]

In *Negative Dialectics*, the former exile self-ironically implicates himself when he associates "the drastic guilt of him who was spared" with the coldness entailed by "mere survival" defined as "the basic principle of bourgeois subjectivity, without which there could have been no Auschwitz."[24] Adorno's "bourgeois coldness" translates into Masao Miyoshi's "asocialized individualism" as a barometer of neoliberal indoctrination: "Those in need of help are held in contempt as inept, lazy, and superfluous, while the entrepreneurial 'winners' are held in awe as capable, quick, and intelligent. Wealth and power are considered natural rewards for such strengths; poverty and marginalization, on the other hand, are the just desserts of the failures."[25] Sanctimonious moralisms and petty retributions buttress a preconscious "right" not to be reminded about how our dull empathetic capabilities and torpid habits victimize those beyond our notice. Kafka remains prescient about today's neoliberal democracies because he stages the toxic repercussions of an apathy too often misconstrued as civility. The threat of ostracism goads a bourgeois craving for assurances that "we" are beyond full-scale betrayal despite our own vaguely intuited worthlessness.

Adorno's representation of Kafka's universe as an expressionist anticipation of the totalitarian mindset *avant la lettre* celebrates him for scrutinizing "the smudges left behind in the deluxe edition of the book of life by the fingers of power."[26] Within Slavoj Žižek's psychoanalytic purview, this scrutiny positions Kafka to serve as a pedagogue of the real, the traumatically resurgent repressed splicing through the fragile misrecognitions that suture social identifications. Fantasies about a fundamental social cohesion deflect repressed anxiety about the violence of self-authorizing norms, the micropersecutions of work and debt payment, the ever-present threat of exposure from isolation, senescence, turpitude, or "poor management." Illusions of solidarity circle the void at the crux of a subject who fails ineluctably to assume a self-certain place in the symbolic order.[27] Kafka rubs his readers' noses in the dire arbitrariness of survival and impels them to notice the threadbare quality of the safety nets through which anyone at any moment can fall. We face the disavowal that hinders norm-abiders from grasping the magnitude of such unpredictable falls, and the impersonal malice that engulfs the fallen. Kafka grapples with the abjection that overcomes those who suffer as the powers that be obscenely enjoy swatting humans like flies.

Judith Butler's account of "precariousness" offers an alternative understanding of the real that opens up the ethical implications of Kafka's fatal performatives. In essays collected under the title of *Precarious Life*, Butler draws on Giorgio Agamben and Emmanual Levinas to examine the rhetoric of the "war on terror" deployed by the Bush administration and its allies as an alibi for their entrenchment of sovereign power through an unbridled decoupling of justice from law.[28] Her analysis illuminates how this rhetoric transfigured a tacitly permitted condition, a special case "state of emergency" proviso, into a blatant euphemism for extraordinary rendition. After 9/11, the Bush administration actualized Kafka in its proliferation of Josef K.'s arrested without charge.[29]

Butler's contribution to a theory of the real hinges on Levinas's commentary about an ethical dilemma that stems "from a constant tension between the fear of undergoing violence and the fear of inflicting violence." These two impulses are "at war with each other in order *not* to be at war," and this volatile paradox lies at the heart of Levinas's promotion of nonviolence.[30] Butler's return to Levinas thus illuminates an axiological version of the fatal performative contradiction: When I disavow the Other as a prospective victim of my violence, I endanger the continuity of discussion, to address the Other and to be addressed in kind, or to work out a solution that would save us both. Since the Other is the condition of address upon which language depends, succumbing to aggression preempts possible outcomes that discourse creates.[31]

Levinas's supposition that "the desire to kill is primary to human beings" nevertheless disturbs Butler. For if "the first impulse towards the other's vulnerability is the desire to kill, the ethical injunction is precisely to militate against that first impulse. In psychoanalytic terms," Butler proposes, this "would mean marshalling the desire to kill in the service of an internal desire to kill one's own aggression and sense of priority."[32] It is not clear to Butler how Levinas's ethics could extricate us from "the circuitry of bad conscience, the logic by which the prohibition against aggression becomes the internal conduit for aggression itself."[33] If the ethical transcends the neurotic movement whereby aggression is "turned back upon oneself in the form of super-egoic cruelty," it is "because bad conscience is, after all, only a negative version of narcissism" that the Other's singular vulnerability interrupts.[34]

Butler's reinvention of bad conscience reiterates a key motif of *Civilization and Its Discontents*, where Freud maintains that socialization renders aggression latent at the same time that its regulation volatilizes the transgressive pleasure of deposing the veneer of civility upon which collective functioning depends. In the *Dialectic of Enlightenment*, Horkheimer and Adorno link this vicious cycle to Nietzsche's conception of bad conscience redefined as *reification*, or the "second nature" of affect-hardened masses, as they internalize the forces of their own domination.

In their analysis of scapegoating from the "Elements of Anti-Semitism" chapter, Horkheimer and Adorno highlight a pernicious outgrowth of bad conscience in the potentially lethal revulsion against survival anxiety and other markers of vulnerability. A sanction-ready second nature globalizes the gory specter of flesh-parceling punishment as emotionally calcified conformists scrutinize each other for signs of incomplete subjection to social-Darwinist protocols against instinctual expression. Such denatured minds despise self-forgetting enjoyment (earmarking animals for contempt, experiment, and mass slaughter) in the same way they revile the all-too-natural goose-pimpled skins of those stigmatized by vulnerability. An aversion toward weakness converts the vulnerable into magnets for projectile self-hatred and *ressentiment*, the by-products of the powers that spur us to keep others in line, or to crush them in order to stave off dreaded encounters with our own precariousness.

As an employee of the Workers' Accident Insurance Institute for the Kingdom of Bohemia, Kafka served a bureaucracy administered by the Austro-Hungarian monarchy, reputed to be the most pervasive of its kind in Europe as it endeavored to keep "different ethnicities loyal to Hapsburg."[35] Kafka's fiction, in Mladek's view, reflects an uncanny intimacy between modern bureaucracy and the human mind. Once it has been internalized as bad conscience, bureaucracy flows "out of the origin of human nature," and if the modern subject "does not act swiftly, no internal or natural life independent of this all encompassing apparatus will remain."[36]

In posing the question of the "Id of institutions," as Mladek phrases it, Kafka conjures a put upon employee whose tank-like [*panzerartig*] shell inversely embodies the petrifying impact of internalized domination. Gregor Samsa's initial reaction to the unnerving spectacle of his six new insect legs waving in the air lasts for a mere two sentences before his thoughts resume what Stine characterizes as an "eager enslavement to routine."[37] He is maniacally obsessed with catching the next train to work even as he bemoans his unappreciated yet grueling labor. If the one-time salesman evinces masochistic desires, as Eric Santner surmises, it is because he has so thoroughly adapted to his bosses' unremitting surveillance as to become a barely sensate limb of their callous regulatory body, his mind a din of orders he would conscientiously fulfill.[38] This disquieting lack of dissonance confirms Santner's reading of *The Metamorphosis* as a fantastic emplotment of abjection.

Santner identifies two orders of abjection in *The Metamorphosis*. The first is associated with Gregor's history before his transformation "as a sacrificial object *within* the family structure," which entails his "introjection of the family debt or guilt." The second order is linked to his metamorphosed state, which ostracizes him and nullifies his ability to assume "a position outside the texture of fate." In Santner's [Lacanian] terms, what the self-sacrificial first order conceals becomes overt in the second: "the lack of a consistent and dependable Other from whom one could expect a determination of one's identity, whose gaze could guarantee one's recognition, even as *an object worthy of sacrifice*." An emblem of inconsistency in the symbolic domain of language, norms, and laws, Gregor's "verminousness" derails the sacrificial order and therefore triggers a desire to destroy him; however, there is no stable image to eradicate, since the beetle's physical features cannot be fixed.[39] To Santner's analysis, I would add that the crux of this instability lies in the readiness for betrayal that Gregor encounters in those closest to him. Gregor cannot escape the devastating consequences of a disloyalty that robs him of his sense of being-for-others and batters him with evidence that no kindness will redeem him.

Santner's logics of abjection echo Adorno's identification of reified "second nature" with the sadomasochistic circuitry of bad conscience. This deforming internalization of the instincts becomes palpable in a peculiar piece of "interior decorating" that absurdly comes into focus for Gregor directly after his waking discovery that he is a beetle and is therefore(!) late for his grueling job: "Above the table on which a collection of cloth samples was unpacked and spread out—Samsa was a commercial traveler—hung the picture which he had recently cut from an illustrated magazine and put into a pretty gilt frame. It showed a lady, decked in a fur hat and a fur boa, sitting upright and extending to the spectator a heavy fur muff into which the whole of her forearm had vanished" (MM 1971, 89/1998, 57; translation modified). Santner suspects this passage might allude to Leopold von Sacher-Masoch's *Venus in Furs* (1870), especially since "Gregor" also happens to be the name that the protagonist Severin assumes after signing a masochistic contract with the dominatrix, Wanda.[40] Yet Santner's citation of the passage leaves out the third person narrator's interjections that locate cloth samples on the table and inform us about Gregor's job as a traveling salesman. These "objective" disruptions accentuate Gregor's (feminine) masochistic fascination with the furry fetish that Santner posits here; they also link Gregor's sexual fantasy life and his unnervingly conscientious obsession with showing up for work, in beetle form no less.

Even his sexual predilections and hobbies gratify his supervisors' interests in producing a worker who enjoys his own subjection. Stine points out that "Gregor's only real pleasures and resentments...arise out of that

admittedly despicable, forgotten, yet indestructible side of being, his animality." As evidence, he cites Gregor's "discovery of the autoerotic freedom
of crawling the walls and hanging from the ceiling." Stine interprets such
interludes of "blissful absorption" as "the freakish and regressive antics of
a sexuality too long deferred,"[41] yet it is also during these moments that
Gregor can breathe more freely, having converted his bedroom quarantine into a playground. He will nevertheless relinquish these delightfully
physical respites in response to his mother's concern that removing all of
his furniture, his desk above all, will destroy his hope of recovering his
lost "humanity" (when he was the creature of mean-spirited bureaucrats).
This willingness precipitates another fatal performative as the prospective
expropriation of his writing table reverts him to masochism: He literally
clings to the framed cut out of the woman in furs and "would rather fly
in Grete's face" than let his sister chase him down from the wall (MM
1971, 119). Once again, we see, with Santner, how the novella crystal-
lizes around Gregor's "peculiar attachment to this piece of pornographic
kitsch" as "an elaborate punishment scenario called forth by guilt-ridden
sexual obsessions."[42] This chain of events metonymically links Gregor's
lost humanity and masochism as if to suggest that regression to the latter
might stand in for the former. Insofar as this linkage begins with Gregor's
impetus to keep his desk, it also connects writing to masochistic desire.[43]

The third person narration of *Käfer*-Gregor's incommunicable thoughts
also divulges his craven attempts to propitiate the chief clerk who hounds
his employee in his own home as soon as the first slip in Gregor's otherwise
reliable subservience provides a pretext. This petty bureaucratic scourge
impudently knocks on a locked bedroom door and lets fly abusive accusations based on rumor. No solidarity prevails apparently, even among
low-level colleagues at Gregor's workplace. Gregor himself agrees with
the chief clerk that "fortunately or unfortunately" men of business "very
often simply have to ignore a slight indisposition, since business must be
attended to" (MM 1971, 96).

Readers must also witness a suddenly tyrannical father fiercely hissing
while he drives Gregor into his room at the conclusion of the first section.
At the close of the second, this malevolent stalker imbeds an apple in his
son's fleeing back, leaving it to fester there for the remainder of his life. In
the penultimate act of Gregor's Passion, readers no longer expect solicitude
from this ruthless fury for his beetle-son's well-being. It is, nevertheless,
stunning to hear Gregor's beloved sister revoke her relation to the shut-in:

"My dear parents," said his sister, slapping her hand on the table by way of
introduction, "things can't go on like this. Perhaps you don't realize that,
but I do. I won't utter my brother's name in the presence of this creature,

and so all I say is: we must try to get rid of it. We've tried to look after it and to put up with it as far as is humanly possible, and I don't think anyone could reproach us in the slightest." (MM 1971, 133)

The sister stridently importunes her weakly protesting father to "try to get rid of the idea that this is Gregor," since believing it "for so long is the root of [their] trouble. But how can it be Gregor?" she exclaims: "If this were Gregor, he would have realized long ago that human beings can't live with such a creature, and he'd have gone away on his own accord. Then we wouldn't have any brother, but we'd be able to go on living and keep his memory in honor. As it is," Grete continues, "this creature persecutes us, drives away our lodgers, obviously wants the whole apartment to himself, and would have us all sleep in the gutter" (134).

In her ensuing frenzy, Grete imagines Gregor is coming after her, *actively* persecuting *her*—a hysterically projected inversion of her own desire to extinguish responsibility for her brother's "still form" (MM 1971, 134). The description of her sudden terror is telling: "And in an attack of panic that was quite incomprehensible to Gregor she even quitted her mother, *literally* [*förmlich*] thrusting the chair from her *as if* she would rather sacrifice her mother [*als wollte sie lieber die Mutter öpfern*] than stay so near to Gregor, and rushed behind her father, who also rose up, being simply upset by her agitation, and half spread his arms out *as if* to protect her" [*auch aufstand und die Arme wie zum Schutze der Schwester vor ihr halb erhob*] (1971, 134/1998, 102; my emphasis; translation modified). The self-conscious tone of *literally* [*förmlich*] and the two *as if*'s [*als* and *wie*, respectively] exacerbates the tensions between the denotative and connotative levels of the third-person omniscient narration limited to Gregor until after his death. These elements not only reinforce the narration's tone of "superior calm" as Walter Benjamin might have described it,[44] but also skew the intentions readers might otherwise impute to the sister and father. Her teary proclamations about the family's benevolent efforts to "look after it and to put up with it as far as is humanly possible," efforts for which "no one could reproach [them] in the slightest," are belied by the paradoxical term *förmlich* ("literally" *or* "ceremoniously"), which divides her own words against themselves. The tone of *förmlich* insinuates a judgment against the sister and her parents who did not take long to slacken their concern for Gregor (she might not reproach herself, but we do). She will ward off this "it" displacing the "he" who would have toiled on in a miserable post to send her to a music conservatory. This "sensitive" girl will even defend herself at her mother's expense if necessary. The father is no better; he spreads his arms before his distraught daughter in a theatrical semblance of protection.

As Grete makes an impassioned plea on behalf of her parents' health ("it will be the death of both of you, I can see that coming"), what becomes manifest is how quickly the daughter's "we" and "us" slides into "one" and then "I": "When one has to work as hard as we do, all of us, one can't stand this continual torment at home on top of it. At least I can't stand it any longer" (MM 1971, 133). Yet her brother remains dependable until the very end: he mildly accepts a verdict that rescinds his right to subsist. He even sympathizes with the rationality of Grete's disgust, which reduces him to an enervating parasite sustained "at her expense." Locking the door in haste after his laboriously slow retreat, the sister's antipathy toward beetle-brother blows the cover from the real to expose his precarious survival as a revocable privilege. Though Grete's pronouncement of a death sentence in Gregor's presence confronts us with a shocking breach of solidarity, he does not disclaim the "justice" of her denunciation; he compassionately grasps the import of his demand on their forbearance. He survives "at the expense of" his family's complacency. His subsistence "persecutes" his parents and sister by not allowing them to forget themselves.

Recalling Nabokov's lectures at Cornell, Stine asks why Gregor does not fly off rather than suffer his family's neglect.[45] However, the vermin-morph's question is why his family "could not think of any way to shift Gregor" if they wished to take a smaller apartment. He sees "well enough that consideration for him was not the main difficulty preventing the removal, for they could have easily shifted him in some suitable box with a few air holes in it." The insightful son intuits that what "really kept them from moving into another flat was rather their own complete hopelessness and the belief that they had been singled out for a misfortune such as had never happened to any of their relations or acquaintances" (MM 1971, 124–125). Gregor's "suitable box" solution differs pronouncedly from cages that permit prisoners to remain visible to spectators. By spatializing his debasement, this pathetic conjuration reveals that he expects only the barest necessities, and he will even forsake the dignity of remaining visible for others, of looking at them and being looked at in turn.[46]

In the end, Gregor seemingly pursues a Levinasian route that priori-tizes his family's well-being over his own: "The decision that he must disappear was one that he held to even more strongly than his sister, if that were possible." After "[t]he first broadening of light in the world outside the window entered his consciousness once more," his head sinks "non-voluntarily [*ohne seinen Willen*] to the floor and from his nostrils came the last faint flicker of his breath" (MM 1971, 135/1998, 103; translation modified). Once again, if a "decision" has been made in this scene, it remains oblique: Gregor will, in fact, die after one night's reprieve *as if* in response to his ungrateful sister's nonreciprocal appeal to his "human" sense of justice. A dramatic irony derives from the ambiguity of his hope (and perhaps ours) that somehow the parents and sister will appreciate his final fatal performance of humanity as an act of martyrdom. He relishes the light through his window one last time, but it comes too late to revive him or imbue his death with religious grace. Gregor Samsa passes wordlessly with the morning light like a worn out workhorse conveniently expiring to accommodate its master, and the charwoman throws out this *"Zeug"* as though she were taking out the trash. After so little nourishment, the neglected body is *"vollständig flach und trocken"* [completely flat and dry] like a piece of parchment, ready for writing.

Gregor's ravaged vulnerability is "too trivial" to attain any sublimely tragic magnitude.[47] No one commits to his survival for its own sake (the "sanctity" of life) or out of respect for his service as the bread-winning son indentured to his father's debts, surrendering his own comfort so that his family could live at his expense. It remains ambiguous whether his starvation-flattened form and final thoughts incrementally carry out a "decision" or merely acquiesce to the cancellation of an existential equation between meaning for others and being for himself. In the grey zone between conscious response and passive submission to the inevitable, his expiration accedes to his family's self-interest in emotionally and physically moving on by relocating to an affordable flat.

Stine cites Kafka's markedly *un*Levinasian admission: " 'I have never been under the pressure of any responsibility,' Kafka wrote, 'but that imposed on me by the existence, the gaze, the judgment of other people.' "[48] Gregor's tender acceptance of his death sentence in a rubbish-filled room nevertheless seems to fulfill a Levinasian obligation to shield the other from self-preservative violence, a demand that Kafka, by his own dispensation, would elude. In the end, this forsaken vermin-corpse corporealizes Derrida's emphasis on the impossibility of present tense justice that should but does not remain open to the singularity of any appeal to continued life, especially the "appeals" of animals. With his last breath, Gregor foregrounds how judgments about the value of a particular living being always capitulate to the exigencies of survival adjudicated by "speaking animals," whether their survival is actually at stake or not. Gregor's love for his family nostalgically abides with the habit of his original humanity, and even though he "cannot communicate, he continues to remember."[49] The desired proof of secure family ties is, nevertheless, not forthcoming; it subsists, not in abeyance, but in a permanent state of retraction.

The reader is left to contemplate whether such a death could register as a sacrifice among those who so quickly shuffle off this "unclean" animal at once "unacceptable to man (*ungeheuer*) and unacceptable to God (*Ungeziefer*)," and thus "unsuited either to intimate speech or to prayer."[50]

When Gregor realizes that "his life of self-abnegation had been, it now appears, a kind of social game he had actively worked to perpetuate," Santner argues, "the long-suffering son" acts out a "sacrifice of sacrifice": He relinquishes "the very sacrificial logic that had given his life its doubtlessly bleak consistency" and thereby reprieves his family from the intolerable wound his transformation rips open in their everyday lives.[51] For this reason, Gregor is not simply a scapegoat figure; his repudiated need for love is an inassimilable remainder. Kafka's fiction thrives on attempts to dispose of such detritus that fatally perform the coldness that produces it. The hunger artist's bones are swept out of his cage to make room for a lively cat, who lustfully eats his fill. Gregor's deflated husk is unceremoniously dispatched by the giddy charwoman. Neither character could find the food he likes. Each hopes others will sustain him by showing solidarity with his sacrifice, but neither receives it.

At the historical moment when the artwork is no longer "nourished by the idea of humanity," as Adorno contends,[52] it seemingly renounces autonomy and "dies as a figural world... redeeming nothing" while casting "the abjection and heteronomy of the outside world in[to] quite horrible relief."[53] Heroic sacrifice is not an option for Kafka's characters who bear witness to this implosion of autonomy, a loss which cannot be compensated for or reversed.[54] The equivocal ethics of Gregor's final 'sacrifice of sacrifice' thus mirrors the contradictory burdens placed on modernist literature as an "epitaph" of the artwork confined to carrying out its own execution by an instrumental modernity. Kafka's vermin metaphor depletes its own vehicle and thereby commits the quintessential fatal performative: Beyond the irreversibility of an unjust verdict, Gregor's unsung demise reveals how "the chance which might have saved was missed," and this thwarted appeal for solidarity outlives his betrayed vulnerability to reproach us now.

Notes

1. Martin Jay, *Marxism and Totality: The Adventures of a Concept from Lukács to Habermas* (Los Angeles and Berkeley: University of California Press, 1984), 187. For Lukács, a realist novel gives us a concrete totality in Marx's Hegelian sense to the extent that it includes "all of the mediations that linked the seemingly isolated facts." (Ibid., 105.)

2. Terry Eagleton and Drew Milne, eds., *Marxist Literary Theory* (Cambridge, MA: Blackwell, 1996), 141. Having previously relegated Kafka's works to the politically incorrect side of literary art, "Lukács finds himself ridiculous," as Simon Critchley suggests, "because reality has conspired to bring about a situation which directly contradicts his aesthetic judgment." (Simon Critchley, *On Humour* [New York: Routledge, 2002], 107.)

3. Max Brod, *Franz Kafka: a Biography*, trans. G. Humphreys Roberts and Richard Winston (New York: Schocken, 1947), 75.

4. Tzvetan Todorov, *The Fantastic: A Structural Approach to a Literary Genre*, trans. Richard Howard (Ithaca, NY: Cornell University Press, 1975), 167. Todorov adds here that, "One can even say that it is to some degree because of literature and art that this distinction [between the real and the imaginary] becomes impossible to sustain." (Ibid.) Paul Reitter and Brett Wheeler also cite Todorov to emphasize that Kafka's stories represent "the operations of fiction itself, *how* literature works, making the unreal real at the end of the period in which this is still possible as hope" (Paul Reitter and Brett Wheeler, "Reflections on Kafka's Urban Reader," *German Politics and Society* 23.1 [2005]: 58–70, 74.)
5. Todorov, 175.
6. Ibid., 167.
7. I am grateful to my colleague Michael O'Driscoll for alerting me to the concept of the fatal performative contradiction in Derrida's explication of Freud's *Moses and Monotheism* in Jacques Derrida, *Archive Fever: A Freudian Impression*, trans. Eric Prenowitz (Chicago, IL: University of Chicago Press, 1996), in particular pp. 63 and 67–68.
8. Jacques Derrida, "Force of Law: the 'Mystical Foundation of Authority,'" in *Acts of Religion*, ed. Gil Anidjar (New York: Routledge, 2002), 244.
9. Ibid., 256.
10. Klaus Mladek, "Gotta Read Kafka: Nine Reasons Why Kafka Is Crucial for the Study of the Law," *Studies in Law, Politics, and Society* 31 (2004): 89–117, 97.
11. Ibid., 98.
12. Ibid., 89 and 98.
13. Ibid., 91 (citing Kafka).
14. Ibid., 91.
15. Friedrich Nietzsche, *On the Genealogy of Morals and Ecce Homo*, trans. Walter Kaufmann and R.J. Hollingdale (New York: Vintage, 1989), section 16: 84–85.
16. Ibid., section 16: 85.
17. Ibid., section 1: 58.
18. Mladek, 91.
19. Ibid. Peter Stine affirms that, "Kafka regarded the ability to forget as vital to survival in the modern world, a way of editing a metamorphosing self for the sake of a parodic wholeness of being" (Peter Stine, "Franz Kafka and Animals," *Contemporary Literature* 22.1 [1981]: 58–80, 60).
20. Ibid., 61. Stine reminds us that Kafka was a "strict" vegetarian and relates an anecdote of Brod's: "Once at a Berlin aquarium…Kafka began speaking to the fish in their illuminated tanks: 'Now at last I can look at you in peace. I don't eat you anymore.'" (Ibid., 70; citing Brod, 74.) In "Force of Law," Derrida foregrounds the ruthless mistreatment of animals among the forms of "hostage-taking" and "terror" that enjoin a reconsideration of "the very foundations of law such as they had previously been calculated or delimited." (Derrida, "Force of Law," 257.) On this cluster of themes, see also Jacques Derrida, "The Animal that Therefore I Am (More to Follow)," trans. David Wills, *Critical Inquiry* 28.2 (2002): 369–418; Jacques Derrida, "'Eating Well': Or the Calculation of the Subject: An Interview with Jacques Derrida," trans.

Peter Connor and Avital Ronell, in *Who Comes After the Subject*, eds. Eduardo Cadava, Peter Connor, and Jean-Luc Nancy (New York: Routledge, 1991), 96–119; and Karyn Ball, "Primal Revenge and Other Anthropomorphic Projections for Literary History," *New Literary History* 39 (special Issue on "Literary History and the Global Age") (2008): 533–563 [for a commentary on Derrida's "The Animal that Therefore I Am (More to Follow)"].

21. Robert Kauf, "Once Again: Kafka's 'A Report to an Academy,'" *Modern Language Quarterly* 15.4 (1954): 359–365, 362. "A Report to an Academy" was published along with "Jackals and Arabs" in the 1917-1918 volume of *Der Jude*, edited by Martin Buber. Following William C. Rubinstein (1952), Robert Kauf (1954) interprets "A Report" as ironically commenting on debates among Western European Jews of Kafka's time about the relative perils of Zionism and assimilationism. Rubinstein previously argued that two courses are open to the ape to extricate himself from an unbearable confinement: "to attempt an escape to freedom (Zionism), or to become a human being (assimilation and conversion)." (William C. Rubinstein, "Franz Kafka's 'A Report to an Academy,'" *Modern Language Quarterly* 13 [1952]: 372–376, 375.) Since the Zionist option is too dangerous, Kauf claims that "A Report" "attacks that type of assimilationism which, based upon opportunism, sacrifices a spiritual heritage and destiny to a crude materialism." (Kauf, 365.) For more recent analyses of Jewish motifs in Kafka, see Iris Bruce, "Kafka and Jewish Folklore," in *The Cambridge Companion to Kafka*, ed. Julian Preece (Cambridge, England: Cambridge University Press, 2002), 150–168; Iris Bruce, *Kafka and Cultural Zionism: Dates in Palestine* (Madison: University of Wisconsin Press, 2007); as well as Vivian Liska, *When Kafka Says We: Uncommon Communities in German-Jewish Literature* (Bloomington: Indiana University Press, 2009).

22. Theodor W. Adorno, "Notes on Kafka," in *Prisms*, trans. Samuel and Shierry Weber (Cambridge, MA: MIT Press, 1997), 259.

23. Ibid., 260.

24. Theodor W. Adorno, *Negative Dialectics*, trans. E.B. Ashton (New York: Seabury, 1973), 362–363.

25. Masao Miyoshi, "Turn to the Planet: Literature, Diversity, and Totality," *Comparative Literature* 53.4 (2001): 283–297, 292.

26. Adorno, "Notes," 256.

27. Slavoj Žižek, *The Sublime Object of Ideology* (New York: Verso, 1989), 173.

28. Judith Butler, *Precarious Life: The Powers of Mourning and Violence* (London: Verso, 2004).

29. Recalling Kafka's "inaccessible functionaries" in *The Castle*, Adorno suggests that Kafka "could have invented the expression 'protective custody,' had it not already become current during the First World War." (Adorno, "Notes," 259.)

30. Butler, 137.

31. Ibid., 138–139.

32. Ibid., 137.

33. Ibid.

34. Ibid., 137–138.

35. Mladek, 107.

36. Ibid., 105 and 108.
37. Stine, 63.
38. Eric Santner, "Kafka's *Metamorphosis* and the Writing of Abjection," in MM 1996, 195–210.
39. Ibid., 199, n. 8.
40. Ibid., 205, n. 5.
41. Stine, 64.
42. Santner, 205.
43. Reitter and Wheeler argue that self-conscious references to reading and writing in Kafka's stories formally instantiate a radically transformed urban reader "who is cognitively truncated by mass culture and anonymous powers of bureaucracy that rob modern subjects of agency altogether." (Reitter and Wheeler, 59.)
44. Walter Benjamin, "Notes from Svendborg: Conversations with Brecht," in *Understanding Brecht*, trans. Anna Bostock (London: New Left Books, 1973), 110.
45. Stine, 65.
46. I am grateful to Ewa Domanska for sharing her observations about this image with me.
47. Mladek, 113.
48. Stine, 61 (citing Franz Kafka, *I Am a Memory Come Alive*, ed. Nahum Glatzer [New York: Schocken, 1974], 191).
49. Stanley Corngold, "Kafka's *The Metamorphosis*: Metamorphosis of the Metaphor," in MM 1996, 89.
50. Ibid., 103. Dwelling on its Middle High German roots, Corngold notes that the word *Ungeziefer* connotes Gregor's status as an unclean animal that can be killed, but is not suitable for sacrifice. He is also *ungeheuer* [monstrous], "a creature without a place in God's order." (Stanley Corngold, Introduction to *The Metamorphosis* by Franz Kafka, trans. and ed. Stanley Corngold [New York: Bantam, 1986], xix.)
51. Santner, 198.
52. Theodor W. Adorno, *Aesthetic Theory*, trans. and ed. Robert Hullot-Kentor (Minneapolis: University of Minnesota Press, 1997), 1.
53. Reitter and Wheeler, 75 (citing Todorov, 175).
54. Mladek, 102.

Chapter Ten
How is the Trapeze Possible?

Christophe Bident

Translated from French by Amelia Fedo, with
A. Kiarina Kordela and Anna Tahinci

1. The Aerial Prison

Dark, labyrinthine, chthonic, or subterranean: in the work of Kafka, as in the world, prison most often rejects brightness, order, and light. What happens to it when it rises up into the air? Is it possible to imagine an aerial prison? A confinement that towers over the world, gazing down on it in hunger?

When one takes even the slightest risk, prison is in sight, consented to, desired without being perverted. It is one of the stakes in a gamble with life, and death.

Once inhabited, a prison curbs, crushes, and destroys; but it also offers the perverse possibility of reconstituting an unequal, unjust, and violent world. The physical prison doubles as a virtual prison, no less real, where orders come down with hatchet-like suddenness. Time does not allow for it to be otherwise: the order is immediately a sanction. Prison accentuates, to a radical extent, the rhythm and space of repetition: an unyielding rhythm in an inviolable mirror.

Walls leave no hope but the sky. Ball-and-chains redouble the gravity of the floor, the weight of damnation. Bars impose striations upon a gaze that is still moved by the possibilities of daylight. Their vertical rhythm inscribes, in its own way, an immense power of negation. In "First Sorrow," Kafka invents, more simply, a trapeze and nets.

One does not get used to Kafka's incongruities. That may be his greatest art—diversifying and multiplying incongruities. Here, in four pages, neither the situation, nor the event, nor the dénouement escape this.[1]

202 / CHRISTOPHE BIDENT

The Situation

The exaggeration is limitless. Kafka places a trapeze artist on a trapeze—but he fixes him there enduringly, permanently. The trapeze artist does not leave, will never leave, his trapeze at the top of the circus tent: he integrates it, so to speak, into his lived-body. All the logic of incongruity is then developed. If the trapeze artist remains on his trapeze, what is to be done with him when the circus takes the tent down to move from one city to another? Kafka invents a few alternative solutions: the trapeze artist travels apart from his colleagues, alone in a train compartment, up in the luggage net; "racing automobiles" which "whirl [the trapeze artist] at breakneck speed"[2] are reserved to transport him through deserted streets, at night or in the early morning, from the train station to the circus tent, already pitched upon his arrival and ready to take him in.

One must therefore imagine the trapeze artist sleeping, washing, and feeding himself on a horizontal bar, perhaps with the aid of two vertical ropes. One must imagine him enduring a long journey by train, sufficiently long for the stagehands to set up the circus tent before his arrival. One must imagine him in despair in those automobiles, which, for all their speed, still bring him down to ground level. In this whole situation, implausibility matters little. Here, it displays the strokes of caricature. A bit like in an Expressionist painting, the stretching of the frame and the violence of the diagonals distort the illusion and advance the representation in zones where another truth is outlined by the image. Kafka's narrative is very visual, and very kinetic. The exaggeration of the situation touches as much on mobility as on immobility. It uncovers an absence linked to the world and destined to be unsatisfied. It invents a superior, atheistic, nontranscendental point of view: the trapeze artist on the trapeze takes the place of the eye of God in the triangle, and we are led to follow his gaze. We, the readers, will not be his spectators; besides, the narrative does not describe any exercise or number, neither show nor rehearsal. The trapeze artist is a trapeze artist in essence, never in action. What does it mean to be a trapeze artist outside of gymnastic time? What remains of the gymnastic body in civilian time, in time of rest? Everything, apparently. The trapeze-artist-being has absorbed the being of the trapeze artist. And he is a being who is lacking, who wanted it all only to end up losing everything. Time sets in to the situation; melancholy arrives, with its crises and tears. That is what the narrative's point of view—its height, its logic, and its distance—asks us to understand.

The Event

Thus the event occurs, in the form of a request, followed by a demand and a flood of tears. A progressive crisis that is also irresistible, for in spite of the favorable responses of the manager to his wishes, the trapeze artist bursts into tears like a spoiled child—like a child that nothing will satisfy, not even that which he has desired and for which he has expressed the desire. However, within the framework of the narrative, the crisis of tears has nothing incongruous about it. One can easily imagine the trapeze artist, eaten away by his solitude, "cracking," like an overly adored celebrity, so that this being who has become untouchable suffers twice as much pain at the exact moment the manager touches him, caresses him, and presses his face against his own. This, then, is the fate of the trapeze-artist-being: a skin that cannot be touched without suffering, like that of the gray, parchment-like bodies of Samuel Beckett's *The Lost Ones*, endlessly evolving inside another geometric shape, that of an enormous cylinder.

However, these visions of the reader—always so ready, and so hasty, to impose their own models—do not correspond to what Kafka makes us read. For if the crisis of tears does not seem at all incongruous, the real reason Kafka provides it *is* incongruous, and disproportionately so. Indeed, what does the trapeze artist ask for—what thing, about which he is unsure whether to rejoice or agonize? He asks for another trapeze. The trapeze-artist-being does not ask for another trapeze artist to break his solitude, to form an ethical circle, to improve his act, or to bring the symmetry to perfection: he asks for another object, and asks for it as an other himself. This is probably the origin, or one origin, of tears—the objectification of being imposes that of demand. Like Midas and his gold, Kafka's trapeze artist can no longer touch anything but trapezes. The world has closed itself up on his desire. It is the source of his happiness and his damnation.

(Two French trapeze artists have plainly experienced this in recent times. Chloé Moglia and Mélissa Von Vépy have told me to what degree the idea of dedicating their lives to the trapeze, after graduating from the National Circus School of Châlons, had become unbearable for them. They could find no way out except by continuing to practice the trapeze, or vaulting, or climbing—but while inventing other supports, forging other narratives, constructing other images, playing in their shows with the human, ethical, physical, and metaphysical borders that living things cannot cross. Kafka does not use the device of the contemporary circus to prolong his story. But, between the lines, that is where he is leading.)

The Fall [*La chute*]

This is a short story, and Kafka has nothing to develop. This is his customary practice, which allows him to turn an incongruous situation into a luminous event. The ending [*La chute*] of the narrative both opens and closes up time: it opens the reader's imagination to a future that nothing seems to be able to divert from the path of repetition. If the trapeze-artist-being has requested, demanded, and obtained a second trapeze, what can arrive from now on but a third, a fourth, a fifth, a sixth, and so on, for infinity? One can read here all the parables one wants, starting with those of the repetition of the object of desire, of the imprisonment within passion, of the solitude to which destiny's great lines deliver their choice. They will all be valid without being able to exhaust the range of the narrative. The force of the tale resides in its ending [*sa chute*] in an indeterminate image: the appearance of the "first furrows" on the trapeze-artist-being's "smooth, childlike forehead." All of the beauty of this image resides in its naivety. This enigmatic revelation, this transparent icon, turns its back on the incongruous complexity of the narrative, which yet accompanies it. The trapeze-artist-being sinks into time. The wrinkles form so many trapezes that scar his face and forehead. Obsession writes the weight of flesh upon his skin. And yet, the narrative does not valorize either these new bars, or the empty space they still demarcate, even if only in the distance.

The Distant

The distant—this could be still another narrative of Kafka's. In "Report to an Academy," the ape scoffs at the aerial freedom of the trapeze artist, whose movement, he thinks, does not escape error, or death, except by regulating itself, borrowing automatic reflexes, on an alarming geometric order of banality, a double symmetry, a double agreement of time and space (RA 1971, 253). What passes for an extreme exploit in the eyes of man is nothing more than simplistic mechanics to an animal. And it is the whole of human architecture that collapses before this sight. "The self-controlled movement" so prized by trapeze artists and their admirers—that is to say, by more or less the entire human species—is a physiological, psychological, and political model: what more can one dream of, as an ethical ideal, than a space where each movement would have to answer to nothing but itself, all while absolutely preserving the movement of others, without which it knows it would be nothing? The most agile animal prefers the animation of disorder—including tigers outside of the hoop, elephants in a stampede, apes clinging to any element of the circus tent and outside of the circus tent.

Indeed. But the trapeze-artist-being, voluntarily solitary, has never been a fanatic about symmetry. He clings to the pinnacle and to the miracle of the multiplication of trapezes. He need only dare to venture, like an ape, the conquest of an animal freedom.

He knows that the "frail, consumptive equestrienne" of "Up in the Gallery," who was able to train her horse and adapt its wildness but was

not, however, able to spin "for months on end without respite...before an insatiable public," can only provoke delirious weeping from the young spectator.³ Domesticating the animal is useless; spinning around indefinitely is impossible. No neutral movement—neither chaos nor balance—has reached it. The trapeze artist prefers therefore to prevent the tears of the young spectator: he weeps instead himself, and develops wrinkles.

But, the image of tears presents itself to us also as a vanity. The trapeze artist, a showman and spectator plunging his gaze down onto every spectacle, knows this. He offers us his vanity like a gift. This transparent vanity cages the childlike, and henceforth adult, being. To be at the top, the eye of the trapeze-artist-being does not escape a—tragicomic—form of reducing the world.

2. The Voice of the Trapeze

Chloé Moglia and Mélissa Von Vepy would then have been able to spend their lives on their trapezes. Upon leaving school, however, they decide to break with the "ordinary lifestyle" of those athletic artists who have seduced the public of all times with the dizzying height of their feats and the great risk to which they expose themselves each time. They found their company and if *they* do not desire a second trapeze, it is because they desire other objects and other materials. They grow. They leave the smooth childhood of trapeze artists who do not age because they have no age other than that of childhood silence, or of a time other than that of pendulous motion opposed to death. They get one or two wrinkles to enter into time. Henceforth, the time of trapeze artists will be counted in a gap between the pursuit of gymnastic risk and the reflection upon the finality of their accomplishments. They listen to voices and prepare for movements other than bends, leaps, and releases. The voices are those of philosophers. While working in the ceilings of circus tents, Chloé Moglia and Mélissa Von Vépy listen to recordings of Bachelard, Deleuze, or Jankélévitch speaking about the void, vertigo, risk, and motion. The voices are bare. They betray the wrinkles that articulate them and pronounce them. They are suffused with their own time. They are deep, funny, accentuated, full of tremolos, split along the cracks, suspended on their pauses. They say what the trapeze artists know implicitly but want to hear from outside.

It is 2005. They are not yet thirty. Chloé Moglia and Mélissa Von Vépy create the show that, to this day, matters the most to them: *I look up, I look down.*⁴ On the ring of the circus tent or on the boards of the theatre they install a large plywood polyhedron, covered in magnesium and fireproof black paint. The only thing to occupy the stage, positioned stage right and turned to face the audience at a 3/4 view, this block with the appearance of a monolith, more than five meters high, is surrounded only by old bits of plaster that have been scattered around, as though tossed at its feet. The two young women appear at the top of the monolith. The whole question, for close to an hour, is to know how, with one or two ropes, harnesses, or bare hands, they will be able to get back to the ground. How, and why; together, or not; and what traces this obstructed descent will leave on their existences.

The Figuration

In other words, a narrative begins: a narrative of borders. What border to oppose to the desire for personal risk and for common enterprise? What border to oppose to the gaze of the living? We, spectators, sense these questions under the empire of a scenic dramaturgy: stage design, lighting, voices and music, physical feats, and choreographed movements are our responsibility to present, to exhibit, to *provide a figuration*. These figures are full of possible meanings, of intersecting logic, of cracks along their borders. How to dramatise such a scenography of risk? How to avoid holding on to the physical performance while holding against the allegorical meaning? What becomes of the nature and the finality of risk? How to expose it while also reserving it? How to construct a movement between the different sources of perception? What place to accord to the voices of the philosophers? How to hold on to them and how to forget them? These are at least some of the questions that Chloé Moglia and Mélissa Von Vépy ask themselves.

Over the course of the spectacle's creation, which takes several months, a poetic question transforms into a narrative representation. The basis of the trapeze artist's motion—his suspension in the void—having become source of astonishment and motive for creation, should not be reduced, according to Chloé Moglia and Mélissa Von Vépy, to a demonstration or an exhibition. We are, therefore, far from the logic of an artistic performance: the issue is neither realizing, nor photographing, nor exhibiting a leap into the void like Yves Klein's, even if the initial dread remains that amazing "zone of immaterial sensibility" that the void constitutes and that many artists and writers of the twentieth century have named "the neutral." We are also far from the logic of an athletic performance: the issue is not still believing in the metaphysics of the body and pushing further its limits with new exemplary acrobatics. Rather, the issue is precisely outlining the borders that neither the body nor the image can cross, to which they can merely appeal with a gesture, and present these gestures in the conduct of a narrative. This does not occur painlessly, for it is the story of an impossible dream and an impossible event that the spectacle is about to unfold. It is thus a matter of the poetics of the trapeze, and at the same time of exiting it; in other words, a matter of the politics of the trapeze in contemporary spectacle, partly serious and partly comical.

Two young women, then, appear at the top of a monolith. They are surprised and worried to find themselves so high up, over the void. They both come down a first time, without too much difficulty; it is like a prologue that harbors, at a smooth pace, the infancy and dream of the technique, and which the narrative that follows will first deny in order to accomplish them better later, and to capture the psychological effects of such an accomplishment. For then the two women go up again, to come down once more, without trying to forget the other, without acting alone. The heart of the representation multiplies the acrobatic figures, the risks of the fall [*chute*], without ever underscoring them, constantly integrating them into the story of a succession of events where the small failures never exhaust the attempts and do not completely cut into the complicity of the two characters. We are witness to both an organic splendor and a moral narrative; at the center, like the nexus of the body and meaning, the spectacle constructs a whole series of images, optical illusions (to the point of creating the impression of a horizontal plane one would see from above), effects of light and shadow, and sonorous creations. The specter of animality (images evoking hanging bats or simian movements) constantly persists under the altruistic gesture of the extended hand. All the constitutive borders of humanity are evoked (animal, mineral, night, death, fiction…), and this is what gives the spectacle its density.

The Dénouement

And this is also what makes the ending violent. Freed of all equipment, and having returned to the ground, the two women wander in despair in a rockslide of broken plaster. They are sorrowful, like Kafka's trapeze artist, at the very moment when they should be satisfied. Suddenly, they rush at the monolith. They bang once on it, hard, and then they begin again. The music that has been accompanying them since the beginning rises dramatically. A voice comes from it, that of Jankélévitch, the only voice retained in the actual show. It is a voice recorded on the radio, on an ancient medium, dozens of years ago. It is an improvised voice, made of flights of lyricism, of precise notations, of solecisms and anacoluthons. Like a Pascalian thought [*pensée*]. It comes out of the music and then falls back into it, partly inaudible. It shivers, affirms, trembles, exclaims: "The desire for nothingness, the lure of nothingness, the game with the perils of death that humans are amused to exalt dangerously—that is to say, humans play at dangerously exalting the permanent condition of their existence in order to make it more passionate, in order to make existence passionate, adventurous. In the end, there will be then a romantic temptation of death, dramatic and extremely intense, in which is affirmed precisely the dramatic character of life and the fact that, in spite of everything, it is worth living it. It deserves to be experienced and lived...."

Thus, something remains of the age of the novel and its illustrations. The bodily risk, here presented both as a figure and as an episode, does not become a metaphor for all vital risk merely because it itself is one. The metaphysical discourse, culminating in a resounding orchestration, maintains its own border, maintains itself as a border, because it claims its due: the exigencies of training and the real accomplishment of risk, without a net, as they say—which also means without the saving nets of translation. On the one hand, the circus starts to signify; on the other hand, the theatre starts to put the body in risk: it is this extreme encounter that both holds on to and overturns the metaphysics of presence, and which resounds the secret echo of passions, at once necessary and unjustified.

The Concatenation

These are, then, at once solitary, communal, poetic, political, and aesthetic borders that this spectacle evokes. It confronts us at the harshness of the border with the double violence that the monolith opposes: its unassailable height and its consistent harshness. The grace with which the two women move down the length of the wall is equaled only by the violence with which they bang themselves against it. The calming down that follows the blows is not entirely reassuring. It takes also salutations, smiles, and complicity. But the spectacle acts like a concatenation. It denounces the sidereal vertigo of imposing triumphs. It accomplishes the dance of the world like a sum of virtually and vitally communicating singularities. "Everyone dances alone," writes Jean-Luc Parant. "But if everyone dances alone, we all dance together at the same time, as though one could hear think only all together at the same time in the silence of the infinite *void*, where the night is darkest and where no one would hear his or her thought but in order to hear the others' thoughts sing..."[5]

The Illusion

In "Report to an Academy," Kafka's ape-turned-man expresses himself: "In passing: may I say that all too often men are betrayed by the word freedom. And as freedom is counted among the most sublime feelings, so the corresponding disillusionment can be also sublime. In variety theatres I have often watched, before my turn came on, a couple of acrobats performing

on trapezes high in the roof. They swung themselves, they rocked to and fro, they sprang into the air, they floated into each other's arms, one hung by the hair from the teeth of the other. 'And that too is human freedom,' I thought, 'self-controlled movement.' What a mockery of holy Mother Nature! Were the apes to see such a spectacle, no theatre walls could stand the shock of their laughter" (RA 1971, 253).

It is because we are not ape enough that we smile without laughing at Chloé Moglia's and Mélissa Von Vépy's spectacle. But we become conscious of this vanity that comes with the exemplary demonstrations of the laws of motion. It is this "sublime illusion," in Kafka's terms, just as sublime as an ideal freedom, that they make us share. That is precisely where they find their freedom. The border is the "sublime illusion" that escapes its own materiality.

Notes

1. Franz Kafka, "First Sorrow," in *The Complete Stories,* ed. Nahum N. Glatzer (New York: Schocken Books, 1971), 447–452.
2. Ibid., 447.
3. Franz Kafka, "Up in the Gallery," in *The Complete Stories*, 401.
4. *I look up, I look down*, spectacle conceived and interpreted by Chloé Moglia and Mélissa Von Vépy. Sound, Jean-Damien Ratel. Lighting, Xavier Lazarini. Costumes, Isabelle Périllat.
5. Jean-Luc Parant, *Comme une petite terre aveugle* (Paris: Editions Lettres vives, 1983).

CHAPTER ELEVEN
WITH IMPUNITY

Henry Sussman

1.

Mercurial, fragmentary, and nonlinear by design, alighting on one discursive tradition and display after the next, randomly and with impunity, Giorgio Agamben's *Homo Sacer: Sovereign Power and Bare Life* is not what one would expect as an early exemplar of full-throttled cultural deconstruction. *Homo Sacer* never escapes the tortured middle-ground or margin that is both its premise and the contested zone of most of the phenomena that it addresses. Political regimes and their ideological and teletechnic underpinnings—what I term in recent work Prevailing Operating Systems[1]—may come and go, the volume reminds us. But the deep wiring that facilitates genocide, large-scale death meted out with alacrity, and the camps and other holding areas fitted out for this purpose, remains implanted within long-standing Western linguistic usage and cultural practice.

As ongoing Middle Eastern politics remind us, intensified by endless war in Iraq, Afghanistan, and other locations, the *ricorso* to the World War II death camps, as strategic actualities and conceptual artifacts, remains invitingly open. The camps persist as a particularly grim figment of the political time-warp that Deleuze/Guattari set out in their *Capitalism and Schizophrenia* diptych, one in which "prior" formations, whether as antecedents or in crass brutality, whether "despotic nomadism" or feudal hierarchy, never go away.[2] In Deleuze/Guattari's implied historiography, the systemic antecedents hang suspended, rather, in a glutinous membrane of cumulative political eventuality, ready for reactivation whenever the triggers permit.

In many senses, *Homo Sacer* positions itself in the direct trajectory of the deconstructive project, downstream from the troping of Western programmatic language into talismans or insignias coordinating linguistic elucidation with symptomatic performance. With pronounced precision, *Homo Sacer* implants itself into core Western concepts and texts, gathering this canon into a broad and discordant array of sources. These in turn, from Plato's *Gorgias* and *The Laws* and Aristotle's *Metaphysics* to Pompeius Festus's *On the Significance of Words*, form a network of key terms rendered mutually interactive by ties to social segmentation, ostracism, and banning, a priori profiling put into practice, and summary justice at the service of large-scale death. In all these tendencies, plus the dramatic nonlinearity it claims as the royal road into the heart of its matter, *Homo Sacer* is in the drift of Jacques Derrida's most trenchant instances of deconstructive critique. I would include *Of Grammatology,* "Plato's Pharmacy," "The Law of Genre," *Specters of Marx,* and *Rogues* on this short list, but then, these particularly focused while at the same time freewheeling windows on embedded metaphysics implicate, by one route or another, virtually everything else he ever published.

Homo Sacer heralds and embodies a slightly different sensibility and practice, though, in the abjectly material dimension of the phenomena it folds into deconstructive performance: the camps themselves, the corpses, human ash and sludge, and the confiscated possessions and wealth that the camps produced. This materiality extends as well to the legal legerdemain, the masses of records and documentation that were the camps' paper underpinnings and simulacrum. In a brilliant poetic coup, Agamben showcases the *Musselmann,* the exemplar of what he terms "bare life," the still-alive but inert vestige of systematically delivered death in the complete withdrawal of social recognition and empathy as the starkest material remain of the collusion, endemic to large-scale genocide, between jurisprudence, ideology, social engineering, and military science. "Bare life" marks the spot at which states and other sovereign entities claim power over the biological status and possibility of groups and individuals inhabiting their domains. (Sometimes over groups and individuals in various respects in absentia.) The notion demarcates Agamben's most serious debt to Michel Foucault, the latter's construction *biopolitics,* whose deployment regulates sexual activity, reproductive possibility, and familial configuration at the same time that it selects "who will live and who will die."[3]

At the same time that the *Musselmann* personifies the debasing of human life that the World War II camps produced industrially, "bare life" serves as the limit-case to the viability, potentiality, and physicocognitive sensibility or mindfulness attending survival, persistence, "continuity of Being." The logic attending the appearance of the *Musselmann* as the persona of bare life runs approximately as follows: The production, with impunity, on the part of the totalitarian regime, or War Machine, of the *Musselmann,* marks the ultimate degradation of civil life to the undifferentiated condition of survival and mindless persistence. The imposed simplification and mind-lessness of bare life extend figuratively, by analogy and metonymy, to the unconditionally violent, blunt, and disrespectful assertion of power on the part of the belligerent sovereign entity.

Agamben's learned recourse to the *homo sacer* and tangential con-structs—at the semic as well as conceptual level—as the enabling legisla-tion for the legal, social as well as geographical banning or quarantine concretized in the camps is a nod in the direction of the more "practical" deconstruction in which perhaps the major share of Derrida's later writ-ings engaged. Insisting on the imagination and execution of the camps as an instance of *biopolitics* strategically deploys the rhetorically motivated and powered historiography that Foucault configured and rendered indis-pensable through his archaeological account of knowledge in the broader modernity. Agamben's broader appeal to Foucault runs this way: "In the notion of bare life the interlacing of politics and life has become so tight that it cannot be easily analyzed. Until we become aware of the political nature of bare life and its modern avatars (biological life, sexuality, etc.), we will not succeed in clarifying the opacity at their center. Conversely, once modern politics enters into an intimate symbiosis with bare life, it loses the intelligibility that still seems to us to characterize the juridicopolitical foundation of classical politics."[4] Agamben freely affirms that he follows Foucault in designating life, in the play between *zoē* and *bios* qualifying the concept in classical Greek philosophy, as the primary bone of conten-tion and assertion of power and sovereignty in modern politics.[5] Assuming the guise of a political historian, Agamben asserts that it is life and only the control, rationing, and sovereign obliteration of life that could explain the pell-mell twentieth-century transformation of middling democracies and constitutional monarchies into totalitarian powers:

> And only because biological life and its needs became the *politically* decisive fact is it possible to understand the otherwise incomprehensible rapidity with which twentieth-century parliamentary democracies were able to turn into totalitarian states and with which this century's totalitarian states were able to be converted, almost without interruption, into parliamentary democ-racies. In both cases, these transformations were produced in a context in which for some time politics had turned into biopolitics, in which the only real question to be decided was which organization would be best suited to the task of assuring the care, control, and use of bare life. Once their referent becomes bare life, traditional political distinctions (such as those between Right and Left, totalitarianism and liberalism, private and public) lose their clarity and intelligibility and enter into a zone of indistinction....
>
> Along with the emergence of biopolitics, we can observe a displacement and gradual expansion beyond the limits of the decision on bare life, in the state of exception, in which sovereignty consisted.[6]

Not only does this striking passage chronicle the rise of biopolitics into the telling political factor in twentieth-century national and international politics. The biopolitical factor emerges as a universal shifter, situated in the crux of a chiasmus, a "zone of indistinction." Where biopolitics operates—everywhere in the twentieth century—political formations are transformed into their political complements, if not opposites. The political contention over life in an ongoing and endless state of exception transforms totalitarian regimes into democracies and democracies into totalitarian regimes.

The life over which sovereign entities deliberate and dispose is always in a process of reversion to its "bare" or stripped-down condition. Once engaged in massive social engineering, demographic control, eugenics, or genocide, twentieth-century states are not thinking, in other words, that they are transforming or liquidating specific individuals or even communities. They are processing, rather, life itself, life stripped bare, life crunched to its lowest common denominator: life, in other words, as the limit-case to survival, endurance, in the social as well as personal sphere. Life-politics is not calibrated to fine distinctions. Bare life is the fundamental issue and condition of politics, community, and social administration. Its fundamentalism extends to the impunity with which it is spared or death is meted out.

Impunity emerges not only as the quasilegal condition of possibility or suspension of rule of law, enabling operations of profiling, banning, segregation, disenfranchisement, quarantine, unsanctioned homicide, and genocide. It is the *performative* tact or bearing, in this sense it is an intangible, bestowing upon sovereign acts of violence their distinctive *qualities*. Impunity is nothing more formidable than an *attitude*, extending from linguistic *expression* to *act*, with irreversible repercussions for the political structure and tenor of habitation within, assistance at, certain distinctive totalitarian formations.

The most compelling *aside* to Agamben's magisterial account of the wholesale devaluation of life in the twentieth century by bureaucratic fiat, sovereign prestidigitation, and military science is indeed the noise or scraping that he allows rhetorical figures to make within the thundering momentum of the death-system. As motivator and shifter of political values, bare life effects *chiasmatic* tension and transformation. Impunity's wide death-swathe is implemented by means of *rhetorical* stance.

The impunity with which the dispensable, wretched, and deterritorialized are liquidated is a multidimensional echo of the bareness of life to which they have been, strategically and systematically, relegated. Hence, the centrality of the *Musselmann* to the figurative constellation that Agamben assembles. As characterized by Primo Levi, this figure stands out vividly in the dramatis personae of the legally disenfranchised, backlit in pure abjection:

> He was not only, like his companions, excluded from the political and social context to which he once belonged; he was not only, as Jewish life that does not deserve to live, destined to a future more or less close to death. He no longer belongs to the world of men in any way; he does not even belong to the threatened and precarious world of the camp inhabitants who have forgotten him from the very beginning. Mute and absolutely alone, he has passed into another world without memory and without grief. For him, Hölderlin's statement that "at the extreme limit of pain, nothing remains but the conditions of time and space" holds to the letter.
>
> What is the life of the *Musselmann*? Can one say that it is pure *zo*? Nothing "natural" or "common," however, is left in him. Nothing animal or instinctual remains in his life. All his instincts are cancelled along with his reason. Antelme tells us that the camp inhabitant was no longer capable of distinguishing between pangs of cold and the ferocity of the SS. If we apply this statement to the *Musselmann* quite literally ("the cold, SS"), then we can say that he moves about in absolute indistinction of fact and law, of life and juridical rule, and of nature and politics. Because of this, the guard suddenly seems powerless before him, as if struck by the thought that the *Musselmann's* behavior—which does not register any difference between an order and the cold—might perhaps be a silent form of resistance. Here a law that seeks to transform itself entirely into life finds itself confronted with a life that is absolutely indistinguishable from law.[7]

This memorable passage conspicuously leaves unresolved whether the devolution to bare life is the result of a systematic incapacitation of linguistic processing, short circuiting all possibility of social interaction or interpersonal support; or, whether it is a material condition, whether of pain, cold, or even mental blackout. Indeed, the passage gains its vividness from a calculated "indistinction" between linguistic muting and tangible, material suffering. In the first movement to this vignette, in the first paragraph, it is muteness, quietly introduced, articulation-meltdown, that defines the *Musselmann's* sublime outsideness to all social interaction, making him/her/it susceptible to the suffering poetically displayed by Hölderlin: an occultation of all experience save the intuitive apprehension of time and space, factored out in Kant's *Critique of Pure Reason* as the baseline objective, universal thresholds of human cognition and experience; the only dimensions not contingent on human striving and attainment.

The second paragraph above specifies the catastrophic damage to linguistic processing and communication delivered in the camps: an "indistinction," read that devastating viral attack on the differentiating function (Derridean "*différance*") at the basis of all articulations, enunciations, media, messages, and information. The *Musselmann* is the broken-down

218 / HENRY SUSSMAN

former resident and noncitizen of the domains of culture, institutions, law, art, and religion. It is in the context of bureaucratically designed and militarily delivered social anomie that the most generic, stripped-down life claims the abstraction and universality of law. (Agamben appropriates the concentration camp, then, as the twentieth-century site of Hegelian "sense-certainty" [*sinnliche Gewißheit*], also determined by the vertiginous fluctuation between stark immediacy and universality.) The convergence of life and law in the abjected figure of the *Musselmann* makes him/her/it one of history's most vivid poster children for the catastrophic outcomes of Foucauldian biopolitics (there are surely multiple others).

At the heart of the politico-etymological-ideological history resulting in death-camps populated by the broken-down remnants of human articulation, custom, community, and law is the schizophrenogenic status of the *homo sacer* from which the study derives its title, an outsider who can be killed with impunity but whose elimination may not be registered in the social loss-column, as a sacrifice. "The very body of the *homo sacer* is, in its capacity to be killed but not sacrificed, a living pledge to his subjection to a power of death. And yet this pledge is, nevertheless, absolute and unconditional, and not the fulfillment of a consecration."[8] The aporetic messages surrounding the *homo sacer* fulfill with a vengeance the underlying conditions making possible all the double-binds formulated and sequenced by Gregory Bateson in his meticulous (and underrated) account of schizophrenic pathologies. From Pompeius Festus to Karl Kerényi, Agamben meticulously traces the archeological (in Foucault's sense) evolution of the disposable human being who can be eliminated but not remembered in any sacramental or historical way. Such a systematically outlandish social component, argues Agamben, requires a space or holding-area neither here nor there, in keeping with the expendable nature of its population, created by edict but outside the civility and protection of the law. The twentieth-century preserve of the *homo sacer* and his/her/its descendents, facilitated by the advances of modern bureaucracy and military science, is the concentration camp and its relatives (the detention center, the holding facility). The camp is itself a chiasmatic space whose overarching double-bind is the conflation of unprocessed brutality with unconstrained destructive possibility:

> Only because the camps constitute a state of exception in the sense which we have examined—in which not only is law suspended but fact and law are completely confused—is everything in the camps truly possible. If this particular juridico-political stricture of the camps—the task of which is precisely to create a stable exception—is not understood, the incredible things that happen there remain completely unintelligible. Whoever entered the camps moved in a zone of indistinction between outside and inside, exception

and rule, licit and illicit, in which the very concepts of subjective right and juridical protection no longer made any sense. What is more, if the person entering the camp was a Jew, he had already been deprived of his rights as citizen by the Nuremberg laws and was subsequently denationalized at the time of the Final Solution.... The correct question to pose concerning the horrors committed in the camps is, therefore, not the hypocritical one of how crimes of such atrocity could be committed against human beings. It would be more honest and, above all, more useful to investigate more carefully the juridical procedures and deployments of power by which human beings could be so completely deprived of their rights and prerogatives that no act committed against them could appear any longer as a crime. (At this point, in fact, everything had truly become possible.)[9]

Even at this rather late point in his study, Agamben pauses in disbelief at the anomaly of "juridical procedures and deployments" that could result in "zones of indistinction" in which "no acts committed" against the victims could be construed as crimes and "everything had truly become possible." These eventualities have all been facilitated by the construct of a "state of exception" hovering inchoate, a malevolent specter, around the ancient figure of the *homo sacer*. (This figure is itself grounded in the even more venerable *topos* or trope of the scapegoat as, say, Derrida elaborates it in his pivotal "Plato's Pharmacy.")[10] In terms of the implied historiography grounding Deleuze/Guattari's "Capitalism and Schizophrenia" diptych, the *homo sacer* is a zombie from Roman law released into the volatility and vindictive tenor of twentieth-century politics. As theorized by Carl Schmitt and others, the state of exception becomes a prevalent feature of the sovereignty asserted by the modern constitutional nation-state, the German Weimar Republic furnishing a notable example. "The sovereign sphere is the sphere in which it is permitted to kill without committing homicide and without celebrating a sacrifice, and sacred life, that is, life that may be killed but not sacrificed—is the life that has been captured in this sphere."[11] The sovereign state of exception that at its outer limits could create monstrosities of the nature and scale of the concentration camps is the juridical deployment of the impunity that Agamben traces all the way back to the *homo sacer*, defining the particular Democlean sword suspended over this figure.

For totalitarian nihilism, impunity remains the starting point, the fundamental temperament, affectively as well as politically. Some of Agamben's most vivid imagery for the impunity prevailing within the "zones of indistinction" demarcated both by concentration camps and strategic states of exception stems from his glosses of Roman law. "The specificity of *homo sacer*" arises, according to Festus, from "the juxtaposition of two traits:"[12]

the unpunishability of his killing and the ban on his sacrifice. In the light of what we know of the Roman juridical and religious order (both of the *ius divinum* and the *ius humanem*), the two traits seem hardly compatible: if *homo sacer* was impure (Fowler: taboo) or the property of the gods (Kerényi), then why would anyone kill him without either contaminating himself or committing sacrilege? What is more, if *homo sacer* truly was the victim of a death sentence or an archaic sacrifice, why is it not *fas* to put him to death in the prescribed forms of execution? What, then, is the life of the *homo sacer* if it is situated at the interstice of a captivity to be killed and yet not sacrificed, outside both human and divine law?

It appears that we are confronted with a limit concept of the Roman social order that, as such, cannot be explained in a satisfying manner as long as we remain either inside the *ius divinum* or *ius humanum*. And yet *homo sacer* may perhaps allow us to shed light on the reciprocal limits of these two juridical realms.... We will try to interpret *sacratio* as an autonomous figure, and we will ask if this figure may allow us to uncover an originary *political* structure that is located in a zone prior to the distinction between sacred and profane, religious and juridical.[13]

Impunity is *unpunishability* within a context (or, following Erving Goffman, *frame*)[14] of *indistinction*, suspended or disabled articulation, distinction, *difference*. The camps, runs Agamben's logic and powered by some of Schmitt's political speculations, are the military-industrial outgrowth of the *homo sacer's* constitutionally tenuous and ambiguous position.

By contrast, Joseph K.'s predicament in Franz Kafka's *The Trial* (*Der Prozeß*) gains a significant measure of its vividness from several intertwined factors: "one fine day" Joseph K. wakes up to find himself already relegated to the status of outsideness, imputed culpability, ambiguous civil and legal status, and lack of protection of the law familiar to us through twentieth-century deterritorialization and genocide practices. Joseph K.'s legal and social circumstances are a projection, within a deliberately *conventional civil* dwelling and habitation, of the practices and conditions that became endemic to any number of systems of concentration camps, work camps, and killing fields. This places Kafka, not only through the virtual horror of Joseph K.'s legal predicament, but also by dint of the uncannily benign holding center known as the "Nature Theater of Oklahoma" in the culminating episode of *Amerika* (alternately, *The Man who Disappeared*),[15] in the position of a cultural seer or lightning-rod who could sketch out, decades in advance, the horrors of the Final Solution and the *gulag*.[16] Lacanian psychoanalytical theory, with its reconfiguration of such Freudian agencies as the superego in the direction of cognitive science, and with its careful attention to such pivotal philosophical constructs as Kantian *Einbildungskraft*,[17] remains the most fertile field for exploring the bizarre prescience manifested by Kafka in his conjuration of Joseph K.'s legal purgatory and the trajectory fatefully leading Karl Rossmann into the midst of the Nature Theater. (In Lacan's strategic revision, the stock-character in the Freudian *comedia del'arte* known as the superego becomes the Imaginary.)[18] There is, then, an uncanny logic prompting Agamben's appeal to Kafka as he spins the figure of the *homo sacer* into the forced indistinction that becomes the archeological as well as material condition of the camps.

2.

It is no accident, then, that in his inevitable *ricorso* back to Kafka, Agamben would highlight the inbuilt and systematic duplicity of the Kafkan law, above all, its serving as a particularly obtuse instrument of *power* while obliterating the gradations and distinctions of semantically delivered meaning. Kant is himself, Agamben discovers, uneasy at legal formalism, a posture structurally capable of welcoming abuse at the ground level of the justice system. Kafka's vivid literary renditions of the double-binds *structurally* attending the assertion and execution of the law—whether activated or not—go back to German idealism's blanket misgivings toward the momentum of conceptual invention and virtuosity unchecked by a grounding in the world accessible through sensibility, perception, and understanding.[19] According to Agamben, the law, as it has worked itself through the traditions of Western metaphysics and Abrahamic theology, has constitutionally both liberated and condemned itself to a permanent state of exception.

Kafka's cameo role in *Homo Sacer* brings out some of Agamben's tersest, epigrammatic, and most poetic writing:

> Kafka's legend ["Before the Law," my inclusion] presents the pure form in which law affirms itself with the greatest force precisely at the point in which it no longer prescribes anything—which is to say, as pure ban. The man from the country is delivered over to the potentiality of law because law demands nothing of him and commands nothing but its own openness. According to the schema of the sovereign exception, law applies to him in no longer applying, and holds him in its ban in abandoning him outside itself. The open door destined only for him includes him in excluding him and excludes him in including him. And this is precisely the summit and the root of every law.[20]
>
> What, after all, is the structure of the sovereign ban if not that of a law that *is in force* but does not *signify*? Everywhere on earth men live today in the ban of a law and a tradition that are maintained solely as the "zero point" of their own content, and that include men within them in the form of a pure relationship of abandonment.[21]
>
> In Kant the pure form of law as "being in force without significance" appears for the first time in modernity. What Kant calls "the simplest form of law" (*die bloße Form des Gesetzes*) in the *Critique of Practical Reason* is in

fact a law reduced to the zero-point of its significance, which is, neverthe-less, in force as such.[22]

And it is exactly this kind of life that Kafka describes, in which law is all the more pervasive for its total lack of content, and in which a distracted knock on the door can mark the start of uncontrollable trials.... So in Kafka's village the empty potentiality of the law is so much in force as to become indistinguishable from life. The existence and the very body of Joseph K. ultimately coincide with the Trial. They *become* the Trial.[23]

Because Agamben has been so attentive to the intangibles of his own writerly performance, he is able to display on the screen of poetic con-densation and vividness the very chiasmatic ambiguity at the heart of the *Musselmann's* conditions and defining the confinement of the camps: "Law applies to him in no longer applying." "The open door destined only for him includes him in excluding him and excludes him in including him." The world of unconditional legal constraint under which Joseph K. lives is the civilian correlative to the extreme sociopolitical deterritorialization and abjection delivered by the camps. Kafka's law, like the state of exception under which the camps were activated and the excuse for a life that the inmates found there, voids meaning (semantics) in favor of pure relation, in this case, arbitrary totalitarian will. Whether wittingly or not, in his characterization of the self-negating blankness of bare life, whether in the cloistered anomie of the camps or amid the civilian trappings of the city, Agamben appeals nostalgically to the analog foundations of meaning that have been obliterated in the ascendance of purely relational regimes of sub-jugation, survival, and death. His bemoaning the obliteration of the *analog* media of culpability, legal recourse, and accountability is strikingly remi-niscent of Anthony Wilden's admonitions regarding the dissemination of *digital* thinking and technologies, which he could realistically assess fully two decades before personal computing was widely available.

With pitched interest at the very outset of the still-actual age of cogni-tive and cybernetic processing, Wilden ponders:

> The relationship between semantics and syntax in these two forms of com-munication. The analog is pregnant with MEANING whereas the digital domain of SIGNIFICATION is relatively, somewhat barren. It is almost impossible to translate the rich semantics of the analog into any digital form for communication to another organism. This is true both of the most trivial sensations...and the most enviable situations.... But this impreci-sion carries with it a fundamental and probably essential ambiguity.... The digital...because it is concerned with boundaries and because it depends on arbitrary combination, has all the syntax to be precise and may be entirely unambiguous. Thus what the analog gains in semantics it loses in syntac-tics, and what the digital gains in syntactics it loses in semantics. Thus it is

that because the analog does not possess the syntax necessary to say "No" or to say anything involving "not," one can REFUSE or REJECT in the analog, but one cannot DENY or NEGATE.[24]

The vestiges of frame, context, relation, communication that once endowed the *Musselmann's* existence with at least a share of meaning have been eliminated somewhere amid the camps' industrially engineered and virtual *indistinction* program. The camps erase communities and communications networks; they generate, and often leave behind, statistics, records, numbers. The numerical simulacra to the camps' functions and modes of production are a *digital* readout to what was once an ecology of *analog* relations. It is more palatable for the perpetrators of genocide to destroy amid the virtuality of digital boundaries and relations.

Under the turbulent conditions of the Kafkan climate, double-logic and arbitrary predicaments become humorous as they shift from the grim officialdom of the court to the countryside, a zone where arrested development at the communal level and shopworn historical tradition coincide. (In his documentary work, Elie Wiesel has noted the beauty of the rustic settings in which concentration camps were often placed, as have others.)[25] As an official of the oppressively interlocked Prague Court, the Klamm of *The Castle* would undoubtedly be as corrupt as any of his peers. As a Castle official charged with administering the benighted village to which K. has been summoned as a land-surveyor, he is a larger-than-life character of fickleness and mood-swings that can only be characterized as comic. "We have a saying here, perhaps you've heard it: official decisions are as shy as young girls," explains Olga to K. as she accounts for her family's systematic ostracism by the Castle bureaucracy and local village populace. This pogrom-like persecution has been prompted by the spirited dismissal by her sibling (Amalia) of the sexual propositions by a minor Castle bureaucrat (Sortini). This repudiation of bureaucratic power impacts with particular repercussions on the third sibling, Barnabas, the only male, whose effort to establish a professional trajectory and to regain the family's respectability begins with his ill-fated assignment as K.'s messenger.

Klamm governs, gets his way with the village women, and disappears back into the anonymity of the Castle bureaucracy with an impunity that in other settings is downright menacing and devastating to those individuals caught in its magnetic field. Klamm steps out of the pages of Max Weber's early accounts of bureaucracy; he is a model citizen and presiding chairman of the civil rather than the military order. According to Weber, bureaucracy gains its impersonality and strict discipline and regimentation through the importation of military values into the commercial sphere.[26] Klamm is a poster child for the charisma that, according to Weber, powers bureaucracies on to the completion and execution of the contracts and understandings under which they and their functionaries operate. His domain of operation may be the stale air of village familiarity, but the taint of imperviousness and immense power still clings to him.

Technically, Klamm works at the behest of the Count Westwest, a vestige of the local feudal hierarchy known only anecdotally.[27] But Klamm, on the other hand, is the highest, most mystifying, and exceptionally elusive official that the villagers ever briefly spy or embroider upon with their fanciful reports. The regulated procedures over which he presides and the impersonality with which he and his underlings fulfill them typecasts him immediately as a bureaucrat, as Weber elaborates the term, even at a moment early in the evolution of large-scale corporate organizations. But the extraordinary if not exactly magical habits and powers that the villagers ascribe to Klamm also endow him with the charisma that Weber earmarks as indispensable to the ascent to and maintenance of power amid putatively democratic conditions of equality before law and administrative procedure. It is only a brief step from the phantom liberties and excesses attributed to Klamm as a transcendental signifier with charismatic power (we would now call him a celebrity) to the impunity with which he and his cohorts act and move through their provincial outpost now updated in accordance with the most modern business procedures.

Even as Weber first sets out the organization and operating principles governing bureaucracy, Kafka configures his virtual fictive display of these conditions into a ribald parody of their corruption. According to Weber, the bureaucratic domain is segmented into "fixed and official jurisdictional areas, which are generally organized by rules."[28] The "characteristic principle" of bureaucracy is "the abstract regularity of the execution of authority, which is a result of the demand for 'equality before the law' in the personal and functional sense—hence the horror of 'privilege,' and the principled rejection of doing business 'from case to case.'"[29]

> The principles of office hierarchy and of levels of graded authority mean a firmly ordered system of super- and subordination in which there is the supervision of the lower offices by the higher ones. Such a system offers the governed the possibility of appealing the decision of a lower office to its higher authority, in a definitely regulated manner. With the full development of the bureaucratic type, the office hierarchy is found in all bureaucratic structures: in state and ecclesiastical structures as well as in large party organizations and private enterprises.[30]

Weber calibrates bureaucracy in this introductory passage from "Bureaucracy" as a system to stand alongside the systemic institutions of church and state. Bureaucracy is a system that has been foolproofed by

Enlightenment considerations of impartiality, disinterest, and consistency in the name of even-handed treatment. The graded architecture of the bureaucratic system—in striking contrast to K.'s initial glimpse of the Castle in the novel's first chapter—pursues the syllogistic logic of rational argumentation and administrative process simulating it. The appeals process is a safety mechanism (or in terms of contemporary systems theory, release-valve)[31] enabling the bureaucratic apparatus to assume self-regulation to the same degree that this has been earmarked as a decisive and indispensable feature of human beings having undergone the emancipation that Kant both surveys and prescribes for them. Bureaucracy is not merely a blueprint of the organization formed by autonomous post-Enlightenment men and women working in concert with one another; in its trappings, settings, equipment, and even its refuse, it is the framework for and generator of the material conditions of modern life. Weber's slippage from the hegemonic traits of bureaucracy as the idealized worksite of the post-Emancipation Western world to the cluttered storage closet (*Rumpelkammer*)[32] of its materiality is precipitous:

> The management of the modern office is based upon written documents ("the files"), which are preserved in their original or draught form. There is, therefore, a staff of subaltern officials and scribes of all sorts. The body of officials actively engaged in "public" office, along with the respective apparatus of material implements and the files, make up a "bureau." . . .[33]

Weber's inventory of bureaucracy's paraphernalia is immediately reminiscent of the hilarious scene in *The Castle* in which Mizzi, the mayor's wife, in concert with his assistants desperately stuffs files back into a secretary (the cabinet) out of which they've accidentally poured; also of mail distribution in the corridors of the Herrenhof Inn in Chapter 19, producing stray documents not belonging anywhere in spite of the procedure's exaggerated fastidiousness. Kafka's attention to bureaucracy's material intransigence, whether in these scenes or accruing from the telephone systems in this novel and in the Hotel Occidental in *Amerika*, is a recurrent source of uncontainable comedy. The humor is slapstick in its most fundamental sense, directly riveting ideation (in this case unpleasant) onto physical objects and absurdities. Indeed, the "physical humor" of bureaucracy that Kafka explores and exploits beginning with his fractured contemporary myths (e.g. "Poseidon," "The Silence of the Sirens") and in *Amerika* is a powerful means of defusing bureaucracy's more uncanny and unsettling epiphenomena.

Chief among these, at least in Kafka's fictive rendition, are the bureaucrat's ubiquity, the fact that he is invariably incommunicado, his ability to "disappear" himself at the same time that he asserts unconditional power asserted with no accountability. The fusion of his intangibility and his blunt, unavoidable impact is uncanny in the full Freudian sense. As characterized by Weber, the bureaucrat is the figment of a Master/Bondsman aporia in relation to his position and his functions. "The individual bureaucrat cannot squirm out of the apparatus in which he is harnessed. In contrast to the honorific or avocational 'notable,' the bureaucrat is chained to his activity by his entire material and ideal existence. In the great majority of cases, he is only a single cog in an ever-moving mechanism which prescribes to him an essentially fixed route of march.... The individual bureaucrat is thus forged to the community of all the functionaries who are integrated into the mechanism."[34] Weber sketches out a Sisyphean predicament for the bureaucrat, who derives any control he exercises from "being chained" to his activities. In the passage immediately above, the bureaucrat's intrinsic insecurity about whether he is masterful or in bondage goes hand in hand with his encompassing "material and ideal" facets. The bureaucrat's disposition, translated into coordinates of mood (and mood disorders), is inherently bipolar.

At the upper register of the bureaucrat's capability and affect, in Weber's sociological analysis, he is distinguished and empowered by his charisma. Kafka agrees whole-heartedly with Weber on this point: the imagined Klamm exerts his metaphysical as well as tangible power over the village only by dint of a charisma deriving in part from communal mystification, in part from uncertainty, an aura as absurd in its arbitrariness as the most extreme religious beliefs and practices. In the secular zone of bureaucratic administration, charisma serves Weber well as the personal attribute providing the high functionary with his cover, the assumed identity under whose aegis he can *perform* his checklist of tasks, whether these are in fact draconian or not.

> The term "charisma" will be applied to a certain quality of an individual personality by virtue of which he is set apart from ordinary men and treated as endowed with supernatural, superhuman, or at least specifically exceptional powers or qualities. These are such as are not accessible to the ordinary person, but are regarded as of divine origin or exemplary, and on the basis of them the individual concerned is treated as a leader. In primitive circumstances this particular kind of deference is paid to prophets, to people with a reputation for therapeutic or legal wisdom, to leaders in the hunt, and heroes in war. It is very often thought of as resting on magical powers.... What is alone important is how the individual is actually regarded by those subject to charismatic authority, by his "followers" or "disciples."[35]

This passage is exceptionally instructive as a viewfinder from which to track and analyze the overdetermined arbitrariness that Kafka is able to construct in and around the character of Klamm. On the widest horizon of theoretical interest, this and related passages hover on the aporetic state of affairs in which routine procedure, specifically engineered for its neutrality, disinterest, and consistency, is powered by charisma, by the ability of strong personalities to gather around them disciples and other acolytes. It is the charismatic personality's "endowment" with "exceptional powers or qualities" from any number of sources, ones setting him "apart from ordinary men," that provide for the multiplicity of his different appearances and manifestations. Klamm is free to become, in Kafka's ex-urban geography on the cusp of hardcore modernization, all things for all villagers. It is consonant with Weber's analysis of bureaucracy that Klamm's arrangements almost never bring him in contact with the villagers; in Chapter Eight, for example, Klamm does not emerge into the courtyard, even though his sled has been waiting there to spirit him away, and K. has also set up a watchpost, in the hope of accosting him there. As landlady Gardena explains to K. in the presence of Frieda, the barmaid who has serviced Klamm sexually until *most* recently, when she has switched over to K.:

> There's no other way of making him understand what we take for granted, that Herr Klamm will never speak to him—*will* never speak, did I say?—*can* never speak to him. Just listen to me, sir. Herr Klamm is a gentleman from the Castle, and that, in itself, without considering Klamm's position there at all, means that he is of very high rank. But what are you, whose marriage we are humbly considering ways here of getting permission? You are not from the Castle, you are not from the village, you aren't anything. Or rather, unfortunately, you are something, a stranger, a man who isn't wanted (*überzählig*) and is in everybody's way.... You are what you are, and I have seen enough in my lifetime to face facts. But now consider what it is that you ask. A man like Klamm is to talk to you. It vexed me to hear that Frieda let you look through the peephole.... But just tell me, how did you have the face to look at Klamm? You needn't answer, I know you think you were quite equal to the occasion. You're not even capable of seeing Klamm as he really is; that's not merely an exaggeration, for I myself am not capable of it either. Klamm is to talk to you, and yet Klamm doesn't talk even to people from the village, never yet has he spoken a word himself to anyone in the village. It was Frieda's great distinction (*Auszeichnung*), a distinction I'll be proud of to my dying day, that he used at least to call out her name. (C 1982a, 63–4)

K.'s status, that of a stranger as delineated by the above passage, marks him as peripheral and in certain respects dispensable. He is "not wanted and in everybody's way." The situation he has backed himself into may not be as dire as the *Musselmann's*, but it is characterized by a very similar tenuousness and constitutional ambiguity. The quarantine, or in Agamben's terms

228 / HENRY SUSSMAN

"ban" that K. faces is first and foremost, as the narrative couches it, a linguistic one. In Gardena's words, Klamm is free never to acknowledge K.'s presence in the community or to address him, all the more so if he never addresses anyone from the village (limiting his speech in this regard to verbal ejaculations to his sexual servers). K.'s ostracism, banning, statelessness, and congenital tenuousness in the community have been situated by Gardena squarely in the referential plane.

So complete is the extent of Klamm's legerdemain and the impunity in which he acts that he has even been exempted from the burdens and constraints of identity itself. He works and functions as an impromptu social force, a designated X-factor, absolved from maintaining a consistent character and from leaving behind an intelligible trace or fingerprint of his actions. Klamm is the indexical figure of bureaucracy as it radiates outward from officialdom into the communal, domestic, and intimate spheres. Olga splices these considerations into her running commentary on her family's predicament to K.:

> His appearance is well known to people in the village, some people have seen him, everybody has heard of him, and out of glimpses and rumors and through various distorting factors an image (*Bild*) of Klamm has been constructed which is certainly true in fundamentals. But only in fundamentals. In detail it fluctuates, and yet perhaps not as much as Klamm's real appearance. For he's reported as having one appearance when he comes into the village and another on leaving it, after having his beer he looks different from what he does before it, when he's awake he's different from when he's asleep, when he's alone he's different from when he's talking with people and—what is comprehensible after all that—he's almost another person up in the Castle. And even within the village there are considerable differences in the accounts given of him, differences as to his height, his bearing, his size, and the cut of his beard. Fortunately there's one thing in which all the accounts of him agree: he always wears the same clothes.... Now of course all these differences aren't the result of magic, but can be easily explained; they depend on the mood of the observer, on the degree of his excitement, on the countless gradations of hope or despair which are possible for him when he sees Klamm and besides, he can usually see Klamm only for a second or two. (C 1982a, 230–1)

Kafka's literary construction of administrative impunity is not so much grounded, like Weber's, in the social reality of large-scale corporate and governmental organizations. (It is notable that Kant's rigorous terminologies can serve Weber as well as Kafka in their respective constructions of bureaucracy and the personalities that legitimate and drive it.) The fictive construction of Klamm arises above all within a constitutional crisis of reference. Klamm's inconsistent bureaucratic rulings have their ultimate derivation in his congenital difference from himself and the ongoing communicative inconsistency and ambiguity that this sets into play. The catalogue of Klamm's intrinsic self-differences in the passage immediately above—from setting to setting as well as from moment to moment—instantiates his status, first and foremost, as an image, in the terminology of German idealism, an appearance (*Erscheinung*).[36] "In detail," Klamm's appearance "fluctuates;" it is as changeable as stable. As the passage clarifies, the image of Klamm is a dual construction, a split image. It is as much the result of his observers' affective issues, their moods, as of any objectivity that can be imputed to the empirical observations they make. In the end, as the narrative ironically notes, the only thing holding the image of Klamm together is his wardrobe, a not very impressive one at that.

At the manic extreme of his register, Klamm serves the fictive world of Kafka's novel as a transcendental signifier, to which any and all village phenomena may be referred. In the language of Ernesto Laclau, Klamm is the empty sign occupying the phallic position of leadership:[37] the administrative fulcrum who is a be-all and end-all for the community, seen everywhere and nowhere, in a bewildering multiplicity of guises. For all this diversity of *Erscheinung*, perhaps by virtue of it, this figure is also, socially as well as semiotically, meaningless, devoid of semantic pith.

It is not clear how seamlessly Klamm's career, had Kafka managed to pursue it into the 1930s and 1940s, would have segued into the administration of the camps and related detention, forced labor, and extermination facilities. Or the degree to which Klamm's charisma is the home-grown, *garden*-variety miniature to the hype and misconception under which the cults of twentieth-century totalitarianism—in the names of Hitler, Stalin, and Mussolini—were able to thrive. Yet in every instant Klamm acts in unrestricted impunity and whimsy. Klamm's legal and extralegal authority is grounded in constructed double-binds pursuant to the vexed wanderings and history of the *homo sacer*. Writing with uncanny prescience in the late teens and early 1920s, Kafka's fondest wish for the figure of Klamm would have been its relegation and confinement to the local and miniature stage of situation comedy.

3.

It is hopefully not too exasperating for a disquisition pirouetting around the figure of the *homo sacer*, specifically around the ideological and juridical legerdemain constituting him and to which he gives rise as well as the industrial sites of mass confinement and genocide that his status predicates, to end up in a radically different zone of production, but one also constituted under the release provided by a statute of impunity. I refer here to the matrix of ethical considerations under which we, as critics, are obliged to think the thoughts that occur to us as we process our running aesthetico-cultural encounters, and to enter them in display in the medium of thoughtful language, without self-censorship or filtration in the name of expediency, whether of a social, professional, or political nature. In this regard, the infinite conversation of critique is grounded in a cultural contract of uncontainable expression, but of a completely different order from the instrumental nonaccountability giving rise to the catastrophic systematic abuse chronicled in *Homo Sacer*.

From the perspective of critique's rendering explicit the conceptual and terminological fixity allowing for politicocultural totalization and reaction, critique contributes to the noise of the system,[38] the accompaniment of unrestricted expression giving the lie to systematic pretentions to rectitude, order, logic, science, intelligibility, propriety, defense, and so on. It is incumbent on critique to access and emit this somewhat inchoate static or noise, whether the entrenched mechanisms of the system drown it out or not, whether the expression is judicious and expedient or not. With eloquence far in excess of anything to which I could aspire, Derrida, in his later writings, demarcates zones of an expression "without alibi," lanes and scenes of thinking and expression that must be kept open at any cost, for their very activity and effectiveness are tantamount to the suspension of communicative and informational censorship. Prominent among these are psychoanalysis and the university, settings whose similarity may not be immediately evident, but that both appeal to and rely upon unrestricted frankness and franchise.

The operating principles underlying Derrida's mission statement for the contemporary university, "the one whose European model, after a rich and complex medieval history, has become prevalent...over the last two centuries in states of a democratic type"[39] are well known. In principle and constitution, such a university "*should* be *without condition*" [Derrida's italics].[40] "This university demands and ought to be granted in principle, besides what is called academic freedom, an *unconditional* freedom to question and assert, or even, going still further, the right to say publically all that is required by research, knowledge, and thought concerning the *truth*."[41] The "unconditional" freedom of thinking, investigation, and related expression in the form of research findings reaches toward a statute of impunity, albeit one arising in a certain framework and with certain very specific restrictions pertaining (more on which below).

It is the mark of the unrepentant philosopher that Derrida remained until his death that the quest for truth should serve as the framework within which unconditional thinking, investigation, and related expression take place. The university does all within its power to establish and safeguard what might be called truth-conditions; it is for him an institution always already calibrated to truth-values. The "*unconditional* discussion" properly situated on campus pivots around "the question and the history of truth, in its relation to the question of man, of what is proper to man, of human rights, of crimes against humanity, and so forth."[42] On the basis of this open-ended and necessarily respectful discussion, the traditional humanities will be recalibrated into the "new Humanities" of our particular (e.g., cybernetically inflected) moment.

Given the irreverent, often outlandish, free-wheeling, performative as well as constative, and nonlinear investigation of the truth that Derrida has exemplified as well as conducted, it is by no means excessive that he militates for the "right to deconstruction" at the contemporary university fitted out for the unconditional discussion. In *Without Alibi, Specters of Marx*,[43] and in essays ranging from "Plato's Pharmacy" to "Faith and Knowledge"[44] and "Hostipitality,"[45] Derrida reaches toward a tangible scenario of the performance and prospects for the interrelated bearings making up the distinctively deconstructive posture. In what would this right, the right to deconstruction, exercised with particular relevance at the university, consist?

> I am referring to the right to deconstruction as an unconditional right to ask critical questions not only about the history of the concept of man, but about the history even of the notion of critique, about the form and authority of the question, about the interrogative form of thought. For this implies the right to do it *affirmatively* and *performatively*, that is, by producing events (for example, by writing) and by giving rise to singular *oeuvres* (which up until now has not been the purview of either the classical or modern Humanities)....
>
> This principle of unconditional resistance is a right that the university itself should at the same time reflect, invent, and pose, whether it does so through its law faculties or in the new Humanities capable of working on these questions of right and of law—in other words, and again why not say it without detour, the Humanities capable of taking on the tasks of deconstruction, beginning with the deconstruction of their own history and their own axioms.[46]

This passage contains some of the most suggestive available intimations as to the interface and potential interactions between deconstruction and the law. To the extent that deconstruction constitutes a mode of cultural intervention consisting in a confluence of interconnected analytical and exegetical postures or bearings, to the extent that deconstruction is invariably not only a legal but also respectful activity, access to deconstructive practice under the aegis of institutions including universities, the humanities, and subspecialties of science, research, and scholarship amounts to a right; its availability is a legal as well as curricular *imperative*. Derrida chooses to define the legal substrate of the deconstructive project in terms of its accessibility or its *dissemination*, the latter a troping of linguistic ramification that he encountered early in his writing.

Along with the university, psychoanalysis becomes a pivotal venue within whose parameters Derrida can imagine the articulation and expression of a discourse without self-justification and excuses and hence without alibi. Although the term "psychoanalysis" refers primarily to a practice and psychological intervention, psychoanalysis, as Derrida makes certain to point out, is no less an institution, is no less storied in the bloodthirsty hostile takeovers making up its history, than the university. It is in this context that Derrida can declare a "States General" for psychoanalysis, a well-publicized plebiscite over its directions and orientations to come. If psychoanalysis, along with the academy, is to rise to *its* "right to deconstruction," it too will institute measures of internal reform; to reprogram its sordid tango with psychical cruelty into an open-ended communications feedback loop from which no eventualities have been expunged. "Psychoanalysis…would be another name for the 'without alibi.' If that were possible."[47]

The convening of the States General, in 1789: a broad and frank forum on major political and economic issues facing French society on the cusp of a traumatic revolution. The revolution for which psychoanalysis can strive on the occasion of its deconstructive reconfiguration is the one both declaring moratorium and impunity for its deliberations and initiating its performative and allegorical phase, as opposed to its confinement to clinical description and diagnosis. "Only a psychoanalytical revolution would be, in its very project, up to the task of taking account of the grammatical syntax, conjugations, reflexivities, and persons that I unfolded in order to begin: to enjoy making or letting suffer, making oneself or letting oneself suffer, oneself, the other as other, the other and others in oneself, me, you, he, she, you plural, we, they, and so forth. With your permission, I will spare us any example of this cruelty."[48] In addressing psychoanalysis, the sovereign state (of therapists, their training, therapeutic protocols and regimens, and so on), as well as the archive of core texts, deconstruction in no way relinquishes the very finite and specific scrutiny it has from the outset afforded language and linguistic features ("grammatical syntax, conjugations, reflexivities"). The revolution standing before psychoanalysis in the pertinent essay from *Without Alibi*, "Psychoanalysis Searches the States of Its Soul: The Impossible Beyond of a Sovereign Cruelty," is the one through which this practice and this institution acknowledges and admits, in several senses, the *indirection* that a discourse "without alibi" perforce assumes.

> What should take place in a certain way at every analytic session is a sort of micro-revolution, preceded by some music from the States General; chamber

group, lending their voices to all the agencies and all the states of the social body or the psychic body. This should start up again each time that a patient lies down on the couch, or, as happens more and more today, undertakes a face-to-face analysis. The analysand would then be initiating a revolution, perhaps the first revolution that matters: he would be opening virtually *his* States General and giving the right to speech within him to all the states, all the voices, all the agencies of the psychic body as multiple social body. Without alibi. After registering all the grievances, griefs, and complaints. In this sense, and by right, a psychoanalysis should be, through and through, a revolutionary process, the first revolution, perhaps, preceded by some States General.[49]

A bit tongue-in-cheek perhaps, with a musical prelude redolent of an official ceremony, Derrida in this passage nevertheless powerfully and rigorously spells out the revolutionary potential of a successful psychoanalysis, in his terms, one "without alibi," for all the states to which the analysand, the reader, the student, and the participant in culture belong and in which they participate. This is a marvelously fanciful passage, but it bespeaks Derrida's unwavering commitment to the revolution that he outlines and his solidarity with its fellow participants, above all a *deconstructive* revolution. First and foremost in this scenario, the analysand, the critic, the cultural participant is herself a sovereign state, "a multiple social body," constituted by a panoply of states and conditions, pertaining to mood, emotion, interpersonal relations, adaptation, and so on. Having undertaken the analytical process, the cultural as well as psychoanalytical analysand gives the "right of speech" within her to all these constitutive states, however mutually discordant, painful, counterintuitive, disruptive, dysfunctional, and inexpedient they may be. This enfranchisement of the contrary states within the psychoanalytical/cultural analysand/witness/programmer *is* a revolution, a basic training for participation within the ongoing public revolution programmed and performed by deconstruction. Toward the end of a career in which he has, on more than one occasion, pointed out the submerged metaphysical shoals concealed within the psychoanalytical constructions posited by Lacan as well as Freud,[50] Derrida continues to return to the psychoanalytical *cabinet*. He does so precisely because psychoanalysis, regardless of its borrowings, injudicious generalizations, and premature conclusions, remains the preeminent *scene* in which culture, as the individuated analysand, comes to terms with its/her *states*.

The counterinstitution of deconstruction studiously avoids training programs in which therapeutic protocols are instituted and credentials accorded at the "culmination" of a program of study, practice, or both. But the working deconstructor implied by the above passage is a revolutionary cadre, one whose radical intervention is grounded in having given the floor (or as the French say, the word) to the discordant and discrepant states, having been attentive to this discord "without alibi." The attentiveness underlying deconstruction's revolutionary thrust or downbeat is by no means a gratuitous accessory. It is a discipline unto itself, the responsibility in which the critic's task of entering feedback without condition into the website of cultural communications is grounded. The critic responds, intervenes, and enters the text she has synthesized with impunity. As opposed to the juridical/military/bureaucratic impunity chronicled in *Homo Sacer*, theorized by Weber, and parodied by Kafka in *The Castle* and elsewhere, however, the conversation "without alibi" that Derrida situates on campus and in psychoanalysis arises with excruciating attentiveness to its responsibilities and the bearing of respect without which it will immediately degenerate into reductive and dismissive polemic.

It is in such an essay as "Faith and Knowledge," in which Derrida inquires at the limit to what degree the leanings and investments of religion might still be binding, that he carefully works through the contractual terms of deconstruction's inherent responsibility and respect. "*Scruple*, hesitation, indecision, reticence (hence modesty *<pudeur>*, *restraint* before that which sacred, holy, or safe: unscathed, immune)—this too is what is meant by *religio*. It is even the meaning that Benveniste believed obliged to retain with reference to the "proper and constant usages" during the classical period."[51] If deconstruction initiates a revolution, if it foments, in an atmosphere of "messianism without messianicity,"[52] memorable and trendsetting critical events,[53] these are hardly bloodbaths. The deconstructive revolution of inscription "without alibi" transpires in the zone of meticulous de- and recoding, of close exegesis and even more reticent alternate programming. Temporally, it emerges radically otherwise than directly or in sequence.

Notes

1. See my *Around the Book: Systems and Literacy* (New York: Fordham University Press, 2011).

2. Note that in a Chinese cultural framework, this meticulous "recycling" of prior philosophies, schools of thought, and religious practices works to a remarkably constructive and innovative effect. Deleuze/Guattari assert the persistence of some of the more violent political formations of the past, such as "nomadic despotism," in a much grimmer context: as they explain, for example, the vast "becoming-death" instantiated by the War Machine in such catastrophes as the twentieth-century World Wars.

3. This phrase recurs throughout the liturgy of the Jewish High Holy Days (also known as the "Days of Awe"). It repeatedly asserts divine volition (or sovereignty) in the appropriation/withdrawal of life in the coming year.

WITH IMPUNITY / 235

4. Giorgio Agamben, *Homo Sacer: Sovereign Power and Bare Life*, trans. Daniel Heller-Roazen (Stanford, CA: Stanford University Press, 1998), 120.
5. Ibid., 1–2 and 9–11.
6. Ibid., 122.
7. Ibid., 185.
8. Ibid., 99.
9. Ibid., 170.
10. Jacques Derrida, "Plato's Pharmacy," in *Dissemination*, trans. Barbara Johnson (Chicago, IL: University of Chicago Press, 1970), 130–4.
11. Agamben, 83 (author's italicization).
12. Ibid., 73.
13. Ibid., 73–4.
14. For Erving Goffman's most systematic work on context and its impact within a sociological domain, see *Frame Analysis: An Essay on the Organization of Experience* (Cambridge, MA: Harvard University Press, 1974), 22–39 and 124–55.
15. I've hopefully opened up some of the ironies surrounding this scene in "Incarcerated in *Amerika*: Literature Addresses the Political with the Help of Ernesto Laclau," in my *Idylls of the Wanderer: Outside in Literature and Theory* (New York: Fordham University Press, 2007), 192–6.
16. No one writes more trenchantly on Kafka's unique ability to predict, within the phantasmatic landscapes of his fiction, the emergent extremes and actualities of twentieth-century politics than Russell Samolsky. See his forthcoming *Apocalyptic Futures: Marked Bodies and the Violence of the Text in Kafka, Conrad, and Coetzee* (New York: Fordham University Press, 2011).
17. For this notion, see, above all, Immanuel Kant, *Critique of Pure Reason*, trans. Paul Guyer (Cambridge: Cambridge University Press, 1999), 211, 225, 236, 239, 256–7, 273–4, and 281–2.
18. For Lacan's basic work on the Imaginary, his cognitively critical successor to the Freudian superego, one is inevitably drawn to the "Of the Gaze as *Petit objet a*" segment of his *The Four Fundamental Concepts of Psychoanalysis*, containing such essays as "The Split between the Eye and the Gaze," "Anamorphosis" (crucial), "The Line and Light," and "What is a Picture?" See Jacques Lacan, *The Four Fundamental Concepts of Psychoanalysis*, trans. Alan Sheridan (New York: Norton, 1978), 67–122.
19. These misgivings find an expression in Kant's *Critique of Pure Reason*, in which the criteria for any *pure* understanding or *pure* reason, that is, definitively severed from sensation and its processing, are, to say the least, high. In the Hegelian metaphysics, the constitutional crisis forcing understanding to take refuge in self-consciousness occurs when its distinctions and resulting abstractions begin to escalate with no grounding in the tangible world; the very "freedom" of self-consciousness places it in a similarly tenuous situation, requiring the intervention of reason. See Kant, *Critique of Pure Reason*, 210–43, 394–410, 470–75, and 484–85; G. W. F. Hegel, *Hegel's Phenomenology of Spirit*, trans. A. V. Miller (Oxford: Oxford University Press, 1977), 94–103 and 131–8.
20. Agamben, 49–50.
21. Ibid., 51.

22. Ibid.
23. Ibid., 52 and 53.
24. Anthony Wilden, *System and Structure* (London: Tavistock Press, 1972), 163.
25. See, for example, comments by Rita Renshaw, recorded by Suzan E. Hagstrom, who, in 2008, accompanied Holocaust survivor Helen Garfinkle Greenspun and family on a return trip to Chmielnik, Poland. Renshaw, Greenspun's daughter, commented as follows: "'Growing up I only heard bad things—about concentration camps and throwing babies into the fire. Poland always had a big X on it,' Renshaw said, marveling at the gently rolling terrain and quaint wooden farmhouses featuring flower boxes, peaked roofs and dormers. 'Mom had never told me about the beauty of the country or the scenery.'" On the Worldwide Web at http://www.jewish-guide.pl/47. Hagstrom is also author of *Sara's Children: The Destruction of Chmielnik* (Spotsylvania, VA: Sergeant Kirkland's Press, 2001).
26. Max Weber, *On Charisma and Institution Building*, ed. S. N. Eisenstadt (Chicago, IL: University of Chicago Press, 1968), 72–6.
27. Count Westwest shares this status with "definite acquittal," the only one of the three forms of acquittal from a prosecution brought by the Court in *The Trial* never to have been recorded—as late in the novel these possible resolutions are spelled out to Joseph K. by Court painter Titorelli in his atelier. "Ostensible acquittal" and "postponement" are, on the other hand, regularly meted out, but vie with one another in the diabolical nature of their uncertainty, endless duration, and potentially multiple jeopardy.
28. Weber, 66.
29. Ibid., 70.
30. Ibid., 67.
31. The need, structurally as well temperamentally, for overextended systems to install release valves ameliorating the pressure they generate, is a key feature of the systems theory that anthropologist Gregory Bateson developed over several decades. See his *Steps to an Ecology of Mind* (Chicago, IL: University of Chicago Press, 2000), 97–9, 105–6, 112–21, 206–8, 212–6, 492, 498–501, and 504–13.
32. I refer here to the setting in *The Trial* where Joseph K. is first exposed both to the sado-masochistic facets of his legal subjection and to some of his deeper psychological motivations (e.g., ambivalence regarding marriage, homoerotic desire), to the extent that we might read him as a fictive "surrogate" endowed with a psychology. I have commented extensively on this scene in "The Court as Text: Inversion, Supplanting, and Derangement in Kafka's *Der Prozeß*," *PMLA*, 92 (1977): 41–45, rpt. in my *Franz Kafka: Geometrician of Metaphor* (Madison, WI: Coda Press, Inc., 1978), 84–93.
33. Weber, 67–8.
34. Ibid., 75.
35. Ibid., 48.
36. See, for example, Hegel, *Phenomenology of Spirit*, 88–9.
37. See Ernesto Laclau, *Emancipation(s)* (London: Verso, 1996), 44–5, 53–5, and 95.
38. See, for example, Wilden, 389–90, 400–3.

39. Jacques Derrida, "The University without Condition," in *Without Alibi*, trans. Peggy Kamuf (Stanford, CA: Stanford University Press, 2002), 202.
40. Ibid.
41. Ibid.
42. Ibid., 203.
43. Jacques Derrida, *Specters of Marx*, trans. Peggy Kamuf (New York: Routledge, 1994).
44. Jacques Derrida, *Acts of Religion*, ed. Gil Anidjar (New York: Routledge, 2002), 40–101.
45. Ibid., 356–420.
46. Derrida, *Without Alibi*, 204.
47. Ibid., 240.
48. Ibid.
49. Ibid., 253.
50. Derrida's *The Post Card* is a treasure trove of formulations and positions indicating his points of commonality and departure with and from Freud and Lacan. (*The Post Card*, trans. Alan Bass [Chicago, IL: University of Chicago Press, 1987]).
51. Derrida, *Acts of Religion*, 68.
52. Derrida, *Specters of Marx*, 59, 65, and 73.
53. Ibid., 10, 21, 28, 57–60, 62–6, 69–70, 104, 117, and 168–9.

INDEX